BY ANNIE HARTNETT

The Road to Tender Hearts
Unlikely Animals
Rabbit Cake

THE ROAD TO TENDER HEARTS

A NOVEL

ANNIE HARTNETT

BALLANTINE BOOKS
NEW YORK

Ballantine Books
An imprint of Random House
A division of Penguin Random House LLC
1745 Broadway, New York, NY 10019
randomhousebooks.com
penguinrandomhouse.com

Copyright © 2025 by Annie Hartnett

Penguin Random House values and supports copyright. Copyright fuels creativity, encourages diverse voices, promotes free speech, and creates a vibrant culture. Thank you for buying an authorized edition of this book and for complying with copyright laws by not reproducing, scanning, or distributing any part of it in any form without permission. You are supporting writers and allowing Penguin Random House to continue to publish books for every reader. Please note that no part of this book may be used or reproduced in any manner for the purpose of training artificial intelligence technologies or systems.

BALLANTINE BOOKS & colophon are registered trademarks of Penguin Random House LLC.

Interior image credits are located on p. 371.

Hardback ISBN 978-0-593-87344-1
Ebook ISBN 978-0-593-87345-8

Printed in the United States of America on acid-free paper

7th Printing

First Edition

Book design by Elizabeth A. D. Eno

The authorized representative in the EU for product safety and compliance is Penguin Random House Ireland, Morrison Chambers, 32 Nassau Street, Dublin D02 YH68, Ireland, https://eucontact.penguin.ie.

For Leora, my favorite little person

Why aren't we flying? Because getting there is half the fun.
—Clark Griswold, *National Lampoon's Vacation*

Shut up and look out the window.
—Paul Hartnett Jr., on every family road trip

PONDVILLE, MASSACHUSETTS

SPRING 2014

Part I

AN ANCIENT KNOWLEDGE

1

Things were falling apart at the nursing home in Pondville, a small town in the armpit of Massachusetts. There was a leak in the roof in the left wing, and water came down the walls when it rained. The food was terrible, but that wasn't new. The staff kept quitting. The pay was shit. People were dying, all the time, but that was to be expected in this line of work. And just that morning, Dr. Gust found the resident nursing-home cat in his office, curled up on the keyboard like a fat loaf of bread. "Shoo," Dr. Gust said, but the cat would not budge. "I'm fifty-seven," he told Pancakes. Pancakes was the hospital's therapy cat. He was supposed to be in one of the rooms of the nursing-home residents, comforting them. That was his job. To comfort people at their end.

But Pancakes was not comforting the elderly residents, some of whom were quite sick, not long to go. No, the cat was in Dr. Gust's office, and he would not budge from the keyboard. Dr. Gust had to answer emails and think about the budget. Pancakes was purring along with the whirr of the computer monitor. Perhaps he likes the heat from the computer, Dr. Gust reasoned. That must be it. "I'm fifty-seven," he said again. Dr. Gust was a short man, with very bushy eyebrows and no hair left on his head. He wore a Saint Michael pendant around his neck, which was supposed to protect him.

Pancakes kept purring. A bit of drool fell onto the keyboard; Pancakes drooled when he was content. That was enough for Dr. Gust, who picked up Pancakes by the middle and carried him down the hall, arms straight, trying to keep the cat as far away from his body as possible. He marched the cat to the common room, where an arts-and-crafts class was under way. The residents were making butterflies out of markers, clothespins, and coffee filters. "Here," Dr. Gust said, dropping Pancakes in the middle of the room. "Have your pick." He gestured at the room full of residents, all of them over eighty. Instead, Pancakes scaled the bookshelf, and once on top, turned and hissed.

"I'm glad you're mad," said Dr. Gust, hands on his hips. "Because I hate you too."

Actually, Dr. Gust loved the cat. He was the one who'd bought Pancakes from a box of kittens outside the supermarket; he was the one who had made him a valued member of the nursing-home staff. He made Pancakes employee of the month more than a few times. But Dr. Gust still didn't want Pancakes hanging around his office, didn't want him lingering in his lap, because the cat had a remarkable talent.

It was Maribeth on the housekeeping staff who had noticed the pattern. Maribeth was in charge of stripping the beds, cleaning and dusting and sanitizing, and after a resident died, she noticed there was always orange cat hair everywhere, much more than in any other room. She pointed it out to Dr. Gust. She said she had heard there was another cat like that, a therapy cat over at a Rhode Island hospital. It wasn't a completely unknown phenomenon.

"Curious," Dr. Gust had said, and he agreed to look into it. In the morning, the cat was found on the chest of another patient, who had died overnight. Soon Dr. Gust was obsessed with the cat's movements. First, Pancakes spent all his time in Mrs. Monty's room. Dead in three days. Then on to Mr. Broomfield's room down the hall. Dead in a week. Upstairs to Mrs. Anderson's corner room. Mrs. Anderson lived another two weeks. One time, Pancakes snuggled with a patient for three months, but the woman was still the next one in the home to die. And so on, and so on, Pancakes made his choices. And the cat was never wrong. Dr. Gust was so excited, he called the reporter for *The South Coast Daily Sun*. The headline read: NURSING HOME CAT PREDICTS DEATH, PROVIDES COMFORT AT END. Dr. Gust planned to frame it for his office.

But after the article ran, there was no more comfort in the Pondville nursing home. Before, no one except Dr. Gust and a few members of the staff had known about Pancakes's knack for prediction. After the article, the residents were in hysterics. Here was a four-legged and -pawed Grim Reaper, walking in their midst! Stalking the halls and picking them off, one by one. One of the patients died jumping out the window, just because the cat had sauntered in.

"Get rid of the cat," the nursing-home patients demanded.

"Get rid of the cat," the nurses said at the next meeting.

But Dr. Gust didn't believe in getting rid of animals. He knew shelter animals were treated like they were disposable. He wished they could euthanize some of the patients in the Pondville nursing home instead. He didn't want to get rid of the cat. But now Pancakes was in his office and Dr. Gust didn't want to die either. He was fifty-seven, and he was newly divorced, and he was having some luck on the dating apps. He had just gone on a date with a woman he'd really clicked with; she was newly divorced too. They'd had a great dinner at Applebee's, and a nice time at Dr. Gust's place after. Her name was Linda. She was into bondage.

That afternoon, the first day that Pancakes had showed up in his office, Dr. Gust went to his own doctor, but the doc couldn't find anything. Blood pressure was normal. No hard lumps in his abdomen. His prostate felt better than ever.

Dr. Gust tried to bravely carry on at work for the rest of the week, but every morning that goddamn cat was in his office. Dr. Gust couldn't handle it. He was young. Or youngish. He had so much juice in him yet. So, he did what he felt he had to do: during his lunch break on Friday, he took Pancakes in the cat carrier to the animal shelter. The sad one on Breaker Road off Main Street in Pondville, with the concrete cells.

"He's only two years old and his name is Pancakes," Dr. Gust said to the woman at the counter. "I hope he finds a good home. He's a wonderful cat," he continued. "But he was a . . . well, he's . . . a killer."

"Did you put a little bell on him?" the woman volunteering at the animal shelter asked. Her name was Alana, and she had six cats at home. "If he wears a jingle bell on his collar, it will be much harder for him to kill birds. Or you could always make him an indoor cat. That's a great option."

Dr. Gust didn't want to get into it with this nice lady at the volunteer animal shelter. He did not want to get the cat a jingle bell. It would do nothing to fix the problem. He shook his head sadly. He would not change his mind. "He's an agent of death," he said to Alana.

"That's a shame," Alana said, shaking her head also. "We'll try to find him a good home. Maybe he'll get lucky." Those were heavy words: *maybe* and *lucky*.

Dr. Gust teared up, but he turned away. I am a good person, he reminded himself. I work with the elderly. I am a good person, he repeated, before driving away from the animal shelter and back to work.

That afternoon, Alana smoked a bowl at her desk. She fed everyone their kibble, refilled their waters, and then locked up for the night. Pancakes enjoyed his dinner before he started working on the lock. Thanks to his claws, Pancakes was able to pick the lock with surprising ease. Once he was freed, he jumped from his cage to Alana's desk to the top of the filing cabinet. Alana had left a window cracked open to air out the pot-smoke smell overnight, and it was through that window that Pancakes slipped out into the night.

Out on the road, Pancakes took a left onto Main Street. He

walked through the town center, past the stone library and the white-steepled Congregationalist church on the right. On the left was the town hall, built in 1856, still coated in a thick layer of lead paint. He went past the athletic club, past the liquor store, past the gun shop, past the crumbling brick fire station. He walked by White Rock Elementary School, a square building with lots of windows, built on land that backs up onto Assawompset Pond. Pondville was named for the network of five ponds in the town, and Assawompset Pond is one of the five. Assawompset is a word from the Wampanoag tribe, and it means "the place of the white stone."

Pancakes kept walking. He followed the main road out to the edge of town, past the cranberry bogs and the cranberry juice factory, past a stone bench memorial for a teenager who had drowned in the bogs nearly fifteen years before. There was an old man who sat on the bench sometimes while he worked through a six-pack, but no one was sitting there now. Pancakes sniffed the legs of the bench. He lingered for a minute. Up ahead was the town border.

LEAVING PONDVILLE, the sign said, at town's edge. BE CAREFUL OUT THERE! it said underneath that. Pancakes had learned to read from one of the patients in the nursing home. Alberta Russet would read aloud from the Russian masters while Pancakes snuggled on her lap. Alberta Russet hadn't made it to the end of *Anna Karenina* before her death, had missed the entire part about the train.

Pancakes walked to the other side of the roadside sign. WELCOME TO PONDVILLE! it read. And then in smaller letters, written in yellow on a white sign, looking like piss in snow, the town motto read: YOU'RE SAFE HERE.

Bullshit, thought the cat, because he had seen his fair share of bad things, and he was only two and a half human years old. No one was safe in Pondville, because no one is safe anywhere. Pancakes knew with certainty there had been violence in the town. He remembered that the first events of King Philip's War happened in Pondville in 1675, and that war was an absolute bloodbath. All cats have an ancient knowledge; it's dogs that are born with a blissfully clean slate.

But this isn't a story about cats, or even about dogs. It's a story about horrible things that happen to people, and how on earth anyone can stomach raising children in a world where doom and disaster lurk around every corner. So, no, it's not a story about a cat. It's just a story that starts with a cat, and it goes from there.

2

Dr. Gust's obituary ran in *The South Coast Daily Sun* two weeks later, on May 3, 2014, to be exact, yet another day that PJ Halliday, a sixty-three-year-old Pondville resident, would wake up, as usual, all alone in his house full of shit. That morning, PJ had no clue, not the slightest inkling, how much his life was about to change. PJ Halliday didn't read Dr. Gust's obituary, even though it was right next to another obituary that day—the one that would change his life—and all of it would be connected in the end. PJ didn't know Dr. Gust, so it wouldn't have meant much to him, that the man died slumped over his desk, using the keyboard as a final pillow. During the autopsy, an extraordinary amount of cat hair would be found in Dr. Gust's nostrils, sucked in off the keyboard during Dr. Gust's last breaths. That wasn't in the newspaper, of course; those kinds of details never make it into obituaries. But again, PJ Halliday didn't read Dr. Gust's obituary. It was another obituary, the one printed right next to it, that would catch PJ's attention and set him off on a new life course.

But first, the day had begun ordinarily enough: Still wearing his pajamas, PJ put on his ratty slippers and went downstairs to the kitchen, where he was greeted by his piles. Piles and piles and piles.

"Good morning, house," PJ said.

Good morning, PJ, the house said back. A house will always talk to you, if you live there long enough. PJ had lived in that house for nearly forty years out of his sixty-three, a blue house on the corner of Clear Pond Road with a white front porch.

PJ sat down at his kitchen table to count out his pills. As he swallowed, he looked up at the wooden sign by the telephone, which read A MESSY HOUSE IS A SIGN OF A HAPPY FAMILY. PJ had bought it at Nifty Gifts & Thrifts, the shop next to the post office. He thought it was a good joke, the bit about a happy family, since the house was empty. But his family had once all lived there, happily, or happily enough, and so the sign was probably PJ's most prized possession, if he had to pick. A reminder of how things had once been.

Then again, his house was chock-a-block full of old memories, so there would be a few other contenders for prized possession: the Sharpie drawing on the living-room wall, for example, a relic from one of his daughters' toddlerhoods, never painted over. Or his ex-wife's wedding dress that still hung in the closet, badly yellowed. The toys in the attic. Or his antique car in the garage.

Upstairs were his kids' rooms, rooms he never dared to go into, because the sadness might crush him. His younger daughter, Sophie, had cleared out most of her things, so it was the emptiness that would hurt. Sophie was all grown-up, twenty-six, and she didn't live far, only twenty minutes away, down in New Bedford. He saw her a few times a month. She was doing all right. He was lucky to have her so close by, even if Sophie wasn't always happy to see him.

It was the room at the end of the hall that really killed PJ. In there was Kate's stuff. His older daughter, his firstborn. Kate's room was the exact same as it had been, the night fifteen years ago she had gone to prom and hadn't come home. Her twin bed, her piggy bank, her posters of half-naked men. Fifteen years later, Kate's softball hat was still hanging on her doorknob outside the room. Maybe that was PJ's most prized possession: the blue hat on the door.

"Hello, hat," he said to it sometimes.

I miss her too, the hat said back. *I wish . . .* the hat always continued, but it never finished the sentence. A hat doesn't know what to wish for.

PJ knew most of what he owned was junk; he didn't think he was sitting on a pile of treasure. He had empty jars on the counters, mail stacked up so high on the table you couldn't see the tablecloth anymore. He knew it had cheery sunflowers on it. His ex-wife loved sunflowers, and PJ liked to think about the tablecloth hidden underneath the mail, but he could never get the strength up to unearth it. And PJ had more crap, spread around, everywhere. He had shoeboxes full of old letters under his bed. There were stacks of books on the floor, books that couldn't fit on the bookshelves. He slept next to a heap of laundry, some of it clean. There were beer cans lined up by the sink. And in the upstairs bathroom, there were still four toothbrushes in the cabinet. Proof that there had once been other people in this house.

After his pills, PJ got up from the kitchen table and made a cup of coffee in the Keurig. "Piece of shit," PJ grumbled, because he had to press every button on it before it started to boil water. He hated the machine, how it made one single sad cup of coffee, but he was not allowed to be at his ex-wife's house until eight A.M., earliest, and had to be there no later than nine. That was the deal. So, PJ had his cup of coffee first, before going back upstairs and putting on a stretched-out T-shirt with beige cargo shorts. He was a large man, overweight, lots of hair on his chest, his long beard was unkempt, his gray hair was down to his shoulders. He wasn't exactly George Clooney, but women always said he had nice eyes. They were green. Women liked him. They always had. They liked that he read poetry and listened to classical music, could play the piano, but they also liked that he loved rock music, and even the new stuff the young people played in the bar. Women liked that PJ knew about cars. They liked that he could tell a good joke, and that he wasn't a snob. They liked that he loved animals. They didn't mind how flatulent he was. They liked his sensitive nature.

PJ slipped on his Birkenstock sandals and his sweater, the zip-up with the polar bears stitched onto it. "If you want to hear a sad story, read about the polar bears," PJ would say to the women at the bar sometimes. He blamed the plight of the polar bear for one of his heart attacks. It was the documentary that had started the chest pain, he told his doctor. The bears were drowning, had the doc heard that? Habitat loss.

"Yes, I've heard that too," his doctor had said. "But I think it's your diet and lifestyle that's causing your heart trouble."

"Genetics," PJ said to that. "Nothing I can do about genetics."

The doctor had given him statins and a pamphlet about diet and exercise.

At 8:05, PJ was out the door for his morning walk. Walking used to be part of his job as a postman, and he walked everywhere still. He'd always gotten plenty of exercise, he was just big-boned, but doctors never listen when you talk about big bones. PJ didn't bother to lock the front door behind him when he went out. People rarely locked their doors in Pondville, unless they were leaving on a long vacation, and that morning, PJ had no plans to go anywhere. Out on the street, PJ waved hello to his neighbor Kellyanne Thomas, headed to work at the cranberry juice factory headquarters. She was in corporate, and PJ felt terrible for her, having to wear a monkey suit to work. PJ used to hate his own work uniform, the navy polyester pants and light-blue shirt, but he had been fired from his mail-carrier job a long time ago. "How are you, PJ?" Kellyanne Thomas called out to him from her driveway.

"We're one day closer to the end!" he called back.

"The end of what?" she asked.

"Our time together! But I've loved every minute."

She laughed. "Well, I have too, PJ."

"You're looking like a million bucks today, Kellyanne," PJ said, although he didn't like the suit. "Don't let the boss get you down."

"Oh, thank you," she said, blushing. "And I suppose you would know what a million bucks looks like!"

PJ chuckled and waved as she drove off. He knew she would smile all the way to work. He liked to make people smile.

It had been $1.5 million, actually, not a million bucks, that PJ had won. Everyone in Pondville knew he had won big in the scratch-off lottery tickets sold at the gas station, ten years ago. He didn't even remember buying the ticket, he'd been so drunk when he bought it. It had been good timing, he had really needed the money, had been about to lose his house, his wife already halfway out the door. But even after the lottery winnings, his wife had left anyway. People might have considered PJ the luckiest man in Pondville, if everyone didn't know how much he'd already lost.

PJ's sandals smacked the pavement. It was fifty-three degrees, the very beginning of spring in New England, the third day of May. It wasn't really sandal weather yet, but it was a short walk.

Every morning, after he had his first cup of coffee alone, PJ walked the ten houses down to his ex-wife's house, where Ivy lived with her boyfriend, the retired judge Fred Sharp, in their home right on the pond. It had been Fred's second home, until Fred moved down full-time so he and Ivy could get serious. He'd taken a big pay cut with the move, too, changing to a district court, but he'd still made a good living, and now he was ready to retire. Fred was also a world-class bird-watcher, and he was taking Ivy on a bird-watching trip, leaving tomorrow. It wasn't just a weekend trip, either; they'd be gone for four entire months to Alaska, which seemed about as far away as they could go. PJ had been steeling himself for it. He walked up the gravel path to their house with heavy legs.

Ivy opened the door; she'd been waiting for him. PJ's ex-wife was still as beautiful as she had been the day he met her. She had just turned sixty-two. She still dyed her hair Marilyn Monroe blond, and she wore red lipstick, lots of jewelry, and colorful ponchos she knit herself. She had been an art teacher at the high school.

"It's not safe to leave me alone," PJ told her, giving his ex-wife his best puppy-dog eyes when he came in, but Ivy only shook her head. She'd explained this before. She and Fred had both retired and it was time for them to travel.

"Live your life," PJ muttered. "Yes, forget all about me. Leave me here to die."

"No one's leaving you to die," Ivy said, rolling her eyes. "We're only gone four months. May until end of August."

"Keep taking your medication," Fred reminded PJ when he came downstairs to join them. Fred was freshly showered and dressed in a V-neck cashmere sweater. "And lay off the booze."

"Yeah, yeah." PJ plopped himself down at the table and picked up the newspaper Ivy had laid out. It was in tatters, because Ivy had cut it up for him before he'd even arrived at her house. PJ wanted to read the news, stay up to date, but he loved animals and children—they were the jewels of the world—and he did not want to hear about bad things happening to them. He was too sensitive. His heart couldn't take it. He'd already had three heart attacks. A fourth might be the one to do it.

So, every morning, after the second heart attack, Ivy had cut up the paper, took out the cruelty to animals or children. She did this back when they lived in the same house together and continued even after she gave up on their marriage and moved out. At first, after she'd left him, Ivy would leave the chopped-up newspaper on his doorstep, but eventually she'd invited PJ over to the house on the pond for breakfast. She still loved PJ, in a different way from before, but she did love him. She wanted him to be all right.

That first breakfast was seven years ago, and now, every morning, PJ took a seat in the clean, yellow-floral-wallpapered kitchen with Ivy and her boyfriend. Ivy would make cinnamon buns or omelets, scones or pancakes, a frittata once in a while. No bacon for PJ, because PJ had accidentally read an article about the factory farming of pigs once, because sometimes Ivy didn't get all the bad news. There was so much of it, bad news, in the paper. She was bound to make mistakes, there was always something she missed.

It was turkey bacon only for Fred, always following a heart-healthy diet. Fred also didn't drink. He exercised. He was a lover of wildlife. A big reader. He was the first Black judge to win the prestigious Noble and Fair Justice Award, and he was known for giving second chances to people who deserved them. He never lost his cool. PJ had tried to hate Fred for stealing his wife, but it wasn't easy to hate Fred, even if he was a dweeb much of the time, always pointing out woodpeckers and titmice, never making dirty jokes, only sometimes laughing at PJ's. "Ivy's Diner," Fred would call the morning meal, patting his stomach, and he would also clean the kitchen afterward, clear the plates and fill the dishwasher and wipe down the counters.

"Apple polisher," PJ would call him, but Fred didn't mind. He did like Ivy's apples and wanted to polish them.

That morning, their last breakfast together before Alaska, Ivy had cut a huge hole in the front page of both newspapers. They had two papers delivered every morning: one for PJ, one for Fred and Ivy to share. They were keeping *The South Coast Daily Sun* in business; most people had made the switch to *The Boston Globe*, or even *The New York Times*, but PJ was resistant to change, and Ivy catered to him. She hardly ever cut up both papers, though, so whatever the front-page news was that morning, it was something extremely upsetting. PJ tried not to think how bad it could be, but imagined Fred and Ivy must have been discussing it before he arrived, and maybe that was why Ivy hadn't made much of a spread. It was simple scrambled eggs and toast, but when PJ took a bite, he found the bread buttered to perfection. PJ reminded himself not to underestimate the simple things. "I hope you always appreciate what you have there," he told Fred, pointing to Ivy puttering around the kitchen.

"I do appreciate her, of course I do," Fred said. "Anyone can see I appreciate her."

"Do you appreciate me, PJ?" Ivy asked, turning around to face her ex-husband. "Because I sometimes wonder."

"I haven't had sex with another woman since you left me. Not once in eight years. How is that not appreciation?"

Ivy laughed and crossed her arms over her chest.

"Okay, fine. Me and Francie Hubble had our thing."

"What about Patricia?"

"Who's that?"

"The woman who owns the Nifty Gifts."

"Oh. Well, yes. A few times. I didn't know you were keeping tabs."

"Will you two stop flirting," Fred said. "I'm right here."

"Jesus Christ, Fred," Ivy said. "No one's flirting."

"I'm always flirting," PJ said. "I'll win her back, someday. You'll see. Maybe once she gets tired of your performance problems in the bedroom." PJ had seen the Viagra in Fred's bedside drawers, one day when he was snooping around upstairs.

"Ha," Ivy said. "Pot calling kettle."

"That's enough of that," Fred said. "But you make a good point, PJ, we should appreciate each other. That's what this trip is about: appreciation. Appreciation for each other, and a new adventure. And birds, of course. New birds to see."

"Here's to adventure then. And birds," PJ said, lifting his glass of OJ, even though he wanted to beg them not to go. They could appreciate each other at home. There were plenty of birds right outside.

"Yes, cheers to birds," Fred said, lifting his coffee cup.

"Cheers to birds," Ivy muttered, with less enthusiasm. But PJ was always cheersing to something, and Ivy had suffered through so many years of it.

"Hey, did you ever think of inviting me?" PJ asked. "I like birds. I could chaperone. I've never been to Alaska." PJ had never been outside New England, except once, to Vietnam and back home again, plus a training camp in Bastrop, Texas, which wasn't much of a place.

"We did discuss it, actually," Ivy said. "We discussed asking you and Sophie to come, too, but ultimately—"

"I'd ruin your time, you think?"

"We knew you'd never go, PJ. We know you don't like leaving Pondville. You don't like to fly. You never even wanted to go on vacation when the kids were little."

"We didn't have the money back then for vacation. You remember how it was—" he started, even though he knew Ivy didn't like to remember. She almost never wanted to talk about their memories of Kate, not even the happy ones.

"Oh, admit it, you're a homebody, Paul," Fred said, sensing PJ was about to try to go down memory lane again. Fred always called PJ by his first name, even though no one else did. "You're a homebody, and Alaska's really far. A man like you doesn't change, Paul. You like the things you like, and you like Pondville. You're not going to turn into Ernest Shackleton overnight."

"I might have gone if I'd been invited," PJ said, huffy, and couldn't remember who Ernest Shackleton was. But it was true Pondville was home, and he was comfortable at home. *The mayor of Pondville*, they called him at the Wild Orchid, because PJ knew everyone at the bar, and remembered their names. Pondville didn't have a real mayor, only a board of selectmen. Bastards, all three of them, according to PJ. But he liked everyone else, mostly, and everyone else liked him. Everyone at the post office had been so sorry when they'd had to fire him. And after PJ won the lottery, his popularity only increased. He'd given money to the church, the farm co-op, the Lions Club. He didn't even belong to the church, the farm co-op, or the Lions Club. He purchased a new playground for the nursery school. If a friend needed money, PJ wrote a check. Ivy and Fred and his daughter Sophie would never take his money, but everyone else in town was glad for a handout. PJ regularly covered a round for the entire bar, sometimes two, except for his estranged brother, Chip, who could pay his own effin' tab as far as PJ was concerned, but Chip had died a year and a half ago anyway. Chip wasn't a problem anymore. Yes, PJ was a popular guy in Pondville. He'd never had a desire to leave, until Ivy and Fred had planned this trip to Alaska without him. He would have liked to have been invited.

There was another reason PJ rarely left Pondville in recent years, but PJ didn't like to talk about the DUIs. Why he had to walk everywhere in town he wanted to go. A decade ago, over the span of two years, he'd been pulled over for drunk driving twice, and rolled his car the third time. PJ had also driven the mail truck into Assawompset Pond before that, but he hadn't been breathalyzed for that accident. He had only been fired, his uniform and pension taken away. He had stopped leaving Pondville, for almost any reason, except to go to the Boston hospital during his heart attacks. He walked to the bar, and he walked home.

"We'll take you on the next trip, PJ, I promise," Ivy said. "We'll all go to Vermont or something. But now I need to go finish packing for Alaska; I just know I'm going to forget something we need. But you boys enjoy your breakfast. Take your time."

Fred pointed to his cheek for a kiss, and Ivy gave him one, and then she bent and gave a peck to PJ too. Both men smiled and watched her walk upstairs before they returned to their newspapers. PJ sniffed and lifted his paper to cover his face. He was tearing up. This was their final breakfast together before the trip. This was the last supper, and Ivy was already headed upstairs to pack as if she didn't even care.

PJ tried to focus on the newspaper. There was a new bakery opening up on Main Street; gas prices were higher than they used to be. There was a war, somewhere really, really far away, and nothing mentioned about children dying in it, so Ivy had left it in. But of course, there were children dying in that war. Horrible things happen around the world every day. PJ didn't forget that, as hard as he tried to. And then there was that huge hole in the front page of both newspapers. It must have involved children, whatever it was Ivy had removed from both papers, and it must have been bad. He tried not to think about it.

By the time PJ got to the obituaries, he was about to go home for his post-breakfast nap, after which he'd walk the mile down to the Wild Orchid Bar for the rest of the day. It was a Hawaiian-themed place. Hank and Moose were always there by eleven, ready to joke around all afternoon and into the night, watch sports, play darts. It filled the time. PJ had a lot of time.

Yes, PJ was about to close the newspaper and get going on the day and everything would have been so different if he had. He might have even gotten back home in time to answer a phone call from a social worker who was dialing him right then. If he had taken that phone call, everything might have been different: it would have meant Fred and Ivy heard about it before they left for their trip, and they would have certainly pushed the social workers to consider other options, probably would have delayed their trip to Alaska. But PJ was blissfully unaware of the tragedy that had struck the Meeklin family two days before, and he didn't know anything about their connection to him. The last name didn't ring any bells for Ivy when she saw it in the paper that morning, and no one had any idea that a social worker with the Massachusetts Department of Children and Families was attempting to reach PJ at his house.

In his ignorance of what was to come, PJ lingered on the last page of the paper, and that was when he noticed the obituary for an old friend. He hadn't seen the man in forty-five years, but he recognized him in the picture. Bottlecap glasses and a doughy face. Yes, he looked nearly the same, it was remarkable. That was Gene Bartlett. As teenagers, PJ and Gene had both been lifeguards at the beach at Clear Pond, and they used to use their keys to unlock the front gate late at night and take girls to look for the mermaid. Local legend had it, you could only see the mermaid of Clear Pond after dark, when she came out of the water to sleep on the raft at night. It was how both Gene and PJ had lost their virginity, taking girls to the beach to look for the mermaid.

Four and a half decades later, PJ had still never seen the mermaid, lumped in among so many other life disappointments, and now, apparently, his old friend Gene was dead.

The obituary read:

> *Gene Bartlett Sr., 63, husband of 41 years this September of Michelle (Cobb) Bartlett, passed away on Friday, following a brief illness. Born in Pondville, Mass., Gene was a proud 1969 graduate of Pondville High. After Gene met and fell in love with Michelle, the couple moved to Los Angeles to pursue Michelle's acting career, and Gene found success in LA real estate. They lived a comfortable life. For the past decade, they enjoyed retirement by traveling the country in an RV, seeing sights such as the Grand Canyon, the Badlands in South Dakota, the Space Needle in Seattle and eating one too many beignets in New Orleans, before settling down last year in a two-bedroom condo in Tucson, Ariz. Gene is survived by his darling Michelle and his—*

PJ stopped reading at that point. "Michelle Cobb," he said, and whistled, remembering how good Michelle had once looked in this one orange sweater. PJ wished there was a photograph of Michelle that went along with the obituary, but it was only Gene, looking like the same goober he was forty-five years ago. Michelle Cobb had been the other love of PJ's life, besides Ivy, but then PJ had gone away to war, and he'd never seen her again. Michelle Cobb was back on the market. *Wasn't this a change of fortune!* Michelle was likely still living at the two-bedroom condo in the Tender Hearts Retirement Community, because that's where the obituary said you could send flowers in memory of Gene Bartlett. The retirement community was in Tucson.

PJ excused himself from the breakfast table and went upstairs to Fred's office to use his computer. The room held a small desk and a computer but was mostly full of cardboard filing boxes, so many boxes you barely had room to move in the swivel chair. PJ assumed they were old court case files, and wondered why Fred didn't just toss them. PJ sat down at the desk and typed into Google: *Florist, Tucson*. He took out his credit card and sent a dozen red roses, and also a small teddy bear. The Valentine's Day package, it was called. *My deepest condolences,* he asked the florist to write on the card. *All my love from Pondville,* he signed it. *Your old friend, PJ Halliday.*

This was the beginning of something wonderful, PJ was sure of it.

And then there was a tap-tap-tap on the door, and Fred pushed his way in. Fred didn't ask what PJ was doing on the computer, because PJ used that computer all the time, he didn't have internet at home.

"Hey, Paul, can I show you something?" Fred asked.

"It better not be disgusting, Fred," PJ said, because Fred had bunions on his feet, and that's when Fred pulled out a ring. It was a sensible size, the diamond, which PJ was grateful for. The diamond on the engagement ring he'd given Ivy, all those years ago, was so small it had probably worn away to a grain of sand sitting unworn in her jewelry box.

"I wanted to ask for your blessing," Fred said. "And I wanted to ask if you'd be my best man. Ours is a strange friendship but it's—"

PJ didn't let him finish, because he grabbed him by the face and kissed Fred on the mouth. He was overjoyed to be asked for his blessing, and that Fred wanted him around for the wedding, wanted him to play a major part. "Of course, I will, buddy. And I'll start planning our big bachelor party."

"No party," Fred said, being a dweeb again.

"What are you two doing in there?" Ivy asked, because the office door was closed. "Freddy, you have to finish packing. PJ, what's this about a party? If you get arrested while we're gone, there's going to be no one to bail you out. Remember we won't have cell service most of the trip."

"I remember," PJ said. "I won't be able to call." This was the worst part; he wouldn't even be able to talk to them. They were leaving him here to die of loneliness.

"So, no parties. No bad behavior. Call Sophie if you get into any trouble. Don't take advantage of your daughter; you should do your own grocery shopping, but I don't want you rotting in jail."

"No bad behavior. Don't call Sophie unless I need to," PJ promised, and smiled at Ivy. It was all PJ could do not to spill the beans, make Fred get on one knee right there among the cardboard boxes, but somehow PJ kept his mouth shut. Good ol' Freddy wanted to propose on their trip to Alaska, of course he did, that would be more romantic than asking in Pondville in front of her ex-husband. PJ couldn't believe it: his ex-wife and his best friend were getting married! They were heading to Alaska tomorrow, and when they came back there would be a wedding. A big one, PJ hoped. He would be the best man. PJ and Ivy's daughter Sophie would be the maid of honor. It would be open bar.

"I'll also need a plus-one on the invite," he whispered to Fred, thinking of Michelle Cobb and how wowed she would be, once she saw the flower arrangement, the teddy bear.

3

The story that Ivy would cut out of both newspapers had happened two days earlier, on the first day of May, three streets over from where PJ lived in his house full of junk, in a small white house on Deerfield Lane.

It all started when a nine-year-old boy named Ollie Meeklin opened his eyes. Ollie thought it was odd that he hadn't heard his mother's alarm go off; she always pressed Snooze several times. In fact, the house was so quiet that morning, that first day of May, Ollie could hear a mouse farting in the walls. His sister was still asleep, but she slept so quietly it was almost like she was dead. She had told Ollie recently she wished she was dead sometimes, and so Ollie had vowed to do something about it. He was going to tell an adult at school why Luna was so depressed. His sister was the smart one, and older by eleven months, already ten, but he would be the brave one today. He would be the tattletale.

Finally, his sister was awake. She wasn't dead, which was a relief.

"You look weird this morning," Luna told him. "Stop being weird."

"Can't help it," he said.

"I know." Luna shook her head. Ollie was the sweet one. Sweet and round like a cupcake, redheaded and freckled like his father. Luna was small and dark-haired. She had been a biter as a child, and her mother had thought maybe she was possessed, but the pediatrician said it was simply because Luna was jealous of Ollie, so close to her in age. The doctor said he usually recommended two years between children, to prevent violent behavior and give the mother time to recover. Their mother had never recovered. In fact, the kids were so close in age that they were in the same grade. Fourth graders.

That morning, Ollie had a spring in his step. He was going to make things right today, get his sister the help she needed. That was the way they talked about sadness on TV.

But on the first floor of the Meeklin household, something was different, something was strange. Their mother was sitting next to their father at the kitchen table. Usually, their mom was running around in the morning, clucking like a mother hen, wearing the fuzzy pink bathrobe the kids' father called "The Bonerkiller." Their mother was always rush-rush-rushing to get things ready for the day, lunches made, homework in backpacks. But that day, she was simply sitting down next to their dad, Officer Frank Meeklin, and staring at him.

"What's wrong, Mom?" Ollie asked. Their mom had to go to the mental hospital for two weeks after their grandpa died, and Ollie didn't want it to happen again.

"Everything's fine," their mother said. She pointed to the counter. "I got donuts."

Their mother had indeed gotten donuts, a whole box. "Whose birthday is it?" Luna asked.

"Mine," their mother said, although it wasn't. Her birthday was in the summertime. The kids weren't stupid. They were fourth graders, and Luna was probably a genius, their teachers said, but their parents never wanted to hear about that, because being a genius meant a special school, school they couldn't afford, especially not for a girl. If only Ollie had been the one born with the brains, their dad often said.

"One minute until you're out the door," their mother warned, which was more like her, but she was still sitting. "Backpacks on, shoes on, let's go." Usually, she would be holding the backpacks in her hands, throwing their shoes their way, but today she kept sitting, watching her husband.

Luna and Ollie's father, Frank Meeklin, didn't seem to notice he was being watched. He was drinking his coffee and having his powdered donut, wasn't paying much attention to his wife or his kids. "I got to get going too," he said, standing up and brushing some white powder off his uniform.

"You haven't finished your coffee," their mom pointed out.

"Oh, I'll stop at Dunkin' later. I've got to get in early. A colleague's birthday. I'm in charge of the flowers. There's a party after work. I'll be late." Frank leaned over to kiss his wife goodbye. He didn't know what had gotten into him really; he never kissed his wife goodbye, and she never tried to kiss him either, but he was in such a good mood because it was Cherri's birthday, the new receptionist at the police station. As things stood, Frank was currently only allowed to touch Cherri's breasts over her sweater, but he was sure that would change tonight, after a romantic dinner, because Cherri had admitted she did have a fantasy about sex in the back of a police cruiser. Frank had cleaned up so much blood and vomit and piss and shit off the plastic seats in the back of the cruiser that he did not share that fantasy, but whatever, Frank would do it anywhere.

The children both grabbed a donut. They put on their shoes. They grabbed their backpacks. They felt nervous and they weren't sure why. Maybe it was the school project they had to present. It was family history day. Ollie had written a report on their grandfather, his dad's dad. Grandpa Meeklin was a firefighter, but he died before Ollie was born. Ollie knew his mom's dad much better; Grandpa Chip used to live with their family, but Ollie would never ever write a report on him. Grandpa Chip was a mean old bastard who hanged himself in their garage two Octobers ago, and that's when their mom had her first breakdown and had to go on those special meds. So, instead, Ollie had made a poster of firefighter pictures, had drawn a house burning and people inside it screaming.

Luna had kept her family project a secret, and she hadn't made a poster; she had done a PowerPoint instead. It was on a thumb drive. Ollie thought he should remind Luna not to forget the thumb drive, because his mother wasn't doing it. No, his mom was rinsing her mouth out in the sink after her husband had kissed her. Ollie knew his parents hated each other, but that was a little much.

Luna had indeed forgotten the thumb drive and ran upstairs to get it after Ollie reminded her. When no one was looking, Ollie grabbed his father's coffee, poured it into a water bottle. His teacher had claimed that coffee helped her with concentration and focus, which was why she drank it all the time. Ollie's most recent report card had said "needs to learn to concentrate," and his dad had whupped his ass over it. So, Ollie had started sneaking coffee. He needed to learn to concentrate. And today he needed to concentrate on being brave.

Outside, at the end of the driveway, Luna and Ollie climbed up the three black steps into the school bus while their father got into his cruiser. Luna and Ollie always sat right behind the bus driver, because Luna got in too many fights when she sat in the back. Their dad turned on his sirens as the bus pulled away, to scare the kids.

"I hate him," Luna said.

"Yeah," Ollie agreed, although his feelings toward his father were more complicated. He knew their parents loved them, even though their father was mean and hit them sometimes, and even if their mom yelled at them for being lazy and slow and even though she did crazy things. She threw out food she'd just bought because she said she saw bugs in it. Lately, she'd been accusing people on the street of following her.

Ms. Deon, the old woman who drove the bus, looked in the rearview mirror and spoke over her shoulder, "Oh, Luna, sweetie, don't you ever say you hate your parents. I know they would do anything for you."

Frank Meeklin was feeling a little funny when he arrived at the Farm & Flower Market, but he chalked it up to nerves. It had been a long time since he'd given flowers to a girl he really liked, with the promise of sex later. So that feeling in his chest? Butterflies, he was sure. It was nice, really, to be a twenty-eight-year-old man in love. He and Elaine had gotten married too young. High school sweethearts, pregnant with Luna senior year, and Elaine wasn't nuts back then. Or she'd been nuts but in a good way. A fun way. Elaine wasn't fun anymore. And everything would have been so different if they had used a Trojan or a Durex that night. Any brand would have probably worked.

It was by the refrigerator of cut flowers when Frank started feeling worse. He couldn't decide between roses or maybe something more creative, *maybe those purple ones?* and the decision seemed to be giving him the sweats. He looked around for someone to ask about their opinion on the flowers, and that's when the chest pains started. He felt like he might faint or vomit or both. He was hot and cold at the same time.

Frank thought some fresh air might help. He was just dizzy, he was sure, from the smell of the flowers. Some of those flowers were strong-smelling. He went outside and sat on the curb next to his cruiser. He put his head between his knees. "I'm in love," he said to himself, out loud. This must be what this was. He was really in love, and he'd never been in love before. Not ever with Elaine, not even in high school, not even that great night on New Year's Eve. He was overwhelmed by love, so it was making him sick. Soon his chest pains would stop, and he could stand up again, and he would go into the flower shop, and he would buy roses, because even if they were cliché, they were classic, and Cherri the receptionist was a classic. Like a Cadillac or an ice-cream sundae, he thought. He would say that to her tonight, that she was an ice-cream sundae, and her breasts were two scoops. *Wow, that was romantic,* Frank thought. It was his final thought before passing out. Frank fell off the curb where he'd been perched, and he lay on the pavement between the yellow lines of the empty parking spot.

No one noticed Frank, because the checkout boy was the only one in the store, and he was addicted to a game called Candy Crush on his phone. If the owner wasn't in the store, Ryley, the checkout boy, was definitely playing Candy Crush. So, Ryley didn't see the policeman curled in a fetal position in the handicapped parking spot in front of the store because he was looking at the candy onscreen. And there were no other shoppers there, because it was early, and most people were either eating breakfast at home, or on their way to school or work, or waiting in the drive-thru line of the Dunkin' Donuts, not stopping for cut roses at the Farm & Flower. Officer Frank lay on the blacktop, curled up. He was not dead yet, but there was foam in the corners of his mouth, and he certainly needed immediate medical attention.

As luck would have it, another customer was on her way into the store, a woman by the name of Gail Quigley, and she was coming into the Farm & Flower because it was where she liked to buy liver for her cat, Mittens, who was a two-time blue-ribbon winner at the southeast Massachusetts cat show. Gail Quigley was distracted that morning because her daughter, who often accused Gail of liking the cat more than she liked her own daughter, had asked to go on birth-control pills. Gail Quigley thought that was quite the ask, coming from a fifteen-year-old. Lily had insisted the pills were needed in order to regulate her period and clear up her acne, but Gail Quigley wasn't born yesterday.

Gail was trying to find the number for an ob-gyn, was looking at her phone when she pulled into the lot at the Farm & Flower, when she felt her car hit something. She assumed it was the dog who belonged to the owner of Farm & Flower Market, that ugly old hound, but when she got out of the car, she saw it was not a dog crushed underneath her wheel, but it was Officer Frank Meeklin. Gail Quigley, who never cursed because it set a bad example for her daughter, said: "Oh fuck, oh fuck, oh fuck." Officer Frank Meeklin had once pulled Gail Quigley over for going 40 in a school zone but let her off with a warning. Gail Quigley started to scream and scream and scream for help, and Ryley the checkout boy came running out. Even though he was honestly having the game of his life in Candy Crush, he still tossed his phone down on the counter to go see what the screaming was all about, but when he saw Gail Quigley trying to pull a limp Frank Meeklin out from under her Jeep, he turned back around to dial 911.

When the ambulance arrived, Frank Meeklin was loaded into the back, and the two EMTs spent a little time hanging around, talking to Ryley and trying to soothe Gail. It was not important to rush to the hospital; there was no one to save. One of the EMTs reached down to scratch the ears of the big brown dog who belonged to the owner of the Farm & Flower, and the man noticed the dog had a tuft of orange fur in his mouth. The dog was known to be a cat killer, which is why Gail Quigley hated him.

An hour later, Elaine Meeklin got a visit from two police officers, her husband's coworkers, regretfully informing her that Frank was dead, and Gail Quigley had killed him with her Jeep Wrangler. Elaine did her best to cry in front of the officers, but when she closed the door in their faces and was alone in the house, she couldn't believe her luck. She wasn't going to get caught. She was going to cash out on that life insurance. Everyone would be so focused on the car accident, they wouldn't ask any other questions. Yes, there would be an autopsy, but Elaine Meeklin was sure they wouldn't be looking for suspicious substances, even though Frank Meeklin had been lying on the ground when Gail Quigley hit him. Cause of death had to be: *Hit by moving vehicle, distracted driver.* Standing in her kitchen in her fuzzy pink bathrobe, Elaine Meeklin hugged herself. What a terrific thing she had pulled off.

He was dead, they said, already, so she didn't need to hurry to the hospital. She could meet them at the morgue to identify the body, but they knew it was him already. It was a small town, and his name was right there on his police uniform. No mystery there.

Elaine went upstairs, took off her Bonerkiller bathrobe, got dressed in her favorite red blouse and jeans, and then got in her car to go pick up the kids early from school to break the news to them. She decided that was what a person would do next, if they were shocked and horrified by their husband's death. They would go pick up their children.

In the White Rock Elementary School main office, Principal McGuffries hugged Elaine when she told him what had happened, even though she certainly did not want to be hugged. She would have preferred a high-five, but she knew that would be a strange ask, even for a principal who high-fived kids in the hallway of White Rock Elementary School all day long. It was a big part of his job, to give the high-fives out. Principal McGuffries walked Elaine Meeklin down to the fourth-grade classroom, where her two kids would be.

Luna was standing in front of the rest of the kids, giving some sort of presentation. "It's family history day, unfortunately," Principal McGuffries said with a cringe as he and Elaine stood in the hall outside the classroom. The kids hadn't noticed them yet. There was a PowerPoint up on the projector behind Luna, and there was a black-and-white yearbook photo of a young man on the projector. Elaine had long ago stopped helping with Luna's homework, and she had not the slightest idea how Luna had gotten hold of her yearbook. "This guy went to high school with my mom."

Under the photo, it read:

> MARK STACKPOLE
> Varsity Baseball, Drama Club, Jazz Ensemble, Crossword Club

"He seems smart, doesn't he?" Luna asked the class. "I don't know what my mom was thinking, why she married my dad instead of him. And get this, now Mark Stackpole is famous. He's on a soap opera, on TV every day while we're at school. He doesn't always wear a shirt. You should see his muscles."

"All right, Luna," Ms. Delaney said. "That's it for today."

Luna ignored her teacher and asked her classmate Gabriel to go to the next slide.

Gabriel clicked the button and revealed a microscope photograph of sperm meeting egg. Some of the kids giggled, while others stared blankly.

"Oh no," Ms. Delaney said. She had noticed the principal standing in the doorway.

Gabriel clicked the button again, and there was a phrase projected on the screen. It was a French phrase, so Luna didn't try to pronounce it. She was a genius, but she was still a fourth grader, and she had never taken French. She had never heard it said aloud, she had only read about it in her mother's diary. Luna looked down at her next index card. "This is when three people have s-e-x—"

"Luna!" Ms. Delaney reprimanded. "Not appropriate."

"Jiminy Cricket," Principal McGuffries said.

"But I spelled it," Luna said. "I didn't say s-e-x." It was on the class list of words the kids weren't allowed to say. "I think Mark Stackpole is my real father. I found my mom's old diary. The timeline adds up. My mom and Frank Meeklin and Mark Stackpole had intercourse together nine months before I was born. Am I allowed to say 'intercourse'?"

Out in the hallway, Elaine Meeklin turned to the principal, the blood draining from her face. Principal McGuffries averted his eyes. Elaine felt sweat bead at her temples.

"Well—" Principal McGuffries started, grasping for something positive. "They'll have sex ed next year. It's state mandated." He hoped that would be a help. He hated to see women embarrassed.

"On second thought," Elaine said, smoothing her hair back, "you know what, I'll tell them about the accident after school. Let them have one normal school day. One last normal one."

Principal McGuffries nodded, and together they backed away from the door, walked back down the hall. The kids hadn't seen them. It was only the teacher, poor first-year teacher Ms. Delaney, who had noticed Ms. Meeklin and the principal, standing there in the dark of the doorway, witnessing how wrong things went in her classroom sometimes, especially when she let Luna Meeklin have the floor.

On the way back to her house, Elaine was feeling a little rattled, and sweaty. She turned left onto Deerfield Lane and almost ran over an orange cat, darting across the street. The cat looked bloody, had possibly been missing an ear. Poor kitty, Elaine thought, but kept on driving. She was almost home.

She pulled into the driveway and went inside. She opened the fridge. She had just dipped into some of her dead husband's leftover cheesecake—he'd gone to the Cheesecake Factory up in Braintree over the weekend, with the woman Elaine knew he was having an affair with, and Elaine had followed them and now she had proof; Elaine wasn't so crazy after all, was she?—and that's when Elaine got a phone call. It was the school nurse.

"Ollie is sick," the nurse said. "Can you come get him?"

"What do you mean he's sick?" she asked. "I just saw him in his classroom. He looked fine." But Elaine *hadn't* seen Ollie, she realized. She had only seen Luna doing her little song and dance about sperm and egg. "He's sick?" she asked. "What's wrong with him?"

"Clammy," the nurse said. "Some vomiting."

"I'll come right now," Elaine said. "I'll be there in ten." She reluctantly put the cheesecake down.

"Thank you," said the nurse. "He seems very sick. He might be hallucinating." Then the nurse told Elaine what Ollie had told her. She whispered it, since it wasn't a comfortable conversation to have in an elementary school. Ollie had claimed their grandfather had exposed himself to Luna. Those were her words, not Ollie's. Ollie had said his grandfather had shown his sister his wiener and asked if the nurse could find his sister a therapist. "It's my job to check up on accusations like that," the nurse said. "Even if . . ."

"No," Elaine said. "It didn't happen."

"Okay," the nurse said. "If you're sure. Otherwise, you know I have to report it."

"I'm very sure it didn't happen. Ollie is an imaginative child."

The nurse agreed. Both Meeklin children were always in trouble for being imaginative.

"And besides," Elaine said, "my father killed himself. Nineteen months ago. He hung himself in my garage."

The nurse was silent for a few seconds after that. "I'm sorry," she said. "I had no idea."

"You couldn't have known," Elaine said. "Don't kick yourself," she told the nurse. She was about to hang up the phone when it occurred to her to ask. "Has Ollie had any coffee?"

"I would never give a child coffee," the nurse said. "I'm a registered nurse."

"Can you ask him? Ask him if he's had any coffee?"

The nurse asked him.

"Just a cup from home," the nurse said, back on the phone. "He said he needed it for bravery. I'm sure I don't have to tell you he's a strange kid."

"How much did he drink?"

"I don't know, Ms. Meeklin, I didn't give it to him."

"HOW MUCH DID HE DRINK?" Elaine demanded.

The nurse asked Ollie, who was lying on the plastic couch next to her, writhing. "His whole water bottle," she reported back.

"Oh my God. Oh my God. Oh my God. Call 911," Elaine said. "Call 911. Tell them he drank Visine and it's deadly. It can be deadly."

"Visine eyedrops? Why did he do that?"

"It was in the coffee. I put it there. It's poison. Please," she said to the nurse. "Call 911. Oh my God, call 911 right now, I'm hanging up, call them now."

And as the call disconnected, the whole town of Pondville heard Elaine Meeklin scream. The early birds at the bar put down their eleven A.M. beers. The mice in the walls stopped their scampering. The deer in the woods by the reservoir raised their heads. The mermaid who lived in Clear Pond shivered.

Elaine Meeklin had read, on the internet late at night, that Visine eyedrops are odorless, tasteless, and deadly if you consumed enough of them. Elaine had used two bottles. They were $4.99 at Target. It had seemed too easy. She had originally picked April 1 to do it, the perfect date to say it was her son's April Fool's joke gone wrong, but she'd chickened out last month and wondered if the affair was only imagined. But she had proof of the affair now, real proof, photos from the Cheesecake Factory, and May was a new month, a second chance, and couldn't a nine-year-old boy pull a practical joke on his father anytime? He could get the idea at any minute at that age. There was a scene in *Wedding Crashers* where Owen Wilson puts eyedrops in the coffee of his romantic rival to give him diarrhea. It's not a crime to give your dad the shits as a practical joke, Elaine had planned to say, if she had to, in court. But she had never meant to give the coffee-and-eyedrop mixture to her kids. It was for their father, who was a cheater and a bastard, a liar and a violent drunk. He had deserved it.

Elaine Meeklin rushed around to get things together, the kind of rushing she usually did in the morning before the kids went to school. She grabbed a duffel bag. She knew she would need supplies for the hospital; she had been to the ER before, many times, for other emergencies with the kids. She grabbed a few books, extra clothes for herself and Ollie, protein bars, mini bags of goldfish. She threw in the rest of the box of donuts. She was buckling herself into the front seat of the car when her cell rang again. It was Ollie's teacher. She scrambled to answer. "I'm on the way to the hospital," she said. "Tell him to hang on. Please tell him to hang on."

On the other end of the line, Ms. Delaney paused. She was a little confused. She had heard from Principal McGuffries that Officer

Frank Meeklin was dead, dead as a doornail, had no more hanging on left to do. She had no idea that Ollie Meeklin was very ill, an hour and a half ago she had sent him down to the nurse's for a tummy ache, which was standard stuff for a fourth-grade teacher. Ms. Delaney was only calling Ms. Meeklin to apologize for what she had seen in the classroom. How upsetting that must have been, to see her fourth-grade daughter talking about her mom's sex life in front of everyone, and on the day of the accident. Ms. Delaney was a new teacher, this was her first year, and she didn't want to get fired, so she was calling to apologize. "Ms. Meeklin, I'm so sorry," Ms. Delaney said, and then she started to cry. Jessica Delaney's own father had died a few months before, had collapsed suddenly on Christmas Eve, and she was still kind of a wreck. "I'm so sorry," she said. "I'm so sorry, Ms. Meeklin. I wish there was something I could do to change it. I wish everyone didn't see it happen. It was horrible, horrible I let it happen—"

"Everyone saw him?" Elaine Meeklin asked, the fear rising in her. "It was horrible? You let the other children see him? I'm on my way. Is it too late to see him? I'm on the way to the hospital. Is it too late?"

"Oh, Ms. Meeklin, I'm so sorry." Jessica Delaney could see what was happening, the first stage of grief: denial. Jessica hadn't believed her father was really gone until she saw him, rigor mortis under the white sheet. "I'm sure you can see his body," she said, trying to help. "They always let the family see the body, if it's not too . . . damaged." Principal McGuffries had told Ms. Delaney about the car crash at the Farm & Flower, so Mr. Meeklin's body might not be in great shape. They might not let her see him, but Ms. Delaney wasn't sure.

On the other end of the line, Elaine Meeklin began shrieking in pain.

"Oh my. I'm so sorry, Ms. Meeklin," Jessica Delaney said, responding to the shrieks.

"I killed him! I killed my baby!" Elaine was pounding on the steering wheel. She was still in the driveway. There was no point going anywhere if it was too late.

Jessica Delaney was twenty-five, and she hated when grown adults called each other baby, but she was not going to judge a grieving woman. Jessica's own mother kissed her father all over his face, after he was gone. Jessica Delaney figured Elaine Meeklin had sent her husband to the store for milk or something, and that's why he was killed, why she thought it was her fault. "Oh, Ms. Meeklin," Jessica Delaney said, wondering if she should call her Elaine instead, during such an intimate conversation. "Elaine—you mustn't blame yourself. It was an accident. My mother always blamed herself but it's . . . it's no one's fault. It was an accident."

Elaine Meeklin was sobbing on the other end of the line. She repeated what Jessica Delaney said. "It was an accident."

"Yes," Jessica Delaney said. "Exactly."

"My baby," Ms. Meeklin wailed. "It was an accident. An accident."

"I'm so sorry," Jessica Delaney said. "I'm so sorry Ms.—Elaine—I'm so sorry, but I have to go. I can call you after school if you'd like to talk more. I'm here for you."

In the background, Elaine Meeklin heard the noise of all the kids, her son's classmates. Recess was over, they were flooding back in. That was more than Elaine Meeklin could bear, and she hung up as quick as she could. She opened her car door and vomited in the driveway. She threw up all the cheesecake she'd eaten. She threw up her pills from that morning, that were supposed to make her feel like a normal mom and get rid of the voices she heard sometimes. The voices that had been telling her to kill her husband for months. She was trembling as she got out of the car and went to her front door. She had killed her baby boy. She had only meant to kill her husband, who deserved it. Her baby boy didn't deserve it. The voices had never said to do that.

Elaine went into Ollie and Luna's room and lay in Ollie's bed for a long, long time, holding his stuffed alligator, one he'd had since he was a baby. She bit the alligator as she cried and cried. Ollie had been such a good boy. He had been her little guy, he had been the one who liked to bake with her, he had been the one who liked to cuddle. She had been a good mom to him, she told herself. Frank was the one who flew off the handle at the kids. He was the one who broke Ollie's arm that time, another time they had to go to the ER. Frank really had deserved to die. She should feel proud for killing him. She had been a good mom. She had only gone a little crazy after her dad died, but who wouldn't? With what had happened. And she almost always took her meds. She could think clearly if she took her meds. She was thinking clearly now, wasn't she?

That was when Elaine realized that she had confessed to the murder, to both the school nurse and to Ms. Delaney. Jessica Delaney had been surprisingly understanding, but Elaine knew the jury was unlikely to think it was an accident that she had poisoned both her husband and son. The practical-joke defense would never hold up, not with the way things had turned out, she could see that now. She would be going to prison if she stuck around for the cops to come get her at this house. Her husband's colleagues. It was only a matter of time before the sirens returned to her driveway.

There was only one thing Elaine could do at this point. She sat up in bed. She wiped her eyes. She had to go be with her son. She knew that with clarity. She was calm suddenly, at the thought of being with Ollie. She took a deep breath. She went to the computer in her bedroom, where she and Frank had slept together the night before. Another lifetime ago.

There was the matter of what to do with Luna. Luna would need someone to take care of her if Elaine was gone. She didn't know anyone who was up to the job of taking care of Luna. Elaine's parents were dead, and so were Frank's, all of them burning in hell. She opened Google and searched: *guardianship choices for your child when you have no family*. Google was quick with its suggestions: *choose a non-relative as a godparent, or a close family friend, a kind neighbor, a clergy member.*

Elaine didn't know any clergy members, but she had neighbors. Across the road was Pamela Korman, with the medicine cabinet full of painkillers, down the street there was Hallie O'Connor with five kids of her own. She mentally thumbed through Ollie and Luna's classmates who had nice or rich parents. Luna hated all her classmates. It would be a great betrayal to leave Luna with one of them.

And Luna needed so much care, especially after what had happened with Elaine's father. Elaine's father, Luna's grandpa, had always been a cruel man, abusive and mean as a rattlesnake, which is probably why Elaine had married another man with anger problems, history repeating itself, et cetera, but she was sure her dad was losing his mind when he did what he did. Elaine knew she shouldn't make excuses. She wished she could stop making excuses.

A year and a half before, in the fall, Elaine had come home from grocery shopping, and the TV volume was up so loud that her father didn't hear her come in the door. When she walked into the living room, her father had his penis out of his pants and was flapping it at Luna, sitting on the other end of the couch, and talking to the little girl in a cartoon voice, calling it Mr. Turtle, saying Mr. Turtle wants a pat, Mr. Turtle is hungry. When Elaine saw that, she had dropped the groceries, breaking all the eggs, and she had taken off her high-heeled shoe and beaten her father with it. He sat there and let her. He had never been the kind of man who let anyone beat him, but he sat there and stared straight ahead.

"Has this happened before?" Elaine had asked once she was done with the shoe. Her father shook his head no, but she didn't believe him. She had to ask Luna over and over before the girl answered.

"He likes to show it to me," she finally said. "But I've never touched it."

"Don't you dare ever touch it," Elaine had snapped at her daughter, as if any of it were Luna's fault, and she felt bad about that, but she was angry, so angry, in the moment, that this was happening in her house, under her roof. Luna said she'd never touched it, and Grandpa had never touched her either, it was just Mr. Turtle, and just for the past few weeks, ever since Ollie went to soccer and Frank had decided Luna's gymnastics were too expensive. Luna told her mother she mostly ignored her grandpa and watched whatever was on television. That day it was *Saving Private Ryan*, which is why it was so loud everything exploding all the time in that movie, and why her father hadn't heard Elaine coming into the house in time to zip his pants.

Elaine promised her father right then she'd be putting him in the old-folks' home as soon as she could. Frank had recently said they couldn't afford that, either, but Elaine would find a way to get her father out of her house and away from her daughter. Her father could show Mr. Turtle to the nurses in the old-folks' home, who had seen hundreds of wrinkled old turtles before. What was another one.

"We're not going to tell your father or your brother," Elaine decided, and told Luna. "Your father will kill Grandpa. He'll shoot him in the head. And as for Ollie, he will never understand. He'll look at you different, but he'll never really understand." Then she sat by Luna, who was crying by then, and she told Luna it happened to most girls. Not this thing exactly, but something like it was bound to happen eventually. It was horrible, but as long as she hadn't touched it, she was sure Luna would be fine. It happened to most girls at some point in some way, she repeated, because the world is full of rotten men.

So, when Frank came home a few hours later, no one told him. He saw his father-in-law's scratched-up face, beat up from the high-heeled shoe, and asked if he'd gotten into another bar fight. The old man was always getting into bar fights. Ollie came in with his dad, the boy was still dressed in his soccer uniform, and Elaine had hugged him tight, hoped he wouldn't grow up like other men. He smelled like freshly mown grass. Then the family all had dinner together. It was chicken and peas. It was back to normal, except that Elaine would spend the rest of the night researching assisted-living homes in the area, anyplace she could dump her father. It could have been so much worse, she told herself that night, and many nights after. She knew it could have been worse than it was, which is why it was so frustrating later, when Luna started getting into fights at school, started moping around for no reason.

Ollie told his mother Luna needed therapy, because that's how he saw people on TV get over terrible things. Luna had told her brother what had happened, and of course Ollie didn't understand, just like their mother had warned.

Therapy wouldn't do shit, Elaine told her son and said Ollie should shut up before their father heard him talking. There was no point in getting Frank riled up about something that had already happened, and nothing left to do about it.

Knowing what Elaine knew now, she wished she had let Frank kill her dad in a fit of rage that night instead of insisting they all have dinner together. Chicken and peas. She wished she'd let her husband blast her father into the next lifetime. If that had happened, Frank would be spending life in prison, and Ollie would still be alive. Her baby boy. Her father would be dead either way, because the next morning, after the turtle incident, she found her dad in the garage, hanging near the chest freezer by a rope. He had left a suicide note, but he hadn't apologized to Luna or to Elaine or expressed any remorse for anything else he'd done. He'd only left a long rambling screed about his brother. He always perseverated on his brother. He was obsessed with the money his brother had won in the scratch-offs.

Elaine, sitting at the computer and remembering all this, everything that had happened in the past two years and how it had all gone wrong ever since, suddenly realized: *Holy shit, she did have a family member in town.* Someone who could take care of Luna. Her dad's brother. They had been estranged since they were young. People could never believe it, that the two men lived in the same small town and never spoke in all those years, not even when they were both sitting at the same bar, a few seats apart. Elaine had never met her uncle, never even shook his hand, although they'd been in the same room together many times, at the pizza restaurant or in the post office, but her uncle PJ never even seemed to recognize her. When PJ's older girl, Kate, had drowned on prom night, her dad didn't pick up the phone to call his brother, not even then.

Maybe it was helpful that her uncle PJ knew something of tragedy if he was going to be the guardian of Luna. She didn't hold it against PJ that her father had hated him; it was a good sign, actually. She did know Uncle PJ drank too much; she'd seen him at the bar. Still, it was Elaine's best option in a world full of really shitty options. Her uncle was a stranger, but he had won the lottery.

On a piece of clean white printer paper, Elaine wrote out her final will and testament with a black ballpoint pen, naming Mr. Paul John Halliday as Luna's guardian, and then she signed it, just like she'd signed permission slips in years before, when the kids toured the cranberry juice factory, or went to the New Bedford Whaling Museum, or when they visited Lizzie Borden's house in Fall River and stood on the floorboards where Lizzie murdered her poor parents with forty whacks.

The mice in the walls pissed themselves fifteen minutes later when Elaine Meeklin shot herself with one of her husband's guns, and she was legally dead by the time a text message arrived and the phone dinged. Somehow, even in death, Elaine's eyeballs still scanned the phone to read the screen. It was the school nurse, and she was at the pediatric ER. *Ollie will be fine,* the text read. *They pumped his stomach. Could you call me back, Ms. Meeklin, please? They're telling me now, Ollie will be fine. Call me back when you can, call when you can please call as soon as you can.*

So, that was the story Ivy would cut out of the front page of both newspapers on the morning before she left for Alaska. Of course, the article missed many important details, and nothing was mentioned about what Elaine Meeklin had said in her suicide note. The newspaper seldom gets the full story, but Ivy would cut it out of the paper anyway.

4

In Pondville, there had always been freak accidents and regular accidents, illnesses, and death, neighbors who hated one another. People who accidentally blew themselves up during fireworks season. There were affairs and gossip and fistfights and drunk driving and drug overdoses and general ugly behavior. Three years ago, the high school hockey coach had been fired for sexual assault, but the school had kept him on the payroll because it really couldn't be proven, a he-said-she-said case. There had been suicides, successful and attempted. There were people who died alone in their houses, their bodies not discovered for months and months. But it had been a long time since something *this* bad had happened. A wife and mother poisoning her husband and son. That was what shocked people so much: that it was the wife who'd done it. People understood when men killed women, because that kind of thing happened all the time. Well, not in Pondville, but elsewhere.

Elsewhere, it was the kind of thing that happened all the time, sure.

But not here in Pondville.

Some people said Elaine Meeklin was on drugs. Other people said it was really the Meeklin girl who'd poisoned her father and brother, and Elaine Meeklin took the fall for her kid. The bus driver had heard Luna Meeklin say she hated her father only that morning, so it was possible. Others said Elaine Meeklin was crazy, had been crazy ever since her dad died; some people said it was schizophrenia and hadn't you heard her talking to herself in the supermarket? Others said it was postpartum depression, even though her kids were nine and ten years old. Still others said Frank Meeklin deserved it; they knew he was the kind of cop who beat his wife.

Everyone was relieved, of course, that Ollie Meeklin was going to be all right. Everyone liked Ollie, he was such a nice and friendly kid. Seemed happy-go-lucky. It was his sister who had always seemed troubled, even before the tragedy, and now people wondered what had been going on in that house. Luna had ruined last year's school play, for instance. People hadn't forgot that, how she'd thrown a punch in the middle of the production of *Peter Pan*. She'd knocked Tinker Bell out cold.

People had heard it had been the girl who found her mother dead.

On the afternoon of that unfortunate May Day, Luna called 911 and first the cops came and then the ambulance, and later, the crime-scene clean-up crew, and ever since then the white house on Deerfield Lane had been covered in yellow caution tape. Over the house, there were often three turkey vultures circling. The Meeklin kids were no longer living in the house, of course, not without their parents. They had been sent away to western Massachusetts to an overcrowded foster home. This placement was temporary, the state social worker assured the kids. Just until the paperwork was sorted out.

At the foster home, Luna Meeklin kept reminding the adults about her real father, but no one was listening to her, because she was a kid and because what she wanted was ridiculous. A DNA test to prove she and her brother were half-siblings, that they had different fathers, and *her* father was a man she'd never met but was someone she'd seen on TV. No one was entertaining that. Their mother had named a guardian, and he was related by blood and not some fantasy on television. He was right here in Massachusetts.

Nearly everyone in Pondville would have told you PJ Halliday was not a suitable guardian, but the social workers weren't local. Most of them lived in Boston or its suburbs. But this wasn't a complicated case for them—a named guardian who was next-of-kin. Things would go slower with a handwritten will, but PJ could have custody of the children, if he wanted them, and if there were no major red flags in the home inspection, but it would all take a few weeks to sort out. And, yes, they had found the DUIs on his record, but DUIs more than three years old could generally be overlooked. That was the policy, but they would ask him about the DUIs in his interview.

One complication was, the Department of Children and Families hadn't yet been able to reach Mr. Halliday by phone. PJ never picked up the phone if he didn't recognize the number. It was for his own protection. Fred had gotten PJ a landline phone with Caller ID, because after PJ won the lottery, random people called him all the time. The names of lottery winners are public information, and everyone needs money for something. Surgery. A dying dog. A child with cancer. PJ didn't have a voicemail machine anymore, because Fred had taken it away after PJ couldn't handle all those sad stories from strangers.

"It's why so many lottery winners commit suicide," PJ always told the women at the bar. "You carry the weight of the world."

5

So, two weeks after the events at the Meeklin house, PJ Halliday still didn't even know there had been a murder-suicide in Pondville. He hadn't gotten a voicemail from the Massachusetts Department of Children and Families, because he didn't have a machine. There were tons of articles about it, but he wasn't reading the newspaper with Fred and Ivy gone. There were no long, leisurely breakfasts with his best friends, sipping coffee and reading the newspaper. They were gone to Alaska, and they'd left him behind. And he didn't hear about it at the Wild Orchid, where everyone at the bar was talking about it. Nothing that interesting had happened in Pondville in a long time, so of course everyone was talking about it.

But PJ didn't overhear it at the bar, because, for once in his life, PJ Halliday hadn't been going to the bar. In fact, PJ hadn't had one single drink since Ivy and Fred had gotten on their plane. He was in so much pain when they left, realizing that he wasn't part of their family after all, he was just the ex-husband who lived down the street. He was disgusted with himself for losing so much in his life, and angry with Fred and Ivy for leaving him, and he thought he might as well punish himself further by not drinking. He knew going cold turkey could cause all sorts of problems, but PJ didn't care. If he died from not drinking, Fred and Ivy would be sorry for leaving him then.

But then he survived all the vomiting and the sweating and the shaking. It hadn't killed him. It had taken nine days, but it hadn't killed him. PJ had never had a detox as bad as that one, not even when he had to go to prison for six weeks for the drunk driving, but once the detoxing was over, PJ had a new outlook. The sun came out. When Ivy and Fred got home in September, he could be a new man. He wanted to be a man who was worthy of being their best man. Without the booze, PJ started feeling hopeful. There was really a lot to be hopeful about. A wedding in the fall. He could drive to Arizona and get himself a date.

In PJ's garage, there was a 1970 Jaguar E-Type convertible kept under a cover. A two-seater, with a dead engine. It wasn't the car he'd rolled into a ditch; that was the family Ford Taurus. But the antique car, that beautiful machine, hadn't been driven in eight years, because that's Massachusetts's law after your third DUI. But PJ had done his time, and the eight-year suspension was almost up. He'd have his license back at the beginning of June, and the car just needed a little fixing up and he was sure he could get it running again. PJ pictured himself driving up to Tender Hearts Retirement Community and leaving with Ms. Michelle Cobb, holding her hand all the way back across the United States. He had been hoping she would have called him up to thank him for the roses. He would have picked up the phone if it had an Arizona area code. But she hadn't called. Maybe she needed time to grieve her husband. Or maybe she needed a bigger romantic gesture, like PJ making a cross country drive in a two seater convertible.

Michelle Cobb had married Gene Bartlett, her high school sweetheart, so she was probably old-fashioned about romance. PJ was sure: Michelle Cobb would want to be wooed.

6

It was eleven A.M. on the thirteenth morning without Fred and Ivy, and PJ hadn't had breakfast yet. He hadn't had dinner last night. He had run out of food. Ivy had always done his grocery shopping. It was easier for her to do it; she had a car, and she would leave the bags on his front porch for him to unpack. Ivy refused to come in the house anymore, the house that still held Kate's neat and clean room, her posters of teenage heartthrobs on her walls, with the rest of the house destroyed, the wallpaper peeling. It was too painful for Ivy to go into that house, so she left the groceries on the porch.

Before Fred and Ivy had gone to Alaska, they had considered this problem, PJ and his groceries. They could ask Sophie to do his shopping, but Ivy didn't want to ask too much of her daughter, who was supposed to be living her own life down in New Bedford. Finally, with some hesitation, Fred had given PJ the keys to his Volvo, his old boxy Volvo station wagon, still in perfect condition, not one chip in the red paint, with the vanity license plate that read BIRD BRN, which was supposed to stand for "Bird Brain" but PJ always told Fred it looked more like "Bird Barn" to him, and that didn't really make much sense. Fred had told PJ he could use the Bird Barn for grocery shopping and other necessary errands as soon as he got his license back in June, and maybe even before he did, as long as PJ was really, really careful and mindful of the speed limit, and drove only when sober, that went without saying, but Fred said it anyway.

So, that morning, thirteen days without Ivy, PJ knew he could drive himself to the supermarket in the Volvo, but he was also pretty sure there was plenty of good food left in his ex-wife's house, and no one to eat it. Most of it was sure to expire. He closed the hood of the Jag. He would need to special order a part, he was pretty sure. It had been a long time since he had worked on a car. He had learned to fix cars in auto shop in high school, right around the time he met Michelle Cobb at a mixer in the spring of 1969. A lifetime ago.

He started his walk to Fred and Ivy's. It felt good to be walking that way again.

As PJ walked, he noticed his T-shirt was smeared with oil, but Fred had a whole closet of clothes, all of them clean. Fred wouldn't mind. Fred was a giver. It was one of the things PJ liked about his best friend. Giving him the keys to the Volvo, for example, despite PJ not having his license back yet. Fred was a judge and had presided over horrible cases involving drinking and driving, and it meant a lot that Fred thought he deserved a second chance. PJ knew he was lucky he had never hurt anyone except himself, but it was wedged permanently in the back of his mind, that he could have. He could have killed another driver, or a pedestrian. A child. One DUI was a mistake; three DUIs made him a scourge on the earth. That was how Ivy had put it. She said she regretted saying it, later, but she said it. And part of her must have felt it, even if she welcomed him over for breakfast every morning and kept him in her life. PJ teared up as he walked down the street, thinking about his dear Ivy and all the ways he'd let her down.

He was wiping the tears from his eyes when he spotted Stan Weiderman, out in front of his house, crouched down by his porch. Stan saw PJ coming and was standing up. He was holding a spray can of some kind and was wearing gardening gloves and woodworking goggles. Stan was a talker. *Shit,* PJ thought. He was lonely, but not lonely enough to talk to Stan Weiderman.

"Got a new cat?" Stan asked.

"What?"

"The cat?"

"What?" PJ asked. He hadn't expected Stan Weiderman to lose it before he did. Stan Weiderman was much younger, and quite spry.

"There's a cat following you?" Stan said, pointing with his floral gardening glove.

PJ turned around. There was indeed a cat following him. A light-orange tabby. The cat stopped and sat and licked his paws. The cat seemed to know they were talking about him, although PJ wondered how well the cat could hear. He was missing part of an ear. "Hello, kitty," PJ said.

"If he's not yours, I should probably call animal control," Stan said. "He looks feral."

"Oh, yes, sorry," PJ said. "Yes, that's my cat."

"Why didn't you say so?"

"I didn't recognize him."

"You didn't recognize your cat?"

"He has a new haircut. Looks like the barber cut off part of his ear, but it'll heal. We're just headed to Ivy's house for some breakfast."

"I thought Ivy was out of town. Fred told me they were going to Alaska," Stan said, then took off one of his gardening gloves. His hand was swelling; it had been stung earlier. The spray can he was holding was wasp spray.

"Ivy is indeed out of town, but someone has to look after the house," PJ explained. "Listen, I've got to get going, but put some ice on that wasp sting, Stan, and then call an exterminator. Don't try to take care of a nest yourself."

"You're probably right," Stan agreed, looking at the size of his hand. "Leave it to the experts."

PJ gave him a thumbs-up and kept on walking. When he looked back a few houses later, Stan was back down in the dirt, lying down, presumably trying to get underneath the porch at the wasps' nest again. Some people never listen. PJ also saw the cat had disappeared off the sidewalk, and he smiled a bit. Even the cat knew Stan Weiderman was a dipshit. PJ was tired of some of these neighbors. You know what, he was tired of all of them, even the ones he loved. Without Fred and Ivy, he was tired of Pondville. All the more reason to get his convertible fixed up and get out of there, on the road to Arizona.

Hell, maybe he would even stay out in Arizona. Maybe he and Michelle Cobb would have a whole new life at Tender Hearts Retirement Community. They probably had air conditioning, a pool, shuffleboard. All the things you need to live a comfortable life. PJ didn't know how to play shuffleboard, but he figured he could learn.

PJ made it to the little brown house on the pond without running into any more of his neighbors. He got the key from under the flowerpot and fumbled with the lock. He wasn't used to this door being locked, and it was sticky in the frame, so he had to put his shoulder into it, and when he finally got it open, he saw something orange dart past his legs and run into the house.

That damn cat had gone in the house! The cat had run upstairs.

PJ was not in the mood to catch a cat on an empty stomach. "I'll deal with you after breakfast," PJ called up the stairs. He went to the fridge and opened it. There was bounty inside; Ivy must have known he would raid her fridge. Ivy knew everything. He took the eggs and cracked three in a bowl. PJ was no chef, but scrambled eggs, that he could do. He finished the eggs, took bread out of the freezer, and stuck a couple slices in the toaster. He took the landline off the hook and called Information for the number for the animal shelter. A woman he knew a little bit picked up the phone at the shelter. Her name was Alana; she was friends with his daughter Sophie.

Alana said no one had called about a lost cat recently, but there was a bulletin board of lost-cat posters outside the shelter; some of the posters had been there for years. She encouraged PJ to come look at pictures and see if there was a match.

"Will do," PJ said, disappointed he wasn't immediately heralded as a hero for finding a cat. "I hope someone will be happy I found him. He seems like a nice enough cat. I always liked orange cats."

Alana paused. "An orange cat?"

"Yes. An orange cat."

"It might be Pancakes. Does he respond to Pancakes?"

"He snuck in the house and ran upstairs. I didn't catch his name."

"Very funny, Mr. Halliday." Alana was used to people underestimating the intelligence of animals. "Can you tell me anything else about him?"

"Well, let's see . . . he's missing part of an ear. But it must have happened recently, there's still blood on his face."

"Oh, I do think it's Pancakes," she said, thinking Pancakes was the kind of cat to get into fights. He had caused trouble in the shelter, showing the other animals it was possible to escape, and he'd only been there a few hours. "He escaped from the shelter a couple weeks ago," Alana said, before explaining to PJ that a crazy man had dropped off the cat. The man had said Pancakes was a nice cat, and he loved him, but that he was a killer. Alana said she'd suggested a jingle bell, but the man insisted the cat was an agent of death.

"I see," PJ said.

"He looked like he'd seen a ghost," Alana said. She said she called the man after Pancakes escaped to see if the cat had found his way back home, but she was told the man had died suddenly at his desk.

"Never understood why people do that," PJ said.

"What?"

"Work themselves to death."

Alana agreed. She liked to work at the animal shelter because she could get high on the job, and no one bothered her.

"Should I bring him back?"

"Well, Mr. Halliday, that's up to you."

"What will happen to him if I do?"

Over the phone, Alana made a noise that usually went with the gesture of running your finger across your throat. PJ couldn't tell if she made that gesture, but he got the gist. Euthanasia, the end of every month. It was part of the drill at the animal shelter.

"Right," PJ said. "So, no one is looking for him?"

"If you want the cat, Mr. Halliday," Alana said, "he's yours."

"I'll think about it," he said, then thanked her and hung up. As bad as he felt for the little beast, PJ did not think he wanted or needed a cat. But he also didn't need to make the decision right now; there was breakfast to be had. He sat down with the eggs and toast and a glass of juice. He didn't bother with the newspaper. If he had a heart attack, he'd be all alone. He didn't want to die alone in his ex-wife's house. He didn't want Fred and Ivy to come home in September to find his skeleton at the kitchen table, the bones picked clean by the agent of death upstairs.

So instead of the newspaper, he pulled out a road map of the U.S. from the pocket of his cargo shorts and got a pen from the junk drawer. The straightest route to Tucson would be to go through the middle of the country, he figured. But maybe it would be more interesting to go to the southern U.S. and see Nashville, Atlanta. Or he could go through the north and see Chicago, and Mount Rushmore, then drive down through Nevada, see Las Vegas, the Grand Canyon. PJ had never seen any of those places. He drew out the three routes in pen. He would pick a route and leave as soon as he got his license back. If he wasn't invited to Alaska, he would have his own adventure. Ivy and Fred could go to hell.

Satisfied with his plan, PJ turned to his plate to finish his eggs, but the plate was empty. The cat was sitting up at the table in Fred's seat, a small scrap of egg still stuck to his whiskers. The cat was staring intently at the map.

"Good eggs, were they?" PJ asked.

The cat looked at him. The eggs had been superb. The cat had eaten only powdered eggs before, since that was all they served at the Pondville Nursing Home. Real scrambled eggs were another food group entirely. He was glad he'd followed when this bearded man mentioned breakfast, instead of staying with that man on the ground dying from anaphylaxis.

PJ reached out his hand to see if the cat would like a scratch, and the cat rose his nose to smell the hand. The cat seemed to approve of whatever he smelled on PJ, and Pancakes rolled his head into PJ's palm for a cuddle. Well, wasn't that nice. PJ got up to grab a rag from under the kitchen sink and then he gently washed the dried blood off the cat's face. The cat sat still as PJ cleaned him up. "Good kitty," PJ said. "Good as new."

The cat purred. PJ understood. The cat was thankful for the help. The cat purred more and started to drool. "I suppose I'll need a traveling companion," PJ said as he stroked the cat. "I'll get lonely on the road, with no one to talk to. You'll have to learn to talk, though."

I'll work on it, the cat promised.

Did cats do well in cars? PJ wondered. PJ had never had a cat before. One of his daughters was allergic. He had forgotten which one and thought he should remember to ask them.

He still thought of both daughters sometimes that way, both of them in present tense.

It would be fifteen years on June 15, a few weeks away, since Kate Halliday had been found facedown in one of the cranberry bogs near the Eagle Neck conservation land, after she'd been missing for days after senior prom. She had drowned in less than two inches of water, found still wearing her prom dress and crown. No signs of struggle. There had been a bonfire in the woods after the prom, a Pondville High School tradition, where the kids would drink beer and toast to the end of high school. But at some point, Kate had wandered away from the party and ended up in the bogs. Drunk and disoriented, she must have fallen, or simply lay down to sleep in the trench.

PJ had wanted to sue the juice factory, but you can't sue anyone for growing cranberries. Ivy wanted to sue the kids who brought the alcohol to the firepit after the prom, but everyone in town thought *that* was something, coming from the Halliday family. PJ was at the bar all the time even then. PJ had always liked to drink. Ivy knew that when she married him.

Kate liked to drink too. She'd been grounded several times senior year for coming home drunk. Kate was the kind of teenager who always looked like she was up to something, and usually was. The kind of teenager who sat on her teacher's desk and batted her eyelashes to get a better grade. After she died, PJ and Ivy heard stories like that. Everyone seemed to have a confession of some kind. That they weren't as nice to Kate as they should have been in middle school, back when she had a stutter. Or that they had helped her cheat on a test once. That they were in love with her, and never had the chance to tell her and they might as well tell her parents. "She was magnetic," the principal had said at the ceremony where they unveiled the memorial bench. "She was my best friend," said several teenage girls, none of whom PJ had ever seen before. Lauren Cleary, Kate's real best friend, had said nothing at the unveiling at all. "She was going places," everyone at the memorial agreed. Kate had been supposed to go to Florida State on a softball scholarship. Her mother was concerned it was a party school. In the articles about her death, the drowning, they listed Kate's blood alcohol level. The newspapers had called Kate a "party girl," as if that meant she had deserved to die. As if that meant other parents didn't need to worry about their own kids, as if any good parent would have seen it coming.

PJ knew Kate stole his beers from the fridge on occasion. She might have stolen some of his beers to bring to the bonfire after prom, but PJ couldn't say for sure, he didn't keep a careful tally of the beers in the fridge. Ivy blamed the two boys who had made some sort of vodka mixture with Kool-Aid powder in a trash can. The high schoolers had been drinking out of a trash can the night one of them died. During the autopsy, the coroner found that Kate's tongue was stained red. That was the one source of relief for PJ, that it wasn't his own beers that had gotten his daughter so drunk she'd laid down in the bog.

Ivy was always mad at PJ for continuing to drink, even after it was alcohol that killed Kate. Ivy gave up wine completely. But PJ couldn't do that. PJ thought, if he ever did get sober, it would be the excruciating pain of being fully awake in a world without Kate that would kill him.

But now Ivy had left him for Alaska and he was thirteen days sober, through the worst of his withdrawal, and it hadn't killed him.

It was almost disappointing.

PJ didn't want to be in town for that day in June, fifteen years without Kate. He wanted to be in Arizona, at the retirement community, playing shuffleboard and hustling everyone in a weekly game of poker. PJ was even more determined than before to go to Arizona now that he had the cat for company. A companion was exactly what he needed. He had seen a movie once, about an old man on the road with a cat. Art Carney had won an Oscar for the movie, if PJ remembered correctly. PJ thought maybe he and Pancakes could watch it, but he couldn't remember the ending, if the cat had lived or died.

So, instead, he sat down in Fred's favorite chair and turned on the cooking channel. As Ina Garten made buttermilk biscuits for her beloved husband, PJ closed his eyes for his post-breakfast nap, and his mind wandered to a memory of an evening spent in a chair like this one, back when their family was intact.

Sophie was about four, pink from a bath, smelling like fresh lavender, and she had climbed into his lap for a cuddle. Kate and Ivy had gone out to the hairdresser that afternoon and would be home any minute. PJ had made them all spaghetti for dinner, one of his only specialties. It was waiting on the stove.

He could hear Ivy in the front hall. "We're doing a fashion show!" Ivy had called.

"We're ready for you!" PJ had called back.

Ivy strutted in. In an entirely new outfit, even though she'd told PJ they had to not spend any more money for a while. She was wearing a yellow coat, and her hair was pixie-cut short.

"You look beautiful, Mommy," Sophie said.

"Doesn't she?" PJ said, squeezing Sophie, loving the honest, open kindness of children.

Then Kate walked in, too, in a new red dress. She did a little turn on the living-room catwalk. She was only eleven, but she already looked something like Barbarella. Kate had always looked like the kind of kid who should be in beauty pageants, but Ivy wasn't the kind of mom to put her in them.

"Kate looks *even more* beautiful," Sophie said, and it was true, Kate did look the most beautiful, but she still had all her long hair that she had left the house with earlier that day.

"I thought you were going to cut your hair too," PJ said.

"I did cut it, Dad. I got bangs."

"But—"

"I didn't let her," Ivy interrupted. "No sense in us both losing our hair." The rest of Ivy's pixie cut would be falling out in the next few months. Ivy had breast cancer, was starting chemo, but the doctor was confident they'd beat it. Ivy would tell PJ the truth later, that Kate had chickened out once she was in the chair. "No other girls in my grade have short hair," Kate had said. "No other girls have moms with cancer."

"I get it," Ivy had said. "It's unfair."

And that's when the hairdresser suggested bangs, brought out a magazine photo.

PJ was disappointed that Kate hadn't gone through with it; he'd thought it was a beautiful way to support her mother. It had been Kate's idea, and then she didn't do it. It wasn't very nice to say you were going to do something and then not do it. He wondered about the girls they were raising, and what would happen to them if he had to raise them alone.

Back then, PJ thought the breast-cancer diagnosis, the months of chemo, the threat of losing Ivy, was the worst thing their family would have to survive, forgetting the ancient knowledge that the worst thing that can happen to anyone is the death of a child.

Then again, PJ never thought that would happen to him.

7

Forty-five minutes into his nap, a new cooking show episode had started, and PJ jerked awake when the phone rang in the kitchen. It took PJ a minute to realize where he was, at Fred and Ivy's house, and he had no business picking up their phone, but he thought perhaps Fred had set up a camera somewhere and was calling to yell at him for being in their house. The cat was sleeping on his chest, so he pushed Pancakes off and ran to grab the phone. "Freddy?" he said into the receiver, hoping it was his best friend.

"Um, hello," a woman said on the other line. It wasn't Fred, and it wasn't Ivy either. PJ didn't recognize her voice. "I'm calling to speak with Ivy Halliday?" the woman said. Ivy had kept PJ's last name after the divorce, which PJ considered a victory. It was their family name.

"I'm sorry, Ivy is occupied at the moment," PJ said. He had always liked saying that to callers, because everyone knew it meant the person they were calling for was on the shitter. "This is her ex-husband; can I take a message?"

"Oh, I can call back another time . . ."

"She'll be in Alaska for a while."

"I'm sorry, did you say you're her ex-husband? I'm currently speaking with Paul Halliday?"

"Everyone calls me PJ, unless you're my mother." PJ's mother had been dead for ten years. "And who's this?"

"My name is Belinda Bell and I'm a social worker with the Massachusetts Department of Children and Families. I've been trying to reach you actually. You're hard to reach. We've been calling every day."

"You're calling from child services? My daughter Sophie's full-grown. If you wanted to take her away, you missed your window." He chuckled.

"No, no, no," Belinda Bell said, although it was perhaps a little alarming to her that PJ was joking about his own daughter being taken away. "You've been mentioned in a family will," she said, because she didn't want to say *family suicide note*. "And we're trying to determine the best path forward—"

"Oh, you can stop yourself right there," PJ said. "I don't want his money. I'm glad he's dead. I'm sorry I didn't kill him myself."

"Mr. Halliday, you're glad Frank Meeklin is dead?"

"No, Christ. I'm glad my brother is dead. Who's Frank Meeklin?"

"You don't know Frank Meeklin?"

"No, I do not. Did he deserve to die?"

"Frank Meeklin was married to your niece."

"Ah," PJ said. "And who's my niece?"

Belinda Bell explained about Elaine Meeklin, who was the daughter of PJ's brother, and married to Frank. She couldn't believe he didn't know this stuff, basic family history.

"My brother and I were estranged," PJ explained. "We didn't speak for over forty years. He burnt our mother's house down, a few months after he tried to kill me."

"I see," Belinda Bell said. It was her job to be unflappable. "Well, Frank and Elaine Meeklin lived two streets down from you. Less than half a mile."

"And Frank's dead?"

"They're both dead." She explained what had happened, the car accident, the poisoning, the suicide, how the kids were left without parents. PJ's heart ached. The boy had made a complete recovery from the poisoning, and PJ was glad to hear that.

"We'd like to get them in a stable home as soon as possible," Belinda said.

"Sounds like that would be best."

"Well, yes, that's why I was hoping to talk to you, PJ. The mother, Elaine Meeklin, named you as the guardian of the children."

"Huh? What? Me? Why? I'm a stranger."

"You're a blood relative."

"I'm an old man. One foot in the grave."

"You're in your sixties, the paperwork said? Not so old."

"Right. Not so old, I guess. If you say so." The cat meowed, and PJ reached to pet him. The cat meowed again, so PJ went to the fridge and poured out some milk, one day away from its expiration date. As the cat drank the milk, and Belinda Bell told him more about these poor children, PJ thought of Pancakes in the animal shelter, waiting for a home, waiting to be euthanized. Of course, the foster-care system didn't euthanize the children at the end of the month, but it wasn't a real home, it was a brick building crammed with children in the worst part of Springfield, that was how Belinda Bell described it. PJ Halliday believed all children should have a real home. But also, he didn't know if he was able to do it. Take care of two kids by himself.

"What happens if I say no?" PJ asked. "What happens if I can't do it?"

"You can say no, of course you can, no one would blame you. If you decide you can't be the guardian of the children, the children will remain in the care of the state. We will find them placement in foster homes. But for many reasons, we prefer to place children in the homes of blood relatives, especially children who have been through extreme trauma, so we believe you are their ideal caretaker."

"I see." PJ liked hearing himself described as an ideal caretaker.

"Do you have experience caring for children, Mr. Halliday?"

"Yes," PJ said. "I have two kids of my own." He did not tell her one of them was dead, because it was none of this woman's business. But when the kids were little, man, you know what, he had been a good dad. He was always home from the post office before they got back from school, and he got on the floor with the Legos, he did bedtime stories, made afterschool sandwiches. He asked them questions about their lives and let them know he was always there to talk about their problems. He held them when they cried. He bought them gifts to make them happy. He tried not to lose his patience. He tried to never yell. He only went to the bar twice or three times a week.

Sure, after the tragedy with Kate, he'd checked out a little. Started drinking more. That was when he started going down to the bar every day. That was when three beers a night became ten a night, and eventually PJ could put away thirty beers in a day. He wasn't proud of it. PJ was sorry he hadn't been the best father to Sophie after Kate's death, during all of Sophie's teenage years and into her twenties. He'd gotten so drunk he peed his pants at her high school graduation, then wasn't invited to her college one. He had missed so many things. Lately, he wished he could get a second chance with Sophie. Well, this was a second chance, on the phone with Belinda Bell. A different kind of chance from the one he'd hoped for, but still a second chance to be a good father figure. A grandfather figure. "Okay," he said into the phone to Belinda Bell. "I'll do it. I'll take care of them."

"I'm very glad to hear that. But I do have one more thing to ask you, Mr. Halliday. We did find the DUIs on your record. Can you tell me about those?"

"Oh, I'm sober now. Been sober for a long time." It hadn't been a long time, not really, but it felt like a long time. He knew Ivy would have scolded him for lying, smacked him on the back of his head and asked him what he was thinking. But Ivy wasn't there.

"Just what I was hoping to hear," Belinda Bell said. "And it was eight years ago? No problems since?"

"No problems since."

"Good. We can forgive things that happened in the distant past, if you've modified your behavior."

The distant past, PJ thought. He liked how that sounded. It was far behind him. "I have," he assured her.

"I'm looking at my calendar now," Belinda Bell continued. "I'll bring the kids to you and check out the house and if everything looks good, they'll be yours."

"They'll be *mine*? Just like that?"

"There's far fewer hoops to jump through with next of kin, and so we will always favor this sort of placement. Let's say the Monday after Memorial Day, that'll give you about two weeks to get ready. Does that Monday work?"

PJ knew he didn't have anything on that Monday, without needing to look at any calendar. And then Belinda Bell was confirming PJ's home address on the phone, and that's when PJ realized, this social worker could not be allowed to see the state of his house. His piles and piles. It was no place for a child, let alone two. "Actually," PJ said. "There's a typo. It's 33 Clear Pond Road, not 13 Clear Pond."

"Oh," Belinda Bell said. "Let me get that changed." She also needed an email address. PJ didn't have a computer, but he had his own email address. His daughter Sophie had set it up for him in case he ever wanted to apply for a job. Belinda said she'd send all the initial paperwork right over. A list of things the kids would need in order for PJ to pass the home visit. To prove he could give children a proper home.

When PJ Halliday hung up, he was shaking. "My brother's grandkids, holy shit," he said. It had not occurred to him that his brother had grandkids. He tried to never think about his brother.

The cat looked at him.

"My brother and I weren't close," he told the cat. When Chip was at the bar, they would sit at opposite ends. Everyone at the bar knew the two men hated each other, but most people didn't know they were brothers. When Chip died, PJ bought everyone at the bar a round in celebration. Some people thought it was in bad taste, since the man had killed himself, but no one turned down the free drink.

PJ went upstairs to Fred's office. He sat at the desk and turned on the computer, put in the password for his email. There it was: *From Belinda Bell, Licensed Social Worker.* Attached was a list of things children needed. Water and food and a place to sleep, pajamas and clothes and books and toys. PJ already knew all this. He had raised two children; he wasn't a moron.

"They'll need new beds, for starters," PJ announced to the room full of filing boxes. The cat hadn't followed him upstairs, so PJ was talking to himself, but some things have to be planned aloud. "And we'll have to clear this room out," he said.

PJ opened the other attachment in Belinda Bell's email. It was a photograph. Two kids, nine or ten years old. Both smiling for the camera. They didn't look too much alike, PJ thought, a big redhead and a small brunette. Then again, he and his brother hadn't looked too much alike, and for that PJ had always been thankful. PJ was the big one, his brother had been thin, and eagle-nosed. PJ typed into the computer: *Where to buy beds for children?*

IKEA, the computer replied. PJ had never been to an IKEA. The nearest one was forty minutes away.

Downstairs, PJ grabbed the Volvo keys and found the cat perched on the kitchen table, sitting on top of the road map, his golden eyes intense, his tail twitching. *You've forgotten our plan,* the cat seemed to be saying. For the past hour, PJ had indeed forgotten about the road trip he had planned, he'd been thinking only about these children, these poor children who needed a home. *Dammit,* he wanted to go on that trip. If Fred and Ivy were going to be in Alaska, he wanted to go somewhere too. And he needed a date for the wedding.

Well. Maybe it didn't need to be called off. They would arrive right after Memorial Day, and children had a summer vacation coming up soon after that, didn't they? Maybe they would like to go on a trip. Michelle Cobb probably loved children. But they would have to take the Volvo. He couldn't drive the convertible, what with it not running yet, and not if he had two children with him, plus the cat. The Volvo had a good safety rating, everyone knows that about Volvos, and people with children cared about things like that. He remembered how angry Ivy had been, way back when, when he'd first bought the two-seater Jaguar convertible for his own fortieth birthday. She had wanted to know how she was going to cart their two children around town in that thing. He had told her it was his midlife crisis, it wasn't about the children, and she hadn't spoken to him for three weeks.

Yes, PJ would have to take the red Volvo Bird Barn on the trip and ask for Fred's forgiveness later. And today, he would go to IKEA to get bunk beds, and to the PetSmart for some cat food and a leash and a harness. Alaska didn't look like such a big adventure now. He had errands to run. Things to buy. PJ knew from experience: Children need so many things. It's how you end up with a house full of crap, once your children have grown up or are otherwise gone.

8

Two weeks later, on a Monday afternoon in early June, the Meeklin children were sitting in the driveway of the foster home, waiting for their ride. The rest of the kids were inside, watching the biggest kid play a single-player videogame. The paperwork, the adults said, was finally done. All they needed now was to make sure their great-uncle's house was hospitable for children, the home inspection was the last box to be checked. The kids were waiting for someone to pick them up and take them to this uncle's house, and they were sitting next to their trash bags full of stuff. They didn't have proper suitcases, because strangers had packed for them, adults who had gone into the house to stuff clothes in trash bags. Ollie hadn't been given any underwear, and he'd been free-balling it for a month. The children hadn't been allowed back in their own house to get their things, after Luna got off the school bus and found their mother with her phone in one hand, a gun in the other. Luna was still wearing the same leopard-print fake-fur coat she'd worn ever since that day, even though it was getting much too warm for it, and a purple dress and her favorite pink Converses. Ollie was wearing a rotation of three T-shirts, one that looked like a ketchup bottle, one that looked like a mustard bottle, and a black WrestleMania T-shirt with two angry men on it. Their dad had bought the wrestling T-shirt for him, even though Ollie didn't like WrestleMania. Their dad always wanted Ollie to like the same things he did, but he didn't care what Luna thought about anything. Luna still wanted to get a DNA test to prove he wasn't her father.

Ollie kept telling her to drop it. "They'll separate us," he insisted. "If they think we're not related, they'll separate us. They'll send you to a home for really bad girls, and I'll go to a loving home."

"We *are* related. I just think we have different fathers, and my dad's still alive, and he's on television. And besides, why wouldn't I go to a loving home too?"

"Because you get into fights."

"I never start fights—" she started to say, but Belinda Bell had pulled up in the white transport van, so Luna shut her trap. When the adults were around, Luna had stopped talking. The social workers said it was a trauma response, the not-talking, but really, Luna was tired of talking to people who weren't listening to her. She had requested a DNA test over and over in the first week they'd been at the foster home, and still everyone kept talking about this great-uncle they'd never heard about, even though he lived less than a mile from them. He lived on the road that took you to the Clear Pond swimming beach.

"I bet he loves children," Ollie said.

"He better be rich," Luna had whispered to Ollie.

Ollie was kind of glad when his sister stopped talking when the adults were around, because he really was sure they would separate them if they found out how bad she could be. He didn't want to be separated from his sister. It was hard enough with his parents dead, and they had been mean so much of the time, his dad especially, and his mom had gotten stranger, started talking to herself all the time.

There were even moments when Ollie was glad both his parents were gone, and then he'd feel guilty about thinking that, and wish and wish and wish they would come back.

"How old is our great-uncle?" Ollie asked Belinda Bell as she was opening the door to the van.

"Not too old," Belinda Bell said. "He sounded young at heart when I spoke to him on the phone."

"Will he die soon?" Ollie asked, climbing into the van, pulling the trash bag behind him. Luna climbed in too.

"I hope not," Belinda said. It was another thing she couldn't promise these kids, that they would be happy or that no one else would die. She had found foster children good homes before and the guardian had dropped dead shortly after. It happened sometimes.

"But if he doesn't die, we're going to live with him?" Ollie asked.

"Yes, and you'll still be able to go to the same school and have all the same friends. You're lucky you have a great-uncle in the same town."

Luna opened her mouth and stuck her finger in, miming that she was going to make herself throw up.

"What's that about, Luna?" Belinda Bell asked.

Luna shook her head to show she wasn't going to answer. Couldn't trick her that easily.

Ollie shrugged. "Luna might be happier at a school for gifted children."

"She'll have to start talking then."

"She *can* talk. She's just choosing not to."

"I know," Belinda said. She started the van.

An hour later, they pulled up to the house on Clear Pond Road. Belinda had stopped for Big Gulp slushies at a gas station on the way. She always bought the kids a treat before she said goodbye, because she had no idea what was going to happen to them next and she wanted them to have one last good thing. Luna picked blue raspberry and Ollie had cherry red. Luna had also stolen a half pack of cigarettes from a woman's handbag while they walked around the gas station. She stole her lighter too. Luna didn't smoke cigarettes, but she thought she might start. She was an adult now, if her parents were dead. Or her mom at least. Her biological father was still alive. He was probably a smoker. She had heard all actors were. The cigarettes were Lucky Strikes. There were twelve cigarettes left; Luna had counted while Belinda Bell had been keeping her eyes on the road. Ollie had seen her do it, but her brother never tattled, except recently, to the school nurse. Luna had been trying to figure out if she had to punish him for that, but he'd already been poisoned, which was pretty bad.

The house on Clear Pond Road was a small cape, with green shutters and natural wood shingles. PJ Halliday was sitting out on the front lawn in a beach chair. He smiled and waved. He was wearing a clean T-shirt he'd taken from Fred's closet and sunglasses, cargo shorts, socks, and Birkenstocks. He'd brushed his hair. His beard needed trimming, but he wasn't going to do that. This wasn't a wedding. He was drinking a Coca-Cola, because he had badly wanted to drink a beer, but he knew that would be unwise. He wanted to impress the social worker.

"So, he's not rich," Luna said when she saw him, as quietly as she could, so only Ollie would hear.

"I'm Belinda Bell, social worker," Belinda Bell said, extending her hand to PJ.

"A pleasure," PJ said.

"And these are the kids, Ollie and Luna Meeklin."

"Hi, kids," PJ said, putting his hands on his stomach because he knew kids that age don't like to shake hands. "I'm your uncle. Great-uncle. The greatest uncle, in fact."

"I'm Ollie," Ollie said.

"Solid name. After Oliver Twist?"

"Who is that?"

"He was a famous . . ." PJ started, but couldn't bring himself to say *orphan*, "he was a famous character in literature. Dickens."

"Oh. No, I don't think my mom named me after anyone."

"We'll watch the movie. Roman Polanski did a pretty good version. And who is this?"

Luna was standing there scowling.

"That's Luna," Ollie said. "She's also not named after anyone. She can talk but she's currently choosing not to."

"I see. Well, you don't have to talk, Miss Luna. Fine with me. Children should be seen and not heard, right, Ms.—Bell, was it?" PJ was trying to be on his best behavior.

"That's an abusive phrase, Mr. Halliday," Belinda Bell said. "I'm sure you don't feel that way?"

"Oh, no. No, no, no. I love when children talk. They say the funniest shit."

"No swearing," she said. "And that movie you mentioned—it's PG-13."

"Well, scratch that too."

"I've seen seven R-movies," Ollie said. "In this one I watched with my dad, two people wake up and there's this man named Jigsaw . . ." Luna elbowed him. She gave her brother a look. "Okay, okay," Ollie said. "Luna wants to know if we're going to have our own rooms."

"Oh," PJ said. "Unfortunately, you're going to have to share. I was told you're used to sharing a room, and it's a small house. Only a two-bedroom." The house down the street was three bedrooms, he thought, but it was full of junk. "Hey, how'd that work, that you knew what Luna wanted to ask without her saying anything? You can read each other's minds?"

"We're Irish twins. It's easy to know what she's thinking."

"What's an Irish twin?"

"I don't think that's a PC term," said Belinda Bell.

"It means we're eleven months apart," Ollie said. "It means we're in the same grade and we're closer than regular siblings, so our minds are connected."

"I've heard about that," PJ said, nodding, glad to know what he had heard about twins was true, that they were a little bit supernatural, even if these children weren't exactly real twins. They were close in age. His own kids had been seven years apart.

"Irish twins also meant our mom never lost the baby weight," Ollie said, repeating something he'd heard so many times.

"Oh," PJ said, uncomfortable at this unflattering mention of their mother, so soon after her death. "Well, do you kids want to see the house? I've got a surprise in the backyard."

"We definitely want to see the surprise," Ollie said. He dragged his trash bag full of clothes through the door. Luna dragged hers in too, and they both dropped them by the coat rack. They were all standing in the front hall with the striped wallpaper and the grandfather clock, and Luna was wondering again if Uncle PJ was rich after all. From there, Uncle PJ led them into the kitchen with its yellow walls and sunflower tablecloth and cherry cabinets with gold knobs.

"This is a beautiful house," Belinda said, walking around, looking at the cabinets Fred had made himself.

"It is," PJ said. He had always admired Fred's taste, and Ivy had added her feminine touches.

"What's the surprise?" Ollie asked.

PJ opened the glass sliding door to the backyard and when the kids saw it, they both squealed and went running out into the yard immediately. *He is rich!* Luna thought with glee. There had been a Walmart next to the IKEA and PJ hadn't been able to stop himself from adding the eight-foot trampoline to the credit card. He'd had to pay for delivery, the package too big to fit in the car.

"Trampolines often result in trips to the ER," Belinda Bell told PJ when she saw the surprise in the yard, but she had to admit it was nice to see the kids smile. They hadn't even smiled when she'd bought them the Big Gulps.

PJ had also left a bag of candy in the middle of the trampoline, and the kids tore into it, packages of gummy frogs and gummy worms.

"Thanks, Uncle PJ," Ollie said, a worm halfway out of his mouth, and even Luna gave him a thumbs-up. PJ smiled at the new name. *Uncle PJ.* He liked that.

PJ and Belinda Bell left the kids and went back inside for the home inspection. Belinda turned on the tap water in the kitchen. She put a little paper strip in the water, waited to see if it turned orange. "No lead," she reported.

"Damn," PJ said. "I'll have to sprinkle it in their cereal."

"Mr. Halliday," Belinda Bell said, and she wasn't smiling, "do I need to remind you that one of these children recently suffered a poisoning incident?"

"My apologies, Ms. Bell. Only a joke. No lead in their cereal, check."

"I'm going to need you to take this seriously," Belinda Bell said. Belinda Bell was frustrated by men who never stopped being children.

"You got it," PJ said. "I'll be serious."

Upstairs, Belinda Bell inspected the kids' room, the new white bunk beds from IKEA. PJ had finally gotten them put together, which had seemed an impossible task, had even called his daughter to help but she hadn't answered. After he'd done it, he'd lain on the floor for hours and waited for the big heart attack to hit, but he had survived.

"New," Belinda said, shaking the beds. "Sturdy."

"It's Swedish furniture. Only the best."

"And what's in the boxes?"

PJ hadn't moved all the filing boxes to the garage yet, because he'd been so tired from trying to build the bunk beds, so there were a few left in the room. "Oh, those are just my ex-wife's things."

Belinda Bell lifted a cardboard lid. On top was a news clipping. *Gas Leak Kills Entire Family, Including Children and the Dog.* She brought out another: *Girl Accidentally Shoots and Kills Baby Brother.* PJ immediately knew what was in the box, in the many boxes, not Judge Fred's old court cases at all, he understood immediately, Belinda Bell didn't need to keep digging. It was all the bad news his ex-wife had collected over the years. For whatever reason, Ivy hadn't been able to throw the clippings away. He understood it, the hoarding impulse, of course he did, making ordinary things sacred. She was holding on to the bad news because she knew what it was like to have your bad news printed in the paper, and then have everyone recycle it the next day. Maybe that happens to everyone who loses a child, that you hold on to things because you know better than anyone else there's nothing in the world anyone can actually hold on to. *Oh, Ivy,* he thought. He wanted to hug his ex-wife, but she wasn't there for a hug and Belinda Bell was standing there instead, waiting for an explanation. "My ex-wife is an art teacher," he said, which was true. "You know how artists collect newspaper. For papier-mâché." Ivy would have never insulted the intelligence of her high schoolers by making them do papier-mâché, but the social worker didn't need to know that.

"Did you recently divorce?"

"Yes," PJ said. "Well, eight years ago. We're still very close." He pointed to one of the photographs on the wall. "That's her and her future husband, her boyfriend, Fred. He's proposing soon. Any minute now. They're up in Alaska. I've seen the ring. Modestly sized diamond. I would get her a bigger one if I were going to marry her again, but I think she's going to be happy with it."

"You keep a picture of them in a frame?" Belinda Bell asked. There were actually a lot of pictures of Ivy and Fred framed, sprinkled around the house, but Belinda hadn't seen them all yet.

"I'm best man in the wedding," PJ said, puffing out his chest. "I'm also hoping she'll let me give her away."

Belinda immediately softened on PJ. "Well, that's lovely, Mr. Halliday. I have to say, I wish my ex-husband would show the same maturity."

He nodded. "She's grateful for me."

"And how about your kids?" she asked. "Do you have a good relationship?"

"We're all very close," he said, which was a lie, because Sophie barely ever picked up PJ's phone calls, and PJ's other daughter had been dead for nearly fifteen years. But this social worker didn't want the truth. PJ could see how this worked. This social worker wanted to hear what she wanted to hear and jot it down on her form. That this was a safe home for children, and her job here was done.

They ordered Domino's for dinner, including a salad no one would eat, but PJ wanted to prove he knew something about healthy eating. He spread out the pizza and the paper plates on the table in the dining room, a room that Fred and Ivy only used for holiday dinners. It was a long narrow room on the side of the house, with a mahogany dining table on one end, and a loveseat and a white grand piano at the other. Luna went right to the piano and sat down.

"That used to be my piano," PJ said, feeling proud the kid had noticed the beautiful instrument. "But my ex-wife got it in the divorce. She said I wouldn't take care of it, and she'd spent too much money on it to watch it fall apart."

"Why is it in your house then?" Belinda asked.

"What?"

"Why is the piano in your house if she got it in the divorce?"

"Oh," PJ said. He tried to think. "Well, she gave it back. She went to Alaska, so she gave it back."

Belinda nodded. "Probably too heavy to take on a plane, a piano that size."

"Yeah," PJ said, getting excited that he'd pulled off another lie. "She would have had to take it on a boat or by truck. And it would be expensive. Too expensive to take with you to Alaska." He bit into his slice of Domino's. "Good pizza," he said.

Ollie was on his second slice, but Luna was still sitting at the piano, hadn't come over to get her pizza. She was staring at the keys.

"Play us a song, Luna," Belinda Bell said. "Play us a song if you're not going to eat. You can be the dinner entertainment."

"She's a good singer but she doesn't play the piano," Ollie explained.

But Luna put her hands on the keys, and she pressed down. *Ting,* said the key. *Ting, ting, ting.* And then her fingers kept moving, and there was music. There was a song, a real one, and not "Twinkle, Twinkle, Little Star" or "Chopsticks." It was something else. It was beautiful.

"Fabulous," Belinda Bell said when Luna stopped.

"Since when do you play the piano?" Ollie asked. He hated when his sister had secrets.

"Debussy. 'Serenade for the Doll,'" PJ said. "That's what that was. My mother taught me to play that. I suppose she taught my brother to play it too. Maybe he taught you?"

Luna looked at this old man, this old man she was supposed to live with, who knew the name of the song she had played. She had not known this man was related to her grandfather, because no one had explained to her what a great-uncle was, but she figured it out now. Luna turned away from PJ and back to the piano, but first PJ thought he saw something he understood in her eyes. A hurt and an anger he recognized. He was worried for her, being so young and having that kind of hurt. Belinda Bell and Ollie both thought Luna was about to play a second song on the piano, another something beautiful, but instead, she vomited, projectile, a brilliant blue, all over the piano, with half-chewed lumps of frogs and gummy worms hitting the keys.

"The Big Gulp," Belinda Bell said. "Oh my God, the Big Gulp."

"The trampoline," Ollie said, somberly. "It shook her up."

"I'll get a rag," PJ said, running for the towels and some carpet cleaner. There was blue goo in the beige carpet, too, pieces of gummy candy everywhere. He was thinking about what Fred would say about the carpet. Fred was tricky about the carpet in this room. It was the formal dining room, that's why Fred and Ivy only used it for holidays, but this had been a special occasion. It was the kids' first dinner in the house.

Luna burst into tears and ran for the bathroom and shut the door. Belinda and PJ didn't run after her; they were focused on cleaning up. Even Ollie didn't bother his sister, at first, because he was worried his red slushie would come up at any second too. He had been shaken up on the trampoline just like Luna had, and he always gagged whenever Luna vomited. They were connected that way. Ollie could never be happy unless Luna was too.

In the bathroom, finally alone for a minute, Luna sat on the toilet, put her head between her knees. Something in the room meowed, and Luna looked up. There was an orange cat, lying stretched out in the empty bathtub. Pancakes had been sleeping in there all day. He offered the girl his white belly. Luna wiped her eyes and sat next to the tub and put her hands into his fur. She felt better immediately. He purred and purred and sniffed her hand with his little pink nose. Her smell was so familiar to him, but at first he couldn't place it.

"I'm going to run away," she told the cat. She looked up from the tub to the window above the toilet. "Do you think I can fit through that window?" she asked him.

The cat sat up and jumped from the tub to the toilet. He looked at the size of the window and the size of Luna. *No problem,* he thought.

"Okay," she said. "I'm going." She used the crank to open the window; there was no screen. The cat watched her climb out the window, watched her balance on the windowsill in her pink Converses for a second, hesitating, before she jumped into the bushes below. Pancakes followed her, much more gracefully, didn't hesitate before the jump.

"Are you allowed outside?" Luna asked the cat, pulling some branches out of her hair.

But the cat went ahead and darted away from her and trotted on ahead down the street. He knew where they were going. The white house over on Deerfield Lane. He had been over there before in the weeks he was a stray and the house was empty. He had slept on Luna's bed. That explained how he knew her smell already. From the purple bedspread he had slept on for several nights. Pancakes knew they were going back to that house, which had reeked of death, but the purple bedspread with the butterfly print had smelled sweetly, from the sweat of a child at rest.

A few minutes later, Ollie knocked on the bathroom door to check on his sister, not knowing she was out the window and off the property. "Are you okay?" he asked. He didn't expect Luna to answer, because she still had her rule against talking when the adults were around, and she wouldn't be able to tell who was listening in with the door closed. He tried the doorknob, but it was locked. "The puke didn't stain," he said. "No one's mad."

"Of course we're not mad," Belinda Bell said from behind Ollie. "Everyone gets sick. Are you all right, Luna? Do you need help?" she asked the door.

But there was no answer from the other side.

"Hey, kiddo, don't worry about it, please. It's my ex-wife's piano, why would I be mad?" PJ reassured her. "She left me for another man. She's marrying him in the fall. Hey, would you like to be a flower girl? They'll need a flower girl." PJ thought that might get her out. He didn't know Luna yet. Didn't know that Luna was not the type of kid who ever wanted to be a flower girl.

"Luna, let me in," Ollie said. "Please let me in, Luna."

"I think Luna just needs some alone time," Belinda Bell said. "She knows no one's mad at her. She'll come out when she's ready. Let's go back and finish our pizza."

So, everyone went back to the dining room, including Ollie, leaving Luna alone in the locked bathroom to sulk. PJ would have stayed longer to try to coax the girl out, but Belinda Bell was the professional. She was paid to know what was best for children.

After dinner, the paper plates were thrown in the trash, and Belinda Bell announced that things looked good here. She was going to head out. "There've been worse drop-offs, believe me," she said when PJ asked if she was sure she didn't want to stay until Luna came out of the bathroom. Belinda said she would check back in a few weeks, and she was always a phone call away. She left a file of paperwork on the counter, the kids' birth certificates and medical records, along with a Post-it with her phone number. PJ tried not to panic. It was happening. It was really happening, and it couldn't be undone. Was it too late to undo it? Then again, he didn't want to go back to being alone all the time. And one of the kids could play Debussy on the piano. Who knows what else they would do together? It might all be wonderful. Everything up ahead might be wonderful.

"Oh," Belinda said, as she gathered her things. "One last thing you should know: Luna thinks Frank Meeklin isn't her real father. When she starts talking again, she's going to ask for a DNA test. She is going through complicated grief, but it's best if you ignore this request."

"I look exactly like my dad," Ollie explained. "His mini-me. It's why he liked me better. But she doesn't really look like him, or my mom."

PJ scratched his head. PJ was glad to hear about this possible loophole. If there was someone else who could take the kids, that might be better. Maybe PJ could just take care of them one night a week; that might be great. "Well, why not give her a DNA test? I mean, maybe Frank Meeklin wasn't her father? It's possible, isn't it? Do you know who the other candidate is?"

Belinda Bell whispered in PJ's ear, the bit about Luna's ménage-à-trois theory. Luna had showed Belinda the PowerPoint before she'd stopped talking. Belinda was not about to say *ménage à trois* in front of a child, even if Ollie had heard about it before, from his sister.

"Oh my," PJ said.

Belinda Bell kept talking, no longer a whisper. "And that's not all—this man who she says is her real father is someone on television, an actor on a soap opera. He grew up in Pondville, but he hasn't lived here since high school. I think you can understand, Mr. Halliday, that it would be improper if we demanded a paternity test from someone who has never met the children and is not listed on the birth certificate, especially someone who is a public figure and lives all the way in Los Angeles. It would bring shame on the Massachusetts Department of Children and Families."

"Shame?" PJ asked. He thought that was a bit overkill.

"Yes," Belinda Bell said. "We have no reason to believe Frank Meeklin is not her biological father. But Luna is going to bring it up with you eventually, probably as soon as she starts talking, so I thought you should be aware."

"Okay, I get it. I would have liked my dad to be a big star on television too." PJ winked at Ollie, but the poor boy looked miserable. PJ felt for the kid. PJ had never met his own father, whoever his dad was had only sent PJ's mother an envelope of cash a few times a year, and PJ's mother wouldn't talk about him, would only say that she'd loved him very much and had met him when she was traveling the country alone. PJ's mother had lots of stories about traveling the country alone, the adventures she'd been on. The things she had seen, outside of Pondville.

Now this little boy, Ollie, would grow up in Pondville without a father too. PJ knew how lonely it would be.

"Wait," PJ said to Belinda. "Now, I don't know how it works, but could you test the boy? Wouldn't a DNA test tell you if they're full-siblings or half-siblings?"

"I don't want you to test me," Ollie said. "I won't let you." He imagined a DNA test would really hurt.

"Like I said," Belinda Bell said, "you're better off leaving it alone, Mr. Halliday. You're only going to cause trouble for yourself if you let the girl have whatever she wants." And then Belinda wished PJ the best of luck with the kids and was out the door and off in her white van. The boy looked sad to see her go.

"You want to play videogames?" PJ asked the boy, thinking of something that might cheer him up. "I bought you a PlayStation, but I'll need your help getting it hooked up to the TV." PJ had gone a little crazy at Walmart.

Ollie nodded and grinned.

9

It was nearly bedtime, and Luna still wouldn't answer when they knocked on the bathroom door, not even when Ollie described the two-player videogames they could play together. Ollie and Luna hadn't been allowed a turn at the videogames at the foster home; that was only for the big kids, the teenagers. But Luna wouldn't come out, not for anything. Finally, PJ was fed up, and he dug out the screwdriver and he took the bathroom door off its hinges. He found the bathroom empty, the window open. "Holy shit, Ollie, she's gone out the window."

"Out the window?" Ollie said, not believing it. "Did she fall?"

"It's not a long drop to the ground. She's probably not hurt, but she's gone. She's run away. I'll call the police."

"No," Ollie said, shaking his head. "You do not want to call the cops. They'll beat you up."

"Why would they beat me up?" PJ asked. PJ was no friend to cops, but he thought he needed the police in this situation. A missing child was exactly why you called the cops.

Ollie crossed his arms. "The cops are all my dad's friends, and they will beat you up for losing my sister. They even might kill you."

"Okay, okay, good point," PJ said, trying not to panic. "We'll go look for her first. She can't have gone far." His heart clutched in his chest. *Not now*, he thought to his heart. He had to find this poor kid. She was probably frightened. His mind went to the bogs, to the edge of town.

"I'll find her," Ollie said. He took off before PJ could stop him.

"No, come back!" PJ called, but it was too late. The boy was fast, and young. PJ tried to follow where Ollie had gone running. The social worker had said the children had lived only a few streets down when their parents were alive, but PJ couldn't remember the street, didn't know where their old house was, and Ollie was out of sight. PJ tried to run to catch up, but he was in no shape for this. "Luna!" he called. "Luna! Ollie! Luna!"

PJ walked up and down the street, but eventually he found his way back to Fred and Ivy's and went back inside. There had to be someone he could call for help. He looked at the number for Belinda Bell on the paperwork on the table, and thought about calling her, begging her to come back. *This was a mistake*, he wanted to tell her. *This was a huge mistake. I've already raised children, and I've been through too much. I lost one and I failed another, I didn't tell you the truth when you were here, and it's all a terrible idea for me to try it again.*

But when PJ opened the folder, there was a photograph of the two children paper-clipped to the top. He looked at the picture of the children, smiling on the front steps of a white house, two kids who didn't look much alike despite being siblings. But he remembered that Ollie and Luna were Irish twins, even if that wasn't PC to say, and that made them a bit supernatural, didn't it? Ollie would find her. It would be all right. It would be nothing like it had been before. Nothing like that.

So. PJ didn't call Belinda Bell. And he didn't call the police, because he realized the police would take the kids away as soon as they found Luna, they would take them away from him and put them back in foster care. What good would that do? And he didn't call Fred and Ivy, because what could they do all the way in Alaska? Nothing. Instead, he called his daughter Sophie, who was only down in New Bedford, close enough to be in Pondville in twenty-two minutes, but of course Sophie didn't pick up the call. He left a long, rambling voicemail, explaining the situation, begging for some help here. Then he took the photo of Ollie and Luna from the social worker's folder of paperwork and went out into the night to show any neighbors who might be out walking their dogs, ask if they had seen these kids.

Three streets over, in the white house on Deerfield Lane, Ollie ducked under the yellow caution tape still wrapped around the house. The cops had left it up, and no one dared remove the yellow tape in the month since, even if it was getting to be an eyesore. The three vultures that were usually circling the house were roosted in the branches of the tree in the yard for the night, and the birds watched the boy go in, and each rocked their weight from foot to foot. The birds huddled closer on the branch, putting their ugly heads together to discuss what would happen next.

Ollie found his sister sitting on the floor, in the spot where Luna had found their mother after she got off the school bus that day. Someone had cleaned it all up. Ollie wondered who had that job. He had never seen the mess, but his sister had described it, and Ollie could see it clearly, how it had looked. But the floor was clean now, and Luna was holding a big orange cat in her arms. Next to her was one of her mother's purses, the big pink one that said MAMA on the side, which Luna had stuffed with some of her things from their bedroom. "Hi, Ollie," she said.

"Luna. You scared us."

"Who's us?"

"Me and Uncle PJ."

"What about Ms. Belinda?"

"Ms. Belinda's gone."

"Oh," Luna said. "Good." She was grateful Ms. Belinda was gone, because Belinda didn't listen. She was another adult who didn't listen. Luna was also grateful Ollie had found her, because she didn't have a plan from here. Luna had meant to go to the bus station next, but she realized she didn't know where the bus station was, and she also didn't have any money for a ticket. She had hoped she would find some money in the house, but it seemed like whoever had cleaned up the mess her mother had left had also taken the shoebox full of cash from under the bed. People had a way of disappointing Luna, all the time. "I found a cat," Luna said to her brother, showing him the cat in her arms.

"Where did you find him?"

"In Uncle PJ's bathtub. He followed me out the window when I was running away."

"You were . . . really running away?"

"Yeah."

Tears were in Ollie's eyes. "You were running away without me?"

Luna stared at him. "Well, you don't listen to me."

"Because you're not the boss."

"You shouldn't have told the nurse what I told you. I told you not to tell. Mom told me I shouldn't even tell you about it. She said you'd never understand because you're a boy."

The cat jumped out of Luna's arms and went to sniff Ollie's feet. One of Ollie's tears fell onto the cat's head, and the droplet was absorbed into the orange fur. "Okay," Ollie said. "Fine. I'm sorry."

"What are you sorry for?" Luna asked. She was testing him.

"For being a boy. And for not listening to you. I'll listen to you."

"Always?"

"Yes. But you can't leave without me again."

"Deal," she said. "I won't leave without you again."

"Good." He wiped his eyes. "Are you coming back to Uncle PJ's?

He's not bad, Luna, he's not mean or crazy like Grandpa, I can tell. He got us a trampoline, and a PlayStation. And bunk beds. Brand-new. They still have plastic on the mattresses. No bugs." There had been bedbugs at the foster home in Springfield. "And he said he loves us," Ollie lied. "He said he loves us already."

"I'll stay there for tonight, I guess," Luna agreed. "I can't stay here," she said, looking around their old house, which seemed so different than it had. Musty. Haunted. But it had never been an especially safe place, when her grandpa lived there, or when her dad got too angry or drunk, or when her mom called their neighbor Michael Hoonhaut and accused him of looking into their windows, which Luna was pretty sure he'd never done. It was a scary and confusing place, where it had always felt like anything could happen at any time, and you didn't know when you woke up if it would be a good day or a bad one.

"No," Ollie agreed, also looking around the house. "I never want to come back here again."

"Should we burn it down?" Luna asked, because she had the lighter from the woman she'd stolen the cigarettes from, but Ollie said no, he didn't want to. Luna knew her grandfather had burned down a house once; he had told her the story. He had tried to burn down the house with a woman inside, but the woman had escaped. Her grandpa had lots of terrifying stories like that, things he'd done or wanted to do. "Uncle PJ really said he loves us?" Luna asked.

"Yes," Ollie lied again. "He did."

Luna could see Ollie was lying, but she let herself be comforted anyway.

"And if he doesn't, we'll run away together. We'll find your dad," Ollie promised.

"Okay," Luna said. She needed to hear that too.

The vultures in the maple tree outside the house craned their long, ugly necks and watched the Meeklin children leave the house on Deerfield Lane, the girl carrying the orange cat. The birds watched the children walking back toward Clear Pond Road, listening to the distant calls of Uncle PJ shouting their names. Luna stayed silent, but Ollie called back: "We're here! We have your cat, Uncle PJ! She's alive!"

Alive, the buzzards agreed, stretching their wings and bobbing their naked heads. *Alive, alive, alive,* they rasped. Vultures don't screech or call like other birds; they only hiss and make clicking sounds. They're otherwise silent animals, like death itself. But here was something new: the vultures chanting the word *alive* over and over, hoping those poor children would stay safe and protected, forever and ever, amen.

10

Back at the ranch, after teeth were brushed and the kids were tucked in and everything had calmed down, PJ sat in a chair next to the beds. It was Fred's office chair that swiveled. The cat jumped in his lap. Luna was on the bottom bunk, Ollie up top.

"So, tell me about this guy," PJ said to Luna. "The man you think is your father."

Luna looked at him for a minute, considering whether she could trust this old man, but she could see the cat liked him, and Luna liked the cat. She reached under her pillow, brought out a glossy portrait. An actor's headshot. It was signed: *All my love, Mark Stackpole.* PJ took it from her gingerly, trying to keep his fingers only at the edge so he didn't leave greasy fingerprints on the photograph. "Oh dear," he said. "He sent you this?"

Luna nodded. It was why she'd had to go back to the house. It was one of the things she needed to get. Her real father had sent it to her in the mail after she'd written him a letter asking him if he was willing to take a paternity test. In return, the assistant of Mark Stackpole had sent her a signed headshot and a coupon to the protein powder that Mark was a spokesperson for.

PJ admired the headshot photo in his hands. "Handsome guy. You do look a little bit alike."

Luna sat up. "You think so?" she asked.

"Yes," PJ said, glad to hear the kid's voice for the first time. "I do. I really do."

"Can you get me a DNA test?"

"Well, I wouldn't know the first thing about a DNA test. But I can take you to LA to meet this guy."

"You can?"

"Well, we'll need something to do this summer, won't we? I was thinking we'd go on a road trip. But you'll have to come with me to Tucson first. It's on the way. We'll drive to Arizona, and then go to California. They're next-door neighbors."

"What's in Tucson?"

"My high school girlfriend. She's single again. A brand-new widow. I haven't seen her in forty-five years."

"You really love her that much?"

"I don't know if I do. But it's worth a shot."

"You're going to drive all that way to give it a shot?"

"Yup."

"What about an airplane? Can we take an airplane? Ollie farts in the car."

"Good question, kiddo, but here's the thing: And I don't want to scare you, because I know your parents just passed away, but I'm getting to be an old man and I've never been on a big adventure. I went on one adventure, but the United States government made me go, and I almost didn't survive."

"You were in the CIA?" Ollie asked, piping up from the top bunk.

PJ shook his head. "I was in the war."

"World War One or Two?"

"How old do you think I am?"

"Ninety," Luna said.

"A hundred," said Ollie.

"I'm sixty-three, and I was in Vietnam, which was a terrible war, and then I came home to Pondville, and got a job as a postman and had a wife and kids and responsibilities and I never left after that. So, I think I owe myself one great adventure. I'd like to see the country."

"We've been to New Jersey," Ollie offered. "That's where our dad was born."

"*Your* dad," Luna muttered.

"Was it nice?" PJ asked.

"It sucked," Luna said.

"It sucked," Ollie agreed.

"This will be better," PJ said.

"Great," Luna said. "We'll leave tomorrow."

"You have school," PJ said. PJ had forgotten a lot of things about parenting, but he remembered kids had to go to school. "We'll leave when summer starts."

"There's only one week left until summer," Ollie said. "There's no point." There were, in fact, three weeks left, but Ollie thought that sounded like too many.

"They already gave us our fourth-grade diploma," Luna said, because they had. Principal McGuffries had mailed it to the foster home, in case the Meeklin children didn't come back for the rest of the year. It was a piece of paper he had printed out on his computer in his office. He had stuck some gold star stickers on it. Principal McGuffries had felt good he'd made the effort.

"It doesn't make sense to send us back to school," Ollie said. "Everyone will stare at us and ask us questions. Kids need time to grieve after tragedy." It was something Ollie had read in one of the books at the foster home. He remembered exactly what the book said, and he repeated it: "We need time to trust our new caregiver and adjust to life after loss. We might withdraw, or act out, or even get violent. We may have an especially hard time in school."

Luna was impressed with Ollie. He wasn't usually clever like this.

She was the clever one, and he went along with it. She was sorry she'd left him behind when she ran away.

"I mean, it's basically summer break already, huh?" PJ said, thinking it over. He remembered Ivy always said there was no real school in June anyway, it was just packing up the classroom and the kids goofing off.

"Yup, we're only going to watch movies for the rest of the year," Luna said, practically reading PJ's mind. "You can show us some movies if you want. Your favorite movies." Luna knew adults love to show kids their favorite movies, and she wanted to leave before PJ changed his mind about taking her to meet her father. And Luna did not want to go back to that school where she hated everyone. The talent show was coming up and she already knew Elsie Dawson, the girl who played Tinker Bell last year, would win, and Luna wouldn't be able to punch her again because the teachers would be watching her the whole time.

PJ thought it over. He did want to get out of town before prom, before he started to miss Kate so much it ached. Kate used to smile and say to him after a softball game: "How much money did you lose betting against us?" It was their joke, that he was always betting against her, even though nothing could have been further from the truth. PJ wanted to leave Pondville before he started seeing balloons in the yard for graduation parties, signs that read CONGRATULATIONS, GRADUATE! because Kate had never made it that far.

"Sure, I suppose we can leave soon," he said.

"Tomorrow?" Luna asked.

"Okay, sure," PJ said. "Might as well hit the road." Michelle Cobb might not wait much longer for him. She was sure to have other suitors. There was probably a line at the door of her two-bedroom condo every morning.

"Wait, tomorrow?" Ollie asked. He didn't want to go back to school, but he didn't know if he wanted to leave the house with the trampoline either.

"It'll be fun, Ollie," Luna assured him.

"Okay," Ollie said, and maybe that was good enough, that it would be fun, and he and Luna wouldn't have to go to school where everyone would look at them weird. He snuggled down into his sleeping bag, the plastic on the mattress crackling. He didn't want to take the plastic off until he was sure there were really no bedbugs.

"Thanks, Uncle PJ," Luna said.

"No problem," PJ said, feeling like a hero. "All right, kiddos, it's time to get some rest. I'll see you in the funny papers in the morning." He used to say that every night to Sophie and Kate when he tucked them in. The girls used to ask him what it meant, and he would say that they were funny-looking enough to be in the comics, but it still felt like a lovely thing to say to kids somehow, and it was soothing to him to say it to children again. But after the light was off, PJ realized he needed to say one more thing to the girl. It was easier to say with the lights out. "Hey, Luna?"

"Yeah?"

"I want you to know, my brother was a total asshole. Your grandfather. He was mentally ill, and that wasn't his fault, but he was also an asshole. A person can be both those things, and you don't have to forgive him for whatever cruel thing he did to you. Maybe you loved him but I'm guessing you didn't."

"Luna, I didn't tell him about it," Ollie said. "I promise. I swear."

"He didn't tell me anything," PJ said. "That's the truth. I just know my brother was an asshole and I could see he hurt you somehow, when you played the piano. I could tell. But he was an asshole, and it's good he's gone now. We should be happy about that."

"Okay," Luna said, quietly. "Thanks, Uncle PJ." Then she closed her eyes tight before opening them again to see if she felt any different, now that she had heard someone say something aloud she had wished and wished her parents had said. That it was good her grandpa was dead, and she didn't have to forgive him. When she opened her eyes there were stars on the ceiling, because PJ had turned on the star projector that he'd bought at IKEA, in case the kids were afraid of the dark. His older daughter had always slept with a nightlight and the door open, even as a teen.

PJ left their bedroom door open a crack. He felt more wonderful than he had in a long time. It was a good thing to put kids to bed. He had done a good thing by telling Luna her grandfather was an asshole; that seemed to have helped her. And she was talking again. PJ thought he should be proud of that. Belinda Bell had said Luna would start talking again, eventually, but it had only taken him one night to get her speaking. He was good with the kids. He was practically Mary Poppins.

Then his stomach dropped. There was sadness mixed in with the wonderful, and he needed something to tamp down the sadness. He went downstairs, looked in the fridge. There were only eggs, the leftover pizza, the orange juice and grapes and string cheeses, yogurts he'd bought for the kids. PJ closed the fridge again, opened the front door, and went down the gravel path, out into the night. He walked ten houses down the street. He wouldn't be gone long, and the kids were safe in bed. He would be back well before they woke up.

"Hello, house," he said to his house full of junk.

I've missed you, said the house.

He opened his own fridge, but the six-pack he was looking for in there wasn't in its usual spot waiting for him. Right, because he wasn't supposed to be drinking. He was supposed to be the best man. He could drink after the wedding, at the reception, after the speech. Well, even if he wasn't going to be drinking that night, he could still take a walk. He needed a walk.

But first, he went upstairs and down the hall. PJ never went into Kate's room. It was Ivy who used to go in there, after Kate's death. Ivy would go in there when Sophie was over at her grandmother's house, and she would lie on the bed and cry her eyes out for exactly an hour. When her kitchen timer dinged, Ivy would get up and remake the bed, and go back to her day. PJ knew not to ask her about it. Ivy had trouble even saying Kate's name. After Ivy moved out of their house, PJ kept the door to Kate's room closed and the egg timer on the kitchen counter, but Ivy never walked into their house again. If she cried somewhere for exactly an hour every week, it wasn't in Kate's room.

Now PJ paused in front of Kate's door.

I wish—said the blue hat on the doorknob, but the hat stopped talking because PJ was picking it up, off the knob, and placing it on his head. He had never done that before, worn the hat. VARSITY GIRLS SOFTBALL, it read, over the brim. He went back downstairs, out the front door, with the hat. He walked two miles to the edge of town, where there was a stone bench looking out across the cranberry bogs. He sat down. The cat jumped up next to him.

"You followed me, huh?" PJ said. "You're a strange creature."

You have no idea, the cat thought, rubbing against PJ affectionately in response, and then sat down on the bench next to him, looking out at the view. The bogs were usually dry this time of year, the big flood not done until the fall to harvest the berries, but it had been a rainy spring, the rainiest on record, and the bogs were uncharacteristically full of water. The moonlight glinted off the surface.

The night Kate drowned, fifteen years ago, it hadn't been a wet spring, fairly dry actually. There shouldn't have been enough water in the bog to drown in, and sometimes PJ still wondered how she managed it. How drunk she must have been when she wandered into the bogs, wearing her prom dress, and laid down in a few inches of water to drown.

The search party for Kate had begun the same way it had begun today when they'd gone out looking for Luna, only with he and Ivy and Sophie out in the streets calling Kate's name. A few of the neighbors had joined in, including Fred, before they called the cops. Everyone kept looking for Kate for three days, the whole town had looked, but they only found her after they brought in the cadaver dogs. PJ wished he had never known they were called cadaver dogs. He wished they had called them *finder dogs,* or *hide-and-seek dogs,* or *hero and savior dogs.* Maybe the end of the story would have been different if those dogs had been called something else.

PJ looked out into the bogs, found the spot where the dogs had once found his daughter. The moon was so big and bright that he could see out into the bogs clearly, but PJ had those bogs memorized anyway. He could close his eyes and picture them, when he thought about what had happened that night. For so many years, when he told people about what had happened to Kate, he hated what they always said: "I can't imagine." *Try to imagine,* he always wanted to say, and sometimes he did. *Try to imagine how our family was destroyed overnight.*

PJ usually walked out to the bogs after he left the bar, he had slept on that bench many times, had been shaken awake often by concerned passersby in the morning, people out walking their dogs. Officer Frank Meeklin had even woken him up once, and driven PJ home in the cruiser, but neither man had known their family connection, and hadn't done enough talking to figure it out. Staring out into the bogs now, sober and clear-headed, PJ thought he saw the flick of a silver tail out of the water, as if a large fish were coming to the surface and diving down. *The mermaid from Clear Pond,* he thought. He knew it was childish, impossible, and still, he was sure he'd finally seen her, after so many years of wanting to see her, looking out at the raft at Clear Pond, wanting for her to lift herself out of the water like the scene in the Disney movie when the mermaid lifts herself up on the rock. *I saw her,* he'd tell the kids in the morning. *The mermaid, she got into the bogs somehow.* He knew the farmers filled the bogs with water from Clear Pond, so really, anything was possible.

Things had been bad for so long, but suddenly, with these two kids and Michelle Cobb, anything felt possible again. The world was opening up.

At just that moment, the bench was flooded with bright and unnatural light, like PJ was being abducted by aliens. It was headlights. A car had come over the ridge.

11

PJ shielded his eyes and saw the approaching car was one he knew; it belonged to his daughter Sophie. Sophie was his younger daughter, the living one, she was twenty-six years old, and she was driving her beat-up Honda Civic. It was the car she'd had since she was sixteen, before PJ won the lottery, the car she wouldn't let him replace with a newer model. Sophie didn't approve of PJ winning all that money. She thought it had hobbled him, enabled him to stay drunk for the rest of his life. She said she didn't want a dime.

PJ looked at his daughter, pulling up. His beloved daughter. She looked a little pale, but maybe that was the moonlight. Sophie wore too much eyeliner; Ivy always complained about that, but PJ thought it suited her. Her black hair had streaks of blue, and she had a gold ring in her nose. PJ could have done without the nose ring, but it was her face, not his. She wore thick leather bracelets on her wrists to cover her scars.

Everyone in Pondville knew PJ slept out here on the stone bench a lot of the time after he left the bar, and sometimes Sophie came out here to pick him up, if Fred couldn't do it. But tonight, when he got into the passenger seat of Sophie's car, holding the cat in his arms, Sophie looked angry, angrier than usual, even though PJ didn't stink of booze. She didn't ask about the cat. She said she'd gone to his house first, but he hadn't been home and *what the fuck did you mean*, she said, on that voicemail, that he'd adopted two kids but that he'd lost one?

"Oh, I found her, I found her," he assured her. "They're both safe. They're back at the house, asleep."

"What the fuck is going on, Dad? Mom leaves you alone for five minutes and you adopt two children? Who gave you these children? Did you walk up to an orphanage?"

"They don't really have orphanages anymore; they were phased out through the foster-care system in the '50s and '60s—"

"Dad, where did you get the kids?"

"Okay, okay." They were his brother's grandkids. They had been orphaned. They didn't have anyone else. He had to say yes, or they would have stayed in the foster-care system and who knows what would have happened to them then. Everyone has heard horror stories.

"Dad, you don't have a brother." Sophie just wanted to hear the truth about how he'd gotten these kids so Sophie could figure out how to return them. If her mother was gone, Sophie would have to clean up this mess by herself. Her mother had told her a thousand times she had to watch her dad while she and Fred were out of town.

"I *do* have a brother," her dad insisted. "Or I *did* have a brother, but he's dead. Died a year or so ago. You're lucky you never met him, but that's not the kids' fault. Or you may have met him actually. He owned the bowling alley."

"Chip Duggins? Dad, he was not your brother."

"He was. He is."

"Why did he have a different last name?"

"Different fathers. Same mother. His father was Roy Duggins. A real asshole."

"And these kids, they're asleep at your house?"

"At Fred's house. Your mother's house. You know I couldn't have kids stay at my house. The kids were orphaned, and they need a place to live," PJ said. PJ reached into his cargo shorts and took out the photo of the kids that had come with Belinda Bell's file. He held it up to show Sophie. "Look," he said. "They're sweet kids. One of them even plays the piano."

Sophie glanced at the photo of the kids. A redheaded boy and a little brown-haired girl. They looked like fine kids to Sophie, but PJ Halliday, Fucked-Up Father Extraordinaire, was not the type of man who should be the sole caretaker of children. He was not the type of man who should take orphans in. He was the type of man who spent his weekends in the drunk tank. He was the type of man who only called you because he needed something. He had called her last week because he was having trouble figuring out how to put together IKEA bunk beds, had left a long, rambling, nonsensical voicemail, which did make more sense now. "So, what's your plan? You're living at Fred's with these orphaned kids?"

"Only temporarily. We're leaving on a road trip tomorrow. The kids have a relative in Los Angeles, and we're going to drive there to meet him. Make sure he checks out. The kids' parents just died in a murder-suicide, so it's a delicate situation."

"A road trip? Are you taking them to the circus too? Disney World?"

"Very funny, Sophie, but it appears that this man in California could be the girl's real biological father. We have to make this man take responsibility for the children. I'm only taking care of the kids until the end of the summer. Then they'll go live with him."

"Oh," Sophie said, and that kind of changed things. Just until the end of the summer. Her dad was more of a transport person than a parental guardian. He just had to get the kids to their biological father in California. "And if he doesn't take the responsibility as their father?"

PJ lied again. He was on a roll. "The social workers have someone else lined up in September. I told them I could take care of them for the summer, and I wanted to try to talk some sense into this guy first. Make him see what he's missing if he doesn't get to know his kids. It's the girl's father, but I'm hoping he'll take the boy too. Seems important that they stay together. They're Irish twins."

It wasn't as bad as Sophie thought, although she didn't see why her dad should be the one to talk some sense into this deadbeat guy, but Sophie didn't really know how foster care worked. Maybe there was no one else looking out for these kids. Clearly, the system was broken. Everyone has heard that. "And who is driving the car on this road trip? Did you get your license back?"

He shook his head. "Not yet. Suspension ends in four days." But he still wanted to leave tomorrow. Wanted to make the most of the kids' summer break and reunite with Michelle Cobb as soon as possible. He had been planning to drive carefully, so he didn't get pulled over. "I suppose you can drive us," he said. "If you want."

"No, Dad. No, thank you. No."

"Okay, okay, just a thought. You don't have to decide immediately. This old hunk-of-junk Honda can't make the trip, but Fred lent me the Volvo for the journey."

"He did?"

PJ nodded.

Sophie thought about it. If Fred thought it was okay for her dad to help these kids, then maybe it was okay. Sophie trusted Fred.

PJ looked at his daughter. It wasn't a complete lie; PJ had the keys, didn't he? Fred had let him use the Volvo for groceries, and so what if he was going to use it for a little more than that? It was an important thing he was doing. PJ knew Freddy would give him permission to take the car if he knew the full situation, but every time he'd called Fred in the month since he left, PJ got the dreaded voicemail recording. But Fred loved children and would want to help them. And Sophie seemed to believe that Fred had really given him the Volvo for the trip, because she wasn't yelling at him about it, and if it was believable, it was almost like permission.

Sophie pulled into the driveway and was relieved to see Fred's house still standing. The red Volvo was in the driveway, waiting to be taken on a trip. Sophie's stomach clutched when she thought of what could have happened to those kids in the house without any adults around; what if a kid fell down the basement stairs, or accidentally drank drain cleaner, or burned themself on the stove. She went into the house, the front door was unlocked, and ran upstairs. She looked into Fred's office and found the kids were in their beds, both of them accounted for, safe and sound asleep. If they were in any kind of pain, it didn't show on their faces.

Sophie leaned against the doorframe to catch her breath. Their parents died in a murder-suicide, and tomorrow they were going on a road trip with her dad. *A fun distraction,* he probably thought. He hadn't even come upstairs with her to check on the kids.

Sophie had been about their age when her sister died, and she remembered how her mom had actually sent her on a trip to Disney World, two years later. Her parents hadn't come, Sophie had gone by herself on the plane with a group of other kids. Some organization had put together a five-day Disney trip focused on bereaved siblings. They gave Sophie a T-shirt that said: SURVIVING SIBLING, as if it were a fun club. The T-shirt was magenta.

All the other kids on the trip had siblings who had died from long, drawn-out illnesses, and that had made Sophie feel a little left out, that she'd never donated bone marrow to try to save her sister. They were all teenagers on the trip, so they weren't all that interested in the amusement park; the magic of Disney was gone, and all the teenagers just wanted to get drunk and touch each other. It was the first time Sophie had a boy put his hand down her pants and jam his finger around like he was looking for something he'd dropped down a sink drain. *You're a woman now,* she could hear Kate telling her in her ear. Kate had lost her virginity a few weeks before she died, to the boy who would be her prom date. Kate had told Sophie all about it, even though Sophie was only eleven at the time, but Kate liked telling her little sister every exciting thing the teenage years had in store.

"Did you have a great time?" Sophie's mom asked when she came back from the Disney trip. "Did you make friends?"

Sophie had nodded, because she knew that if she was happy, her mother could be happy. Sophie put the T-shirt they'd given her in Kate's bottom drawer, where she knew no one would find it. A few months later, when they learned about Queen Victoria in history class, how Queen Victoria wore black for forty years after Albert's death, Sophie started coming to school in all black too. It was cliché, perhaps, but it wasn't a pink T-shirt that proclaimed you had survived.

"Shit. I need to help these kids," Sophie said out loud, looking at their faces, serene and innocent under the slight glow from the star projector. Someone had to help them. They couldn't be left alone with her idiot father. And what else did she have going on that prevented her from going on a trip? Nothing. She had nothing. Sophie remembered the kindness of one of the counselors on the Disney trip who had promised her she wouldn't be so sad forever. Even if it hadn't exactly been true, it had been so nice to hear at the time.

Sophie closed the door to Fred's office and went back downstairs to find her dad lying in Fred's armchair, the cat in his arms.

"See?" he said, looking up. "They were fine, weren't they? Both in dreamland?"

"Dad. You can't leave children alone in the house again. Ever. Something bad could have happened. Something really bad."

"I'm sorry. You're right, of course you're right. I thought they would be fine, since they were asleep, but you're right."

"Of course I'm fucking right," Sophie said. "They could have been seriously hurt."

"That's a horrible thing to say, Sophie."

"It was a horrible thing to do."

"I said I won't do it again."

"Good." And then Sophie lingered. She didn't want to stay there arguing with her father, but she also did not want to drive back to her apartment in New Bedford. For the past two months, she had been alone in her bedroom in that apartment, eating Cheese Curls and watching mindless television. She was unemployed, had been unemployed for two months. She had four roommates, and she hated three of them. "And when did you get a cat?" she finally asked, although she wasn't sure she was up for one of her dad's long stories.

"I got the cat two weeks ago; he was a stray," PJ said, simply enough. "He followed me home. His name is Pancakes." He stroked the cat's back.

"You know I'm allergic to cats."

Ah, PJ thought. *There's my answer. Sophie is the one with the allergy.* "We'll get you some Claritin. He's my little pal; I'm not giving him up. It's a very exciting time for me to be alive, Sophie, it really is. And there's something else—you'll never believe it, but I've quit drinking. I've been off the sauce since your mother left."

Sophie looked at him. She wasn't born yesterday. It had been a month since Fred and her mom had left, although he did appear to be sober that night. He usually sang in the car all the way home from the bogs, and this time he'd been having a conversation with her. A strange conversation, but coherent. "That's great, Dad," she said, not fully believing it was possible. "How? Have you been going to AA?" He had never stuck with AA before, the few times Sophie's mom had gotten him to go.

"No AA," he said proudly, because AA was a bunch of losers in the church basement. "I dried out all on my own for the wedding. I am going to be the best man in your mother's wedding."

Sophie was surprised her dad knew about the wedding; she didn't think they were going to tell him. "Fred told you about the engagement?"

"Of course Fred told me! I'm his best man. And I'm going to take Michelle Cobb as my plus-one. And I'm going to stay sober until then, so that I do a good job as best man."

Sophie took the bait. "Who is Michelle Cobb?"

"Oh, she was my first love. The one who got away. She married someone else when I went to Vietnam. And she's finally single again.

She lives in Tucson, Arizona, and the kids and I are going to stop and see her on the way to California."

"You've been talking to Michelle on the phone?"

"Oh, she doesn't know I'm coming. Don't want to spook her. Her husband only recently died."

Sophie put her face in her hands. "Why can't you be normal about anything?"

"I'm a romantic. I'm just an old guy looking for a date to my ex-wife's wedding."

Sophie raised her eyebrows. *Well, okay,* Sophie thought. Let him go find Michelle Cobb. Maybe she would be good for him. She was glad he wasn't upset about the wedding. Seemed happy about it even. And her father needed someone to take care of him. Maybe Michelle Cobb was up for the job. Good luck to her. "Okay," she said.

"Okay, what?"

"I'll help you with the kids. I'll come on your road trip. I don't have a job anymore, so I can do it."

"What happened to your job?"

"The company closed," she said, which was only a small part of the story, but she wasn't going to tell the whole thing to her dad. Since Sophie had lost her job as an assistant to the CEO of a greeting-card company, Fred had been giving her money for rent and groceries. Fred said he was happy to do it as long as Sophie didn't tell her mother she was unemployed. Fred thought Ivy worried too much, and he wanted her to relax. He wanted to take her to Alaska where she could relax. "She has spent her whole life worrying," Fred had said, as if he had been around for Sophie's mom's whole life. "Just give her these few months to relax. And maybe—think about applying to grad school? That would make her happy." Fred told Sophie she should really consider speech pathology. It was a stable and well-paying career, and it would be a beautiful way to honor her dead sister. Kate had once needed to see a speech pathologist when she was in middle school, and her mom must have told Fred about it, which surprised Sophie, because her mother barely ever talked about Kate.

But Sophie hadn't applied to any graduate programs, hadn't yet taken the GRE. She had been lying in bed, smoking weed and watching episodes of *Arrested Development*. "The point is, Dad, I can help."

"Well, that's great. That's really great, Sophie. We'll leave tomorrow."

"But why don't we fly to California? We can get that situation sorted out for the kids, and then you can get another flight to Tucson from there."

"Sophie."

"What?"

PJ didn't care for airplanes, they had always seemed too dangerous, and he had always avoided them ever since the U.S. government flew him back from Vietnam. Besides, PJ had a romantic vision for the trip, wanted to do it the way his mother had once traveled across the country, by car and by train. He needed Sophie to get on board. "Sophie. You're a late arrival to this plan. I think it's great that you want to help me with the kids, I appreciate it, but I'm doing this my way. I need to see the country. Michelle Cobb and her husband went everywhere. It was in his obituary, it said they went all over the country in an RV. In New Orleans, they ate beignets. Do you know what a beignet is?"

"It's like a French donut?"

"Exactly. A French donut. And I've never had one. I'm sixty-three years old and I haven't been anywhere. I haven't done anything."

Sophie pressed her lips together. Since her sister died, her dad hadn't done anything except work on drinking himself to death. But she hadn't gone anywhere either. *Failure to launch,* she'd seen it called. People in their twenties who didn't move far from home. She'd gone to the local state college twenty minutes away from home and then stuck around the area for her job after that. "All right," Sophie said to her dad. "Fine. We'll drive."

PJ smiled. "That's my girl."

12

Sophie went back to her apartment to pack and to say goodbye to the one roommate she liked, Aimee, who was also the one who sold her weed. Sophie bought a small baggie of gummies from Aimee for the trip, and then she emailed Blanche that she would miss therapy this week. Blanche was her new therapist, a woman in her sixties, planning to retire soon, so it barely made sense for Sophie to start seeing her, but therapists were hard to find. Fred had been paying for the weekly sessions so that Sophie wouldn't unload her problems on her mom. It was the deal. Fred would give her money; Sophie wouldn't worry her mother about any of her problems until they were back from Alaska.

Sophie emailed Blanche to say that she was missing therapy because she was going on a road trip with her dad. Sophie wondered what Blanche would say about that. "Now that you're an adult, you can decide how much contact with your father is healthy for you," Blanche had said in their meetings. "Sometimes limiting contact is healthy. Family obligation is not as important as mental health."

But Blanche wasn't so smart about everything. Sometimes Blanche would tell Sophie that she needed more friends her own age, and she had seen some young people at the casino. Sophie couldn't believe her therapist was telling her to go to the casino, but maybe Blanche thought that Sophie needed to try something, anything, other than what she'd been doing.

An out-of-office email bounced back, with the complete lyrics to that song asking if you like piña coladas. It turned out Blanche had gone to Acapulco for the next three weeks. A second honeymoon with her husband of forty years. He'd surprised her, so she apologized to her clients for suddenly leaving. She left the number for another therapist who was available in emergencies, someone Sophie didn't know, and also a number for a suicide hotline.

"Great, thanks, Blanche," Sophie said, feeling the sting of abandonment, and got ready to go out for a run. It was already one A.M., but Sophie did that sometimes, went running at odd hours. Fred wanted her to sign up for a marathon, but Sophie didn't understand why everything had to be productive. Why running had to have a goal, and why anyone would ever want to run in a group with other people and pretend it was fun. Running was painful, and that was the point. Sophie put on her SATAN IS MY REAL DADDY T-shirt, and a headlamp that flashed red so cars could see her—a light that blinked steady as a heartbeat, or the timer on a bomb.

Part II

LEAVING PONDVILLE

DAY ONE
TUESDAY

13

In the morning, while the kids jumped on the trampoline, PJ waited for his copilot. He couldn't believe Sophie had agreed to come. He packed the kids' trash bags in the back of the Volvo. He thought about how he would have to buy the kids some proper suitcases. There were so many things he would have to buy them. So many things kids needed.

I miss her—the hat said, from on his head. Kate's hat. When had he put the softball hat back on his head? He couldn't remember. He hadn't slept in it, he was pretty sure, but he was wearing it again. It was off its doorknob, where it belonged, but the hat seemed glad to be worn again. A hat is meant to be worn, to shield someone's eyes from the sun so that they can catch a pop fly. He could close his eyes and picture the softball field at the high school, what the grass smelled like, the rust-red dust from the diamond swirling in the air. He could hear the girls chanting their chants as they sat on the bench. The softball players had more cheers than cheerleaders, only their cheers were more like taunts. There was one cheer PJ remembered about a boyfriend, and *that boyfriend's name was Ed, but Ed rooted for the other team, so they shot him in the head!* PJ chuckled to think of it.

PJ wondered if Ollie and Luna knew how to catch and throw a ball. It didn't say anything about their sporting ability in the chart where it said there had been domestic disturbances reported at their home. If the kids stayed with him, if they didn't go live with this Mark Stackpole character in Los Angeles, maybe they would want to play baseball and softball. He and Michelle Cobb could raise them in Tucson, in the warm weather, they could play all year round—

It won't be like it was, a voice said, and it wasn't from the hat; the hat never had that much to say. It was another voice from somewhere below. A gravelly voice. PJ looked underneath the car. Pancakes was there, with a dead bird in his mouth. He couldn't see how the cat could talk if he had a sparrow in his mouth. PJ was only hearing things. He hadn't been sleeping well lately, with the alcohol withdrawal, and he'd gotten up so early to finish mapping out the trip. PJ felt a pang of guilt that Pancakes had killed a bird on Fred's property, he knew that the death of a bird would be upsetting to his best friend. "Come here," PJ said, reaching under the car and grabbing Pancakes around the middle. "Spit that out, it's time to get on the road. We're going to go see America."

Pancakes dropped the bird, even though he had only just caught it. He could smell that PJ had packed the cat treats in his duffel bag, and they were the good ones, made of *real salmon!*, chicken liver, and guar gum, and molded like tiny little fish. PJ had put a litterbox on the floor of the backseat, in the flat area between where the children's feet would go.

And then Sophie pulled up in her old shit can Honda Civic, and PJ called to the backyard for the kids to come on and get in the Volvo; they were burning daylight and there were things out there on the road to see.

* * *

Fifteen minutes later, they were all crammed into the red Volvo with the Bird Barn license plate, headed to the edge of town, where the sign cautioned them to BE CAREFUL OUT THERE!

"Why does *she* need to come?" Luna asked. She was suspicious about Sophie, who had showed up that morning without warning. Who had a ring in her nose like a cow. Who was behind the wheel, when Luna had assumed Uncle PJ would drive.

"I'm helping my dad out with you," Sophie said. "And I'm driving the car."

"He doesn't need help with us," Luna said, her arms crossed. "We're not babies."

"Yeah," Ollie agreed, although he liked that Sophie had blue streaks in her hair.

"She's an instrumental part of this trip," PJ assured Luna. "She'll keep me in line. And don't worry, Luna, Sophie only looks scary with all the makeup she wears. She's a marshmallow."

"I'm not a marshmallow," Sophie grumbled.

Luna reconsidered this woman driving the car. A marshmallow in black eyeliner. It might be helpful to have another person to help her find her dad. "Do you know the plan?" she asked. "Did Uncle PJ tell you the plan?"

"We're going to California to find your father." Sophie probably hadn't asked enough questions before getting in the car with her father and these kids, but she was also glad to be driving away from Massachusetts, where there was nothing for her after the job she'd had for nearly four years had evaporated. She was glad to be driving away from the men in Red Sox hats she'd been sleeping with lately. "You're my first goth chick," they all said. Sophie didn't like being an item on a bucket list, but she went home with them anyway. Blanche said that was her clinical depression making the decisions for her, and someday she would have to make the clinical depression stop driving the bus. Well, right now she was driving Fred's Volvo, and helping her dad with two orphaned kids. Clinical depression wasn't doing that.

Luna was glad this marshmallow wasn't telling her that it was impossible to find her real dad. "He doesn't know he's my dad, but he is. Ollie and I don't look alike because we're only half-siblings. We had the same mother, but she killed herself."

Well, that was a lot for this early in the morning, even if Sophie already knew the story. Sophie had googled what had happened to the kids, had read the articles, but she didn't expect the kids to talk about it, not so directly. "I'm so sorry for your loss," she said. That felt awkward to say to a kid.

Luna hated when adults said that. She wasn't going to keep talking to Sophie if she was going to be stupid like other grown-ups were. Luna looked through her big pink purse for something else to do; the purse was packed with things from her old room, and her mother's yearbook and diary. She could look at the yearbook again. Mark Stackpole's face was circled inside. Luna hadn't even been the one to circle it; her mother had done that.

"Sophie, let me know when you get tired, and I'll take over," PJ said.

"Dad, you can't drive."

"Why not?" Luna asked, looking up from the yearbook. "Is there something wrong with you?"

"Yes," Sophie said.

"I drink too much," PJ said, because there was no point in hiding it. "But I'm getting better."

"Our dad could drive," Ollie said. "He was a police officer. And he drank too much beer too."

"They let police officers do anything," Sophie said.

"I'm not the kind of drinker your dad was," PJ said, because he had seen some notes from a social worker in the file, and he got the gist. "I'm a happy drunk. I'm a loving guy."

Sophie rolled her eyes. It was terrible to have any kind of alcoholic as a father, a happy drunk or a mean one. It's always confusing and scary. It's always someone who chooses booze over taking care of you.

A white sports car whizzed by them, cutting them off, and PJ reached over to Sophie's side and pressed the horn.

"Dad!"

"I can certainly drive better than that asshole."

"You are not allowed to touch the steering wheel. And don't swear in front of the kids."

"I know all the swears already," Ollie said proudly. "Do you want me to list them?"

"Yes," Luna said.

"Yes," PJ said.

"Absolutely not," Sophie said. "Dad, talk to the kids. Tell them a story or something."

"Oh, it's a little early for one of my stories, but—oh, wait, I've got something to keep them busy!" He went into the tote bag at his feet. At the Walmart, the saleswoman who'd helped him with the trampoline and the PlayStation had told him that if he was really going to be babysitting children, what he truly needed was an iPad. It was her number-one parenting trick, the iPad. PJ pulled the tablets out of the bag. He'd bought two of them, and headphones too. He'd even charged them up for the trip. He handed them back.

"You bought us iPads?" Ollie said, his eyes wide.

"Are you rich, Uncle PJ?" Luna asked.

Sophie snorted. "He didn't tell you?" she asked.

"Didn't tell us what?" Ollie asked.

"He's a million-dollar lottery winner. It's his greatest life accomplishment. He even wears the sweatshirt they gave him." It was true, the Massachusetts State Lottery had given PJ a zip-up hoodie. They gave it to everyone who won over a certain amount; it was good advertising. To prove that there were real lottery winners out there.

"It was a million and a half," PJ said proudly. "From a scratch-off ticket."

"Wow," Ollie said. "You really won the lottery?"

"Thank you," Luna whispered, bringing the iPad to her chest.

PJ smiled, feeling good. Kids understood how impressive it was to win the lottery, it wasn't something anyone could do. He hated how Sophie looked down on it like it was a white-trash thing to play the scratch-offs. He'd won, fair and square, and he'd done good things with his money. He'd been a contributing member of the Pondville community.

"Can we stay in a fancy hotel tonight?" Ollie asked.

PJ laughed. "Sure."

"And order French fries from room service?" Ollie had seen a movie about a rich kid who lived in a hotel by himself, and he'd always wanted to live that way. Gorge himself on French fries and ice cream served on a silver platter.

"Absolutely. We'll get you French fries."

"A hotel with a pool?" Luna asked.

"No," PJ said, his face darkening. "No. No pools. Absolutely no pools on this trip."

"She didn't drown in a pool, Dad," Sophie said.

"Who?" Luna asked. "Who drowned?"

"My daughter, Kate. When she was eighteen, she drowned. The tragedy of my life."

"Not in a pool, though," Sophie said. "In a cranberry bog."

"How does anyone drown in a cranberry bog?" Luna asked. "They aren't very deep." Everyone in Pondville knew about cranberries.

"It's the greatest tragedy of my life," PJ said.

"I'm sorry for your loss," Ollie said.

"That's very kind, Ollie," Sophie said. She liked the sweet boy. He had a gap between his teeth, so when he talked there was a soft whistling sound.

"I hate when people say that," Luna said. "It's not what sorry means. Sorry is when you hurt someone else and wish you hadn't."

Sophie regretted telling the girl she was sorry for her loss. It was an empty thing to say, Sophie agreed. It had never fixed anything for Sophie either.

"Luna punched Elsie Dawson in last year's school play," Ollie said, breaking the silence. "And she wouldn't say sorry."

"I'm sure Elsie deserved it," PJ said.

Luna smiled. She hadn't expected Uncle PJ to say that.

"We'll get a swanky hotel when we get to Niagara," PJ promised. PJ had planned out the trip, had printed a map off Fred's computer, and he had decided Niagara Falls was their first stop. "We're going to do so many wonderful things."

"But no swimming," Ollie said.

"No swimming," PJ agreed.

"Dumb," Luna said.

Dumb, Sophie silently agreed. The best part of staying in hotels as a kid was the pool. When they went on vacations, before Kate died, they always went in the pool. She remembered once they went to New Hampshire for a wedding, and Kate had taught her how to do a chicken fight, lifted Sophie up on her shoulders. Sophie had scratched another boy across the face, and he had gone crying to his mother. Sophie and Kate had both gotten into trouble, but it had been worth it. They had won the battle. They were undefeated chicken-fight champions by the time they left the pool. Sophie's eyes watered. "Effing cat," she said. She pulled off at the next exit to look for a CVS.

"Are we almost there?" Ollie asked, looking up from his iPad.

They had five and a half hours to go before Niagara Falls.

"No, I'm only stopping for allergy medicine," Sophie said. "Does anyone need anything?"

"Snacks," Ollie said.

"Rubbers," PJ added. He didn't know what Michelle Cobb had been up to since Gene died, and he'd seen the special on *60 Minutes* on venereal disease in retirement communities.

"Gross, Dad. No."

"I'll come in with you," Luna said, unbuckling her seatbelt.

"Okay, sure. That would be great." The girl made Sophie a little nervous. Sophie wanted the girl to like her, but the girl seemed like she might not like anyone. The girl scowled most of the time, or when she smiled it looked like it was because the devil had whispered something in her ear and she knew he was coming for you.

14

Inside the CVS, the fluorescent lights gleamed like the gateway to heaven. Luna put some snacks in Sophie's basket: chocolate-covered pretzels and peanut-butter Ritz, a can of Pringles. Then, when Sophie went off to the back aisles near the pharmacy to find the Claritin, Luna went to look for things to steal. She put a purple bottle of pills that said SLEEP in yellow on the side into her big pink purse that had once been her mother's. The bottle was decorated with stars and moons that made it look like a potion.

In other aisles, Luna pocketed a ChapStick, a candy bar, a lollipop, and an eyeshadow with four shades of blue, and more and more things, putting them into her purse or tucking them into the deep pockets of her fake fur coat. It was so easy to steal things, Luna wished she'd been doing it all her life. Before the cigarettes that Luna had stolen when Belinda Bell stopped for Big Gulps, Luna had never stolen anything. Her dad was a cop. But now it seemed like she deserved to steal. Her parents were dead. One of the bigger girls at the foster home said the best thing about being a parentless kid was the rules weren't the same for them anymore. They were expected to screw up. It was part of the whole deal.

Luna saw Sophie walking toward her, with two plastic bags heavy with the snacks. Sophie had already checked out. But Sophie had seen Luna first. She had seen her pocketing a Jolly Rancher from the big display. "Hey," Sophie said. "I saw that."

Luna went red. "I'll put it back."

But Sophie remembered what it was like to steal things. From her years of teenage shoplifting at the South Coast Mall, she remembered how it gave you a momentary feeling of power. Sophie leaned in. "Take one for your brother too."

Luna grabbed another candy and stuck it in her pocket. A green apple, which wasn't Ollie's favorite, but Luna didn't have time to be choosy.

"Now, act natural. Hold my hand."

Luna wasn't sure about holding this strange woman's hand, but she did it. It had been a long time since she had held anyone's hand. Her mom didn't even make her hold hands when they crossed the street anymore.

"Now, walk fast but not too fast."

Luna did what she was told. The boy at the checkout counter of the CVS, who Sophie knew was stoned out of his gourd, didn't say anything, didn't even watch them leave. The alarms didn't go off. They don't keep security sensors on Jolly Ranchers. Sophie didn't know about the rest of the stuff stashed in Luna's purse and pockets of her coat. She thought they were only stealing two small candies, ten cents each. Didn't know about the bottle of melatonin worth $12.99.

"Our first heist," Sophie said, once they were outside and in the clear.

"Thanks, Miss Sophie. That was fun."

"You can call me Sophie. I'm not your teacher."

"Okay."

"And no more stealing stuff. I got banned from Macy's when I was a kid for stealing. They interrogated me in a back room in the mall. They used a bright-white light."

Luna's eyes widened. "What'd you steal?"

"A bunch of shirts. Some underwear. A bottle of tester perfume."

Luna smiled a little. The combat boots Sophie was wearing were dorky, but maybe Sophie wasn't so bad. Who knew what else Luna could get away with on this trip if Sophie was the one in charge.

"Did you get the rubbers?" Sophie's dad asked, back at the car. He had taken Pancakes out of the carrier, and the cat was sitting on his lap.

"No, I did not."

"You'll be sorry when I die of VD."

"You'll be sorry when I die of cat dander."

"Oh, come on, you'll be fine. You've got the Claritin. And Pancakes is a key member of our party. I'm not getting rid of him."

"I didn't ask you to get rid of him, I asked that you keep him in the carrier."

"No can do; can't cage a wild beast."

Sophie shook her head and pulled out of the parking lot. There was never much use arguing with her father; he would continue to do whatever he wanted, forever. She kept her eyes up ahead and tried not to scream when Luna handed up a baggie full of rubber bands to the front seat and asked Uncle PJ if those were the kinds of rubbers he wanted. Sophie knew immediately the girl had stolen the bag of rubber bands as a gift. It would be almost sweet, if it wasn't disturbing.

PJ laughed so hard, and Sophie half hoped he'd choke on that laughter, for being so gross in front of the kids.

After Uncle PJ finished howling at a joke Luna didn't get, Luna began reading her magazine while sucking on her watermelon Jolly Rancher. The magazine was an old issue of *Soap Opera Digest*. Luna had taken two of her mom's magazines when she'd gone back to get the yearbook, including the issue with the tour of the Stackpoles' house—a big mansion with a fountain out front. Luna wouldn't need to steal anything once she lived there. The Stackpoles probably kept endless candy in big glass jars in the pantry. Some people have everything.

Uncle PJ didn't have everything, even if he was a lottery winner, because Luna had seen Uncle PJ's house, and it was nowhere near as good as Mark Stackpole's. Uncle PJ's house was an ordinary house with a trampoline.

There was other good information in the magazine, not only the pictures of the mansion. Mark was married to a woman named Christine, a former beauty-pageant winner. Christine's favorite holiday was Valentine's Day, and she loved her children "more than life itself," she said in the interview. The Stackpoles had just had a fifth baby. They had named the baby Sassafras, which didn't seem like a real name to Luna. There was a picture of the baby and then even more pictures of the six-bedroom house. It had two fireplaces. Luna's mother used to drool over the issue, what she could have had, if only things had been different. A man who loved her, and two chimneys. Luna had always agreed with her mother on that: their life could have been a lot better if it were different.

"I really hate green-apple flavor," Ollie whined, which annoyed Luna, how ungrateful her brother could be, and then she remembered the sleeping pills. The pills were in gummy form, just like the candies they'd eaten yesterday, the ones Luna had puked up. She offered Ollie two purple gummies, and he snatched them and put them in his mouth. "Vitamins," she said, even if he didn't ask. She felt a pang for secretly drugging her brother so soon after he'd been nearly poisoned by their mother. Well, he shouldn't be so annoying, and then no one would drug him. And then Luna took two gummies herself. She gave four gummies to PJ; he was a big man. She didn't offer any to Sophie; she needed Sophie awake to drive.

Sophie wondered why Luna hadn't given her a vitamin and decided the girl probably needed more time to get to trust her. Like her dad had said, Sophie was a late arrival to this trip. Sophie peeked into her canvas messenger bag at the weed gummies, unfortunately shaped like teddy bears. She would have to make sure the kids didn't get to those. She would have liked to eat one now, but she would wait until that night at the hotel. She was nothing like her father, she would never drive impaired. Sophie was responsible; she just liked a little weed.

"What the hell is this music?" PJ asked.

"It's Björk, Dad. It's my music."

"I don't like it. Too sad."

"Music is supposed to be sad. And I'm driving, so I'm supposed to pick the music. Road trip rules."

"Since when are those the rules?"

"Since always. Driver picks the music."

"Well, that's not fair, because you'll be driving the whole way. Invalid rule." PJ rolled the dial and turned to the radio. He found an oldies station. It was a John Prine song, one of his favorites, about two people in love, a woman who looks down her nose at money, a man who drinks beer like it's oxygen.

But PJ fell asleep not long after John Prine finished singing, suddenly extremely drowsy, not knowing he'd been dosed by a ten-year-old with a triple-whammy of melatonin and L-theanine and chamomile, so Sophie put the Björk back on.

"Uncle PJ is right," Ollie said. "Why would you listen to this?"

"Watch your iPad," Sophie told him.

"I love it," Luna said.

Sophie looked back in the rearview and met Luna's eyes and gave her a small smile.

But it didn't really matter what anyone thought about Sophie's music, because soon both the children were asleep, and it was Sophie alone with the cat, who was perched on PJ's lap and staring intently out the front window as if he were going to give Sophie directions any minute. On the shoulder, a small white cross marked where a teenager had once crashed his parents' car into the guardrail, going 90 in a 65.

15

There was a sign up ahead for the visitor center at Niagara Falls. "We made it," PJ said when Sophie poked him awake. "We're really here."

"Yup," Sophie agreed. She had driven a long way by herself, with her dad and the kids all sleeping. Even when she'd stopped for gas, they hadn't woken up. She'd turned off Björk and downloaded an audiobook on her phone: *100,000 Words You Might Need to Know for the GRE* and played it over the speakers in the car. She might as well use the time productively, she figured, and if she was really going to apply to graduate school like Fred wanted her to, she would need to take the GRE. On the GRE-prep audiobook, a man first read the word, the definition, and then used it in a sentence. "Epicure," the man droned over the speaker. "A person with fine tastes, especially in food or wine."

PJ heard the word *wine*, and even though he was a beer and hard-liquor guy, he wanted a drink, and he'd take a wine. It was getting to be the time of day when it was the hardest not to drink. He wished he hadn't told Sophie he'd stopped drinking. That had been a mistake. Now she would be spying on him, all the time. He wondered how much longer he could hold out. It had been thirty-one days since his last drink. Since Fred and Ivy had left. He had made it to the one-month mark, somehow. He almost wished he'd been going to AA so they would give him the prize of the thirty-day gold coin. He would like a prize for making it this far.

"We're here?" Ollie said in the back, sounding groggy. "Luna, wake up, we're here."

"We're here?" Luna wiped her eyes.

They were in the parking lot. It cost ten dollars to park, which seemed like highway robbery to PJ. They all got out of the car. PJ held the cat in his arms, buckled his leash into the loop on his harness. The leash said #1 PUP in stitched white lettering. PJ put the cat down, and the cat acted like he'd been walking on a leash all his life. "A superb traveling companion," PJ declared.

At the edge of the parking lot, near the visitor center, a man in a green vest was smiling at them and blocking the path. ASK ME ABOUT THE MAID OF THE MIST, read a yellow button pin on his chest. "Hello, folks," he said. "Here to throw that cat over the falls?"

"Excuse me?" PJ asked. He bent over to pick up Pancakes.

Throw the what over the what? thought the cat.

"Sorry, sorry," the man in the green vest said. "I forget not everyone knows the story of Annie Edson Taylor. She went over the falls in a barrel as a stunt. But as a test, first she sent a cat in the barrel."

"Did the cat survive?" Sophie asked.

"Without a scratch." The man chuckled.

Sophie didn't think that was true. She imagined the cat had died shortly after from the trauma, but the man was still talking: "Annie Edson Taylor went over in the barrel the next day. She survived too. The first person to survive going over the falls in a barrel."

"What a moronic idea," Luna said.

"Stupid," Ollie agreed.

"In 1901, people were very impressed," the man in the green vest said. "We are all a product of our own times." The man turned to PJ.

"Now, may I interest you and your family in tickets to get on the *Maid of the Mist*? An all-electric boat ride, right up close to the falls. There's one more boat ride this evening, or I can get you on a boat tomorrow."

"He's not my family," Luna muttered. "He's an old man who put me in his car. I barely know him."

"I think we'll skip the boat," PJ said, giving Luna a side-eye. He did not want to get questioned for kidnapping this close to the Canadian border.

"But, sir, it's not a trip to Niagara Falls without a ride on the *Maid of the Mist*. Most people say it's the most alive they've felt in years."

PJ took a pamphlet, hoping it would shut this guy up.

"The falls are right up ahead," the man said, finally stepping out of their way.

"I can hear it," Ollie said, excitedly. "I can hear the water."

And when they turned the corner, they could see the falls, cascading down. It wasn't as tall as PJ had imagined it would be, but it was much, much wider. He knew he was a better man for having seen this waterfall. It jolted him back, out of wanting a drink, reminding him that this was his great life adventure, and he hadn't been this far from home since Vietnam, and he hadn't gone to Vietnam for long. He'd been shot in the ass and sent right home.

"It's beautiful," Ollie said.

"Wow," Sophie said. "Wow. It's glorious."

"It's the best thing I've ever seen," Luna agreed.

Pancakes pulled on the leash and sniffed a sign that said DON'T JUMP! A man in his forties in a bright-yellow windbreaker was standing near the sign, and he moved away, looking at PJ strangely, as if he'd never seen a cat on a leash before.

PJ looked over the railing at the water rushing below. He had only thought of jumping off anything once, at that big powder-blue bridge down in Fall River a few months after Kate died. He had climbed onto the other side and looked down at the water. If he had slipped, it would have been all over. There was no angel to appear from *It's a Wonderful Life* telling PJ how rotten the world would be without him. It was just PJ, afraid to jump.

They all stared at the rushing water for a good long while. How powerful it was, how vast. How small and insignificant they were against the majesty of nature.

But eventually, both kids said they needed to pee. It's hard for children to stare at anything, no matter how majestic, for too long.

16

After the bathrooms, Sophie said she wanted to go into the Niagara Falls Wax Museum. It boasted "Every Public Figure Who Has Ever Visited Niagara!" There was a misshapen wax figure of Marilyn Monroe in the window, wearing her signature white dress. She had filmed a movie in Niagara. She is strangled by her husband at the end.

"Okay, sure, let's go in." PJ picked up the cat and held him in his arms and walked into the museum.

"No cats," said the woman at the door. She was wearing a red silk scarf and silver earrings. She pointed to a sign: NO PETS, MUST WEAR SHOES, $8 ADMISSION, DO NOT TOUCH THE WAX FIGURES. SERVICE ANIMALS ALWAYS WELCOME.

"He's a service animal," PJ said, thinking fast.

"What for?" asked the woman, who was used to hearing bullshit from tourists. "What condition does he assist you with?"

PJ paused. He didn't think it was legal to ask that. His friend Hank brought his pit bull to the bar all the time, and if anyone asked,

Meatball was a service dog. No one ever asked what Meatball assisted with. "The cat monitors my heart," PJ decided. "He goes crazy if my heart gets out of rhythm." PJ's heart was, in fact, always out of rhythm. He had an arrhythmia. The cat was listening to it beat out of whack right now. "I have a long history of heart attacks."

"It's true," Sophie said. "He's had three heart attacks."

"Uncle PJ could die any minute," Luna said. "That's why it's very important we find my real father."

"I hope he doesn't die," Ollie said. "I don't know who I'd live with."

The woman sighed. It was too late in the day for this. "Welcome to the Wax Museum of Niagara History." She took their money and stamped each of their hands with a rubber stamp of Marilyn Monroe's famous face.

"Thank you, ma'am," PJ said.

The museum was mostly one long hallway, with a few small rooms off to the side. The wax figures were terrible, perhaps melted over time or never very good to start with, and they were all spot-lit from the floor, so they looked extremely creepy. There was a Princess Diana figure with a bulbous nose and a bad wig. Nearby, Mark Twain and his silver mustache sat on a bench.

Ollie banged his fist on a metal barrel on display. It looked like an oil drum. There was a statue of someone named Bobby Leach next to the barrel. The sign explained that Bobby Leach was the second person to go over the falls in a barrel and survive. "But how many people went over in a barrel and died?" Ollie asked.

"Good question," PJ agreed. There wasn't a sign about that.

Instead, there was an orange-peel display on a little velvet pillow, like Cinderella's slipper. "Well, look at this," PJ said. "Bobby's luck ran out." A few years later, according to the little gold plaque, famous stuntman Bobby Leach had slipped on an orange peel and badly hurt his leg. His leg would need to be amputated, and Bobby died of complications two months later.

"That kind of death doesn't *a-peel* to me," PJ said, and Ollie laughed. PJ was glad to make the kid laugh. He looked around for the girl to see if she liked the joke, but Luna had gone off somewhere alone and missed it.

In a small room off the main hallway, Luna was with Abraham Lincoln, six feet, four inches tall and holding his hand out in greeting.

"Hello, sir," Luna said, reminding herself to stand up straight as she practiced what she would say. "My name is Luna Meeklin, age ten and a half, and based on what I have read in my mother's diary about the events at a New Year's Eve party, I believe you are my real father."

Luna switched to a deeper voice: "I remember that night well, little girl. Would you like to come live in my house?" Abraham Lincoln said, in the role of Mark Stackpole.

"Can my little brother come too?" Luna asked.

Lincoln shook his head. "Unfortunately, no, he cannot. I don't think there's room in the mansion. He can stay with Uncle PJ and Sophie, can't he? I heard they have a trampoline and a PlayStation. He'll be all right."

"Well," Luna considered. "He does eat a lot, and he doesn't always listen to me. But I promised I wouldn't leave him."

Mark Stackpole/Abraham Lincoln thought it over. "Well, Luna, you know I would do anything for you. Yes, you can bring him. He can sleep in your closet, but you have to pinkie-promise he won't be much trouble."

Luna touched Mark Stackpole in a pinkie-promise, and when she touched him, she felt the hand of her real father, a man who would never have hurt her or made her feel afraid, who would have kept her safe and told her how smart she was and also pretty, too, who would have called her "my gorgeous child"—and that touch from this real father, as they held pinkie-to-pinkie, wax-to-flesh, vibrated down to her bones and into her veins and healed her a little, to feel the love she'd always wanted from her dad.

But perhaps the vibration of love was too much for Mr. Lincoln, because when Luna pulled away her pinkie, Lincoln's hand and his forearm broke right off, at the elbow, and fell with a heavy clunk to the floor. "Oh no, oh no," Luna said. "Oh shit," she added, because who was around to scold her? Her parents were dead. This was only a stupid wax figure. There had been that big sign at the front about not touching the statues.

"Stuff the arm in your purse," Abraham Lincoln whispered. *"No one saw."*

"Thanks, Mr. Lincoln," Luna said. She grabbed the arm, then hesitated and bowed to him before she left the room. She didn't know how else you showed respect to a former president who was also a father figure to you. He smiled kindly at her as she left. Back out in the main hall of statues, Luna found everyone else standing around Julia Roberts.

"There you are," PJ said, smiling.

"I'm ready to go," Luna said.

"Sure thing, kid. Me too. Let's bust this popsicle stand."

And they all began to walk to the front door. Luna was in a cold sweat. She held the purse tightly to her chest as they exited, but no alarm sounded, no one chased after her. Ollie provided a good distraction, asking the woman at the front desk of the museum what the fanciest hotel in Niagara was. The woman recommended the Roger Woodward, a hotel named after a young boy who had survived going over the falls, and not protected by a barrel either. He'd fallen out of a boat and gone over, was mostly fine when they pulled him out, and no one could believe it, but sometimes people survive the impossible without even trying to pull a stunt.

When they were back to the parking lot and in the car, Luna breathed a sigh of relief. She had Lincoln's arm in her purse. Her second successful heist. She was an outlaw. She was an orphaned child; no one cared what she did.

As they drove away from the falls, Pancakes jumped up onto his hind legs to look out the back window. When the Volvo turned the corner, they had a view of the cascade again from a distance. Pancakes was the only one in the car to look back, the only one to notice the bright-yellow speck drop off the edge and plummet into the frothy rapids below. The neon windbreaker standing by the DON'T JUMP sign. Some people will always ignore the sign, no matter how clear and direct it is.

17

"He's a service cat," PJ explained at the front desk at the Woodward Hotel about the orange beast in his arms, and the concierge in her maroon uniform said service animals were always welcome at the Woodward, as are pets. The owner was an animal lover, a real softie once you got to know her.

After they ordered room service to their two adjoining rooms, Sophie said she was going up to the gym, to do sprints on the treadmill, and then she planned to take a weed gummy and soak in the hot tub in the spa on the fifth floor. She didn't say the second part of the plan. She left that part out. There was no pool at the Woodward, but there was a gym and spa, Sophie had seen the sign. She hoped her dad hadn't seen the sign for the bar.

"Your mother says you exercise too much," he said, as she put on her sneakers.

"Better than getting blackout drunk every night."

"Hey, I wasn't the one who said it. Don't shoot the messenger."

Sophie held up her fingers like a gun, pretending to fire at her father, and then she retreated into the hotel hallway.

PJ was alone with the kids, and it felt like a small betrayal, being shot at and then deserted. Sophie had promised to help him out with the kids.

Ollie turned on the TV and flipped through the channels. Luna wanted to watch a documentary about killer whales. PJ thought it would be depressing, but he let them. It was educational. Besides, he didn't think killer whales would be as depressing as the polar bears. The orca whales didn't need the melting icebergs, did they?

PJ must have dozed off at some point, because he woke up when Luna smacked him on the chest. "Wake up, Uncle PJ. Movie's over. We need a bedtime story."

PJ coughed. "Careful, kid. I've got a weak heart."

"Where's the cat?" Ollie asked. "He'll tell us."

"No, no, I'm not having a heart attack. Don't worry, kiddo, I'm fine. The cat is probably under the bed."

"Tell us a story," Luna whined. "I don't like to go to sleep without a story."

"Well, all right, kiddo, what about?"

"Mom used to tell us about high school," Ollie said. "Or about when she was a little girl."

"Okay, then. I'll tell you a story about high school. I'll tell you about when I met Michelle Cobb, the woman we're going to meet. The woman we're driving all the way to Arizona for."

"It better be good," Luna said. "I'll scream if it's boring."

"Won't be boring," PJ promised, because he'd told this story before, at the bar, and it was always a hit.

It was 1969, in the spring of PJ's senior year of high school, only a few weeks before graduation, and the high school was having a mixer with another high school on a Friday night. A mixer was what they called dances back then.

At this dance, this mixer, Michelle Cobb was standing by the punch bowl, a redhead wearing an orange flower-print dress, with an orange cardigan over that. She looked like a pretty glass of juice. PJ told her he'd never seen someone so beautiful, and he asked her if she'd like to dance. She said she would. She was from the next town over, Middleborough, and went to Sacred Heart Academy for Girls. Her father owned the pie shop in Middleborough on Center Street, and she wanted to know if PJ had ever been. "Sure," he said, because everyone in the area knew Ed Cobb's pie shop, and everyone liked Ed Cobb. But even though Michelle had her father as a model for what a man should be, it seemed like young Michelle didn't have such great taste in boys. She had come to the mixer with Ricky Fafard, whom PJ knew from shop class, and Ricky was a real jackass.

Ricky walked up then, and he was pissed. "What the heck are you doing with him, Michelle?" he asked. "I said I'd be right back."

"It's only a dance, Ricky," Michelle said.

"It's only a dance," PJ agreed, although he was already coming up with a plan to marry Michelle Cobb. He felt like he'd known her all his life. He was glad he'd have someone to write letters to once he went off to Vietnam. He was set to go to training camp eight days after high school graduation. His number had been called. Ricky's number had too, PJ knew that. They'd be going to the training camp together in Texas.

Ricky stormed off, and PJ and Michelle Cobb danced the night away. It was more than one dance. They did the Monkey, the Frug, the Mashed Potato.

"Those were the names of dances?" Luna asked.

PJ nodded at the girl's question, but in his mind, he was staring into Michelle Cobb's blue eyes. How they had sparkled that night. They talked and talked and wondered how they'd never met before as her boyfriend Ricky sulked in the corner. Michelle kept telling PJ to ignore him as PJ felt Ricky's eyes burn into his back. But soon PJ was too caught up in Michelle's blue eyes and the way her body moved when she did the chicken-wings part of the Frug to worry too much about Ricky.

Eventually, PJ had to excuse himself to go to the restroom, and on the way to the little boys' room PJ looked back over his shoulder and

Ricky had followed him in. "I don't want any trouble," PJ said. "It's only a dance. Only a couple of dances. Your girl's a great dancer."

Ricky's face went darker, had a murderous look in his eyes. PJ hadn't pegged Ricky for that kind of violent boy, the kind who would fistfight over a girl, but then again, Ricky was about to be sent away to war, both him and PJ goats to the slaughter. Then PJ saw a glint of silver in Ricky's hand. Ricky Fafard had a knife. It was his older brother's knife, a switchblade, that he'd given to Ricky on the night of the draft. It was time for Ricky to be a man now.

"Whoa, whoa, whoa," PJ said to Ricky in the bathroom of the high school cafeteria, where the mixer was being held. "Let's talk. She said you just started going steady, she said you're getting too serious about her." PJ looked around the bathroom. He was hoping someone would pop out of a stall to help him here, but there was no one else in there with them. It was him and Ricky Fafard and the knife.

"I told him it was only a dance; I told him I was a peaceful guy," PJ told the kids.

But Ricky Fafard didn't care. He swung at PJ with the knife. PJ held up his hand to protect himself, and his finger was cut badly. There was blood everywhere. It was a geyser.

Well, Ricky Fafard had never cut anyone with that knife. And it turned out that Ricky Fafard didn't do well with blood. He fainted straight away and hit his head on the sink on the way down. He lay on the tile floor, out cold, as PJ started wrapping his hand in toilet paper, trying to stop the blood.

That was when another boy came into the bathroom. Gene Bartlett.

PJ saw Gene, and he was covered in blood, sitting next to a body on the ground, and PJ smiled at his friend and said: "Hi, Geney! You're a little late!"

"What did Gene do?" Ollie asked.

"Poor Geney turned and ran. I scared him. Of course, I was loopy from the blood loss. By the time the cops got there, I tried to explain

I'd only wanted to dance with Ricky's girlfriend, but I wasn't making much sense. The cops assumed I'd beaten up Ricky; he was the one lying on the floor, and they took me straight to the slammer and locked me up," PJ said. "My finger was hanging off by a thread, and if it didn't get sewn back on soon, I wouldn't be able to go to war."

"Why not?" Luna asked.

"It was my trigger finger. Can't shoot a gun without one. Can't go to war without a gun."

"But you did go to war," Ollie said. "You said you did."

"So, you already know part of it. I'll tell you the rest tomorrow, but that's all the gas I got for tonight."

"But what happened to Ricky?" Luna asked.

"He hit his head pretty hard on that sink, and he's been in a coma ever since. Forty-five years in a coma. At the Pondville hospital, third floor, first room on the left. His mother still visits him every day. She's ninety-one now, and I heard when she dies, they'll unplug him. I go see him sometimes. The nurses let me trim his beard; it's never stopped growing."

"Is that true?" Ollie asked.

"It's a bedtime story. Who cares if it's true."

"So, it's not true."

"When we get back to Pondville, if we ever go back to Pondville, I'll take you to see Ricky."

"I'd like that," Ollie agreed.

"Uncle PJ?" Luna asked.

"Yeah?"

"Thanks for not telling us a story for babies. Thanks for telling us a real story."

PJ understood why Luna wanted a real story, that she wanted to be treated seriously, and why she didn't want to be bored. It wasn't fun to be bored. It was another one of the things alcohol was good for. But PJ had something else that might excite the kids. He reached into his pocket and pulled out a small box. He showed them the ring he had for Michelle Cobb. A small sparkly diamond ring.

"Wow," Luna said. "Is it real?"

"It is. I'm going to ask Michelle Cobb to spend the rest of her life with me."

"Serious," Ollie said.

"It's an exciting time for me, and I'm so glad you kids can be part of it. But good night, now. I'll see you both in the funny papers in the morning."

"Good night, Uncle PJ," both kids said, and they said it so naturally, as if they had wished their Uncle PJ good night a thousand times before. Kids are so adaptable, PJ thought. It's amazing.

PJ couldn't wait to tell Sophie what a good job he'd done with the kids, but in the adjoining room, PJ found Sophie already asleep in her queen hotel bed, under the covers and completely dead to the world. He'd never seen someone so asleep, in fact, wondering what could have tuckered her out like that. He didn't know about the five miles she'd run on the treadmill, followed by taking two weed gummies, and the thirty minutes she'd spent sitting in the hot tub upstairs in the hotel spa, all while the kids were watching the documentary on killer whales. But PJ wanted someone to talk to, so he wanted Sophie to wake up. She didn't stir when he turned on the TV or stomped around the room.

PJ knew so little about Sophie's life, he realized, and what he knew he knew from what Fred and Ivy said at breakfast. He knew she'd had a job as an assistant somewhere doing something. He knew she had been running a lot lately, and her mom thought it was too much exercise. He knew Fred thought Sophie should go back to school to be a speech pathologist. He knew Fred had thought he was so smart for suggesting that, even if PJ thought it went against Ivy's golden rule: not to talk too much about Kate, because Sophie wasn't going to be defined as the kid who had a dead sister. Ivy had made that rule early on.

We cannot talk about Kate all the time, Ivy had said, even in the early days of their grief. *We have to focus on Sophie.* Ivy was obsessed with making Sophie happy, giving her everything, taking her everywhere. Piano lessons and dance classes and soccer practices and swimming. Ivy had her one hour of crying in Kate's room a week, and other than that, she focused on Sophie.

Sophie put up with all her mother's attention. Even after Sophie started wearing all the black clothes, looking dark and rebellious, she still did all the activities her mother signed her up for. She got good grades. She got into NYU, but she hadn't gone. PJ had thought Ivy should have made her go. Ivy had said it was Sophie's decision, but PJ thought Ivy seemed too happy when Sophie chose to go to the state school twenty minutes away. All those extracurricular activities to pad her résumé, and Ivy didn't even care if Sophie went to the best college she got into.

PJ would have liked to talk to Sophie about all this, if she had any regrets. PJ opened and closed the hotel nightstand drawer next to Sophie's head, but she was either in a deep, deep sleep, or the best faker PJ had ever seen.

Well, there *were* other people to talk to, upstairs at the bar. But PJ really wasn't supposed to go to the bar. He was really going to try not to drink until the wedding, when he would have a glass of Champagne with his best-man speech.

Then again, just because he went to the bar didn't mean he had to drink. There was a man back in Pondville named David Keller, who came to the bar every night to talk ever since his wife died. He always ordered plain Dr Pepper. But everyone at the Wild Orchid treated him the same as everyone else. They let him talk, sometimes people bought him a round, sometimes he bought you one. PJ could go up to the bar, just for the company. It sure would be nice to have some company.

18

After Uncle PJ had closed the door between the rooms, Ollie was snoring nearly immediately, so Luna was left alone in the dark. She got out of the bed they were sharing, because once he'd wet the bed when they went to New Jersey and stayed in a hotel. She moved to the other queen bed, the empty one, where Uncle PJ had been sitting, and she tossed and turned for what felt like a really long time.

There was a knock on the door.

Luna waited for Uncle PJ to answer it, but he didn't. It was the adult's job to answer the door, wasn't it? Where was he? Where was Sophie?

The person knocked again, louder, so Luna went to the door. She tried looking through the peephole, but she wasn't tall enough, so she decided just to open the door and see who was on the other side. *What was the worst that could happen?* she asked herself, as if the answer to that wasn't a very, very long list of bad things.

A big man was standing there, wearing orange swim shorts and flip-flops, a white T-shirt. He was holding the cat. "The front desk said he belongs to you," the man said. "I found him in my room. Don't know how he got there." Pancakes had slipped out on the bottom of the room-service cart, but no one knew that.

"Oh," Luna said. "Do you want a reward?"

"Well . . . um, are you offering a reward?"

"No. I'm a kid."

"Okay, but is this your cat? I just wanted to give back the cat."

Luna nodded and took Pancakes from the man and closed the door without saying thank you. "Bad kitty," she whispered in his ear, but she didn't mean it. She loved the cat. He was the easiest thing to love that she'd ever met, and she liked that he had a mind of his own. She told herself Pancakes hadn't wanted to run away, he just wanted to explore the fancy hotel. She brought him into the bed with her. She stroked him and he purred.

"What's going to happen to us?" Luna asked the cat. "What's going to happen to me and my brother?"

Suffering, the cat answered. *And joy.*

Luna couldn't understand the cat, but she was comforted by his little warm body nevertheless, and she felt he was a good listener and the first new friend she'd had in a long time, and Luna didn't have any other friends. Her brother, of course, didn't count.

DAY TWO
WEDNESDAY

19

Sophie had woken up next to many strange men in her life, but never once next to an old woman. The woman on the pillow next to her had gray hair and a pink silk sleeping mask. "What the fuck," Sophie said. "Who are you?"

In the other bed, her father sat up. "Oh, Sophie, don't be rude. That's Edith."

The woman lifted her eye mask. "Edna," she said. "Edna Gardner, owner of this hotel. And you've got a sailor's mouth."

"Dad!" Sophie said, getting out of bed to hit him with a pillow over and over. "When I was in the room? Are you crazy? Are you out of your fucking mind?"

"Oh, Sophie-Soo, you could sleep through a freight train."

"Oh my God. I need a shower. I need a long shower."

"Don't worry, honey," Edna said. "He's messing with you. We had our fun in the Presidential Suite. But your father wanted to be here when the kids woke up. He has a kind heart. And then, well, I guess I got back in the wrong bed after I got up to use the bathroom in the night. I don't see so well in the dark."

Sophie hit her dad with a pillow again.

"Pillow fight!" Ollie said, standing in the doorway between rooms. "Luna, throw me a pillow!" The kids had been up for hours, waiting for the adults to wake up. Ollie had made himself a cup of coffee in the pot in the room. Even after the poisoning, he found he was still addicted to caffeine. He put in six sugars and three creamers, like his dad used to drink it.

Luna appeared in the door next to him, without a pillow. "Who are you?" she asked.

"Kids, this is Edith—Edna. She's a wonderful woman I met last night."

"Are you going to marry Uncle PJ?" Ollie asked.

Edna laughed. "I don't think so, honey, but it was a lovely night. Brought me back to life."

"I need a shower." Sophie went and closed the bathroom door. She really needed to scream, and curse, and punch something, but a hot shower would have to do.

Edna got out of bed and smoothed the sheets, fluffed the pillow. She was wearing a flannel nightgown. "Who wants breakfast? We do a great continental."

"You work here?" Luna asked. "Are you a maid?"

"I do work here. Are you enjoying your stay?"

"Sort of."

"Well, dear, don't write that review up online. I'm the owner of this hotel, and we aim to do better than *sort of*."

"The owner?" Luna asked.

"It's really nice," Ollie said. "It's *decadent*."

"Where'd you learn that word?" Luna looked at her brother, her eyes narrowing. She didn't like when Ollie was too smart.

"It was on Sophie's audiobook." Ollie had heard some of the GRE words as he drifted in and out of sleep in the car the day before. Ollie liked learning new words.

Luna let it go and looked back at Edna. "You must be really, really rich. Richer than Uncle PJ."

Edna laughed. "I live a comfortable enough life. When my husband was alive, we were very happy. But my husband died three years ago."

"We bonded over that. We both lost our spouses," PJ explained.

"Mom's not dead," Sophie said, opening the door to the bathroom, wearing a white bathrobe, not showered yet, and still looking angry, angrier even than before.

She has lasers in her eyes, Ollie thought, watching Sophie, like the superheroes in the comic books Ollie had left back at his house. Luna had gotten some of her things from Deerfield Lane, but Ollie hadn't gotten to take anything except for the clothes the social workers had packed. He still didn't have underwear. He missed his Wonder Woman figurine, with the blue streaks in her hair just like Sophie had, even though his dad said he shouldn't play so much with a fucking Barbie. She wasn't even a Barbie. She was Wonder Woman.

"Don't you dare say that Mom is dead," Sophie said. "Don't you dare use that line to pick up women."

"I know, I know," PJ said, putting his hands up to show he was innocent. "She's not. But she's getting remarried in the fall. I did lose her. A divorce is like a death."

"It's not, Dad. It's really not. Not even close."

"And you're the best man," Edna said, pointing out the bright side. She smiled kindly at the children. "I heard all about it at the bar."

"I can't believe you went to the bar," Sophie said, her arms crossed.

"Hey, you were here with the kids. I didn't leave them alone again."

"Again?" Luna asked. This meant there were no adults Luna could count on. Except maybe Mark Stackpole. She had to find him. The situation was dire. She went back in the other bedroom to play with the cat. She'd been pulling feathers out of the down pillow and throwing them in the air and letting Pancakes chase them.

PJ sat up in bed and looked straight at Sophie. "I'll have you know I did not drink last night. Diet Cokes. Had about twenty of them."

"It's true," Edna said. "I'm in recovery, and he was an absolute gentleman about it."

"Okay. He's an alcoholic too. You two are a club."

"Yes, he said you would say that. But he didn't have a drop. A perfect gentleman."

Sophie didn't believe it for one second that her father had gone to the bar and hadn't had a drink. He had probably paid Edna to lie for him.

"Well, I've got to go get freshened up before work," Edna said. She took the other white hotel robe hanging on the door and wrapped it around her over her nightgown. She had left her clothes in the Presidential Suite. "You kids enjoy your breakfast," she said. "We do a waffle bar. Strawberries and whipped cream on a Belgian waffle."

"Do you have chocolate chips?" Ollie asked.

"We sure do."

"Let me walk you to the elevator," PJ said.

"Such a gentleman," Edna said, blushing. "Your family should appreciate you more."

Ollie looked at Sophie. *Here come the laser eyes,* he thought. He loved to see them. Yup, there they were, burning hot and red into the back of Edna's tufted gray hair as she walked out the door, the lasers most definitely liquefying her brain. Sophie even wore bracelets on her wrists, where Wonder Woman wore her gold arm cuffs, which are impervious to fire, bullets, arrows. *Impervious* was another GRE word, but Ollie already knew that one, from the comic books.

20

After breakfast, when they went to the front desk of the Woodward to check out, they found both rooms had been comped. "It's been taken care of," the woman at the desk said. "Compliments of Ms. Edna."

"Whatta woman," PJ said, holding Pancakes in his arms. People in the lobby kept coming over to pet the cat. Both PJ and the cat loved the attention. PJ felt awfully proud of himself that morning, for going to the bar and not having a drop of alcohol. It had helped that Edna was the only other person at the bar that night, and she didn't drink. That had been lucky.

"Can I get something from the gift shop?" Luna asked.

"Me too," Ollie said. "I want a snow globe. And a T-shirt. And candy. I need a lot of candy."

"How about I give you some spending money for the road trip," PJ said, putting down the cat and pulling out his wallet. "Then you can decide how to spend it." But when PJ opened his billfold, he was low on cash. He'd spent what he had in there the night before, on the Diet Cokes. Edna had said there was no sense in him paying for her drinks at her own hotel, but he'd insisted. He was a gentleman. That was around the time when she'd mentioned the Presidential Suite.

"Is there a cash machine around here?" PJ asked the concierge, who pointed to the small black ATM in the lobby. PJ walked over to the slim plastic black box. He typed in $2,000 because he didn't think he would need more cash than that. The machine spat out the money in hundred-dollar bills, and automatically printed a receipt. At the ATM in Pondville, you could ask for no receipt before it gave you your money. PJ glanced at the slip of paper and put it in his wallet with the bills, then walked back over to Sophie and the kids, feeling sick.

He wished he hadn't looked at that damn receipt, he wished he'd crumpled it up without looking at it, but he'd seen the number: $21,000 in his checking account, plus change.

That was not anywhere close to a million and a half dollars, what he had started with, eight years ago, before taxes. *You should have invested,* he could hear Hank at the bar saying. *I could have doubled your money,* Hank always said, as if Hank knew crap about investing. Hank lived in a one-bedroom condo off the highway. PJ thought he had spent his money well; he just hadn't known he was going to end up with two kids who needed things. He had thought for years he was going to die any minute, and so he had given back to his community instead of hoarding it away for himself. He had some things to be proud of. The playground at the nursery school.

He opened his wallet and gave Ollie and Luna one crisp hundred-dollar bill each. They ran into the gift shop.

"One hundred dollars?" Sophie asked. "Dad, Jesus, what are they going to do with one hundred dollars?"

"Not drugs, I hope. You want some?" He held up his wallet.

"No."

"Why don't you ever take money from me? I'd like to take care of you."

Sophie glared at him. She wanted to tell him there were better ways to take care of someone than money, but she didn't see the use.

Sophie would never survive this road trip. *Why had she come?* She thought of *Thelma & Louise* and understood why they drove themselves off a cliff at the end.

PJ hoped his daughter couldn't tell something was wrong with him, hoped she wouldn't somehow sense that he had just discovered at the ATM how very little money he had left. But Sophie didn't look like she knew anything. She looked pissed, as usual, but she didn't look suspicious. He was hiding it well, he thought. And by the time the kids had picked out their souvenirs, matching snow globes, plus a bottle opener Luna swiped and put in her jacket pocket, PJ had figured it out: Once they settled in Arizona, he could get a job. Simple as that. Yes, once they got to Arizona, PJ would figure it out.

PJ went to the front desk one more time and asked the concierge if Edna was around; he wanted to say thank you and goodbye to her, and he also wanted to ask if the cash machine in the lobby had accurate information. The concierge said Edna was currently tied up in meetings.

In fact, the concierge had no idea where Edna was. The entire Woodward staff was also looking for Edna, right then. They needed her for damage control. A man had gotten trapped in the sauna last night, right after he'd returned the lost cat to that strange little girl. The latch on the sauna was tricky, and the cleaning crew had found the man that morning. He was still warm but long dead, his skin crisped like a baked potato. He was traveling alone; his family would have to be called. The staff needed Edna's help with this, it was urgent, but right now Edna was up in the Presidential Suite, having a nap.

21

Back on the road, the Bird Barn Volvo passed billboards that read: WE REJECT ANIMAL ACTIVISTS, and another that read: IN PAIN? CALL WAYNE. And several billboards that asked people to protect the babies.

"From what?" Ollie asked, but no one answered him.

As Sophie drove, she got angrier. "You know, Dad," she said, "I said I'd help you take the kids to find their father. I didn't say I'd take over for you. This is still your job. It's your job to look after the kids. You can't go to the bar while you're watching the kids."

"Pull over," he said.

"What?"

"Pull over!"

Finally, Sophie found a safe spot on the side of the highway and pulled over. She figured her dad needed to vomit, but instead he said: "I'll walk the straight line if you want to see me do it. Here, hold the cat."

"Dad, Jesus Christ, I don't want you to do a sobriety test. It's not even ten A.M. That was not the point I was making."

He touched his finger to his nose, the way cops make you do. "See? I said I didn't drink, and I didn't drink."

Sophie shook her head and pulled back onto the road, kept driving. She wasn't going to entertain this shit.

But her dad was still talking: "Sophie, listen, I didn't ask for these kids, so stop making this my fault. They showed up on my doorstep like a pair of lost puppies, and I did the kind thing and took them in. I'm a kind man, Sophie; you don't give me enough recognition for that. Your mother always says—"

"Dad, you have no idea what Mom always says. You don't listen to her. She would think this is an absolute disaster. I can't believe Fred let you take the Volvo."

And as Sophie said it, she realized: *Fred hadn't let her dad take the Volvo.* There was no way in hell. Even if it was for orphaned children, Fred would not let a man with three DUIs and no license drive children across the country in his car. Sophie had been dumb as fuck to believe her dad. Her dad probably hadn't told her mother and Fred anything about the kids, because if Fred and her mom had known about the kids, her mother would have been calling to check in. Sophie couldn't be the one to tell her mom now. Her mom would freak out. "Dammit, Dad. You took Fred's car."

"*We* took Fred's car," PJ corrected. "Because he left us behind."

Sophie flinched. It did hurt Sophie, that her mom hadn't invited her along on her trip. Of course she had wanted to go.

"Uncle PJ, we're not puppies," Ollie said from the back. "We're kids." He didn't sound angry. He sounded sad.

"Oh, I know that, bud. I know you're not dogs."

"I thought you wanted us because your daughter died," Ollie said. "I thought you wanted us as replacements."

"Oh no, no, it wasn't like that. They just called me and said I had to take you because everyone else in the family is dead. They said I was your best option."

"You didn't apply to adopt us?"

"I have enough problems, bud. I wasn't seeking to adopt."

"Oh," the boy said.

Sophie took her hand off the wheel and punched her father's arm. "You might not be drunk, but you sure are an asshole." She looked in the back. The boy wasn't crying, but he had shrunken himself into a ball. "I'm sorry, Ollie," Sophie said. "He has brain damage from years of alcohol abuse. My father doesn't mean what he says."

In the other backseat, behind Sophie, Luna's eyes narrowed. It didn't matter what Uncle PJ meant, he still said it, and it had hurt her brother. She rooted around in her purse. She understood not being wanted; she was almost one full year older than Ollie. Some kids had everything, like Baby Sassafras and that stupid Elsie Dawson at school, and Luna and Ollie had nothing. Luna reached into the purse and found the arts-and-crafts kit she had brought. Luna leaned forward in her seat and snipped off a large chunk of Sophie's blue-black hair with her scissors.

Sophie had felt the release on the side of her head, a sudden weightlessness where the hair had been, and her hand went to her head. "Oh my God!" Sophie said, feeling the blunt ends of her hair, so much shorter than it should be. "Oh my God! What the fuck? You little fucking brat!"

"Now, let's not say something we regret," PJ said.

"She cut my hair!"

"Maybe you needed a trim."

"I didn't need a trim! Luna, if you're angry at someone," Sophie said, "be angry at *him*. Cut *his* fucking hair!" Sophie had vowed not to swear in front of the kids, her friend Sara from work used to talk about how she tried not to swear in front of her kids, but all Sophie's promises to herself were gone now. Squashed like that skunk they'd seen on the road back there, its pink intestines spilling out.

"I'm sure Luna didn't mean it," PJ said. "You didn't mean it, did you, Luna?"

Luna didn't answer. If she opened her mouth, she would start to cry. And she didn't want to cry. Adults hate it when kids cry, and she didn't want to do anything to make herself more unwanted.

"Who cares if she meant it?" Sophie said. "My hair is gone."

"Well, not all of it," said Ollie. "Just one spot. It's gone in one spot."

Sophie shook her head. It had been a terrible idea, coming with her dad on this trip. With these two damaged kids. Sophie remembered in middle school, when her guidance counselor had called her that. Damaged. Damaged by her sister's death. After Sophie had cut her wrists, she'd been made to go to the school guidance counselor twice a week instead of lunch, even though Sophie and her parents tried and tried to tell everyone she hadn't meant to try to kill herself, that it was only an accident. Well, if Sophie had been damaged, these kids were damaged, too, and Sophie didn't feel sorry for thinking it. She was missing a chunk of her hair.

"I'm sorry," Luna said, quietly. And she was sorry. She was really sorry, not like the time she'd punched Elsie Dawson. She was actually, truly sorry. Because Elsie Dawson had deserved it. Right before the *Peter Pan* curtain went up, Elsie had been making fun of Ollie. Elsie had deserved it for what she'd said about her little brother, even if Ollie hadn't heard what Elsie had said. It had felt so good to hear a grown-up say that maybe Elsie deserved to get punched. No one had ever been on Luna's side before.

But Sophie hadn't deserved the haircut, not really. She was driving the car to take Luna to meet her real dad, which was more than most people did. "I'm sorry," Luna said again.

Sophie didn't respond. She didn't say *It's okay*, or *I forgive you*, or *Hair grows back*. She stared straight ahead and continued to drive.

"Don't forget, Sophie," PJ said, whispering, even though everyone in the car could hear him. "Their parents just died."

"I didn't forget, Dad."

"Mom would have whooped your butt for that," Ollie whispered to Luna. "Dad would have killed you." And everyone in the car heard that too.

22

"I need a snack," Ollie announced, as the car was hurtling down I-90 along Lake Erie through Pennsylvania and headed to Ohio. Sophie was annoyed by the request, said Ollie could pick out something from the bag of snacks they'd bought at the gas station yesterday, but PJ looked in the bag and it was only wrappers left.

"They ate it all?" Sophie said, in disbelief. "They really ate it all?"

"They're growing kids," PJ said. "You don't remember how you used to eat."

Sophie thought if Ollie had eaten more than whipped cream for breakfast, he wouldn't be so hungry. He hadn't touched his waffle. Sophie didn't hear Luna complaining back there, who had eaten a proper breakfast, but then again, she didn't really want to hear from Luna right now. Little Edward Scissorhands.

Off the next exit, Sophie could see a Target, the familiar red-and-white circle, and if the kids really needed to eat so often, they could go to Target and fill up on groceries. They parked the car and Sophie grabbed a red plastic shopping cart. PJ grabbed one too, and put the cat in the little basket, where people usually put their toddlers while they shop. The cat was happy in there, so many people cooing when they saw him sitting in the cart like a little king. Several people asked to pet him, but Pancakes took a particular liking to a sharp-nosed woman with purple glasses, purring and purring as she walked by.

"He knows I need the love today," the woman said, scratching under Pancakes's chin.

PJ saw that this could be a good way to meet women if it didn't work out with Michelle Cobb; he could walk around shopping centers with the cat. The woman told PJ she was having a minor surgery later that day, and she was feeling a little nervous about it.

"I'm sure you will be fine," PJ said. "She'll be fine, won't she, Pancakes?"

She will not, Pancakes thought, but PJ was too busy flirting with the woman to hear the cat. Her name was Avelina Sunderhook, and she would bleed out on the operating table in a matter of hours, but for now, she was enjoying the delightful sight of a cat in Target. *Not something you see every day!* she would go home and tell her husband, one of the very last conversations they would ever have. He would mention in her eulogy in fact, how happy she'd been to see the cat. How his dear Avelina had always pointed out the simple pleasures that other people often missed.

Elsewhere in the Target, Sophie had gone to the cosmetics aisle, where she found haircutting shears. She abandoned her cart and took the scissors straight to the checkout, and then took the scissors into the bathroom and opened the package. She surveyed the damage in the mirror and evened out her hair as best she could. She cut five inches off; it was up to her chin.

She looked at herself in the mirror. She was no Audrey Hepburn. There were a few pimples near her mouth. The skin on her oval face was pale and dull, and her eyes looked sad, but they always did.

"Bad breakup?" asked a Target employee, who came out of the

bathroom as Sophie was staring at herself in the mirror, a pile of hair in the sink. Her name tag said Debbie, and she was wearing a red polo.

"Not exactly."

"You know," Debbie said, "in some cultures, they believe haircutting sheds past trauma."

Sophie smiled weakly. "Guess I'm all better then."

Debbie laughed. "I hope so."

Sophie knew she should go find Luna, even if she was still angry with the kid. She had to be the adult here. Sophie remembered once when she'd gotten mad at her sister for telling her she looked stupid in her dance recital outfit, that she looked like a penguin in the leotard with the coat-and-tails jacket over it, and Sophie had gotten so mad that she'd thrown one of Kate's softballs through the living-room window. She remembered the impulsiveness of her anger, the pleasure from the release, and then the regret and shame that followed.

But Sophie also remembered how her mother had forgiven her. She remembered her mom telling her it was hard to hear criticism about things that mattered to you. She remembered her mom had lied to her dad that night and said a bird flew into the window and broke it.

"Was the bird all right?" her dad had asked.

"No," her mother had said, shaking her head sadly about this imaginary bird. "It was a hawk."

"A hawk! What did you do with it?"

"Buried it," Kate said, in on the lie. "Had a funeral. I sang 'Danny Boy.'"

"Wow," Sophie's dad had said. "Now I wish I was there."

It did sound great, Sophie had thought, and she wished that was what really happened, even though she would have felt sad for the hawk. But it probably would have died instantly, crashing into the window and breaking its neck. If it had really happened, the hawk would have never felt any pain.

Sophie knew she should try to be more like her mother, kind and forgiving. Sophie knew Luna was most likely shoplifting somewhere in the Target. Sophie did not want the girl to get in trouble with security, because she had heard Target security was the real deal.

Sophie looked in the clothing aisles, the toy aisles, the food aisles, and finally found Luna by the magazine rack, reading *Soap Opera Digest*, staring at a picture of four black-and-white headshots of square-jawed men. It made Sophie smile a bit, that she had caught Luna lusting after the men in the magazine, even if they were too old for her. She should be looking at a teen magazine, the *Tiger Beats* Kate used to read. "Hey," Sophie said, approaching Luna slowly like she would a wild animal she was trying to trap. "I cut the rest of my hair. I kind of like it. Do you like it?"

Luna looked up. "It's fine," she said. Then she looked down at the magazine again. "That's him," she said, pointing to the one in the middle. "That's Mark Stackpole."

"Your crush?"

"Ew, no. That's my dad. My real dad."

Okay, Sophie thought, *the girl is crazy with grief.* Delusional. She thinks her dad is an actor from a soap opera.

"And we don't even need to go all the way to California to meet him," Luna said. "Look."

Underneath the four headshots, it said, in neon pink lettering: KICK OFF YOUR SUMMER WITH THE HUNKS OF DAYTIME TV. It was a meet-and-greet, sponsored by Soaps.com. It was three days away, on June 7, in Sugar Land, Texas, at the Sugar Land Country Club. "Isn't Texas closer than California?" Luna asked, excited. "Aren't we going through Texas anyway? We can go there and meet him, and then he won't be impossible to find." Those were the social worker Belinda Bell's words: *A man like that would be impossible to find. Security, et cetera. Regretfully beyond the capabilities of the Massachusetts Department of Children and Families.*

"We're only going through north Texas," Sophie explained. "Sugar Land is down south. Near Houston, I think."

Luna began tearing up. "We're never going to find him. We don't even know where he lives." She knew what the mansion looked like, but she didn't know the address.

"Hey, hey, hey, now. Don't cry. You really think this is your dad? This guy from TV? Why do you think that?" She didn't say: *Are you off your medication, little girl?* but she thought it.

Luna told Sophie then, about her mother's ménage à trois back in high school, the one Luna had read about in her mother's diary. She mispronounced the phrase, but Sophie got the gist. Luna said Mark Stackpole went to Pondville High with her mother. That's why they were going to California. To find a soap opera star. A needle in a haystack. Sophie's ears and neck and eyelids were hot. She never would have agreed to this. No one in their right mind would agree to this.

After that, Sophie bought two copies of the magazine, one for Luna so she wouldn't steal it, and one for herself, and then went outside to hit her father with it. "What the fuck was your plan here?" she asked. "Do you know what this kid thinks? She thinks her dad is a television actor on a soap opera."

"Yes, yes, yes, I know that."

"You know that? You knew that this was the plan? You were taking her to Los Angeles and—what? Stand on the street and ask if anyone knows any actors?"

"I'm sure he has an agent."

"Dad, this is stupid, even for you."

"It's plausible! He went to Pondville High School!"

"It's idiotic!" She hit him a bunch more times with the magazine, and then she got in the car. Everyone sat there in silence, waiting for someone to do something. Say something. Sophie didn't start the car. She didn't know where to go—turn around and go home? She could call the social workers; she could ask them about this backup plan they had for September, if there was any way the backup plan could take the kids now. She should do that.

"Listen," PJ finally said. "Sophie, I'm sorry for lying to you, but when I met the kids, well, the girl . . . she wasn't talking at all. The social worker said she hadn't spoken one word in two weeks and then I said, hey kid, what if we went to LA and looked for this guy, and it was like magic, bam, she got her voice back."

"She did," Ollie said from the back. "She was happy because someone listened to her. Adults never listen to us. They never even asked me what I wanted from my room." Uncle PJ had bought Ollie new underwear at the Target, and a suitcase, new clothes, and a Barbie, a real Barbie, and hadn't even made fun of him for wanting it. But Ollie would always miss his old things.

Sophie stared ahead, listening to them talk. She still hadn't moved to turn the key in the ignition. The fact that the girl had a period of selective mutism after a major loss should interest Sophie as a possible future speech pathologist, but Sophie didn't know what to think. She didn't know what to do. She didn't really want to go back to Pondville. It had felt good to leave.

"I'm sorry, Sophie, I am. I'm trying to help these kids. The girl really wants to meet this guy, and well, I think we should try."

Sophie breathed out. She could see her father had lied to the kids. He probably never intended to take them to LA. He just wanted to get to Arizona, to see this Michelle Cobb woman he was suddenly obsessed with, and he lied to get the kids in the car. A car he had taken from Fred. She could see that now. Well, she wasn't taking him to Arizona so he could get laid. He could do that part alone. "Fine," she said. "We're going to Texas."

"Texas?" PJ asked. He pulled out his map. There was a line right through North Texas, the part that looks like a top hat. "Yes, you're right."

"Nope." Sophie was sure now. "We're going down to Sugar Land, Texas. It's down by Houston. We have to be at a country club in three days. There's a meet-and-greet for soap opera stars. We are finding Mark Stackpole."

"Really?" Luna asked. "You'll really take me there?"

"I don't know how else we are going to track this guy down, if he's a celebrity."

"Minor celebrity," PJ corrected.

"If he'll be there, we should be there," Sophie said. "If we want to talk to him, this seems like the only way."

"It's in three days?" PJ asked.

"Yup."

"Is it free?"

"I think so?" Sophie said, thinking that was a weird question from her dad. If they wanted to find Mark Stackpole, this was their chance. They would pay an admissions fee if they had to. He was a lottery winner, wasn't he? He'd never had any problem paying for things before.

"Yup! It's free!" Luna said. She handed the magazine up to PJ in the front, open to the page with the advertisement for the event. *Free to all soap opera fans, cash bar, sponsored by Soaps.com*, it said. There was a word bubble coming out of Mark Stackpole's mouth in his headshot: "Meet me in Texas!" Another word bubble said: "Let's get rowdy!"

"Looks like fun," PJ said. "Let's do it. Let's go meet Mark Stackpole."

"Really?" Luna couldn't believe these adults were listening to her. They weren't saying her ideas were stupid or weird or impossible.

"Really?" Ollie asked, feeling like there was kind of a good reason why adults didn't usually listen to Luna.

"Really," PJ said.

"Great," Sophie said. "Let's go to Texas." And she turned the key and the Volvo started up, and Sophie felt the tiniest bit of hope. If Mark Stackpole went to Pondville High School with Luna's mom, maybe it was possible. Maybe he could be the father. She saw paternity lawsuits against celebrities in the news all the time, and sometimes the women won. Maybe it was possible.

But then again, as she drove on through Ohio, the GPS rerouted toward east Texas, Sophie wondered if there was anyone on the planet dumber than her, listening to two kids and a crazy old drunk.

23

In Ashtabula, Ohio, they stopped for lunch at a diner, and the waitress came over in a turquoise uniform and matching eyeshadow. She had cigarette lines around her mouth. She said her name was Traci, and she didn't say anything about the cat they had in the carrier. PJ asked Traci for some Ashtabula history, and she said she didn't know any. "I grew up in Nevada," she said, holding her pen to the pad of paper.

But first PJ wanted to know how Traci had gotten all the way here to Ashtabula from Nevada, and then Traci put down her pen and she told the story about her ex-boyfriend Rodney and his motorbike, and the road trip they'd been on when one day she woke up in the Ashtabula motel alone. She'd been stuck there ever since.

Sophie was worried her dad was going to offer Traci a ride back to Nevada, and wished her dad was the type to leave waitresses alone, but instead, her dad said: "I'm so sorry he abandoned you," and told her how much more she was worth than that guy, who was clearly a dumb shit.

When Traci brought out their food, she also had a small plate of plain grilled salmon on the tray. "On the house," she said, "for our extra guest." She pointed to the cat carrier.

PJ looked adoringly at Traci. "What a real dipshit that boyfriend was, letting you go. Cheers to Traci, for her beauty and her kindness to animals."

Luna lifted her lemonade and Ollie lifted his coffee cup. "Cheers," they said. "Cheers," Sophie said, but didn't lift her ice water.

At the end of lunch, Traci gave PJ a hug and told him to stay in touch.

"Don't get any ideas," Ollie said. "He's marrying Michelle Cobb."

Traci laughed. "I wouldn't dream of it."

When they were back in the car, everyone well fed including the cat, Ollie asked for the rest of the story about Michelle Cobb.

"Yes, Uncle PJ," Luna agreed. "What happened after you went to jail?"

"We were supposed to save that for bedtime," PJ said, but then again, they did have a long way to go in the car. Ohio was a big state.

Eighteen-year-old PJ lay on the bench in the single jail cell at the Pondville police precinct. He was bleeding to death, he was sure. Most people don't know you can bleed to death by losing a finger, and PJ's finger was barely hanging on. At some point, in his daze, PJ realized his head was in the lap of another man, who smelled strongly of piss. He looked up into the man's face. The man was missing some of his teeth. "Hi, dear boy," the man said. "Are you awake?"

"Am I in heaven?" PJ asked. "Are you my dad?"

PJ had never known who his own father was and didn't know if his dad was dead or alive. His mother, Regina Halliday, had once been married to a man named Roy Duggins, but she had walked out on her family when PJ's older brother, Chip, was ten. Women never did that back then, it was men who went out for a pack of smokes and never returned, but Regina Halliday was ahead of her time. She had left her husband and child, and she hitchhiked around the country. She saw the Grand Canyon, she rode horses in Wyoming, she made friends with a young Frank Sinatra. She was in a movie too, but the film was lost in a fire. She had seen the whole country. She camped out in Death Valley and came out alive. She'd been bitten by a snake and sucked out the venom. She carried a pistol in her bra, she sang on stages for money. She had eaten an entire ten-foot submarine sandwich and won free lunch at a café in Roberta for the rest of her life. She had dozens of boyfriends, and each one loved her more than the last. But when she got pregnant again, she decided to come back to Pondville. She said it was a safe place to raise children, even if she had failed with her first. She moved into a house down the street from her ex-husband and her son. Her ex-husband was married again, and never acknowledged her return, but her son Chip egged her house once a week.

As PJ grew up in Pondville, his mother told him many stories of her travels, how wonderful it had been on the road, but she never told him about who his father was, not even when he begged. Whoever he was, he always sent PJ's mother white envelopes full of cash, no return address on them.

His father could be anyone. So maybe it was this man, holding PJ's head so tenderly in his lap in the jail cell. "Are you my father?" PJ asked the man again. Maybe the man hadn't heard him the first time.

The man stroked his hair like a father would. "Here now, you're going to be all right. You're not going to die here, don't you worry about that, I can see you thinking about that. But no, son, I'm not your father."

PJ looked up at this man, and even though he smelled terrible, and he wasn't his father, he loved him. PJ loved this man as much as he'd ever loved anyone. This man who said he wasn't going to die.

"No, you're not going to die anytime soon," the man said. "Not today and not in Vietnam either."

"How do you know?" PJ asked. "You're an angel?"

The old man said he wasn't an angel, far from it, but he could still tell PJ three things about the future: the worst thing that would ever happen to him, the best thing that would happen to him, and how he would die. "It will cost you though," the man said. "Like I said, I'm not an angel."

PJ had money in his wallet, but the cops had taken everything in his pockets. "I can pay you," he said. "When they let me out of here. I've got money."

The man shook his head. "I don't want your money. But there's a vending machine in the lobby." They could see it from the jail cell.

"They had vending machines back then?" Ollie asked.

"They did," PJ assured the boy.

And the old man said, in exchange for telling young PJ his fortune, PJ would need to buy him a bag of pretzels from the vending machine, after PJ got bailed out, which the man was sure PJ would, very soon.

"A bag of pretzels?" PJ asked. "Why a bag of pretzels?" They only cost about a nickel, but PJ wanted to know what the hitch was.

The man smiled. One of his silver teeth glinted. "Well, boy, it's how I'm going to die. I'm going to choke on a pretzel from that vending machine. But someone else has to buy them for me. That's the prophecy, as I see it. Some good young person kills me, in an act of kindness."

PJ got a shot of adrenaline after that. He didn't want to kill anybody, not in this jail cell, not in the boys' bathroom at the dance, and not in the war somewhere far away. He got the strength to get up and move away to the other side of the cell. He banged on the bars. He was wrong to love this man. The man was deranged, perhaps dangerous. "Can someone help me?" he called. "I need a doctor!"

Thankfully, PJ heard a voice then, someone he recognized. It was Gene Bartlett. He was there to pay PJ's bail.

There was another voice with him. A girl's voice. It was Michelle Cobb. Michelle and Gene had met when the cops took their statements, and Michelle told Gene how it was all Ricky's fault, all of it, she was sure. Gene agreed, it wasn't like Pauly Halliday to start a fight, and Gene and Michelle decided to drive over to the jail to vouch for PJ. By the time they arrived at the police station, Gene was already deeply in love with Michelle Cobb. She was beautiful, and kind.

After Gene paid the bail, the police officer released PJ, and PJ fell into Gene's arms.

"Hey, kid," the old man said. "How about our deal?"

PJ shook his head. "I can't, sir."

The man snarled, gnashed his teeth, gripped the bars. "You're a boy. You're a little boy. You're a little boy going off to war to kill innocent people."

"Shush," Michelle Cobb said to the man. "Who does that help? It's not his choice to go."

The old man looked at Michelle Cobb and his whole body relaxed. His face softened. She was a vision, a vision in orange, like sunshine herself had walked into that grimy jail. "I'm sorry, miss," he said. "I don't know what's gotten into me."

"I'm sure you've had a hard night too," Michelle said sweetly.

"I can tell the best thing that'll ever happen to you for free," the old man said to PJ, who could barely stand and was leaning against Gene Bartlett. "It's that girl right there. She's the best thing that will ever happen to you. And to you too," he said, looking at Gene. "Don't screw it up, boys."

"I won't," young PJ and young Gene Bartlett promised, at exactly the same time.

Gene helped PJ out to the car, and then Michelle said she had to go back inside. She'd forgotten her purse on the bench in the precinct. She went back in to get it and was back out a few minutes later.

"That poor man in the jail," she said, returning with her purse and climbing into the backseat of Gene's Pontiac GTO. "He was hungry. He was only hungry. He didn't mean it, Pauly, what he said about killing innocent people."

"Did you buy him something to eat?" Gene asked.

"Of course I did. A bag of pretzels."

PJ wondered if he should say anything, but instead he closed his eyes and waited to get to the doctor. Michelle Cobb was so sweet, it would have scarred her forever if she knew. Better let her think she helped the man by buying him the pretzels from the vending machine. Better let her think she had done a good thing.

"So why didn't you marry Michelle Cobb?" Ollie asked. "If she was the best thing to ever happen to you?"

"Did they sew the finger back on?" Luna asked. "Can I see the scar?"

PJ held up his hand and there was a visible jagged scar that wrapped around his pointer finger. "It's faded with time," he said, but Luna was satisfied. "As for Michelle, well, she chose Gene. He was the safer choice, I understood. He'd gotten a medical deferment, so he didn't have to go to Vietnam. Bone spurs, my ass. Have you ever heard of bone spurs?"

The kids had not.

"But I get a second chance with Michelle Cobb now. The best thing that's ever happened to me could still happen. It's not too late."

"And the worst has already happened," Luna said.

"The worst is over," PJ agreed.

"I can't wait to meet her," Ollie said. "She sounds really nice."

Sophie rolled her eyes. If Michelle Cobb was the best thing that had ever happened to her dad, her mom sure had put up with a lot of shit.

But Sophie did like the part of her dad's story about her grandmother; she'd always liked Grandma Regina's stories. Grandma Regina used to take care of Sophie and Kate every Tuesday after school. Kate and Sophie particularly loved to hear about all the boyfriends Grandma Regina had once had.

"Goodbye, my brave and smart girls," Grandma Regina used to say, when their mom picked them up. "You take care of those beautiful faces until I see them again."

"You too, Grandma Regina," Kate used to say back, and Sophie never knew if Kate was being mean or not. Their grandma had suffered nearly full-body third-degree burns in a house fire. She was missing part of her nose.

She died five years after Kate.

24

They checked in to a Days Inn in Hellsgate, Kentucky, where PJ insisted on stopping because of the name. "The gates of hell!" he said. "Sophie, your mother has been trying to get me to come here for years!"

"Very funny, Dad."

"I thought so."

As the kids were getting ready for bed, Sophie announced she was going out for a run. They'd had McDonald's for dinner, because Ollie begged for it. He said that he liked McDonald's because it was the same everywhere. Pancakes had been fed several bites of hamburger, and he agreed with Ollie, they should go to that restaurant every day. But Sophie's Big Mac was sitting in her stomach like a rock.

"You're going for a run? It's nine P.M.," her dad pointed out, as if Sophie couldn't read the time. Sophie told him she had a headlamp, and she did it often, went running at night. She told him he was going to stay with the kids in the hotel and not to leave under any circumstances.

"Got it. Call me if you get lost or mugged," he said, as if he were the adult here. And what number would she call anyway—he didn't have a cell phone. Fred and her mother didn't think it was a good idea, said PJ would only pick up more phone calls from strangers asking for money. Fred and her mother infantilized him. They didn't even let him have a computer in his own house, they said he had to come over and use Fred's. They didn't want him to get scammed.

Sophie went out and let the Days Inn door close behind her, heard the satisfying click of the automatic lock. She was alone with the night, and her feet on the pavement. She put in her headphones, put on her sad music, and started to run. The first mile was always her hardest, but she got into the flow after that. She liked to run seven miles. Seven always seemed the most perfect number to her.

Hellsgate was a small city, no big buildings, but residential streets mixed with commercial ones. There was a Kroger supermarket, a brew pub. Many of the homes were ranch-style, red brick. She used the running app on her phone to map out a loop around the city.

As she ran, Sophie thought about her mom and Fred. If it had been worth it to go to Alaska. Her mom had sent her a few pictures, but not much else, and Fred had said so many times not to call, because he was afraid Sophie would tell her mom that she had lost her job and that would ruin her mom's ability to relax. Sophie wondered what they were doing now. She kept running, before the sadness engulfed her. It hurt that Fred and her mom had left her behind. They were cutting her out.

At mile three, Sophie ran by a place called Heaven for Dummies. She didn't like to stop that early in the run, but curiosity took over and she had to stop to read the sign. Heaven for Dummies, it turned out, was a ventriloquist museum, with thousands of puppets inside. A small sign said that dummies are what ventriloquists call their puppets, because the ventriloquist is the one who gives a puppet its brain. One of the dummies was sitting on a chair in the window, brainless but still smiling with its rows of square teeth. Sophie felt a chill, and she swore the puppet's eyes followed her as she ran off.

She ran faster.

She ran by Mount Olive Elementary school. In the fall, Ollie and Luna would have to go back to a school like that one and the teacher would ask them what they'd done over the summer. They would probably have to write a whole report on this road trip. Sophie had to do that on the first day of sixth grade after her sister died, talk about the summer, because that's what everyone did on the first day of school. Sophie had been sent to the principal after she said she'd seen a dead body for the first time and that it was *totally unforgettable*, the way the other kids had described their sleepover camp. The teacher accused Sophie of disrupting the class.

"She was being sarcastic," her mom had said to the principal. "The kid is in *pain*."

Her dad had joined them in the principal's office then, still in his postal-worker uniform and obviously drunk, and the principal had asked them all to leave. It was the only time Sophie could remember that her dad's drinking had helped her. She didn't have to stay in the principal's office and got to go home instead.

Sophie's heart ached for Ollie and Luna, for what they would go through when they went back to school. She hoped someone could help them. Children go through lots of pain when they're at school, and often no one helps them.

Sophie ran by the national cemetery, rows and rows of white stones with little white crosses on them, all the same. The soldiers in uniform, even in death. Kate was buried in the Pickens Cemetery in Pondville. BELOVED DAUGHTER, SISTER, AND FRIEND, the stone said. Her parents had already bought the two plots next to her so they could be with Kate forever. They hadn't gotten Sophie one, and when she asked her mother about it, her mom told her not to be morbid.

Sophie ran by the library. She ran by a large fountain, a Smoothie King, a bank. It was nice to run somewhere she hadn't run before; she had been running the same routes for so many years.

Mile six, almost done with the run, finishing her loop back toward the Days Inn, she ran by a pet shop. There were puppies in the side window, all asleep, but in the center window, a red parrot stared out at her. The bird was in a large cage, some kind of macaw. She stopped to admire him. She thought about breaking the glass and setting him free. She didn't think a pet shop was anyplace for a parrot, although neither were the streets of this small city in Kentucky, so setting him free wouldn't do him much good. Sophie didn't want a parrot as a pet. The bird whistled. One of the windows was open a crack, so she could hear him through the glass. He whistled again, like he was catcalling her.

"Hi, pretty bird," Sophie said.

"Pretty bird," the bird repeated. When he opened his mouth, Sophie could see his tongue was black.

"Are you okay in there?" she asked. "Are you happy?"

"Are you happy?" the bird responded.

Sophie knew it would be stupid to answer the bird. It wouldn't help anything. It didn't even really help to talk to Blanche about not being happy in therapy; she certainly wasn't going to say so to a bird.

"I hope you kill yourself, you cocksucker," the parrot said next. "That'll be forty dollars."

Sophie burst into laughter. She wished she weren't the only person to hear the bird say that. It was the type of thing that would have been better to share with someone.

Sophie walked away from the pet-shop window. She wasn't going to free the parrot; there was no point in pretending. She hadn't finished all seven miles, but she couldn't keep running after what the bird had said. It had to be the end of the run. It was the perfect finish, and she had lost the flow anyway. So instead she ate two weed gummies she'd packed in her little runner's belt, where she kept other things she needed for the run.

Sophie loved getting high after a long run. How her legs turned boneless. She'd read somewhere that 80 percent of professional athletes get high after a workout, that it helped with the pain. She would walk back to the Days Inn. It was about a mile away. It would be a nice walk. Her legs began to turn to rubber.

Ahead, she saw a Waffle House, with the yellow neon lights and the glass windows. Waffles sounded great. She hadn't wanted waffles that morning at the Woodward Hotel, but she wanted them now. Sophie had never been to a Waffle House, a chain nonexistent in New England. It would be a shame not to try it. The Waffle House was open twenty-four hours, and inside, there were several clusters of people eating and laughing, being drunk and rowdy. Sophie sat at a booth with red plastic pillowing. She looked at the menu. She wanted to order one of everything. She had her credit card in her running belt.

The waitress came over. Her nameplate said Yvonne. "Just so you know," Yvonne said. "Someone overdosed in the bathroom last night and I had to be the one to find him, so I am kindly asking you not to shoot up in the bathroom tonight."

"Oh. Wow. Okay. No, I won't do that."

"So, what can I getcha?"

Sophie ordered a pecan waffle and a patty melt and hash browns.

Yvonne walked off with her order, leaving Sophie alone in the booth to look at her phone, and when she wasn't paying attention, two men slid into the booth with her. One sat next to her and one across. They were huge men; it was like two rhinoceroses had just joined her at the table. The one across from her was wearing a Frosted Flakes T-shirt, with a tiger giving a thumbs-up. "We were thinking you looked awfully lonely, so we thought we would join you for dinner."

"No, thank you," Sophie said. "Not lonely."

"Where's your boyfriend, sweetie?" the one with a face tattoo said, putting his arm around her. "Can I be your new boyfriend?"

"Not my type."

"I get it," Face Tattoo said. "But I can make anyone my type."

"Bag over the head," Frosted Flakes agreed.

Sophie felt the chill of fear, real fear, worse than the fear she'd felt when she saw the creepy ventriloquist puppet. That was only horror-movie fear, and this was real fear. Nothing fun about it.

The rhinoceroses stank of booze. *This is why women shouldn't run alone at night,* she heard someone say in her ear. She wasn't sure if that voice was her mother or Fred or her therapist, but whoever it was, it was someone wiser than her. Then again, Sophie wasn't running right now. She was in a well-lit Waffle House. She had a tiny bottle of pepper spray in her running belt, which Fred had given her to take on her runs, but she couldn't reach it right then, with the man's arm around her. Sophie remembered how proud Fred had been when he'd given her the pepper spray in a handy-dandy keychain, as if it were a magic wand that would protect her forever.

"So, Wednesday Addams," Frosted Flakes said, and then chuckled as if Sophie had never heard that Wednesday Addams line before. "Can we get you a drink?"

"It's not a bar," Sophie mumbled.

"We make a good cocktail."

"It's a double." They chuckled again. Sophie tried to move her hand behind her to get to the pepper spray in the sack on her belt.

"Hey," someone called from behind the counter. "Hey, idiots! Leave her alone!"

"What's the problem, Brandon?" Frosted Flakes asked. "You call dibs?"

"I did actually," the Waffle House cook said. "That's my new girlfriend."

"New girlfriend? You finally left your bitch wife?"

"Brittany kicked me out."

"Did she take the kids?" Frosted Flakes asked.

"Sure did."

The Waffle House cook was fit and tattooed, Sophie noticed, and he was valiantly coming to her rescue. If he needed a new wife, Sophie could do it.

"Hey, doll," Brandon said. "Come back here and eat with me."

Sophie looked at the rhinoceros next to her, blocking her way, and she prayed he would move. He did. He backed away and got out of the booth and stormed off to another part of the restaurant. His friend followed. It was like watching a pair of T-rexes decide they were going to hunt and eat someone else. Sophie stood and scrambled over to the kitchen, where Brandon welcomed her to the other side of the counter. "Thank you," she said. Her heart was pounding.

"You have to wear one of these if you're back here," he said. "May I?"

She nodded, and he put a hairnet on her like she was a queen. She loved him.

"They're just drunk," Brandon said, as if that excused them. Sophie was glad at least that he didn't say those two drunk men were harmless. She could feel from the hairs on her neck that they were not harmless.

Brandon served her the pecan waffle and the patty melt and the side of hash browns on three separate plates. She picked up the waffle and ate it without cutting it up, the way she had seen Luna bite into hers that morning. It was phenomenal.

"This," she said, chewing, "is the best waffle I've ever had."

"Glad you think so."

"We don't have Waffle House where I live."

"A Yankee, huh?"

"Massachusetts."

"A *real* Yankee. What brings you to Kentucky?"

"I'm on a road trip with my dad."

"Where's he?"

"Back at the hotel. I was going for a run, and I was walking back to the hotel when I saw the Waffle House. It seemed like a good idea at the time."

"I'll take you back to the hotel," Brandon offered. "Can't have you walking home this time of night."

"Okay," Sophie agreed. "It's just the Days Inn. It's only a mile down the road."

"Hey, Diamond," Brandon said to another one of the cooks. "Cover for me? I'll be back before the rush."

"I got you," Diamond agreed.

Brandon took his apron off, and he pulled off Sophie's hairnet. She felt a little tremble of pleasure when he touched her.

"Hey, Brandon, where are you going?" Frosted Flakes called, when he saw Brandon leaving in the middle of his night shift.

"I'm taking my girlfriend home," Brandon announced to the room, and the rhinoceros men applauded, as if Brandon had just announced their engagement. Sophie smiled, and she felt special. As if she really were the chosen one.

In the parking lot, Sophie found out that Brandon drove a white catering van. "Look at this," he said. "Isn't this sweet?" He opened the sliding doors, and in the back, there was a bed. "I'm living here for now," he told her. "After my wife kicked me out."

"Brittany, your bitch wife," she said, repeating what the Frosted Flakes douchebag had called her.

"Yup. My bitch wife. She's got the kids right now."

"How many kids?"

"Three. I'm going to try to get fifty-fifty custody in the divorce, but the courts always favor the mother. And I probably don't have a shot getting custody at all for the eldest, since I'm not her real dad. I'm going to try, though."

"Good for you."

"She calls her dad by his first name. Jeremiah. She won't even call him Jerry, as if they are total strangers. She has no affection for him. She calls me Daddy."

"That's nice. I mean, it's nice that she calls you Daddy."

"Glad you think so. Maybe you can write me a character reference."

"Sure."

"You want to get high?"

"What kind of high?" she asked, because she remembered the waitress warning her not to use heroin in the bathroom. She was, also, already high.

"Just weed. I grow it myself. Mellow stuff."

So, they smoked Brandon's weed in the back of the van. Sophie noticed his necklace strung with white shells, or maybe the teeth of an animal, and when she asked about it, he said it was the baby teeth of all his three kids. *Sweet,* Sophie thought, *and weird.* Super weird, but people who had kids did strange things. And then, Brandon leaned in and kissed her. He was a good kisser. He took off his shirt, and there Brittany's name was, right above his nipple, along with three other names below, probably the names of the kids. Sophie took off her shirt, too, didn't wait for him to do it. She stank a little, from the run, but Brandon didn't seem to care. He put his hands underneath the elastic of her sports bra.

Afterward, she lay wrapped in a blanket in the back of the van. It was a *Paw Patrol* blanket with the girl dog on it, brown ears in a pink superhero outfit. Sophie wondered what Brittany and the kids were doing right then, and she pictured Brittany in a bed next to one of the children, who was awake from a nightmare, and she was scratching the child's back with her fake fingernails, trying to calm the kid down back to sleep. She imagined Brittany was a good mom. "Were you and Brittany ever happy?" she asked.

He shrugged. "Yeah. We were really happy once. She was my best friend."

"What happened?"

"I don't know. She started being a bitch. She wants me to figure out my life. She wants me to aim higher. But I *have* figured out my life. I'm going to work two years as a short-order cook at Waffle House, and then I'll be able to work in any kitchen I want. Everyone knows if you can handle the pressure at Waffle House, the drunk customers starting fights you have to break up, combined with the speed of the cooking, then they'll hire you anywhere."

"Oh," Sophie said. "I mean, that does sound like a good plan."

"Thanks."

"It's much more of a plan than I have."

"You got a job?"

Sophie shook her head.

"Kids?"

Sophie thought of Ollie and Luna, but they weren't hers. "No. No kids."

"You'll need something," he said. "If you expect to be happy. My dad always said a person needs three things to be happy: something to do; someone to love; and something to look forward to."

Sophie didn't know if she had any of those things. She didn't look forward to anything, not right now. Well, that wasn't true. She looked forward to getting into the clean sheets of the hotel bed. Ollie had checked all the mattresses for bedbugs when they first checked in, the boy was neurotic about bedbugs, so Sophie knew it was safe to just crawl in. "Can you take me back to the hotel now?" she asked. It was already one A.M. Sophie hoped her dad was worried about her. She hoped he hadn't left the kids alone in the room.

He nodded and started the van. "You should get a hobby. Besides my kids and my job, I play poker once a week. I look forward to it, every week. Time with my friends. They're the craziest bastards. You wouldn't believe the stories."

"I'm sure I wouldn't," Sophie said, thinking about the man in the Frosted Flakes shirt, wondering if he was part of the poker club. She didn't want to ask.

Brandon pulled his van into the lot at the Days Inn, and the headlights shone on the window where Sophie's dad was sleeping, and there was Pancakes, peering out between the maroon curtains. "Is that your cat in the window?"

"Yup. That's Pancakes."

"He's waiting up for you. That's so sweet."

"He's my dad's cat, really. I don't think he likes me. I'm allergic."

"He likes you enough to wait up and see if you got home safe. He wants to make sure the serial killer of Hellsgate didn't get you."

"There's a serial killer in Hellsgate?"

"Of course there is; there are serial killers everywhere. But I've got to get back to work tonight. Don't have time to dispose of a body before the three A.M. rush." Brandon winked.

"Oh," Sophie said, and she knew he was probably joking, he was *almost definitely* joking, but she felt the fear in her rising again. The hairs on the back of her neck standing up. The necklace made from human teeth looked awfully sinister now. She didn't want to show her fear, so she leaned over and kissed Brandon on the lips. Not a make-out, but a quick and simple kiss, as if Brandon were her boyfriend and he was dropping her off at home after a date. She thanked him and climbed down from the van, then tried to walk quickly but not too quickly to her room and looked back once to make sure he wasn't following her. She opened the door with the plastic keycard, and then she was inside. The automatic lock clicked behind her, and that click was the world's most beautiful sound.

DAY THREE
THURSDAY

25

When Sophie opened her eyes in the morning, she touched both sides of her face, and put a hand in the middle of her chest to feel herself breathe. "I am alive," she whispered. "I am okay." She looked at the crappy artwork on the wall of the Days Inn, and she thought it was a masterpiece.

"Good run last night?" her dad asked.

Sophie didn't answer. She couldn't tell him what happened, and how scared she'd been. How it probably hadn't been smart to climb into a strange man's van. But she had survived. "You stayed here with the kids?" she asked. "All night?"

"All night," he said proudly. "I told them the story about meeting your mother."

"That's nice," Sophie said, and she found herself wishing she had been there, to hear how her dad had loved her mom at first sight when he saw her in the Wild Orchid forty-three years ago.

They packed up and went down to the lobby of the Days Inn, where there was a continental breakfast set up. They all ate mini boxes of cereal and fat fluffy Otis Spunkmeyer muffins for breakfast, and then they all got back in the car. Sophie was glad to be getting out of Hellsgate and wondered if places always find a way to live up to their name, the way people do. Sophie had heard that people whose last name is "Doctor" become doctors at a much higher rate than the rest of the population. The GPS was pointed at Sugar Land, Texas, still fifteen hours and fifty-eight minutes away, and maybe everything would be sweet there. Maybe Mark Stackpole would in fact be Luna's real dad and would welcome both kids with open arms.

Sophie adjusted the rearview mirror so she could look at the backseat. Luna was making a collage out of one of her *Soap Opera Digest* magazines with those scissors she had and a glue stick she'd gotten somewhere. Sophie knew she should probably take the scissors away, not only because she didn't want to lose more hair but because it probably wasn't safe to use scissors in the car, but Sophie also knew the kids needed to keep themselves busy on such a long trip. She appreciated that Luna could keep herself occupied. Ollie was on his iPad. Her dad was reading a book he'd found in the free pile in the lobby of the Days Inn, called *How to Survive in the Woods*. As far as Sophie knew, her dad couldn't even build a fire.

In the backseat, Luna turned to the middle of her magazine, the sacred part she wasn't slicing up with her scissors, the three pages in the center about Mark and Christine Stackpole and their new baby, Sassafras, as well as "glimpses into their home and busy life with five kids." There was also something in the magazine about how much Mark Stackpole loved Jesus, and that was why he'd had five children already, because he and his wife believed Jesus had called on them to have as many children as they could.

Luna considered the information in the magazine. The part about having lots of kids was a good thing, and Luna didn't have an issue with a half-sister named Sassafras, but she didn't know how she felt about Jesus, or how Jesus would feel about her.

26

"I'm getting awful sick of the highway," PJ announced after another two hours on the road. "We need to experience more of the country. Let's stop and do a little sightseeing."

"We need to get to Texas," Sophie reminded him. "You promised the kids you would take them to Texas."

"You promised Luna," Ollie muttered. "I don't really want to go to Texas."

"We've got a few days to get to Texas," PJ said. "We've got time to stop. We've only seen Niagara Falls and nothing else. Nothing else of this great country of ours."

"We only have *two* days to get to Texas," Luna corrected, looking up from her project with the magazine and scissors. "Today and tomorrow. The event is on Saturday morning. Do you want to see the advertisement again? Ten A.M. to one on June seventh."

Ollie looked at the clock on the car dashboard for the time. 11:36. If they were at school, it would be math time right now. "Can we please stop and do something?" Ollie begged. He didn't want to think about what they were doing at school, or if he and Luna would get in trouble for missing it. He was sorry he had lied to Uncle PJ about how much school they had left in the year, and his iPad had died and he knew Luna wouldn't let him use hers.

Sophie had to agree it would be nice to get out of the car for a while. She was glad to have woken up alive today, and it would be good to not spend the whole day in the car. Up ahead was a billboard for BIG KEVIN'S BIG ALPACA RANCH! with a photo of an alpaca wearing sunglasses. "How about stopping there?" Sophie asked.

"Perfect," PJ said.

"Yes," Ollie agreed. "Perfect."

The next billboard they passed advertised Deedee's Diner, also off Exit 28, with "the best pie in Kentucky!" They took Exit 28. They passed the diner, a silver canister baking in the sun with a pink neon sign. There was green farmland all around. Up ahead, BIG KEVIN'S RANCH was written across a big wooden gateway.

"This must be it," PJ said.

Sophie turned in, and as they drove on the long driveway, the alpacas ran to the fence to see the newcomers. They were shoving one another out of the way with their shoulders to get the best look at who was driving in. It was a sea of alpacas, in many colors—brown, white, gray, black. They had long necks and huge eyes, looked kind of like baby giraffes mixed with sheep.

"Is there such thing as wild alpacas?" Ollie asked.

"They look too dumb to survive in the wild," Luna said.

"Maybe there are in Peru," Sophie said. "Aren't they from Peru?"

"Big Kevin will tell us," PJ said.

Big Kevin was standing in the driveway outside the barn, waiting for them. He was wearing a T-shirt that said ASK ME, I'M BIG KEVIN! on it. He was a large man, six-foot-six or so, and round, red cheeked. He looked like John Candy.

"Howdy, folks," Big Kevin said when they got out. "Welcome to the largest alpaca farm in this part of Kentucky! So happy you're here! You brought a cat! Can't say anyone has ever brought a cat before."

PJ held the cat in his arms. Pancakes was not sure about the alpacas, or Big Kevin. Everything about this place smelled strange. "Hi, Mr. Big Kevin. It's really the largest alpaca farm?" PJ asked.

"The largest alpaca farm in this part of Kentucky."

"Well, look at us, kids, we're really sampling America! We're seeing the sights!"

Sophie rolled her eyes, but she was a little glad to see her dad happy. It was hard not to be amused sometimes, by how much her dad loved new things and new people. Especially after last night, Sophie was glad to be around it.

"What's that noise?" Luna asked. It sounded like there were bees in the air, a constant hum.

"Oh," Big Kevin said, smiling. "That's the alpacas. Takes everyone by surprise. They're singing. Humming, really. They're excited to see you. Sound like a bad high school band, don't they?"

Sophie loved it. A band of alpacas.

"Wow," Ollie said, looking over the fence. "I didn't know llamas made noise."

"Mine are singers, and they're not llamas, they're alpacas. Different species, although they can interbreed. Now, where you folks coming from if you're out sampling America?"

Ollie stood up straight and faced Mr. Big Kevin, the way his dad had taught him to talk to adults. "We're from Pondville, Massachusetts, sir. We're fourth graders at White Rock Elementary. We used to live on Deerfield Lane, but we—we don't anymore."

"Fifth graders next year," Luna said, crossing her arms. "But I'm not going back to that fucking school."

"Luna!" Sophie scolded.

"What? You say curse words. So does Uncle PJ."

"Well. Okay. New rule: no swearing outside the car."

"Oh, don't worry about it," Big Kevin said. "I like a little spice in my language. And I wasn't much for school either, kid. You can be an alpaca farmer like me. It's my second career, but I recommend it."

"I want to be an astronaut," Luna said.

"Since when?" Ollie asked.

"Since forever."

"You're going to have to go to school if you want to be an astronaut," Sophie said. "They don't let anyone be an astronaut."

"She'll be going to school," PJ said. "I promised the state." It had been in the paperwork Belinda Bell had given him. "But first, we'll enjoy the summer," he said.

Ollie gulped.

"*If* I stay with you," Luna said. "I probably won't."

"Sounds like a tricky family situation," Big Kevin said. "Now, who wants a tour of the farm? You guys want to pet some baby alpacas?"

Everyone did.

Big Kevin led them to a big red barn. "A baby alpaca is called a cria," he explained. "And when an alpaca gives birth, it's called an unpacking."

Inside the barn, the baby alpacas came to the edge of the stall. The crias. Big Kevin said that they could go in with the babies, said they liked to be scratched behind the ears, and gave them some apple slices as treats. The baby alpacas ate the apples greedily, the whiskers on their lips tickling their hands. Luna laughed.

"I love them," Ollie said. "They're so gentle."

"Yeah," Luna said. "I'd never be sad if I had one."

"Me too," Sophie agreed.

Ollie looked up at Uncle PJ, wondering if he had heard what Sophie and his sister had said, about not being sad ever again. Wondering if they could put an alpaca in the backyard with the trampoline. He wanted his sister to be happy, but he didn't want to go live with Mark Stackpole. It would be easier if they could just go back to Pondville and ask Uncle PJ to get them an alpaca, who would hum in delight when it saw them, like a big, dumb, long-necked dog. No one else at school had an alpaca, not Gabriel or River or Johnny or Elsie Dawson. To Ollie, that sounded like a much better plan than finding Mark Stackpole in Texas. Ollie was sure that Texas was going to be a disaster, but no one was asking him.

"Sweet kids you've got there," Big Kevin said to Sophie. "I've got three kids myself. Three boys. All grown-up now."

"Do they live around here?" Sophie asked. She didn't want to explain to Big Kevin they weren't really her kids.

"Not close enough, but not too far either. They all live over in Eddyville, where the prison is."

"They're all in prison?" Ollie asked.

Big Kevin snorted. "No, no. They're all corrections officers like I was. That was my first career, before I found my passion in alpacas. I was a corrections officer at Kentucky State Penitentiary."

"Quite a career shift," Sophie said.

"I left part of my heart back there, though. I'm glad my boys are still there, and I get to visit. We call the prison the Castle on the Cumberland, because it's quite a pretty building, looks like a castle, and right on the river. It's haunted, though; you hear people screaming all the time, even when none of the prisoners are. Lots of folks have died there, of course. Plenty of ghosts walking around. But it was a second home to me."

"I love horror movies," Ollie said. "But my sister gets scared."

"I do not." Even though Luna did.

"I've got stories that would make your horror movies look like Disney movies."

"I bet you do," PJ said.

"But maybe let's not tell the kids," Sophie suggested.

"Hey, y'all want to see something cool?" Big Kevin asked. "My sons got it for me for my birthday a few years back. I don't show it to most folks, but you guys seem like you'd enjoy it. Are you folks interested in American history?"

"We certainly are," PJ said.

"Well, come on then, it's in the other barn."

"Is it scary?" Ollie asked.

"A little."

Big Kevin led them away from the crias to a second barn, behind the first. It was more dilapidated, and it was quiet over at this barn, no alpacas humming—so quiet it was almost eerie. Kevin lifted the bar that locked the big door, and it swung open. A few chickens scattered. In the middle of the barn, there was what first appeared to be a plain wooden chair, but there were leather straps on the arms and legs of the chair, and at the top there was a metal cap, and thick silver wires.

The cat hissed and jumped out of PJ's arms and skittered out of the barn. *Absolutely not,* thought the cat. *Evil, evil, evil.* The cat did not approve of those kinds of deaths.

"I guess he'll wait for us outside," PJ said.

"That's a real electric chair?" Sophie asked.

"Yup, it's a real electric chair," Big Kevin said proudly. "Last of its kind in the state. We've switched over to lethal injection in Kentucky, don't ask me why. Nothing better than the drama of an electric chair. Prisoners still have the option of choosing the electric chair, but I guess no one picks it, so they got rid of Ol' Sparky."

"Ol' Sparky? They really call it that?" PJ asked.

"Yup. Ol' Sparky was built in 1897 to replace hanging, and on July 13, 1928, it electrocuted eight men in one day, which is the electric chair world record. They last used it in 1997, but it's been sitting there in the prison since then, until my boys bought it for my birthday and brought it here. Bought it for six hundred dollars at auction."

"Can I sit in it?" Ollie asked.

"Absolutely not," Sophie said.

"No way," PJ agreed.

"You can," Big Kevin said. "My boys fixed up the chair so that it gives you a little shock, not enough to really hurt you, just enough to microwave what you ate for breakfast. You sit here and then we flick the switch. But only if your mom says it's okay."

"She's not my mom."

"Sister?" Big Kevin guessed.

"Um, second cousin I think," Sophie said.

"You folks are an interesting family."

"Let me zap Ollie," Luna begged.

"I'll sit in it," PJ offered. "If the kids want to zap someone, they can zap me."

"What about your heart?" Sophie asked, although she agreed this was better than letting the kids sit in the chair.

"I'll be fine," PJ said. He had seen some of the killer-whale documentary, and he hadn't had any heart palpitations. Maybe he was healthier now that he'd stopped drinking, and he was thinking about what the man in the green vest had said at Niagara Falls, about how people reported that being on the *Maid of the Mist* boat ride was the most alive they'd felt in years. He didn't want to say no to every opportunity on the road trip. He wanted to show the kids how to be alive, and that meant saying yes to new opportunities.

So, PJ sat in the chair. The wood was smooth. He let Big Kevin strap his arms and legs in. PJ's whole body felt cold. "They used to put a wet sponge on your head for the electric current," Big Kevin said. "But we won't do that to you."

"Just one quick shock," PJ said. "Right?"

"There's two buttons here," Big Kevin said. "Two guards did it together, each pushed a button so they could share the responsibility."

Ollie reached over and pushed both buttons at once. He couldn't help himself.

"Ouch!" PJ yelped.

"Did it hurt?" Luna asked.

"Yeah, it hurt," he confirmed. It had hurt worse than he'd thought it would. "You want a turn pressing the buttons, Luna?"

Even though Luna badly wanted a turn, she hesitated. She'd been all set to zap Ollie if he sat in the chair, but he was her brother and Uncle PJ was an old man. A shock could hurt him. She remembered what Mark Stackpole said in the magazine, how the devil had tested him many times, but Jesus always helped him find the right answer. But then Luna reached over and pressed the two buttons anyway.

PJ was expecting the shock this time, but he yelled in pain again anyway. His blood pulsed, he could feel his fingertips throb at the tips.

"That was amazing," Luna said. She was glad the devil inside her had won.

"That was the best thing ever," Ollie agreed.

"Let's get going before you kids fry me," PJ said.

"Yes, I think three shocks might be too many," Big Kevin agreed.

But before he was unstrapped, Sophie reached over and pressed both buttons. *Take that,* she thought, and her dad yelped. She didn't want to give him a heart attack, didn't want to kill him, but she wanted to cause him a little pain. Luna and Ollie fell down laughing when she did it. And it did feel pretty good. There had been so many times he had messed up her life, and today she got to zap him for it.

"Jesus Christ, Sophie, what was that for?"

"Sorry," she said, shrugging. "I thought we all got a turn."

"I love you, Sophie," Ollie said, and then they were all silent for a minute, letting the *I love you* echo around the barn and settle like dust.

"Let's go find the cat," Sophie said, because she knew it was too late to say it back.

Outside the barn, they didn't see Pancakes at first, but they found one dead bird on the gravel path, freshly killed, which PJ felt sorry about. "He's an agent of death," he told Big Kevin, but Kevin wasn't concerned. Things died on the farm all the time.

They found Pancakes on the porch of Big Kevin's white farmhouse, warming the lap of a frail-looking woman in a rocking chair. Her eyes were black hollows, and Big Kevin said it was best if they gave his wife her space when she was staring like that. PJ brought out the Meow Mix treats from his pocket and shook the bag and the cat jumped off the woman's lap and came running.

"Isn't he a marvelous little creature," Big Kevin remarked as he watched the cat trot along, headed obediently with the group back toward the car.

27

They were back in the Bird Barn with a stack of new alpaca wool sweaters that were much too hot to wear, and Luna decided she should ask a few questions to Sophie and Uncle PJ. She had some things to figure out before she got to Texas and met Mark Stackpole. "Does God love everyone?" she asked. "Or does he just love some people?"

There was a long silence in the Volvo, and Sophie waited for her father to answer, but he didn't. He was busy reading his book about how to survive in the woods.

"Um, I think that's the idea," Sophie finally said. "Yes, if there is a God, he loves everyone."

"What about Jesus?"

"I think they're supposed to have the same opinions. I think they are kind of the same person in different bodies. If God, um, has a body." She wasn't really prepared for this conversation. She knew Jesus had a body. *Did God?* Sophie wasn't sure.

"Well, does God love murderers?"

"Well, um, no, I don't think he loves murderers."

"That's what hell is for," Ollie said helpfully. "Murderers."

Sophie's heart skipped one beat. She still felt she had narrowly escaped something back in Hellsgate, something really bad.

"What about people who steal things?" Luna asked.

"Stealing isn't like murdering. So yes. God loves people who steal things."

"Do you think our parents are in hell?" Ollie asked.

"No," Sophie said quickly. "I don't think that they're in hell." Even though Sophie had a SATAN IS MY REAL DADDY T-shirt, she was not comfortable sending Luna's parents to hell.

"I don't believe in it," PJ agreed, finally looking up from his book.

"Don't believe in what?" Luna asked.

"Hell. It doesn't make any sense. Why the actions over your short life-span would determine what happens to your soul for the rest of eternity. If you live for eighty years, that's a tiny blip against the scale of eternity. It seems overkill to me, to have one short chance when God is supposed to be endlessly forgiving."

"Well, what do you believe in then, Uncle PJ?" Ollie asked.

PJ didn't really know what he believed about the afterlife or God or any of it; it had been hard to believe in a higher power after Kate died, but he also didn't like to think that Kate's spirit, that her soul, was gone completely. There had to be some answer for where all that life went. "Well," PJ said, considering what to tell the kids if there was no hell. Surely not everyone could go to heaven. Surely not everyone deserved a free pass. "Past lives. That's a theory I think I like. You might come back a better animal than a human, or you might come back a worse one."

"What were you in your past life, Dad?" Sophie asked, relaxing after her dad took over the conversation.

PJ pet the cat in his lap. "Well, I think in *his* past life, Pancakes was a goat herder in Mongolia. And I believe I was one of his goats."

"A goat?" Ollie asked, laughing. "You think you were a goat?"

"Yup. Or perhaps a yak. But Pancakes and I found each other again, in this life, which is a beautiful thing."

Pancakes purred at this attention, amused at PJ trying to make sense of the afterlife.

But Luna nodded. She liked the idea. "So, like, maybe our parents could be worms now."

"Maybe," PJ agreed.

"Yeah," said Ollie.

Sophie wondered if she or her dad should suggest a more dignified animal their parents could return as, but for Luna, it wasn't so bad for her to imagine her parents as earthworms, easier than imagining them tortured for eternity, which is what she'd heard about the few times her parents had taken her to church. Luna hated her parents, and loved them, too, and didn't want them tortured for eternity. She closed her eyes and thought of them eating lettuce in someone's compost, how peaceful that seemed. It didn't have to be terrible. Luna vowed to move the earthworms off the sidewalk next time it rained.

28

They stopped in Nashville to see the Honky Tonk strip, to walk down the street and hear all the live music coming from every restaurant. When they got back in the car, PJ played Elvis Presley and Dolly Parton songs using Sophie's phone, having finally figured out how to use the music app. They played card games. Twenty questions and the license plate game, and the game where you try to think of the most movies that begin with a certain letter.

By nightfall, they were in west Tennessee. Headlights lit up a stretch of rural highway. Above them, the bats were eating mosquitos, the bloodsuckers big as moths down there. There was an inn up ahead, two red cherries painted on a yellow sign. THE GOLDEN CHERRY INN & SUITES. VACANCY. There wasn't much else on the road, except for an abandoned Laundromat. "Let's stop here," PJ said.

"I'm fine to keep going," Sophie said. "We can get to Memphis. We're in the middle of nowhere now."

"We're not in the middle of nowhere," PJ said, and smiled. "You're never going to believe it, Sophie-Soo, but we're in the middle of

Somewhere. That's the town name. Somewhere, Tennessee. I saw the sign a mile back. It's perfect. We all wanted to go somewhere, and now we're here." It was too perfect, they had to stay in Somewhere. Besides, PJ was pretty sure that rooms in the Golden Cherry wouldn't be expensive.

Sophie pulled into the hotel lot. If her dad wanted to stay in this creepy hotel, whatever, it couldn't be worse than the town named after the gates of hell. There were five other cars in the lot, and one motorcycle. Sophie turned off the car and immediately escaped into the glow of her phone. A guy she'd slept with last month had texted wanting to know if she was around to do it again. Her friend Sara from work had texted to ask if she'd been doing all right since they'd both lost their jobs.

No, Sophie texted back to Sara. *Are you?*

Things have never been bleaker, Sara responded, which is why she and Sophie were friends. Ever since the layoffs two months ago, Sara had been home alone with her kids while her dumb husband got to go to work.

If you think that's bad, wait until you hear about the road trip I'm on with my dad—Sophie typed back.

"You guys stay here, I'll go check in," PJ said. He hesitated a second and then grabbed the cat. He figured if he was going to tell the hotel that the cat was a service animal, it was more believable if he brought the cat with him.

PJ walked into the lobby of the Golden Cherry Inn & Suites, where he was met with a mustard-yellow carpet, cherry wallpaper all over the walls, an old couch, a coffee table with a chess game set up on it, and a big fish tank with tropical fish inside. To his left was the reception desk. Two people were leaning against the desk, making out. They were in their thirties probably, the man wearing a leather jacket and the woman in a short white dress. She had bleach-blond hair. It must have been their motorcycle PJ had seen out in the parking lot. They didn't notice PJ at first; they were too busy sucking face. The cat jumped down from PJ's arms and began to rub against their legs, snaking in between them. "What the fuck?" the man said, looking down. HELLS ANGELS, the man's jacket read. "Where did this cat come from?"

"Sorry," PJ said. "He gets a little too friendly with strangers." There had been an incident at a gas station earlier that day where Pancakes had tried to jump into a van of old ladies on a road trip to a bingo convention.

"Come here, pussy cat," the woman said, and picked up Pancakes. Pancakes liked the nickname, and the Hells Angel liked to see his woman happy. If she liked the cat, he liked the cat.

"Sorry for the PDA," he said to PJ. "We're on our honeymoon."

"Oh, congratulations. That's wonderful. So happy to meet you both at this happy moment."

The man smiled and dinged the bell on the desk that came with a little sign that said: RING BELL FOR SERVICE. "We still have to concentrate the marriage before it's legal."

"It's *consummate*, baby," the woman said, and then smiled at PJ. "I didn't marry him for his brain." Then she rang the bell herself, six times in a row. "Who do I have to blow around here to get a room key?" she yelled toward the back.

"That would be me," a man said, coming around the corner. He had a mustache so thin it looked like it had been drawn on, and he had a gold earring in one ear. His name tag said Gregor. "Let's get you your keys, thanks for your patience," Gregor said. After a few minutes of paperwork, he handed the couple two plastic key cards. "Upgraded you to the honeymoon suite, Room 101," he said. "Thanks again for your patience. And I do have to apologize, our pool is broken. The heater is out of whack. Repairman coming tomorrow—"

But the couple was off down the hall now, groping each other.

"No worries about the pool," PJ said. "The kids aren't swimmers."

"I thought it was just you and the cat."

"No. It's me and my daughter, and the two kids."

"Ah," Gregor said. "Well, I've only got one room left. Two queen beds. The couple in front of you took the suite with two rooms."

PJ was annoyed. The couple did not need two rooms, not when they'd spend the whole night in one bed. "Do you have a cot?"

"I'm using our only cot in my office. But I can do a sleeping bag for an extra fifteen."

PJ wondered if Sophie would be willing to share a bed with him, go half-and-half, but he didn't think so. That was all right. He could sleep in a sleeping bag for one night; despite his older bones, he slept on the bench by the bogs all the time back in Pondville. And there were no other rooms available; it was a small inn. The price was right, and Gregor seemed fine with the cat. "He's an assistance animal," PJ said. "If you were wondering. He tells me if I'm going to have a heart attack."

"As long as he doesn't smoke in the room."

PJ laughed. Maybe Gregor was all right. Maybe Gregor would be his good friend. "Is there a bar in the hotel?" he asked. "Or somewhere nearby?"

Gregor shook his head. "Somewhere is a dry town."

"Oh," PJ said, cursing the whole place.

29

For the first night of the trip, the kids would have to share a bed, since there was only one room. Luna made Ollie promise he wouldn't pee in it, and he blushed and said that had been only once.

"No shame in pissing the bed," PJ said. "Done it many times."

"Gross, Dad," Sophie said, even though she knew it was true.

"Are you going for a run?" he asked her.

"No," she said. "Day off."

Her dad nodded. "Good to give yourself time to recover," he said, as if he knew something about what happened last night. But he just meant that muscles need time to rest.

"We'll need a bedtime story, Uncle PJ," Luna said. "A good one. Another one about high school. About Michelle Cobb."

PJ didn't have any more stories about Michelle Cobb. He'd gone away to Vietnam, and she'd left town with Gene and he'd never seen her again. The only contact he'd had with Michelle in the past forty-five years was right after Kate died; she and Gene had sent flowers to the funeral home. PJ had been deeply touched, had wondered how they had heard about Kate's death all the way out west. "How about instead I'll tell you a story about when my kids were kids," PJ offered. "I'll tell you a story about my daughter Kate."

"Kate is Sophie's dead sister? Your daughter who drowned?"

"Yup. Kate is the dead sister."

"Great. I want to know about her."

"Me too," Ollie agreed.

Sophie didn't know if her dead sister made for a good bedtime story, but Sophie did like to hear stories about Kate, and she rarely did. Her mom kept her memories of Kate locked away like the boxes of news clippings she kept in Fred's office. Her mother didn't even hang any old pictures of Kate on Fred's walls when she redecorated his house. Sophie would have thought it would be good to remember.

Sophie remembered Kate only in flashes, brief scenes of childhood. There were times Kate paid a lot of attention to her, like when they were on family vacations or home on Saturday mornings, but there were many more times when Kate told Sophie to buzz off, to stop spying on her and her friends. And Sophie had loved spying on Kate and her friends.

"What are you doing up here?" Sophie had asked once, climbing up after Kate and two other girls into the treehouse. Kate was already eighteen, much too old to use the treehouse. "Are you smoking cigarettes?" Sophie asked. She knew cigarettes killed you. She had learned that in school.

"Not cigarettes," Kate had said with a smile. "Come over here and I'll share some."

And Sophie, because she was eleven and worshipped her big sister, stood there as Kate and her friends Lauren and Hannah took turns blowing smoke in her face. Sophie tried not to cough. "If you tell Mom and Dad, I'll kill you," Kate said when they were done. "Now you're a woman."

"Now I'm a woman," Sophie repeated, and then Kate told her to scram. Sophie had gone inside and watched cartoons and it was the best television she'd ever seen. It was a happy memory for Sophie, and it took her a long time to see how fucked up that was. But siblings did fucked-up things to each other, didn't they? It was part of the rules. It was why kids with siblings were lucky. They made you tough against the rest of the world.

"I'll tell you about the first time Kate died," Sophie's dad said to Ollie and Luna now, in the dingy room at the Golden Cherry. "And how she came back to life."

"Is it true?" Ollie asked.

"Shut up and listen," Luna scolded, and so Ollie did.

The first time Kate died, she was twelve years old, about to be a seventh grader. It was late summer, and she was riding her bike down the street to Clear Pond to get an ice cream at the snack shack. Kate loved riding her bike. The bike was pink with a white seat, and Kate was wearing a red helmet over her blond hair; Ivy always insisted on a helmet. PJ was following Kate, on foot. He had never been the type of man to ride a bike. Sophie wasn't with them, she was only five, and she was at home with Ivy, having a nap.

It might have all been a nice August night, ice cream on the beach with his daughter, but Mrs. DeAngelis was backing out of her driveway without looking, off to pick up her boys from summer football, and she backed right into Kate and her pink bicycle, sending Kate and her bike flying. She was in flight for several seconds before she fell splat on the pavement, three driveways down.

PJ ran to her, his baby, his first baby, limp as a doll on the pavement. He looked around her helmet for blood, but there was none. There was no blood, but he also couldn't find a pulse, but maybe he wasn't checking in the right spot. He felt on her wrist, and then back again on her neck. She was limp in his arms. He looked up into the bright, bright sun, a sun that was hotter than usual, and he begged it to take him instead.

PJ's eyes rolled back in his head, and he collapsed as if hit on the back of the head with a frying pan. He felt his face hit the concrete.

It was his first heart attack. He had asked for it. He had wanted it to happen. He had willed it. The sun watched from above. She had a perfect view, no clouds out that day. The sky was robin's-egg blue.

PJ woke up in the hospital; a defibrillator had brought him back. He immediately started calling for his daughter Kate, who was elsewhere, in the children's wing. "The helmet saved her," the doctors said, but PJ knew it was the deal he'd made, his soul for her soul, with the sun or God or the devil or the universe, *someone* had been listening.

So, miracle of miracles, they both had lived. PJ had saved Kate. But Ivy hadn't treated him like a hero, wouldn't hear anything of the sort. He was the one with Kate when she was hit. Ivy would never have let either child get hit by a car. It had to be someone's fault, and it was PJ's. PJ would have liked to blame Mrs. DeAngelis.

And even though Kate had survived, she still had a long road ahead, the doctors told them. She had suffered a traumatic brain injury, which can cause all sorts of problems, short-term and long-term. A few weeks after the accident, Kate was still having trouble speaking. The accident had caused nerve damage, which caused her to have difficulty controlling the muscles in her mouth and tongue. She had trouble making words, and she stuttered when she spoke.

That's when Kate started to see the speech pathologist, Miss Kristen. And Miss Kristen was a genius. One session, a few months in, Miss Kristen came up with a clever plan to strengthen Kate's speech muscles: Kate would suck on lollipops. Dozens a day. It was just crazy enough to work.

And it did! Slowly, the words came back. Kate still stuttered, but she was making improvements. Ivy said they would deal with the cavities later.

Everything was looking up, until one day at the end of winter, PJ came home from a long day delivering mail. He wanted to put his feet up and have a cold one, but Ivy was blocking the TV. "Kate is being bullied at school," she said. "You need to do something about it."

"What is she being bullied for?"

"The lollipops. They are making fun of the lollipops."

"She's making great progress! She was hit by a car!"

Ivy scowled. "That girl Winnie Gleason is a hyena."

PJ shrugged. "What can we do about it? Kids are cruel; they always have been."

"I don't know what you'll do," Ivy said, arms crossed. "But I'm sure you'll figure something out."

PJ would forever be punished by his wife for letting Kate ride her bike down the street, even though she'd always been allowed to ride her bike down the street. He said he would need a day to think about it. "Let me walk it out," he said to Ivy, which he often said when there was a big problem. He would spend the day delivering mail, walking, and ruminating on the problem. So that's what he did. And when he came home that night, he had it all figured out. Excited, he told Ivy: "We just need kids to think differently about lollipops."

"I think children like lollipops fine!" Ivy said, mad again. "It's candy!"

"But Kate is the only one who is allowed to have candy in class. She's different. Kids hate different. They see it as unfair, or weird."

"It's for medical reasons!"

"I'll take care of it," PJ said. "Don't you worry. But it will take me a few days. Give me a few days."

"Fine. You handle it," Ivy said.

"I'll need to get permission from the teachers," PJ said, tapping his chin and walking away.

On a Friday, Kate and Sophie woke up and went down for breakfast, same as usual. But when they went outside to walk Kate to the bus stop, everything looked entirely new, and spectacular. It was the first day of spring, and the trees were dripping in what looked like small pieces of colorful stained glass. There were lollipops, wrapped in plastic, growing from every single tree outside. Orange ones, yellow ones, green ones, red ones, purple. The sun glinting off the lollipops. No one in Pondville had ever seen anything like it.

And at school that day, all the kids had lollipops in their mouths because they'd picked them off the trees. PJ had gotten permission from the teachers to let all the kids have lollipops. He had also paid the janitor fifty bucks to write *Suck it, Winnie,* on Winnie Gleason's locker, and pretend it was the handiwork of another kid.

Kate ran into the house that day after school and gave PJ the longest hug he'd ever had in his life. Ivy had timed it.

"It repaired my marriage, for a little while," PJ said, after the story. "Not forever, of course. You know Ivy left me for Fred."

Ollie and Luna nodded. "So, how'd you do it, Uncle PJ?" Luna asked. "How'd you get all the lollipops in the trees?"

PJ smiled, remembering. Another life. "The best thing about being a mailman is you get to know everyone. I knew the candy-store owner, and she made a call to her supplier, and I knew the bread baker, and he made a call to the company that makes the twist-ties they put on bread bags, and then I had all the men in town twist-tying lollipops to tree branches overnight. It all came down to the good friends I had in Pondville. They helped me out."

"And it wasn't on *every single tree* in town," Sophie said. "Just one tree outside every middle schooler's house."

"Sophie," PJ grumbled, annoyed. "Don't spoil the story."

"Sorry."

"Uncle PJ?" Ollie asked, sounding very sleepy.

"Yes, buddy?"

"When we get home, will you make us a lollipop tree too?"

"Sure I will. Of course I will."

"I'm not going back to Pondville," Luna said.

"*We know,*" Ollie said. "Because you say it all the time. You don't have to keep saying it."

"Now, now, let's be kind to each other tonight," PJ said. "It's been a long day."

Indeed, it had, Sophie thought, but she'd been glad to hear the story, even if her dad had exaggerated the number of lollipop trees—it was a happy story. Good for bedtime. Made everyone feel cozy and safe. Well, it was happy if you stopped the story early enough, didn't stick around to hear the very end. It was an ugly-duckling fairy tale: Kate had learned to talk again, recovered miraculously from her brain injury, and she grew up to be beautiful, so beautiful they made her prom queen on the night she died.

30

PJ found it was awfully hard to sleep in the sleeping bag, his legs so constricted, so eventually, he got up and picked up Sophie's cell phone off her bedside table. Sophie was asleep, and so were the kids, but he knew this is what other people did when they couldn't sleep: they looked at their phones. The amazing miniature computer that was ruining everyone's brain. He opened the internet search bar and typed in: *Pictures of Beautiful Women Ages 50 and Up,* but no, that didn't feel right. Didn't feel right to ogle women, not in the same room as Sophie and the kids. And not with Michelle Cobb right on the horizon.

But it was harder to feel excited about Michelle Cobb and their future at the moment. He felt so heavy after telling that story to the kids about the first time Kate died, and maybe that was the real reason he couldn't sleep. Maybe it had nothing to do with the sleeping bag, maybe it was about dredging up the old memory of that long hug Kate had given him. He had wanted the kids to see he was a hero, but really, that story just made him hate himself more that he hadn't been able to save Kate twice.

PJ's fingers hovered over the little phone keyboard: *Prolonged grief after losing a child*, he finally typed. The search returned a list of suicide hotlines, the top one the same number that Sophie's therapist had included in her out-of-office. But PJ didn't know about Sophie's therapist, the one Fred was paying for. He didn't know Sophie was taking money from Fred. It would have hurt him, that Sophie needed money and didn't ask her own father, a lottery winner.

Talk to someone, the Google search suggested.

"I'd like to," he agreed.

I miss her—said the hat on his head.

"Shut up," PJ told the hat. He didn't want to talk to the hat. He wanted to talk to a person, and he wanted to talk about Kate, and how much he missed her, and how he knew there was no way to speak about grief in anyone's normal day.

He took Sophie's phone out into the hallway. Ivy was the only person who would understand. He dialed her number. It went direct to the recording that said the voicemail box was full. So, he called Fred. No room left in his voicemail box either. He opened Sophie's text messages. The autocorrect function kept changing what he wanted to say, but finally he got it right: *Ivy*, he wrote. *Can we talk about Kate? It's fifteen years coming up, and I hope you are enjoying Alaska, but I am having a hard time. This is PJ, by the way.*

PJ thought about adding that he was on a road trip with Sophie and his great-niece and great-nephew, but that would take too much explaining, since Ivy had never heard about the kids. She would ask too many questions; Ivy always did. She would ask what the hell PJ was thinking, and PJ didn't want to talk about that.

PJ watched as three dots appeared on the cell phone screen. *Ivy was typing! Look at that!* He wasn't all alone in the world. She hadn't abandoned him. If he still needed her, really needed her, to talk about their daughter, she would always be there for him. Even if she was in Alaska, getting engaged to another man.

Paul, the text read, which meant it was not from Ivy at all, but it was Fred on the other end of the line, typing from her phone. *Paul,* he had written. *We are in Alaska. We need to focus on being in Alaska. We have to focus on what is happening right now. We love and miss you and will call when we can.* And then he sent a picture of a puffin, one he'd presumably seen somewhere on the Alaskan coast.

"I don't care about your goddamn seabird," PJ said, grumbling, although of course normally he would have been thrilled by the puffin photo, how cute they were, how they look like penguins dressed up as clowns. But right now, he didn't care to see it. He went back in the hotel room, and he put the phone on the bedside table so Sophie wouldn't know he had touched it. Then he shook Sophie awake by the shoulder.

"Wha—?" she asked, sitting up. "What's wrong? Who's hurt?"

"*Shhhhhh.* Don't wake the kids. But I need to talk to you. I don't think your mother should marry Fred. He was very rude to me just now."

"Oh my God. Dad. She's basically already married to Fred. And they asked us to leave them alone." Sophie lay back down and put a pillow over her head.

"I just wanted to talk to my ex-wife for a few minutes. I think I should be allowed to do that. I think someone should be there for me."

Sophie groaned from underneath the pillow. She didn't want to hear it.

PJ's heart fell. Sophie had rejected him too.

PJ had nothing. He had the lottery money, but that didn't count for anything. Would they put that on his tombstone? PJ HALLIDAY, LOTTERY WINNER. He wanted it to say BELOVED HUSBAND AND FATHER instead, but it wouldn't. He had been a failure of a husband, and a failure of a father, and now he was expected to do it again? Care for Ollie and Luna? He couldn't care for them. He couldn't even care for himself. He couldn't even care for his lottery money. It was all gone. He was alone with his sadness and failure and grief. PJ couldn't take it.

There was only one thing to do now. There was only one thing anyone would do in this situation. PJ needed to get good and spectacularly drunk.

But where to get alcohol in a dry town? At this hour?

PJ thought maybe the honeymooners next door might still be awake, and they might have some hooch they'd be willing to share in this prison. He leaned his ear against the wall, but he heard only silence. PJ went to the other wall to listen if anyone was over there, and he startled the cat on the bed. The cat jumped off the bed, darted across the room, and hopped up onto the radiator. Pancakes pawed at the closed window. *Fresh air!* he said. *I demand it!*

"It is a little stuffy in here," PJ agreed, so he walked over and opened the window.

Pancakes pawed at the other window too. PJ opened that one as well, and the night air felt fresh and cool, but then the cat took a dive, leapt straight out the window and landed in the parking lot below, went chasing some invisible mouse or bird. "Shit," PJ said, watching the cat dart off into the night. "Come back here!" he growled, trying not to wake the kids. He shook the bag of fish-shaped treats.

But the cat didn't come back. The cat wasn't a golden retriever. "Dammit all to hell," PJ said. He would have to spend the rest of his night looking for the cat. PJ would have to go find the cat before a coyote ate him. He didn't know if there were coyotes in Tennessee, but there probably were. Or stray dogs, roaming the streets, or maybe the cat would simply wander off and get lost. They were in the middle of nowhere. Nothing good ever happens in a dry town. Yes, it wasn't safe to leave the cat outside overnight. Something bad could happen, and PJ couldn't live with himself if it did.

But first, PJ would stop by the front desk and ring the bell. He thought it was likely his friend Gregor had some liquor hidden in the back office, that little room with the cot in it. Yes, first, he would talk to Gregor about any liquor he might have lying around.

And then he would go outside and search for that goddamn cat.

DAY FOUR
FRIDAY

31

The children were standing above her, breathing on her. "Jesus Christ," Sophie said. "What now?"

"It's nine A.M.," Ollie said. They had never been allowed to wake up their parents before nine on weekends or vacations. It was Friday, so not a weekend, but it was kind of a vacation.

"And Uncle PJ's gone," Luna added.

"What?"

"Flew the coop," Luna said. "Left us high and dry. Will you still take us to Texas?"

Sophie looked over at the sleeping bag on the floor. An empty nylon carcass. Sophie wanted so badly to call her mom at that moment, tell her what her dad had done this time. Maybe she would call her mom later. Just once. Not tell her the whole story, only part of it. But Fred had asked her not to call. He wanted Ivy to relax. Her dad was right; Fred could be a real dick. "Let's go ask the front desk," she told the kids. "Maybe they've seen him." She saw the car keys still on the bedside table. "He can't have gone far."

The kids grabbed their suitcases, so Sophie grabbed hers and her dad's suitcase too. They would check out and then go find him. At the front desk, Sophie rang the bell, but the clerk didn't come to answer it. She could see his boots poking out from the edge of his cot in his office. She rang once more, but the man still didn't stir.

"We found him!" the kids called from outside.

Sophie ran out the front doors, carrying all the bags like a mule. Her father was in the front seat of the Volvo, reclined, clutching the cat to his chest. The cat was wearing his harness and leash. There was a bottle of Colt 45 on the passenger seat.

"Is he dead?" Luna asked.

"Better be," Sophie said, feeling anger rising. So that was why the desk clerk didn't get up when she rang the bell. He was probably passed out too; he and her father must have been up all night drinking. Her dad could make drinking buddies wherever he went. Sophie opened the car door and he sputtered to life. "What are you doing out here?"

"Oh, Sophie, what a night," he said, rubbing his face. "The damn cat jumped out the window and I spent all night looking for him, but look, I got him! Safe and sound. Is it time for breakfast?"

"You smell like beer," Ollie said.

"Yuck," Luna agreed.

"It's malt liquor, actually. All Gregor had in his office. Old, warm malt liquor. Terrible stuff."

"Do you have a single ounce of shame?" Sophie asked.

"Not remaining. But it was one night, Sophie. I'm back on the wagon this morning."

"That's not how it works, Dad. It's not like, a free trolley around town. You don't hop on, hop off."

PJ ignored his daughter. He knew he could stop drinking, because he had done it before now, for over a month. Long enough to get the thirty-day gold medallion from AA, if he wanted one. He knew he could do it again. Now that he had done it once. "You don't understand," PJ said. "Fred was very hurtful. And you didn't want to hear it either. I wanted to talk to your mother about Kate, and how the anniversary of her death is coming up, and she didn't want to talk to me. What else was I supposed to do?"

"Not drink malt liquor, for starters," she said. "Dad. Listen. You can't keep fucking doing this."

"Can't keep doing what? Can't keep being sad about my dead daughter?"

"Yes, Dad, you have to stop being sad about Kate if that's what it takes. You have to stop being a fucking burden to everyone."

"You don't think everyone sees the black clothing? I don't say anything about you being sad. I don't criticize."

Sophie's eyes narrowed. "I might be sad, but I am a good daughter to both you and Mom. And you've made it impossible for me to have a normal life. I feel like I'm buried under a collapsed building, and I'll never climb out from under the rubble." Sophie's eyes teared up. *Don't fucking cry right now,* she told herself.

"I'm sorry you feel that way," he said. "I'm doing my best. Your mother left and that's very hard for me. I've never been without her."

Sophie shook her head. This was no one's best, waking up in a Volvo with a bottle of malt liquor and a cat. She looked at the kids. Ollie and Luna were sitting in the dirt in the parking lot, drawing patterns with their fingers. "If you actually want to do your best, you need to focus on Ollie and Luna. You promised you'd help these kids, so you have to help them. You can't go out drinking if you are taking care of kids. Something really bad could happen."

PJ remembered all the times Ivy had said this to him. That they had to keep the focus on Sophie. That he had to stop drinking so much just because he missed Kate. "You're right," he said. "I know you're right. I need to focus on the kids. On Ollie and Luna."

Sophie wiped her eyes. "Yes," she said. "I *am* right."

PJ knew it was what Ivy would have told him to do, if Ivy had come to the phone. He knew what Ivy would say, even if Ivy didn't get on the phone to say it. "I'll stay focused on helping out the kids. I won't focus too much on the past."

"Good."

"So, speaking of the present, did Gregor make breakfast? We'll all need some breakfast."

"No. We'll get something on the road."

"Really? No breakfast?"

"No, Dad. I didn't see any breakfast in the lobby. Hey, kids, let's get in the car. Time to go."

The Golden Cherry wasn't such a nice hotel after all. PJ should probably learn to lower his expectations now that he wasn't a millionaire, and maybe the days of complimentary hotel breakfasts were over. *What did they call a man with $20,000 in his bank account?* It was like a bad joke. He got in the car, in the passenger seat, moving the malt liquor bottle, but then he remembered: he should say goodbye to his friend Gregor. They'd had such a nice chat last night about how much Gregor hated his mother. PJ should make a gentle recommendation that the Golden Cherry should serve breakfast in the morning; it might make the online reviews go up. People are more charitable on a full stomach. Gregor had complained about the reviews people left on Tripadvisor. That it was dirty; that things were broken. Right now, it was the pool heater that was broken, but that wasn't Gregor's fault. *Sometimes things broke!* Gregor wanted to know if any of those assholes behind their computer could do a better job running a hotel. He'd like to see them try.

"I'll be right back," PJ told Sophie and the kids. "Just saying goodbye to my friend Gregor."

Sophie groaned, but her dad was already headed toward the entrance of the Golden Cherry Inn. "Be quick about it!" she yelled out the window.

"Let's leave without him," Luna said, and Sophie was tempted. Sophie was pissed, so pissed at her dad that morning, but also it was somehow reassuring that he was still drinking. That he couldn't change. He would die long before he could change, so Sophie shouldn't bother hoping for him to be any different than he was. She was off the hook. She didn't need to hope anymore, because it was hopeless.

Sophie had prepared herself for her father's death so many times, had been prepared to be the one to find him; there were countless times she'd had to walk into the house on Clear Pond Road expecting to find him dead. Her mother had started asking her dad over for breakfast so they would have proof that he was alive every day. If her dad didn't show up for breakfast, Fred was sent down the road to get him. If Fred was at work, or off bird-watching on weekends, her mom called Sophie to drive up and check on him, because her mom refused to go inside her old house.

Sophie would usually find her dad lying in his chair in the middle of his piles of crap. If he wasn't there, she'd find him on the bench by the cranberry bogs. Or sometimes she'd find him lying by the bonfire pit in the woods. She always expected to find him dead, choked on his own vomit, or bled from an ulcer, or from the fourth and final heart attack. And he would deserve it. It would be his own fault. That is what she'd thought would happen when the kids woke her up that morning and said he'd flown the coop.

But now Sophie's dad came out of the Golden Cherry Inn & Suites, still alive. "We've got a problem," he said.

"What?" Sophie asked.

"Gregor's dead."

32

They sat quietly in the Bird Barn in the parking lot of the Golden Cherry until two cop cars and an ambulance arrived. Two policemen and three of the EMTs rushed into the hotel together. They did not stop to say anything to the people in the red Volvo sitting out in front of the inn who had called to report the death a few minutes before.

"Okay they're here, let's go," Luna said.

Ollie poked his sister. "Luna, Uncle PJ's friend *died*. Be nice for once."

"I *am* nice."

"Well, he's not really a friend. An acquaintance," PJ said.

"Was he old?" Ollie asked.

"No," PJ said. "Extremely young."

"Um, he was about forty-five," Sophie said. She hadn't looked at the desk clerk closely, but that was a safe enough guess.

"Pretty old," Ollie said, feeling better.

"Was he sick or was it a do-it-yourself thing?" Luna asked.

"Jesus, Luna," Sophie said. "We don't know."

In the backseat, Pancakes was walking back and forth between the kids, purring. "Look at the cat!" PJ said. "He's trying to comfort the kids! How sweet!"

"Ew," Ollie said. "He's drooling on me."

"Bite him, Pancakes," Luna said, but Pancakes refused.

Over at the front entrance to the Golden Cherry, all the cops and the EMTs came out together. They didn't come out with a body on a stretcher under a white sheet. They were empty-handed. There was a cop walking over to their car.

"Something's up," PJ said.

"Bet they think you killed him," Luna said. "In a drunken rage." Frank Meeklin used to go into rages and say he didn't remember it in the morning. Luna hadn't forgotten about that. What the man who claimed to be her father had done.

"I'll be your alibi," offered Ollie.

"Thanks, bud," PJ said.

Sophie put her forehead against the wheel. If her dad got arrested for suspected murder, it would be the icing on the cake. The cop was tapping on the passenger-side window. PJ rolled it down. Luna put her window down too, so she could hear the cop better. She wanted to know what the deal was, so they could get back on the road toward Mark Stackpole.

"What seems to be the problem, Officer?" PJ asked, the way they teach you to say in the movies. The police officer was a short, round man. His gold name tag said Officer Mario Pienta.

"Did y'all stay here last night?" Officer Mario Pienta asked. "In this hotel?"

"Yes," PJ confirmed.

"Yes," Sophie said. "We're the ones who called 911 when we found the poor man dead."

"I see," Officer Mario Pienta said. "And you've got children with you. And y'all are feeling all right? No lightheadedness?"

"No. Why?"

Officer Mario Pienta looked in the back, and the children nodded. They felt fine. "Well, you folks are very lucky. There was some kind of carbon monoxide leak last night in the hotel."

"A gas leak?"

"Yes, ma'am. The fire department and the gas company are on their way. I think we're looking at a mass casualty event. We opened a few guest rooms, and looks like everyone's dead."

"What the fuck," Sophie said. This had not been on her bingo card of the things that could go wrong if she went on a road trip with her father.

"It was the goddamn swimming pool," PJ said. "The heater was broken."

"Ah," Officer Mario Pienta said. "Well, that's very useful information." *Gas leak, pool heater,* he wrote down on his notepad. Next, the cop took PJ's name down, and his phone number, and the car license plate. He said he didn't really need a statement, other than that he was glad they survived. "We'll be in touch if we need anything else, but you folks need to get out of here in case there's an explosion."

"An explosion?" Ollie asked. "Everyone inside is dead and now the building is going to explode?" He was sad and also kind of excited.

"Told you idiots that we should have left earlier," Luna said. "But no one ever listens to me."

"These are unusual circumstances, Luna," Sophie snapped. "We do our best to listen to you. But right now, we needed to do the right thing and report what happened."

But then the fire truck arrived. If the building was about to explode, they should go. They should save themselves. So, Sophie pulled out of the parking lot. They drove a long way in silence. Tears welled in Sophie's eyes. It was sad, those people who had died. She hadn't known any of them, hadn't even talked to the front desk clerk or any of the guests, but of course it was terribly sad.

"Those poor honeymooners," PJ said. "So full of hope."

"But how did we survive?" Ollie asked. "Why us and not everyone else?"

"Well, it was a freak accident," Sophie said, pulling herself together for the kids. She wished she believed in God so she could tell the kids that God had saved them, that God had some bigger plan for them all and that's why they were spared, but the conversation about God and murderers yesterday had made her so uncomfortable, she didn't want to get into it again. And Sophie didn't believe in God, not really. She didn't know what she believed in, but it wasn't a good and benevolent God. Too much bad shit had happened in Sophie's life to believe in that. "And with a freak accident—sometimes, people get lucky. We were lucky. Maybe . . . maybe your parents are watching over you." She wished she hadn't said that last part.

"They're earthworms now," Luna said. "I don't think they can help us."

"Oh my God!" PJ said. "The cat!"

"Luna has him," Sophie said. "Don't worry, we didn't forget the cat."

"No, no, the cat saved us. Pancakes made me open the windows. In the hotel. Both windows. He asked for fresh air. Before he jumped out the window, he made me open both windows. Both of them! Fresh air! He saved the whole family."

Luna gasped. She squeezed the cat, tightly, like you would hug a teddy bear, and Pancakes bit her; he didn't like to be squeezed that tight. Luna released him. "Thank you," she said. "Thank you."

"You saved us, Uncle PJ?" Ollie asked.

"That cat did."

"You opened the window, Dad. You listened to the cat."

"I did." He nodded. "Me and the cat. I did a good thing," he said. He marveled. "There is a reason I am still alive. I am still alive so I can protect you kids."

"Guess so," Sophie agreed.

PJ had told Sophie he didn't have an ounce of shame left, when, in fact, he had a ton of shame. He knew he was a drunk loser, and he knew he'd done the wrong thing, asking Gregor if he had any alcohol lying around, but this time, this time, he had saved the kids. He had saved his daughter. He had drunk a warm bottle of Colt 45, but first, he had saved the kids.

"Wow, Dad," Sophie said. "Thank you."

It sure felt good to hear his daughter say that. And then PJ realized something: his license suspension was up today. After eight long years, it was over. He could be a different man.

33

No one could agree on what music to listen to, somber or upbeat, glad they had survived but also so sorry other people had died, so finally Sophie put the GRE audiobook back on. It was soothing, listening to the man drone on and on about the words Sophie was supposed to know if she ever actually took the test.

They drove for an hour before the kids started complaining about their hunger, so Sophie stopped at a Cracker Barrel, which she was sure the kids would like, even Ollie, who still campaigned for McDonald's at every meal. But her dad said he didn't want anything to eat; he wanted some time to himself in the car. It wasn't like him to miss out on a meal, especially after skipping breakfast, but it had not been an ordinary morning. Sophie asked him for his credit card, and he forked the Visa over, but he also asked if he could use her phone.

"What for?" she asked.

"Entertainment," he said. There were some things he wanted to google. He wanted to see what they were saying about the Golden

Cherry, if anything was online yet, if the survivors had been mentioned on the news. Sophie reluctantly gave her phone to him, and the car keys so he could put the air on so it wouldn't get too hot for the cat, and they left him and Pancakes alone in the car.

Once Sophie and the kids were gone, PJ got out of the passenger seat and climbed into the driver's seat of the Bird Barn. The key was in the ignition. His hands were on the wheel. He wanted to take the car for a little spin. He had saved them all from a gas leak; he deserved to drive. Just around the block. It wasn't like it was his first time driving in eight years, he'd already taken Fred's Volvo to the grocery store and the IKEA and the Walmart, but today it would be different. Today he would be a licensed driver again. Practically. He still had to go to the DMV. He wondered if they would make him take a driving test again. The point was, PJ was a free man.

The cat put his paw on PJ's hand.

"You don't think I should do it?"

Don't do it, thought the cat.

"You don't trust me?"

I don't trust you, the cat agreed.

Sophie's phone started ringing from where it sat in the cup holder.

Who's calling? asked the cat.

"Well, it's Sophie's phone," PJ said, "so I shouldn't answer it." But across the screen, it said clearly: MASS DEPT OF CHILDREN. "Shit," PJ said when he saw that. "What do they want?"

The phone kept ringing, and then it went to voicemail. PJ hadn't answered it, but they had left a voicemail. After a minute of hesitation, PJ played the message. It was Belinda Bell. Belinda told Sophie that she was listed as Paul Halliday's emergency contact, and she said she was sure Paul had told her about the two children who were under his care. She was concerned, because she had heard from the teacher at White Rock Elementary that the kids weren't in school, and she had gone by the house and Paul Halliday and the kids weren't there—Belinda was wondering if Sophie had heard from him.

"Shit," PJ said again. PJ wanted Belinda Bell and the Massachusetts Department of Children and Families to go the hell away. The children were happy now. They had iPads. They were safe.

PJ pressed the red button and deleted the voicemail off Sophie's phone. That would take care of it. Surely Belinda Bell wouldn't call again. Surely she would get busy with other things.

PJ changed his mind and decided he wouldn't drive the car. Not yet. Not if the social workers were watching him.

Hallelujah, thought the cat.

When Sophie and the kids came out of the Cracker Barrel, PJ was back in the passenger seat where he belonged.

"Hey, Uncle PJ," Luna said when she got in the car. "We got you something." She was holding a little Styrofoam box and passed it up.

"The kids noticed it on the menu," Sophie said. "It's a big thank-you for saving our lives."

"Didn't I pay for the meal?"

"Just open it, Dad."

"I already had one. They're really good," Ollie said.

PJ opened the container. It was a takeaway box of Cracker Barrel miniature beignets, sprinkled with white powdered sugar. "French donuts," he said, and he burst into tears. "Wow. How thoughtful. I don't think anyone has ever done anything this nice for me. Ever."

Ollie and Luna grinned, and Sophie rolled her eyes, but she let him have it. This sweet moment with the kids.

34

As they approached Little Rock, Sophie decided she needed another coffee; the coffee at Cracker Barrel had been terribly weak. They stopped at a place called She's Got Big Mugs, and PJ bought himself a coffee mug made of two ceramic breasts wearing a bikini; the coffee was poured into the neck where the head should go. Ollie thought it was the funniest thing he'd seen in his life, and he begged to drink a cup of coffee out of it, but Uncle PJ told Ollie he should really stop drinking coffee, it would stunt his growth, and try switching to soda instead.

Sophie watched Ollie laughing at the boobs mug—the boy laughing so easily and freely after their weird, sad morning—it's one reason why adults don't think children are affected as seriously by death, because they can go back to laughing and playing so quickly. *Resilient*, that's what people say about kids. But playing and laughing can be a child's way of processing, it doesn't mean they've recovered. Blanche had told Sophie all about this in therapy, talking about Sophie's childhood. Sophie worried about these kids, what they had just gone through so soon after losing their parents. Sophie's chest ached, but she didn't really know how to make this situation better for them. She'd never even figured out how to make things better for herself.

Leaving the coffee shop, Sophie noticed the Purse and Handbag Museum across the street. Despite wearing all black all the time, Sophie liked to look at beautiful clothes, and thought maybe a museum would be soothing. Art gave life meaning, didn't it? It was a small museum, and admission was only ten bucks. "Let's go in," Sophie said.

"No," Luna said.

"Just for twenty minutes."

Luna refused. "I'll wait in the gift shop."

"Fine. Don't steal anything."

"Here's my credit card," PJ said to the girl. "Buy anything you want."

"Jesus, Dad."

"It's my money."

Sophie shook her head, before she walked off to look at the displays of purses. She just wanted a little time alone to look at beautiful things, and to pretend everything was fine.

Away from his daughter, PJ walked around the purse museum, holding the cat in his arms. The woman at the counter said it was fine to bring in the cat, so long as he was leashed. PJ was prepared to be bored in the museum, but the purses were divided up by decade, and his heart seized when he saw the display of purses from the 1950s. He could picture his mother carrying one. The purple velvet one with a silver clasp. PJ's mother had been dead ten years now, and she could still pop up every now and then in his mind, totally alive. He thought about how proud she would be of him, for traveling the country just like she had. For finally seeing there was more to the world than Pondville. All the fantastic stories his mom used to tell him about her travels at bedtime, cuddled together with their dog, Arthur, a Yorkie-terrier mix, and now he had stories of his own. He felt overwhelming gratitude for these kids, the kids who had gotten him out of the house and onto the road.

"It's really wonderful for me to do this with you all," PJ told the kids and the cat once they were back in the car. "I'm sixty-three and I've never traveled. Never been anywhere."

"What about Vietnam?" Luna asked, as she held Pancakes in her arms. "You've been to Vietnam. And you said you've already been to Texas before." They would be in Texas soon, crossing the border from Arkansas. Luna couldn't wait.

"Yup, Bastrop. But I was stuck at the training camp, didn't travel around at all. Nothing special about Camp Swift."

"What about Vietnam?"

"Well, I was only there for three weeks before I was shot."

"You were shot? Did it hurt?"

"Like a motherfucker."

"Dad!" Sophie scolded, even though she was the one who said the f-word the most.

"Who shot you? The enemy?" Ollie asked. "Did you shoot him back?"

"Nope. I looked him in the eye, and I told him I was sorry."

"Oh." Ollie was disappointed. "Right, because you were a pacifist."

"Well, that. And because the man who shot me was my brother."

"What?" Luna asked. "Really?"

"Our grandpa?" Ollie asked.

"Are you sure about this story, Dad?" Sophie asked. Sophie didn't know this story, or not the version he was about to tell. In the versions of the story she'd heard, it was her dad's mentally ill friend who shot him, not her dad's brother, because Sophie hadn't known about her dad's brother until a few days ago. Chip Duggins, the crazy old man who owned the bowling alley before it closed. Her uncle. The man who was the grandfather of these kids. "Are you kids sure you want to hear this?"

"I do," Luna said. Her eyes were bright like a hamster's. "I definitely do. I want to know why Grandpa shot Uncle PJ."

"I do if Luna does," Ollie agreed. "And don't worry, Sophie. We already knew he was crazy. We lived with him."

Sophie shrugged. She had tried.

PJ nodded. He knew these kids liked stories, real stories, good ones. "Well, one day, my brother, Chip, older than me by eleven years, and a commander in the army, he found me in the canteen and told me to run. He shot me twice in the ass when I did. When I was on the ground, he stood over me, and I think was going to kill me, but I said I was sorry, and I loved him, and I was sorry we weren't real brothers. Chip didn't know what to do with that, because no man had ever told him he loved him before."

"So, what did he do?"

"He walked away."

"Why did he shoot you?"

"Chip hated me all his life, blamed me for the crap deal he got, blamed me that our mother raised me when she'd left him. I always thought my mother never should have come back to Pondville after she'd left the first time, that she should have raised me someplace else, but she'd wanted to try to be in Chip's life. But Chip was too angry by then, mad at her for leaving. And that anger would only grow with age, morph into putrid hatred. So, when Chip and I both ended up in Vietnam at the same time, in the same camp, and he saw the chance to shoot me, he took it."

"Did they put him in jail?"

"Nah. They dishonorably discharged him, though. He went to a mental hospital, then he went home to live with my mother."

Ollie leaned forward in his seat, straining against the seatbelt. "With your mother? But he hated her! He shot you!"

"She was trying to help him out; his father was dead, he had nowhere to live, and I think she felt that because he hadn't killed me, it was all right. She was trying to make it up to him, for leaving him behind when she did. But then he burnt down her house."

Luna remembered the story. Her grandpa had told it to her. How he'd burnt down a house with his mother inside. How he didn't regret it. How he wasn't sorry. He had told Luna that story several times, after school. And then he would put on a war movie, one with explosions. He loved war movies with explosions.

"My mother escaped with third-degree burns all over her body. She was badly disfigured, and in pain for the rest of her life."

"That's who caused the fire?" Sophie asked. She'd always heard it was her grandmother's tenant, someone renting a room. She had been lied to all her life about why her grandma was a burn victim.

"Yup," PJ confirmed.

"I wish you'd shot him back," Luna said. "In the canteen."

"Yeah, kiddo. Sometimes I wish that too."

"And you came back to Pondville after Vietnam too?" Ollie asked. "And you never left?"

"Moved in with a buddy of mine. And then I met Ivy, and we got married, and she got a job, and I got one too. And I vowed never to leave my family like my mom had left hers. I understand why my mom did what she did, but I vowed I would never get a divorce. I would never leave my kids."

"But you *did* get a divorce," Ollie said.

"Not my choice."

Sophie was annoyed. "Dad, you really can't act like it's Mom's fault you got a divorce—"

"I didn't say I blamed your mother for leaving me. I would have left me too. But I never wanted a divorce. I would have loved her until the end."

"But then you wouldn't have gotten a second chance with Michelle Cobb," Ollie pointed out.

"You're right," PJ said. "I wouldn't have gotten a second chance with Michelle Cobb."

"And Michelle Cobb is the best thing that will ever happen to you."

"Yes, that's right, Ollie, that's right."

"Give me a fucking break," Sophie muttered.

"What?"

Sophie exploded. "*Mom* is the best thing that ever happened to you. She divorced you because she had to, because she needed to take care of me and because you were killing her, but even after that, she stayed your friend even though you're a jackass. She makes your breakfast every day. Does your shopping. Cuts up your fucking newspaper. She takes care of everything."

"Sophie, I know that. Don't you think I know that? But, Sophie, your mother is getting married again. To my best friend. What am I supposed to do now? Sit on my ass and wait to die?"

"Yes."

"Oh." PJ was quiet for a minute. He folded his hands and looked like he was praying.

"I didn't mean that."

He didn't answer her.

"I just meant . . . I just meant I think you should appreciate Mom and all she's done for you. Which means not saying another woman is the best thing that ever happened to you."

"Okay. Fine. I won't say it again."

"But it might be true," Ollie pointed out.

"Shut up, Ollie," Sophie said, and instantly regretted it. "I'm sorry, Ollie," she said. "That was wrong. I'm mad at him, not at you."

"It's okay," Ollie mumbled. "I don't care."

"She didn't mean it, kiddo," PJ said. "You talk all you want. Children should be seen *and* heard, that's what the social worker said."

"I said it's fine," Ollie said. "Leave me alone." The cat walked across the backseat and tried to climb in Ollie's lap, but Ollie pushed Pancakes away.

They drove in silence for a while. Sophie felt terrible.

After another few miles, Luna leaned forward. "Hey, Sophie?"

"Yeah?" Sophie waited for Luna to yell at her for being mean to her little brother. She waited for Luna to take out her scissors.

But Luna didn't say anything about Sophie telling Ollie to shut up. Luna told Ollie to shut up all the time. "I got you a present," she said instead. "Uncle PJ got French donuts, so I thought you needed something too."

Sophie sighed. "What did you steal?"

"I didn't steal it, I bought it." Luna handed something forward. Sophie kept one hand on the wheel and took what Luna was handing her in the other. She glanced down, and oh, how it glittered! It was a purse; one she'd admired in the museum. They sold a replica of it in the gift shop. It was a rhinestone-encrusted clutch in the shape of a pineapple. The strap was a delicate gold chain.

Sophie never in a million years would have bought this purse for herself, but now that she had it, it was perfect. It really was. "I love it, Luna," she said. "I really, really love it. Thank you."

"The lady in the store said that pineapples are a symbol for home," Luna explained. "I wanted to thank you for taking me home. Home to my real dad, where I am finally going to be happy, because of you."

Oh no, Sophie thought. The girl was going to get her heart broken. This man they are going to meet in Texas would break her heart. Sophie didn't know exactly how he'd do it, but she knew he would.

"You bought it with the credit card?" PJ asked. "How much was it?"

"Two thousand dollars," Luna said proudly. "The shop lady said the crystals are real."

"Jesus Christ," PJ said, and put his face in his hands and laughed, then looked up again. "Well, Sophie-Soo, you can't say I never gave you anything."

"It's a gift from Luna," Sophie snapped. She could see the price tag still on the chain. The girl wasn't lying. It was a $2,000 pineapple purse.

35

It was eight P.M. when they pulled into a tiny town called Purity Springs, Texas, thirty miles outside of Lufkin. They had made it to Texas. In the morning, they would drive the rest of the way to Sugar Land, two hours and forty-two minutes away. They were cutting it close if they were going to get there by ten A.M. the next day, but Sophie couldn't keep driving. Sophie didn't know how truck drivers did it. Then again, truck drivers didn't have kids in the back who needed to stop and pee every hour.

There was only one motel in Purity Springs, called the Boar's Tooth Motel, with rows of red doors that faced out onto the street. On the corner of the building, right under the neon Vacancy sign, there was an office with big glass windows. Ollie and Pancakes waited in the car, Ollie still sulking a bit, and everyone else went to check in. Luna skipped to the front door, so happy they were finally in Texas.

In the office, a woman in her forties with fake nails and fake eyelashes and smooth black hair was watching TV. Luna would have considered it a good omen if the woman were watching *The Tears of the Rich,* Mark Stackpole's soap opera, but it was a crime investigation show. Luna's mom had liked those too. It may have even been where her mom got the idea to use the Visine in the coffee, but Luna wasn't sure.

"Welcome to the Boar's Tooth Motel," the woman said. Her name tag said Destiny. "One room or two?"

PJ asked for one room, two beds, and a cot, if she had one. Destiny said she had a room with two beds and a foldout couch, which would work. It was certainly better than a sleeping bag. Destiny gave him a gold key to the room—a real gold key, not a plastic key card—and PJ loved the look of it. He thought he might keep it for a souvenir when they checked out, and Luna thought the same thing.

Sophie asked if they had a treadmill to run on, but Destiny apologized and said they didn't. Sophie's legs twitched. She had been running several miles a day for years, ever since college when she'd slept with one of her professors and had to run off the shame. Sophie wished she could go for a night run outside, but she was still too spooked from the other night. She vowed she would wake up early the next morning and run outside in the daylight, but she knew that was unlikely to happen. She had never been an early riser.

PJ went back to the car to get Ollie and the bags, while Sophie and Luna went straight to the room. PJ didn't notice when Pancakes slipped out of the car and ran off, he thought Luna already had the cat.

Once PJ brought up the bags to the room, he pulled out the foldout couch and lay down for a minute to try it out, but was snoring a few seconds later, still wearing his clothes and sandals and baseball cap.

"Uncle PJ didn't brush his teeth before bed," Ollie reported. "He's going to get cavities."

"I don't think it matters at his age," Sophie said, putting a blanket over her father. "He'll need dentures soon anyway."

"Yeah," Luna agreed. "He'll start falling apart soon. Piece by piece. One day his ears will fall right off his head."

"Really?" Ollie asked.

"No, dummy."

Ollie scowled.

"Let's handcuff Uncle PJ to the bed, so he doesn't wander off tonight," Luna said. "We'll need to be on the road tomorrow to get to the meet-and-greet."

"With what handcuffs?" Sophie asked. She wasn't opposed to the idea.

"These ones." Luna held them up. Luna had rolled down her window while the cop at the Golden Cherry was taking down Uncle PJ's phone number and information. They had been dangling off his belt. It hadn't been hard.

"Jesus, Luna, you have to stop stealing. Especially from police officers."

"He didn't notice," Luna assured her. Luna fastened one side to Uncle PJ's wrist and the other side of the cuffs to the metal bar of the pullout couch. "There," she said. "Perfect." She put the tiny silver key in the motel drawer next to the Bible, and then she got into bed. "Tell us a story," she begged Sophie. "I can't sleep without a story."

"My dad's the storyteller. Can I read you something instead? A book? *How to Survive in the Woods*?"

"No," Ollie said. "We want to know your secrets."

"Hmm, okay," Sophie said, trying to think which of her secrets were appropriate for kids. And then Sophie remembered she had a good one. "It's about how I lost my job," Sophie said. She hadn't even told this story to her mother. She had told it three times to her therapist, after Blanche kept requesting it. Blanche said she told the story at parties, which Sophie was pretty sure was against the patient-therapist contract, but Sophie was glad someone was thinking of her.

"Sit in the middle of us." Luna beckoned. Sophie crawled in the middle of the bed between the kids, and they both rested their heads on her shoulders. Ollie had forgiven her for telling him to shut up, which was a relief.

"So, you were fired?" Ollie asked.

"Not exactly."

"But you were bad at your job," Luna guessed.

"Nope. I was good at it. *Remarkably capable,* that's what my boss always said about me."

Sophie had worked for nearly four years at the Diamond Greeting Card Company in New Bedford, first as the assistant to the CEO Alan Diamond, a good and kind man who gave Sophie her first job out of college even though she knew nothing about how an office worked and when she only really wanted to stay in the area so she could be near her mom. At first, Sophie liked the job, but the company was struggling. E-mail was really taking over. People were using Facebook for birthday wishes.

And then, things really took a dive last year at the company when their poor, good, kind CEO Alan Diamond suffered a stroke while visiting a children's hospital dressed up like a giant baseball. The Diamond Greeting Card Company was a sponsor of the minor-league team, and the team was at the children's hospital doing charity work, and Alan Diamond had volunteered to be the mascot. After the blood clot hit his brain, Alan fell face forward, and his giant baseball head rolled away, and he was dead before he hit the ground. The children's hospital had brought in therapy dogs for a week straight, although none of the children had been that upset about the death of a giant baseball. He wasn't Mickey Mouse.

But Sophie had been heartbroken. She had loved her boss. Alan thought she was smart and quietly funny and full of potential. He said he'd love to have a daughter-in-law like her one day, although he admitted his own son was a loser so she shouldn't marry him. Instead, Alan had offered to introduce her to one of the minor-league baseball players, even though they're not paid very much at that stage. Sophie was open to it, but Alan was dead now, had been dead over a year. Some of the players had moved on to the major leagues.

After that, Alan's loser son, Wyatt, took over as CEO of the greeting card company, and Sophie became Wyatt's assistant, and that's where the rest of the story begins.

* * *

It was two months ago, in early April, in the dead season in the greeting-card industry—between Valentine's Day and Mother's Day—and Sophie was running late to work. She parked her Honda and ran up the stairs and navigated through the maze of cubicles to get to her desk. She was sharing her desk now, with Patrick, the new assistant, but Patrick was already in the meeting room with the boss. Wyatt Diamond was planning something for the Monday meeting. Something stupid, Sophie knew. Wyatt had been driving the company into the ground, and that day, the company was doing layoffs. It was a bad day to be late, but Sophie had to go fetch her father from the stone bench by the bogs, where he'd spent the night, and bring him home before she headed into work.

"Good morning, you look horrible," Sara had said when Sophie plopped down at her desk. Sara always looked polished in a sweater and black jeans. Sara was Sophie's only friend at work.

Sophie probably always looked horrible to Sara, in her black hoodie pulled over her head like she planned to rob the place. But there wasn't a dress code at the company. Maybe no one else except Sophie had read the handbook, because most of the men came in suits and ties. "Thanks," Sophie said to Sara. "I feel horrible too."

"Oh, buck up, Soph. Something good is coming your way. You'll be better off without this job."

That had made Sophie feel worse. Everyone assumed Sophie would be axed during the layoffs that day, figured that would be why the boss, Wyatt Diamond, had hired a new assistant to replace her two weeks ago. But Sophie knew she wasn't on the layoff list; she was instead being promoted to Sara's position. She knew the noble thing would be to quit instead of taking your friend's job, but Sophie needed the money. Probably not more than Sara did, though. Sara had two kids.

But it was also true that Sara was no longer very good at the job. Sara was the writer of the romantic cards, the Valentine's Day cards, the anniversary cards, the "Just Because I Love You" cards, but ever since she came back from maternity leave after her second kid, the quality of her cards had gone downhill. *Happy anniversary to a day I consistently regret,* read one. *Do the fucking dishes,* read another, although that was a surprisingly strong seller.

Sophie had only written three cards last year—anyone in the company was encouraged to write cards and submit them for approval and printing—and Sophie's cards were the three top performers in the romantic section. *I only have eyes for you,* one read, underneath a cartoon drawing of a jar full of eyeballs. Quirky cards were in. Another one read, simply: *Don't worry, we'll figure it out.* This seemed to Sophie like the most romantic thing anyone could ever say to anyone else, even though Sophie had never been in love herself. She specialized instead in one-night stands, but no one gives out cards for those.

"What's a one-night stand?" Ollie asked, but Luna shushed him. She was into the story now.

At ten A.M., the entire company crammed into the big meeting room. Layoffs would be after lunch. Sophie knew that was the plan. There would be a half-day of team-building work first. Their boss, a former Boy Scout, loved team-building activities.

"I know it's been a tough year," CEO Wyatt Diamond said to the room. Wyatt Diamond was only twenty-four, awfully young to run a company, and he was also trying hard to grow a beard but without much success. Wyatt had never wanted to take over the Diamond Greeting Card Company, but he'd stepped up when his dad died. He was now standing in front of a giant envelope, a cardboard display, a Father's Day promotion from years ago. The outside of the envelope said: *Dear Dad, my hero* in giant loopy handwriting. "I was a Boy Scout, as many of you know," Wyatt Diamond said. He said that Boy Scouts believe in bonding activities during tough times, and today was going to be tough on all of them. "Me especially," he said, and the whole room suppressed a groan.

While Wyatt was talking, Wyatt's new assistant, Patrick, handed out small slips of paper with a strange texture. There were all kinds of specialty paper lying around the greeting-card company, but Sophie didn't know what kind of paper this was. She had not been involved in helping prepare for this bonding activity, because she wasn't Wyatt's assistant anymore. Wyatt and Patrick had done this alone.

"Is this homemade paper?" someone asked.

Mr. Diamond shook his head. "Not homemade. But it is magic paper, I assure you. Now, on this magic paper, I want you to write down what you are most afraid of."

"What we're most afraid of in our office?" someone asked.

"Or generally?" someone else asked.

"What you're most afraid of," Wyatt Diamond repeated.

"Losing our jobs," someone muttered.

Sara wrote hers quickly, and Sophie glanced at it. It said: *Outliving my children*. Sara covered the paper. She knew about Sophie's dead sister. How it had ruined their family.

Sophie's pen hovered over her own paper. *This is it*, she finally wrote. And then, because there was more room on the paper, she wrote it again: *This is it, This is it, This is it, This is it, This is it*. She kept writing it until Patrick came around to collect the papers in a big glass fishbowl. "We won't read them," he promised. Sara threw hers into the fishbowl. Sophie folded hers three times and tossed hers in too. This was her biggest fear, this room that they were in now. That this was all her life would amount to, working this boring job, dating terrible guys, living with roommates she hated. *This is it*, she wrote. *I am afraid this is all I will ever have, and that I will feel sad and empty forever.* That second part she didn't write, but that's what she meant.

"It's been a rough, rough year for all of us," Wyatt said, holding the fishbowl of paper strips of worst fears. "Losing my father was the worst thing to ever happen to me."

"Me too," said someone in the back of the room.

"Appreciate that," Wyatt said. "When he was alive, my dad was my biggest supporter. When I wanted to be a Boy Scout, he signed me up. When I wanted to be a magician, he paid for the magic classes. That's where I learned about this special, magic paper. It's called flash paper, and it's called that by magicians because it burns up in a flash. We're about to burn all your fears, all your negativity, and get rid of it. Get rid of it all."

From his suit pocket, Wyatt pulled out a matchbook. It took him three tries, but he got one lit. He threw the match in the fishbowl and the slips of paper—all those worst fears, all the cheating spouses, the dead children, the unhappy marriages that never ended, dying single and alone, a life wasted at a job they hated, plus the "spiders" and the "nothing" with a question mark—all the fears and the nothingness and all of Sophie's *This is it*s, they burned up in a flash.

A huge flash.

The problem was, Wyatt Diamond had never been a good student, and he had skipped magic class the day when they had covered one very important detail: flash paper is best used in small quantities. Someone with more magic experience than Wyatt Diamond would have seen it coming.

But Wyatt Diamond didn't see it coming, not until it hit him right in his face. All those fears burned up so fast and so hot that the fishbowl coughed up a giant fireball, spat it out of its mouth with such force that the fireball climbed up Wyatt Diamond's tie like a monkey up a rope, and then Wyatt Diamond's patchy beard was on fire and soon his entire head. He fell backward into the giant envelope that was behind him and soon the cardboard display was on fire too.

It was very lucky Wyatt had hired his new assistant, Patrick, when he did. Wyatt Diamond had only hired Patrick because he was an Eagle Scout, which is the pinnacle of Boy Scouting, and Eagle Scouts go beyond learning how to tie knots and build a campfire, they learn how to deal with emergencies. Seeing his boss on fire, Patrick the Eagle Scout took off his suit jacket and he ran right into the flames and smothered and smothered them until the fire on Wyatt's face and body were put out. But the giant cardboard envelope was still ablaze. Someone had grabbed fire extinguishers, but the giant envelope was too flammable. The flames had climbed to the ceiling.

Sophie watched all this, openmouthed. She might have sat there while the whole place burned, except Sara grabbed her and pushed her and made her run.

"Pretty good story," Luna said, and that made Sophie feel proud, that she could tell just as good a bedtime story as her father did, even if it had been terrible to watch someone burn.

"We're afraid of the future too," Ollie said. "I would have put a lot of my scary thoughts into the fishbowl."

Sophie said maybe they could make a fishbowl together, but use regular paper, and Ollie said that sounded good.

"I'm not afraid of the future," Luna said. "Not at all. We're going to meet Mark Stackpole tomorrow. I can't wait."

Dread filled Sophie's throat. The girl's hopes were too high, which meant it probably wouldn't go well. "I think most people are at least a little afraid of the future," Sophie said. "Anything could happen."

"This hotel could blow up like the Golden Cherry," Ollie agreed.

"But it probably won't," Sophie said. "I'm sure it's safe."

"I hope so," Luna said. "I finally have something to live for."

Oh shit, Sophie thought. It is a giant mistake to live for your father, the real one or the man you sometimes pretend is your dad. Sophie had been let down by so many father figures in her life. Her college professor who had kissed her in his office and asked her if she could be discreet about an affair. Alan Diamond for dying when she still needed him to help her figure out her life. Even Fred, who had been giving her a hard time about making her mom worry too much. Weren't parents supposed to worry about their kids?

"That was two stories about fires in one day," Ollie pointed out. "The fire at your job, and the one our grandfather set in Uncle PJ's mom's house."

"Oh," Sophie said. It had been a long day. "You're right."

"I liked both stories," Ollie said, as if it were a competition. "Did you know our grandfather on our dad's side was a firefighter? I did a school report about him."

"No, I didn't know that."

"We never knew our firefighter grandpa," Luna said. "We only knew our mom's dad. The one who shot Uncle PJ and set the fire."

"I see."

"Did you know most fire deaths are caused by smoke inhalation and not the fire itself?" Ollie asked.

Another thing Sophie didn't know.

"I never got to do my presentation about my firefighter grandpa, actually, because it was the day everything bad happened. But it was a really good poster. I used crinkle paper for the flames."

Sophie's heart hurt. On the day both his parents died and he had almost died, too, the boy made a school project he was proud of and didn't get to present it, and he was still sad about it. "Well," Sophie said, "maybe your teacher still has it."

"I hope so."

"When I get back to Pondville, I'll ask her. I'd like to see it."

"That would be really nice. Thanks."

"I'm glad some bad stuff has happened to you, Sophie," Luna said. "It means we're not so weird."

"Oh, Luna. You're not weird at all. Bad stuff happens to people all the time."

"It does?"

"To everyone, at some point."

Luna sighed. "My mom said something like that. That bad stuff happens to almost every girl."

"Oh," Sophie said. "Well, not just girls. Something bad happens to everyone at some point, even when it feels like you're the only one who bad stuff is happening to right now."

"That's good," Ollie said. "It's good to not be alone."

"You want to know a secret bad thing that happened to me?" Luna asked.

"She doesn't," Ollie said. "I'm sure she doesn't."

"If Luna wants to tell me something, of course I would like to know," Sophie said.

"Okay." Luna nodded. "I'll tell you." And Luna told Sophie what her grandfather used to do while they watched war movies after school when Ollie was at soccer. And how afterward, after their mom found out, their grandpa hanged himself with a rope.

"I told you that you didn't want to know," Ollie said.

"Jesus," Sophie muttered, but then she pulled it together. "I'm glad to know. I'm glad Luna trusted me enough to tell me. I'm so sorry it happened but I'm glad to know."

Luna looked at her. She did think Sophie was sorry. Not sorry she had done it, because Sophie hadn't done anything, but Sophie looked like she would change it if she could. That helped. "I think my mom hated me after that," Luna said, and looked down at her fingernails, her cuticles badly chewed.

"Oh my God, Luna, no. I'm sure she didn't and if she did—it wasn't your fault. It sounds like he was a very sick man who needed help. You should have been protected from him."

"That's right," said Ollie. "I should have protected you. I shouldn't have gone to soccer practice."

"No, it was an adult's job to protect you. It was an adult's job to protect you both."

"And then Mom went crazy," Luna said. "She had to go to a hospital for two weeks and Dad had to take care of us."

"Dad didn't like to take care of us," Ollie said.

"Fuck," Sophie said, rubbing her face. "I'm so sorry." These kids had been through all this, and here they were, listening to her dumb problems. Losing her job she didn't even like anymore. A fire where no one even died. Her boss had to get skin grafts, but he had lived, and he wasn't even someone she loved. He was just her idiot boss. She thought about telling the kids one of the other things going wrong with her life, to prove to them she did have real problems, big ones, things she couldn't talk about with anyone, but she stopped herself. The kids didn't need to hear anything else about her.

"Luna and I are also super lucky," Ollie added. "We have each other."

"Yup," Luna said. "And we're going to have Mark Stackpole. And his mansion and his wife, Christine, and baby Sassafras and all the other kids."

Sophie took a deep breath. "You also have me," she said. "You have me, and you also have Uncle PJ. And we're going to try to help you any way we can. My dad isn't perfect, but he really cares about you kids."

"You can visit us in our mansion," Luna offered. "You can visit us anytime. Uncle PJ can bring Michelle Cobb. And Pancakes, obviously."

Sophie had to say something. Luna and her dad might both be delusional about this trip—it might work out for one of them, but it probably wouldn't work out for both of them, and it might not work out for either. Sophie had seen so many things not work out before. "Luna, I need to tell you something before tomorrow. If I'm going to take you to meet Mark Stackpole, I have to tell you this first."

"Tell me what?"

"I need you to know, that if this man isn't your father, or if he's a big disappointment for whatever reason, you can still have a great life. If he isn't who you want him to be, I want you to know you'll be all right without him. You can still be an astronaut or whatever you want. Okay?"

Luna didn't answer for a minute. "Okay," she finally said.

"And I promise I'll help you figure out how to be an astronaut if that's what you really want to do," Sophie said, and she meant it, even though she had no idea how anyone becomes an astronaut, and she couldn't even figure out what to do with her own life. But for Luna, she'd do the research.

"I want to be a firefighter," Ollie said. "Or a comic-book artist."

"I'll help you do those things too."

"Cool."

It was quiet for a minute. Outside the door, someone in the parking lot was yelling at someone else, but inside the room they were quiet. Peaceful. Sophie looked down at her hands folded on her chest and wondered what else she could say to the kids to help them. She looked at the leather bracelets on her wrists. They had always made her feel stronger. "Here," she said, taking off one of the bracelets and handing it to Luna. "This will protect you." It was a gesture, an empty gesture, but Sophie didn't have anything else.

"Wow," Ollie said. "You're really lucky, Luna. Those bracelets are impervious to bullets."

Sophie smiled. She didn't know where he'd gotten the idea that the bracelets were impervious to anything, but she gave Ollie the other one.

"I probably don't need it as bad," he said. "Because I'm not a girl." But he put it on and clenched his fingers into a fist, like Wonder Woman did when she was feeling powerful.

"Thanks, Sophie," Luna said. "These are really cool."

Without the bracelets, Sophie knew the kids would see her scars on her wrists, the thin purple lines that had never really faded all that well. *It's not what you think,* she wanted to say to the kids, like she always did when people saw the scars. She wanted to tell Ollie and Luna it was an accident, but she didn't, because she didn't know what they thought about the scars. They were only kids. Maybe they didn't know why someone would have scars on their wrists, and why that was worse than scars anywhere else. Sophie had the scars ever since she was twelve, and whenever people noticed them, they thought they knew everything about her. "Sometimes I think you act sad because that's what people expect from you," her therapist had said recently, and Sophie wondered if Blanche was paying attention, to just how bad everything was.

"Where's Pancakes?" Luna asked.

"He's under the covers with Uncle PJ," Ollie said, because he swore he had seen a cat-shaped lump under the covers while Luna was handcuffing their great-uncle to the bed.

"Okay," Luna said, disappointed that the cat wouldn't be sleeping with her. "Hey, Sophie?"

"Yeah?"

"Will you sleep here with us tonight? In our bed?"

Sophie absolutely did not want to sleep in that bed with the kids. There was an empty queen bed only two feet away, with her dad sleeping in the pullout couch. No one was going to use that empty bed if she didn't use it, and it was made up with fresh, crisp hotel sheets. But Luna had asked, and it would be horrible to say no, wouldn't it? If the kids wanted to stay in one bed, Sophie would have to do it. "Sure. Of course. I'll stay."

"Yay," Luna said quietly, and they all settled into the pillows and both children threw their limbs around Sophie, and soon there was an elbow in her face, and a foot stuck to her leg, hot, stinky breath on her neck, and Sophie felt so uncomfortable and sweaty and smothered and oxygen-deprived and it was something close to torture to try to fall asleep that way and yet—oh man, it was weirdly wonderful.

36

The clock on the bedside table said exactly 10:00 P.M., and Ollie could hear them all steadily breathing. Everyone was finally asleep, so he inched away from where Sophie lay in the middle and rolled out of bed like a ninja. He slid open the drawer of the bedside table as quietly as he could and took out the tiny silver key next to the Bible. He had lots of experience playing with his dad's handcuffs. He knew how to unlock a pair of handcuffs, and that's what he needed to do.

Because Ollie figured if Uncle PJ disappeared in the night, if they had to go find him in the morning, if he got really lost somewhere, they might not make it to Sugar Land in time for the meet-and-greet. Because Ollie didn't want to meet Mark Stackpole. He didn't want to go live in a mansion, the way his sister had promised he would. She had said his room would be a closet, and that he would have to promise not to be too annoying. Because Ollie would not be Mark Stackpole's real kid, he would be a charity case. That is how Luna had put it. Ollie did not want to be a charity case. He wanted to stay with Sophie and Uncle PJ, who had bought him a trampoline and an iPad and Sophie had given him and Luna leather bracelets for protection, and they had actually gotten him a vanilla milkshake from McDonald's when he asked for a vanilla milkshake and didn't call him a *greedy little piggy* like his parents used to.

Ollie undid the handcuffs, and then he got close to Uncle PJ's ear. Uncle PJ's ear had wiry gray hairs sprouting out of the canal, but Ollie put his lips up to it anyway. And then he whispered one word, from his sweet, pouty, nine-year-old lips.

"Beer," he said.

Three minutes later, PJ snorted and sat up abruptly. He must have fallen asleep, he thought, he didn't remember going to bed. Someone had covered him with a blanket on the fold-out couch. The kids and Sophie were asleep, it was dark in the room. The clock glowed 10:03 P.M., not too late. The bars would still be open. PJ needed to drink. He badly needed to drink. He could not wait any longer for it. Yes, he knew he shouldn't, but he needed to. He had seen a dead man that morning, poor Gregor, and what's more, he had saved Sophie and the kids from the same fate. He deserved to drink. He was a hero.

Beer, beer, beer, chanted the hat on his head. Well, that was a new word for the hat. PJ looked in Sophie's messenger bag for the keys to the Volvo.

No, PJ told himself. He had been through this earlier. He could not drive the Bird Barn, not with that social worker breathing down his neck. He would have to walk to the nearest bar. Then he could get as drunk as he liked without guilt. So he didn't take the car keys, just the small baggie of gummy candies he saw Sophie had in her bag, because PJ liked a little sugar late at night. Then he let himself out of the motel room, quiet as he could, and walked down the cement sidewalk in front of the red doors.

When he got to the office at the corner of the building, he could see Destiny through the windows. She was still watching TV, eating a bag of chips with her feet up on the desk. He opened the door, and the bell jingled. "You open?" he asked.

Destiny threw her feet off the desk and brushed the crumbs off her sweater. She hadn't seen him coming. It was a good *CSI* episode. "Can I help you with something, Mr. Halliday?" she asked. Destiny had a knack for remembering guest names.

"I'm looking for the nearest bar. Something in walking distance."

"I'm sorry, honey, there isn't one. Not unless you've got a nine-mile walk in you."

PJ considered it. "Any taxis?"

"Not in Purity Springs."

"Well, I can't sleep without a nightcap. How much would it cost for you to drive me over to the bar?"

"I'm not supposed to leave my station," Destiny said, shaking her head. "We're known to be a twenty-four-hour motel. Truckers stop in here late, and . . . well, other folks come in late too. I have to be here to check them in."

"Leave a note, say you'll be back in twenty minutes. I'll pay you."

"I'm sorry, honey, I can't."

"Name a price. Everybody's got a price."

Destiny shrugged. This guy was a piece of work. "One hundred dollars."

"I'll double it," he said. He opened his wallet, counted out the bills.

"Shit," Destiny said, getting out of her chair. "Okay." She slid on her shoes, the comfortable black mules she liked to wear to work, and grabbed her keys off the rack. She put a sign on the door that said: *Be back in five.* As she hung up the sign, Pancakes came out from under her desk, licking his whiskers.

"Excuse me, sir," PJ said. "How did you get out?"

"That's your cat?"

"Yes, that's Pancakes. Sorry if he bothered you. He's a tricky devil. Always getting out."

"You didn't come in with a cat when you checked in."

"Oh. Well, damn, I must have left him in the car, but I usually bring him everywhere."

"Well, I thought he was a stray. I gave him some tuna fish. He seemed hungry."

"Thanks. He's always hungry. I'll go put him in our room and then we can go." He hoped she wouldn't say anything about the No Pets sign behind the desk now that he was giving her two hundred dollars in cash for driving him nine miles to the bar down the road and leaving him there.

"Actually—" Destiny said. "Do you mind if . . . could I keep him for the night? It's nice to have some company overnight. I've asked my boss if I could bring my dog, but he won't let me."

"Sure," PJ agreed. "I'll come get him in the morning." He put Pancakes down, and the cat jumped up into Destiny's empty office chair, still warm from where she had been sitting.

I'll wait here for you, the cat thought.

Out in the lot, Destiny's car was a red Mazda, and PJ opened the passenger door for himself. There was a stack of papers on the front seat. PJ picked them up so he wouldn't sit on them.

"Oh, just throw those in the back," Destiny said.

"Sure," PJ said, but he saw what was written at the top. ONCOLOGY, it read. The Mercy Clinic. PJ wasn't the smartest guy in the whole world, but he knew enough to know that oncology meant cancer. He and Ivy had been to the oncology center in Boston many times, but Ivy had beat her cancer. Maybe Destiny was going to beat it too. Maybe this would be a hopeful ride. Destiny started the car.

"None of my business, I know," PJ said, placing the papers as gently as he could in the backseat so they wouldn't get out of order back there. "But are you gonna be all right?"

Destiny shrugged and kept her eyes on the road. "No. I'm dying, and there's nothing all right about that."

"No, there isn't," he agreed.

"I'm not going to see my daughter's high school graduation. She's a junior now. I won't make it to next year, the doctor said. He said I should pray for a miracle if I want a miracle."

PJ remembered Sophie's high school graduation, how he got so blitzed before the ceremony, he peed his pants during the valedictorian's speech. He didn't know he'd done it until Ivy dumped ice water in his lap to both punish him and cover up the smell. PJ thought about telling Destiny about that. He also thought about telling her that high school graduations are long and hot and boring, that when they were married, Ivy used to make him go every year even though no one cares if the art teacher's husband attends their high school graduation. But PJ used to go anyway, because he had tried to be a good husband to Ivy. PJ also wanted to tell Destiny that he would have given anything—anything, his right arm, his left leg, a kidney or a lung—to see his eldest daughter graduate, but he hadn't, because her prom was a week before. But PJ didn't say any of that. This was Destiny's life and her tragedy, not his. "I'm sorry," he said instead. "That's a shit deal you've been given."

"Thanks, honey," Destiny said, and she turned right into a dirt parking lot, with a bar with a Pabst Blue Ribbon neon sign in the window. The Half-Moon Bar. "Here we are. Tell Miguel I sent you."

There were three other cars in the lot. A red Ford Taurus, an F-150 truck, and a classic 1970s orange Dodge Challenger. The Challenger had a sticker on the bumper that read HOOK'EM HORNS! the Longhorns football team's rallying cry. PJ didn't have an opinion on the football team, but he loved that kind of car. "I'll tell Miguel that Destiny sent me," he promised, "and I'll see you back at the motel a little later."

"Yup. I'll see you later. Miguel will give you a ride home at the end of the night, if you ask."

PJ nodded, and he hoped Miguel was the one who owned the Dodge Challenger. He asked Destiny to slip a note under the motel door so Sophie would know where he was and tell them that she had the cat in the office. "So that they don't worry," he said.

"All right, Mr. Halliday. I'll tell them."

"Wait," PJ said, before he closed the door. "I've got something else for you." He took his checkbook out of his cargo shorts. He wrote a check for $1,000. "For your kid. Graduation gift."

"All right, Mr. Halliday, all right," she said, her eyes getting wide. "You take care now, honey. You take care."

PJ liked that Destiny didn't thank him too much, or actually, she hadn't said thank you at all, did she? He wished he could have given her more money, but he was running out. He still had the kids to take care of, and those kids were big spenders. Two thousand for a pineapple pocketbook, for chrissakes. But PJ would figure the money situation out later, and Destiny had helped him now. She had gotten him to the bar.

37

The Half-Moon Bar was the kind of bar PJ liked, a dark bar with wood beams and lots of posters hung up to look at. A dartboard. It felt like home, even though it didn't have the hula girls painted on the walls like they did at the Wild Orchid back in Pondville.

"What'll you have?" the bartender asked, in a white T-shirt with a sleeve of tattoos on his arm. This was probably Miguel.

PJ ordered a Bud Light. "Destiny says hello," he said.

"Oh yeah? Who's that?"

"From the Boar's Tooth Motel," he said. "She said you knew her. She gave me a ride."

Miguel shrugged. "Have Destiny introduce herself again next time she's in."

"I don't think she'll be in here again."

"And why's that? Too good for my bar?"

"No sir, no, you see, she's dying. She's got cancer. She wants to spend all her time with her kid before she goes."

"That's a sad story you walked in here with."

"Well, I only meant to say hello for her. And goodbye for her."

"That's really some sad shit, about her kid," Miguel said, wiping down the bar. "You have kids?"

"Two. Or four, depending on how you count. Or three, depending on how you count."

"You'll need to explain."

"I've got two biologicals, one of whom is dead, and I've recently inherited two new ones."

"Inherited?"

"Well, my niece died. Left her kids to me in the will. I guess she'd heard I was a lottery winner. And because she had no one else. Everyone else is dead in our family on my side. And then there's my daughter Sophie, she's alive. She'll be the angry young woman who drags me out of here. You'll like her."

"How much did you win?" another man at the bar asked. He was wearing an orange Longhorns jersey, was probably the owner of the Dodge Challenger.

"A million and a half," PJ answered. He liked that question. It put him back on stable ground. He was a lottery winner, he was at the bar, he was here to have a good time.

"Shit, man," the Longhorn said. "Wow. Drinks are on you."

"Sure," PJ said, but then he sighed. He had come here to talk. He needed to talk. He needed someone to tell the truth to, and it was easier to tell the truth at the bar. A bar was where PJ felt safest, even so far from home. "Well, the money's almost all gone," he admitted. "Got twenty thousand left in the bank, last I checked, and I gave one thousand two hundred dollars to Destiny for driving me here from the motel. And now I have two young, orphaned kids to take care of. I'm all those kids have since their parents died. A murder suicide, from what I hear. I would have read about their parents' deaths in the newspaper, but I can't read the newspaper on account of my heart condition. Can't hear bad news. Too sensitive."

"Never mind," the Longhorn said. "Let *me* buy *you* a drink."

"That's nice," PJ said. "But I'm keeping afloat. The kids are having a good time on this trip. We saw Niagara Falls. The largest alpaca farm in Kentucky. A purse museum. We've met some nice people. And we survived a gas leak." PJ finished his beer. That was good. He felt better. He was having a good time.

He told the Longhorn about his eldest daughter's death, how she'd died fifteen years ago, how she got drunk at a party after prom and drowned in only a few inches of water. He said, back at home, the school had raised money to put up a stone bench so people wouldn't forget her. It had her name on it. But he still felt people had forgotten her. The kids in town were still drinking at that firepit in the woods behind the airplane hangar, as if a teenager hadn't died doing that fifteen years before. Sometimes PJ would go down to the firepit and drink with them. He wanted to imagine what the last hours of his daughter's life had been like. The high school kids all knew him, knew he was harmless and wouldn't get them in trouble with their parents. They called him "Coach PJ," even though PJ had never coached anything.

At the bar, the Longhorn nodded. He took a sip of his drink. "My sister died in a plane crash," he said. "And my dad spent the rest of his life researching the engine of that plane, wanting to know exactly what had gone wrong. It can make a man crazy, needing to know what the last seconds of their kid's life looked like."

"You get it," PJ said, feeling glad, so glad he had made it to this bar. "My ex-wife doesn't want to talk about it with me anymore. She says she's had enough with talking about it."

"Oh, a man needs to talk," the Longhorn said. "You know why they take World War II veterans around to give talks at libraries and community centers every year?"

"The preservation of history?"

"Nah. They take those old farts around because they don't want the war to come back in their minds, they don't want their aging brains tricking them into thinking they're back in the trenches again. And the only way to do that is to tell the story. To retell and retell the story. You tell the story in order to control the story."

"Huh," PJ said. That made sense.

"If you don't talk about it, it'll haunt you," the Longhorn said.

PJ nodded. He was haunted. He needed to talk about it, or he needed to drink to erase the pain of it with booze. Or both. He needed both.

"It'll drive you to drink, not talking about it. You drink a lot?"

PJ nodded.

"Well, that's also why Alcoholics Anonymous works for some people," he said. "The storytelling. It's a safe place to tell your stories. Share with your friends who've been there too. I always tell my AA buddies: show me the horrible things you've done, I'll laugh about it with you."

PJ had never liked hanging out with the other sad losers in a semicircle. He didn't like trying to swear off new relationships for a year, or taking a moral inventory, or all the other shit you had to do in the twelve steps. But maybe if PJ had thought of AA meetings as a place to tell his best stories, he could get on board. Ivy would be happy if PJ was going to meetings. She'd always said it was the only way anyone could get sober. Well, you know what, PJ was sober now. Practically. It had been one beer. He could stay sober, he knew that. He'd been doing great before he fell off the wagon at the Golden Cherry. He could do it again. "You're a really smart man," PJ told the Longhorn. "I'm fortunate I met you."

"I'm nothing but an old drunk," the Longhorn said. "AA never worked for me. But hey, try it. Tell me your worst story. The most horrible thing you've done, and I'll laugh about it with you."

"Well," PJ said. He thought about it. It wasn't the worst thing he'd ever done, but it was one of them.

Sophie was twelve when it happened, the same age as Kate had been when she'd been hit by a car. An unlucky year for the Halliday children. Sophie was outside, playing by herself. She was in the very last gasp of childhood, before your imagination leaves you for good. She was walking along the stone wall in the backyard of the house on the corner of Clear Pond Road, pretending to be a tightrope walker. Earlier, she'd been a strong man, and a fire-eater, a lion tamer. She was a one-girl circus. PJ was supposed to be watching her, but a twelve-year-old doesn't need watching all the time. PJ was in the house, watching baseball. It was Saturday, and he was eighteen beers in, one beer for each year his older daughter had lived. Ivy was away for the weekend, on one of her bird-watching trips down the Cape. The friendly bird-watcher with a second home down the street invited her. A man named Fred, a judge up in Boston, who came down to Pondville on weekends to relax, and organized trips on the Cape to look for birds. PJ had encouraged his wife to go.

So, PJ was home alone with Sophie, and he was passed out in front of the game. Outside, Sophie was still up on her tightrope, up on the three-foot-tall rock wall, and Sophie slipped on a thick patch of moss. She tried to steady herself on the side of the garage, but there was a windowpane right there, and she fell straight through the window, tumbling through it, badly slicing both wrists. PJ was inside, but he didn't hear her screaming, passed out from the beer, the baseball game up too loud.

Mrs. DeAngelis found Sophie in the driveway, blood streaming down her arms, unable to speak from the shock, and she put Sophie in the car and took her to the ER in the same old Buick that had run over Kate and her bike seven years before. Sophie bled all over the cloth interior and caused much more damage to the car than her sister had.

Mrs. DeAngelis and a cop came to PJ's door two hours later, and that's when they woke PJ up.

"Your daughter tried to kill herself," the cop said, not mincing words.

"I took her to the hospital," Mrs. DeAngelis said. "I thought no one was home. I didn't know you were home. But I got her there in time. They stitched up her wrists. She'd sliced them open."

No one said she'd done it accidentally, because everyone had assumed it was on purpose, the Halliday girl whose sister had drowned the year before. She must not be coping well with the loss. PJ shook his head, dazed. The cop wanted to take PJ into questioning for endangering a minor, leaving her unsupervised, even though most people leave twelve-year-olds alone all the time.

When PJ got to the hospital, Sophie told him what happened, about the window, and how she'd called for him, and how scared she'd been, all alone at the hospital, where no one was listening to her and everyone was saying scary things. When Ivy arrived hours later, back from the bird-watching, she hit PJ in the face with her binoculars, cracked the lenses, broke one of his teeth.

"It was really the end of our marriage," PJ explained to the Longhorn. "Ivy took it worse than any of the drunk driving accidents, blamed me for it more. The doctors didn't believe us, they didn't believe Sophie, that she'd only gone through a window, that it was only an accident. They put her on a mandatory seventy-two-hour psychiatric hold. They asked that poor kid questions no kid should need to be asked."

The Longhorn lifted his finger to signal Miguel for another drink.

PJ waited for the Longhorn to ask which tooth it was that Ivy broke, like Ollie and Luna would have asked to see, the proof that the story was real. But the Longhorn didn't ask, and PJ had never really broken any of his teeth; that was the one part of the story PJ had made up. Ivy hadn't hit him. Instead, at the hospital, Ivy let Fred, the strange man from down the street, hold her while she cried. She wouldn't let PJ near her.

"But after that," PJ continued to the Longhorn, "Sophie did okay. She got good grades. She could have gone to NYU. She got into NYU! She didn't need to stick around Pondville. NYU's a great school. But she didn't, because she thought she needed her mom, and thought her mom needed her. I didn't think it was healthy."

"Sounds codependent," the Longhorn said.

"Yes, that's the word for it. Codependent. But after Sophie went to college, Ivy got more serious with Fred, he moved down to Pondville full-time to be with her. I think Sophie started to feel like a third wheel after that, like I did."

"Fred is the bird-watcher? She left you for him?"

"Yup."

"He's an asshole, huh?"

PJ thought about it. Fred's recent texts, telling him to leave them alone, that he and Ivy needed to focus on being in Alaska. Getting engaged in Alaska. Not inviting him or Sophie to Alaska. "No," PJ finally said. "Fred's not an asshole. I love him very much." He wiped his eyes. "I miss him a lot."

"Well, that's sweet."

"I thought you were going to help me laugh at this."

The Longhorn shrugged. "Sometimes it's good to cry instead. The important thing is feeling something."

"I get it," PJ said. "It was pretty bad, what I did."

"You want to hear my story? It's also about how I lost my wife."

"Sure. Of course I do."

"I killed her driving drunk one night. I killed my own wife."

PJ's mouth opened a little. He knew he'd been lucky, that he'd never hurt anyone driving drunk. No one had ever been in the car with him. No one had ever been on the road when he swerved into the other lane and rolled the car or drove the mail truck into the pond. He had been lucky. "That's a horrible story," PJ said. "I'm sorry about that."

"That's not the story. The story part is, on the anniversary of my wife's death, two years ago, I checked into the Boar's Tooth Motel."

"We're staying there."

"It's the only lodging in town. And it's well known to be the best place in town to kill yourself."

"Oh. I don't plan to do that."

"Well, that's precisely why I checked in. When someone local checks into the motel alone, the staff there pretty much knows what to expect in the morning. The motel manager marks the room on the booking calendar with a red X."

"Destiny," PJ said. "She's the manager."

"Exactly," the Longhorn said. "Destiny."

"Doesn't Destiny try to stop the person from killing themselves? If she knows they're going to do it?"

"I think she figures it's not her business. But she does make you pay up-front."

"Huh," PJ said, thinking it would be hard to sleep at night if you knew someone was going to die a few doors down and you didn't do anything about it. Maybe that's why Destiny kept the TV volume up so loud.

"So I paid for my room, and I had a gun with me, a six-round revolver, and I sat on the edge of the bed, disgusted with myself that I had crashed a car into a tree and killed my own wife, but I'd kept on living, not a scratch on me. I put the gun in my mouth. I pulled the trigger, and it clicked. I pulled again. Clicked. No bullet. I pulled it all six times. Still alive. I threw the gun across the room, disgusted, frustrated, that I couldn't even manage to kill myself properly, with a car or with a gun. I threw the gun, and it hit the wall and went off, and the bullet came around and shot me in the leg. Couldn't even kill myself." The Longhorn started laughing. He couldn't stop. He started laughing as if someone had told the funniest joke he'd ever heard. PJ watched the poor man, about to fall out of his chair and onto the floor.

"I'm so sorry," PJ said, putting his hand on the Longhorn's shoulder to steady him.

"Don't be. Don't be sorry for me."

"All right," PJ said. He didn't know what else the Longhorn wanted, if not pity. "Listen, thanks for talking tonight, but I have to get going. Back to the kids." *Focus on Alasha,* he heard Fred say in his ear. *We have to focus on what is happening right now.* Sophie had said that morning that he needed to focus on Ollie and Luna. Just like Ivy had told him once to focus on Sophie instead of Kate's death. PJ needed to focus on those kids. They needed him. They needed him bad. He had promised he was going to take Luna to meet Mark

Stackpole, and he was a man of his word. "You take care, now," he told the Longhorn, and he left $100 on the bar to cover both their tabs, even though PJ had only had one beer. For once in his life, PJ had stopped at one beer.

"Can't even kill myself," the Longhorn muttered.

"I'm sure something will, someday," PJ said, because he knew the feeling. He had been stuck in that feeling for years—half wanting it to be over already and half wanting to find a way to keep living and hope things would get better. But he didn't want to die tonight. He had kids back at the hotel. He needed to stop drinking. And maybe he would even try AA. Sit in the church basement with the other losers. That would make Ivy happy. He wanted to make Ivy happy. He wanted to make them all happy. Sophie, Ivy, Fred, the kids.

"Headed home?" Miguel asked, as PJ headed to the door.

"Yup," PJ said, puffing out his chest. "One drink tonight. I'm on the way to meet the woman of my dreams. And there are kids back at the hotel who need my help. I have a second chance at life. I am one lucky bastard to have survived this far."

"Amen," Miguel said.

"Good luck to you," the Longhorn agreed.

"It's a straight shot back to the Boar's Tooth Motel?" PJ asked, pausing at the door.

"Yup," Miguel said. "Take a left, and it's thirteen miles straight back that way."

"I thought it was nine miles."

"It's nine miles here," Miguel said. "It's thirteen miles back."

That didn't make any sense, but PJ gave him a thumbs-up anyway, and went out the door. He was a former mailman; he could walk thirteen miles.

38

PJ was pretty sure he remembered the road Destiny had driven to the bar had been paved, and the way home was a dirt road, full of ruts, places an old man might sprain his ankle if he wasn't careful. It was warm, even at midnight, and PJ was already sweating through his shirt. It was muggy. The mosquitos swarmed and buzzed in his ear, reminding him he was on the right path, that the Boar's Tooth Motel was just up ahead, to keep walking, because walking kept the blood warm and pumping. The mosquitos dined on his neck, and on his legs, and PJ loved them, because he wasn't all alone on this walk. But then the mosquitos were gone, flew off like a flock of birds, leaving PJ by himself in the dark. He would be bitten up in the morning. He looked forward to the morning. He wanted to get home to the kids, to Sophie, to Pancakes. How good they would all look in the daylight. He walked. He walked and walked.

A few miles in, PJ's feet hurt, bad enough that he couldn't ignore it. PJ had walked all his life—well, since he was ten months old, an early walker by most standards—and he had always been able to walk through pain. He had delivered mail through blisters and sprained ankles, a splinter once that had gotten infected. But he wasn't the young man he'd once been, and he wasn't wearing good walking shoes either. He stopped walking to take off his sandals. The dang things had given him blisters on the sides of his feet, two oozing boils. *How long had he been walking?* Barefoot now, PJ looked up to admire the stars. With the mosquitos gone, it was so quiet he could hear the earthworms digging. They were eating something, PJ supposed, something dead.

He was glad it was not him.

He knew he'd been killing himself, these past fifteen years, with the amount of booze he drank. His doctor said three drinks a night would be fine for a man his size. Or was it three drinks a week? He couldn't remember, but he'd blown right past three drinks a night for many years. It was no wonder, really, that all his money was gone. He felt sick about it.

PJ remembered the gummy candies in his pocket, the three lonely gummy bears Sophie had saved in a plastic baggie for some reason. He needed sustenance. He dropped them in his mouth and chewed. The sugar helped, and PJ had the strength to keep walking, and after a bit, even with the blisters, even with the bare feet in the mud, PJ felt like everything might work out for him.

Up ahead, PJ saw a light. *A flashlight!* Someone had come to save him! Someone cared about him after all! Sophie! Sophie, his dear Sophie, she still loved him despite everything! No, not a flashlight. The light was too steady to be a flashlight. Had he walked in a circle? Was he back at the Half-Moon Bar and that was the sign for Pabst Blue Ribbon? How had he walked so far and come right back to where he had started? Oh, it was the office light of the Boar's Tooth Motel! It was Destiny's office, where she and the cat were waiting for him! He walked faster toward the light. He was practically running. He felt like he might sprout wings any minute.

Getting closer, PJ saw it wasn't the light of the office, and it wasn't the light of the bar, either, it was the single headlight; the other headlight smashed out in an accident weeks back. In fact, it was the headlight of the Longhorn's Dodge Challenger. PJ had two seconds to register that, had enough time to think HOOK'EM HORNS! before he bounced off the hood of the car and was thrown off the road down into a ditch.

DAY FIVE

SATURDAY

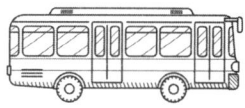

39

"He escaped!" Luna yelled in the morning. "How the hell did he get out?" She looked under the bed. The cuffs were there but they were unlocked.

"The cat?" Sophie asked, wiping her eyes. "Did the cat get out?"

"No, Uncle PJ! Your dumb dad! How did he get out of the handcuffs?"

Ollie shrugged. "Magic, probably," he said.

"Well, we're going on without him," Luna said. "We can come back for him later. We can't miss the meet-and-greet."

"Let's look around for a few minutes first," Sophie said. She got out of the bed she'd shared with the kids and looked out the window. The red Volvo was there, safe in the lot. Wherever he'd gone, he'd gone on foot. Sophie knew Luna was right—they probably should go on without him. He should be punished, *really* punished, for *something* for once. But she couldn't leave her dad behind, no matter what he'd done. Couldn't leave him here to die in Purity Springs. Her mom had asked Sophie to take care of her dad while she was away.

"Oh my God. Pancakes is gone too," Luna said, frantically looking under the beds and in the bathtub and behind the pillows. "He took the cat."

Ollie was pleased. It was all working out. He would not have to live in a closet in a mansion now. He would not be Mark Stackpole's charity case. Luna would never leave the cat behind, not even to go meet the guy from TV she wished was her dad.

Sophie saw there was a piece of paper on the carpet, near the door. She picked it up. At the top, the stationery said: A NOTE FROM THE STAFF AT THE BOAR'S TOOTH MOTEL:

> Your cat is downstairs in the office with me, keeping me company. Your father went to the bar. He didn't want you to worry.
>
> Sincerely, Destiny, Office Manager

"Didn't want us to worry, huh?" Sophie said. But Sophie could barely feel anger at her dad at this point. She was numb. She told the kids to grab their bags and they went down to the office to get the cat.

Destiny was in the office. She was wearing a new outfit, a yellow jumpsuit. Red lipstick. She hadn't slept, but somehow looked more rested than Sophie or the kids. The cat was having his breakfast, another can of tuna fish. "He's a special cat," Destiny said. "Thank you for sharing him with me."

Luna's eyes were dark slits. "You shouldn't have stolen him. We don't have time for this shit this morning." She grabbed the cat and walked out of the office.

"She's not supposed to swear outside of the car," Ollie said to Destiny, as an apology. "She can say whatever she wants in the car though."

"Can she?" Destiny asked, amused.

"Thank you, Ollie," Sophie said. "Go outside with your sister. And thank you for looking after the cat," she said to Destiny. "Do you know which bar my father might have gone to?"

"He didn't come back last night?"

"No."

"Oh my. Well, he most likely went to Miguel's bar. The Half-Moon Bar." Destiny was not going to mention that he had paid her $200 to drive him there. Destiny was not stupid. "It's straight down the road, nine miles after you take a right out of the parking lot. I expect he'll be somewhere along the road, walking home."

Or sleeping on a bench or under a tree somewhere, Sophie thought, because this wasn't her first rodeo. She knew her dad slept outside so he could try to be closer to what had happened to Kate, to tempt it to happen to him. There was almost something beautiful about it, if you didn't have to be the one to find him in the morning. But Sophie also had thought she'd finally gotten through to him yesterday, that he needed to focus on Ollie and Luna and their well-being instead of his own grief. "Thanks for your help," Sophie said to Destiny.

Destiny wished her good luck.

Luna and Ollie were already in the car, Luna holding the cat and looking ready to murder someone. They would be late to the meet-and-greet. She had wanted to be first in line to meet Mark Stackpole, who would probably recognize her immediately and take her in his arms in front of everyone.

Ollie sat smugly in his seat; his hands folded. It was all working out. They would never make it to the meet-and-greet; they would stay with Sophie and Uncle PJ. They would find Uncle PJ, Ollie wasn't worried. They always found him, so far. Ollie put his window down, because he knew his sister hated wind in her face. He loved his sister and wanted her to be happy and not depressed, but he also was going to make her life totally miserable today. She wanted him to live in a closet. He wanted to punish her, because she wanted him to be the one kid in the family whom no one loved, the only one who didn't belong to anybody. He didn't belong to anybody now, not really, but he had a trampoline at Uncle PJ's. The trampoline belonged to him.

Nine miles later, Sophie, the kids, and the cat pulled up to the Half-Moon Bar. They hadn't seen anyone walking on the road, and the parking lot was empty. The Pabst Blue Ribbon neon light was not illuminated. Luna and Sophie got out of the car, but Ollie stayed strapped in. He had turned on his iPad, as if none of this were an emergency, which really ticked Luna off.

Sophie pulled on the door handle of the bar, but the door was locked. She and Luna peered into the windows. No one was inside, no one sweeping or cleaning up. A sign said they were open from one P.M. until two A.M.

Luna stamped her foot in anger. "We need to leave right now if we're going to make it on time."

"I'm sorry," Sophie said, and she really was. "We can't leave him."

"I know. I'm not stupid."

"I know you're not."

"And I'm not mean either. Everyone at school thinks I'm mean, but I'm not, and it would be mean to leave Uncle PJ here, even if he always screws up everything."

"I know you're not mean."

"Don't worry, Sophie, we'll find him!" Ollie called, still in the car but leaning out the window. "We'll never give up on him!"

Sophie shook her head. She wanted to cry, hearing that. It would be hard for these kids, if they never gave up on her dad. Sophie looked at her phone. She knew what she had to do next. She had to start calling around to the hospitals, and to the county jail after that. But there was no cell service at the Half-Moon Bar. She would have to drive back toward the Boar's Tooth Motel. "Let's get in the car," she said.

"Where are we going?" Ollie asked, when Luna and Sophie climbed in.

"Not to Sugar Land." Luna sighed. It was already eight A.M. They were running out of time, even if they left now. They were supposed to leave first thing.

"We have to go to the motel," Sophie said. "And make some calls." Sophie started to drive, hoping she would see her father walking along the road. She felt terrible, letting Luna down. It was such a stupid idea, driving to a soap opera meet-and-greet to get a paternity test—except, it also really was possible Mark Stackpole was Luna's father. Sophie had seen the diary entry. The timeline added up.

"Oh my God!" Luna screamed. "Oh my God, oh my God, oh my God!"

"Oh no, oh no, oh no, oh no," Ollie said.

"What?" Sophie asked. "What?"

"Stop the car!" Luna yelled. "Stop the car! Don't hit him!"

Sophie slammed on the brakes. "What happened?"

"I'm sorry, I'm sorry, I'm sorry," Ollie said. "I had my window open."

Luna had opened her car door, was running toward the woods at the side of the road.

"Luna!" Sophie called. "What are you doing?"

"The cat jumped out of the window," Ollie explained. "I had my window open, and he jumped right out."

"Oh my God!" Sophie unbuckled her seatbelt and opened her door. "He jumped out of the car? What the fuck?"

"He's suicidal without Uncle PJ," Ollie said. "I ruined everything."

The cat was always jumping out of windows. The cat was always escaping. But he had never jumped out of a moving car before. That was a first. Thankfully, there were no other cars on this rural stretch of road. "We'll find him," Sophie told Ollie. Ollie was crying. "Look, Ollie. He's fine," Sophie said, pointing. "Look, he's right down there. Luna has him."

Luna had already slid down the dirt bank and had the cat in her arms. Everything was fine. No one was hurt. Luna had caught the cat.

"Everyone get back in the car," Sophie said, and then something crunched underneath her feet. Broken glass. There had been an accident. And then, down off the road, Sophie saw a Birkenstock sandal in a bed of poison ivy. Holy shit. Sophie slid down the dirt bank. "Dad!" she yelled. "Dad!"

And there he was, behind a bush. Missing his sandals, but he was breathing. He was bleeding from his head, but he was breathing. He groaned. "Sophie-Soo-Soo," he said. "Is it morning already?"

"Dad, are you okay? Is anything broken?"

"No, no," he said. "I only had one drink. One beer and then I said, you know what, Sophie needs me. Those kids need me. And I started walking home. And then that damn Longhorn, he ran me over with his car."

"Hit-and-run," Sophie said. "Bastard." She did not know what a Longhorn was, but she could see that some asshole had hit her father then driven away and left him there. Left him there to die.

It had not been a hit-and-run, actually, but there was no way Sophie could know that. Only an hour ago, an ambulance and a tow truck had been on that stretch of road to clean up the Dodge Challenger and the deceased man in the Longhorns jersey, whose name was Wade Fletcher. They had seen the blood on the hood and the windshield, but they figured that Wade had hit a deer, and the deer had limped off into the woods. The guy who drove the tow truck had hit a moose once, and he swore the moose walked away without a scratch on him. They had assumed only a deer could have left a dent in the hood of the Dodge Challenger that size, and PJ's body was hidden by that bush. They had not seen the lone Birkenstock in the bed of poison ivy. They had not smelled him, the way the cat did. It had been easy for the cat to catch a whiff, driving by him with Ollie's open window. With the heat of the Texas June morning, PJ already stank.

"Uncle PJ, I'm so glad you're alive," Ollie said. "We were so worried."

"I wasn't going to leave you," Luna said. "Even though you were ruining my chances of happiness, I wasn't going to leave you." Both kids were hugging him now.

PJ closed his eyes. Right, it was the day he was supposed to take the kid to meet the man Luna was convinced was her father, and she had spent the morning looking for him instead, finding him in a bush on the side of the road.

"Careful, kids," Sophie said. "Don't hug him too much. We don't know if anything is broken."

"Just my head. Just my head hurts."

"Okay, can you stand up?" Sophie asked. She looked at her phone to see if she could call an ambulance, but she still had no service.

But PJ could stand up, and slowly, he did. He put his arm around Sophie's shoulder, and they walked up the bank toward the Volvo. PJ was shaking like a baby alpaca on new legs, but he could walk. He could get up the steep embankment.

"Put him in the car and let's go," Luna said. "Let's go to the meet-and-greet."

"No, no, no," Sophie said. "We have to go to the hospital."

"Over my dead body," PJ said, and his voice was firm now. He didn't sound at all like someone who had been hit by a car. "We are taking the kid to meet Mark Stackpole. We are giving her closure on this thing that she has wondered all her life. Even if I die, it will be worth it."

Sophie shook her head.

"Listen, Sophie, we have to do this. I'll be fine. Look, I'm not even bleeding that much." He looked in the mirror in the sun visor. "Fred keeps a first-aid kit in the trunk of the car. We'll bandage the wound and then we'll get on the road."

"Great idea," Luna said. If they left right now, there was still time to get to the event, to meet Mark Stackpole. To tell him why they were there, to get him to fall in love with her and Ollie too.

Ollie didn't say anything, because it was his fault the cat had jumped out of the car. He was done meddling. He had done enough.

"Dad, what if there's a bleed in your brain?" Sophie asked. "We need to take you to the hospital. You were hit by a car."

"Then I'll die happy. Being with you and the kids. Doing something for someone other than myself."

"Jesus." Sophie sighed. It was no use arguing with her dad, and you know what, she didn't want to deal with Luna's heartbreak either. If they were going to meet Mark Stackpole, this really was their only chance. "All right. I'll get the first-aid kit. And then we'll go."

Please don't die, Sophie thought as she drove toward Texas, her dad's head wrapped up like a Halloween mummy. *Please, please, please don't die. I still need you.* She didn't know what she needed her dad for, exactly, he was no help to her or to anyone else, but she needed him. To be a burden, maybe. To be a total and constant pain in the ass.

40

PJ woke up as they were approaching their destination, his head throbbing. There was a bus stop outside the country-club gates with a poster taped on the side for a lost cat. Always a sad thing, to see a poster like that. Heartbreaking. And then they drove the Volvo inside the iron gates of the country club, and the lost cat was quickly forgotten.

"Have I died and gone to heaven?" PJ asked, looking out the window. The parking lot was flooded with women, all over forty, and all these women were dressed up like they were going to a summer wedding. PJ had never in his life seen so much floral, so many beautiful flowers, each woman a garden. PJ wondered if there was time for one more fling before they got to Michelle Cobb. Then again, maybe not, because oh man, did his head hurt. They had made it to the meet-and-greet, and PJ wasn't even sure he could get out of the car. "I'm going to stay in the car and rest," he said. "You take them in."

"You're feeling all right?" Sophie asked. "Should we go to the hospital now?" Sophie thought maybe she could just leave the kids here and pick them up later.

"I'm fine, I'm fine," PJ said. But he didn't want to go with Sophie and the kids. He didn't want to look Mark Stackpole in the face. Luna's real father. Because in his headshot, the picture PJ had seen, Mark Stackpole did look a lot like Luna. And maybe PJ really was about to lose these kids forever. The kids who were his final shot at a new life. He hoped Mark Stackpole was a decent man. The kids would be better off, he told himself. Better off without him.

"Let's go," Luna said.

"Let's go," Sophie agreed. She had a paternity test in her bag. She had picked it up at a CVS on the way. It was an at-home paternity test; you swabbed your cheek and then it was sent away to a lab. There was a man cuddling a baby on the box.

Ollie followed Luna and Sophie reluctantly. He wondered if he would even have a bed when he slept in the closet, or if it would just be a pillow and a blanket on the floor.

The check-in table at the meet-and-greet was staffed with women wearing pink fuzzy cowboy hats. They were handing out free samples of the same protein powder Luna had already gotten in the mail. Everyone got a goody bag, with bumper stickers that said HONK IF YOU LOVE SOAP OPERAS! and heart-shaped red sunglasses, and there were several sticks of packaged beef jerky in each bag, custom labeled with I ♥ BEEFY HUNKS. They were giving out Vitamin Waters. Everything was sponsored by Soaps.com.

"Excuse me," Luna asked one of the women in hats. "Where can we meet the stars?"

"That's the Hunk Area," the woman said, pointing to the white tent on the other side of a small pond, down the path. "All the actors are inside."

"Our Hunks sure know how to pitch a tent," another pink hat said, and someone else slapped her arm.

"Oh, Elvira, you're so bad!"

"Not in front of the kids!" Everyone giggled. They couldn't get enough. They had waited for this day all year. Last year's event had been such a big success.

"Hi, little girl, are you a *General Hospital* fan?" Elvira asked Luna. "Or *Invitation to Love?*"

"*The Tears of the Rich*," Luna said. "My father is Mark Stackpole. I'm surprising him today."

"I'm her brother," Ollie said, wanting to be included.

"Half-brother," Luna corrected, never letting Ollie get away with anything. "We have the same mom, but we're pretty sure we have different dads. We're going to ask Mark Stackpole to take a paternity test."

"Oh my," said one of the fuzzy hats. They all looked at Sophie, who was standing behind the kids.

Sophie turned red. "No, I'm not their mother. I'm the nanny."

"Okay," Elvira said. "Where's the camera crew?"

"There isn't one," Luna said. "We drove all the way from Massachusetts."

"Massachusetts?" another woman asked. *Betsy*, it said on her stick-on name tag. "That's awfully far."

"Our parents just died," Ollie explained. "It's a road trip with our great-uncle. But he was hit by a car last night so he's taking a rest with the cat."

"I've never been on reality TV," Elvira said, looking around. "Do I need to sign a waiver? I don't want you to blur my face. I'll give you permission to use my likeness."

"No, no," Sophie said. "I promise, we didn't bring any cameras. We just want to meet Mr. Stackpole. We won't cause any trouble."

"Alrighty," Elvira said, not believing one word of that no-trouble BS. There was trouble at the Meet the Hunks luncheon every year, but viewership always went up for all the soaps in the three months after. Viewers like to see people on TV that they've met in real life, the television execs had figured out. It gives them a false closeness. Makes them feel like they're watching a good friend on the screen.

And personally, as a volunteer, Elvira hoped for trouble. It gave her a good story for the rest of the year, for all her dinner parties. Last year, a woman had bitten one of the Hunks, because he was *so delicious*. That particular Hunk had declined to return this year, so they'd booked a new actor in his stead, but it was good to mix it up anyway, year-to-year. "New blood," the planning committee had joked.

"Go meet Mark Stackpole in the tent down that path," Elvira directed the children and their nanny, the only children she'd ever seen come to the Hunks meet-and-greet in her seven years of volunteering.

"And don't be scared of the alligator in the pond," the volunteer named Betsy assured them. "He's the mascot of the country club, we all love him here." Betsy played golf at the Sugar Land course three days a week. Betsy had been happy since her divorce, deciding how to spend her own time. Playing golf and watching soaps.

"I thought there were only alligators in Florida," Ollie said.

"Oh, we got 'em in Texas too. And they're bigger in Texas. That one in the pond there is named T. Boone Pickens, and he's eleven feet long. Gentle giant, though, never bothers anyone. You can walk right by him."

"Okay," Ollie said, feeling nervous. He'd never seen an alligator before, and he always assumed you couldn't walk right by an alligator, that you had to outrun them. He remembered his stuffed alligator, the one he'd had as a baby, and how his mom used to pretend to eat him with it. The stuffed alligator was still in the house on Deerfield Lane, unless someone had cleaned out their things by now. Thrown them all away.

Sure enough, when they walked by T. Boone Pickens, the gator stayed where he was, lying half in and half out of the water, looking like a fallen tree.

Inside the big white tent, there were five lines of people queued up, all women, everyone waiting for each Hunk. The *General Hospital* hunk's line was the longest. Women had glossy pictures to sign, and calendars, and TV guides, and DVDs. Several women had loose bras in their arms, waiting to be signed on their satin cups.

"I can see him," Luna said. "I can see him! Can you see him, Ollie? He's over there, in the corner! He's glowing!"

Ollie nodded. There was a stone in his stomach. There was the man that their mother always said was Luna's father, whenever their dad wasn't home and their mom had a few glasses of white wine. She told them stories at bedtime about the life she could have had if she had only left Pondville with Mark Stackpole, who had been obsessed with her in high school. There he was. And he *was* glowing, but Ollie was pretty sure that was called a spray tan.

Now all they had to do was stand in the line and wait.

Their line seemed to be barely moving, but soon one of the other lines was getting a little rowdy, with one of the actors from *Invitation to Love* taking his shirt off and giving out lap dances. Taylor Selfridge was the actor who hadn't been here last year, a newbie to the circuit, and Taylor had such a minor part on the soap that he felt he had to give these women a little *somethin'-somethin'* to get their attention, and maybe then the fan base would demand his character get more lines, more time onscreen, maybe someone would even start a petition for the show writers to give Taylor's character an evil twin so he could play two characters at once. That happened often enough on soap operas, and it might as well happen to Taylor, as long as he could get these fans worked into a frenzy over his abdominal muscles. No one had told Taylor about what had happened last year, the medical care the other actor had to get after the meet-and-greet, how hard the crazed fan had bit him, that she'd not only broken the skin but had also partially ruptured an organ.

While Sophie and the kids waited in line inside the white tent, PJ and the cat got out of the car. It was hot in the Volvo, and PJ couldn't put the air conditioning on because Sophie hadn't left him with the keys. Sophie didn't trust him anymore. It hurt him, that his own daughter, his only living daughter, didn't trust him.

But of course, he couldn't blame her. PJ could see himself clearly enough to get it. So, because there was no air conditioning in the car, and it was hot in June in Texas, he decided to take Pancakes out on his leash, and they would go for a walk. His head still hurt, but he felt steady enough to walk, and sometimes it helped to walk off the pain. They started a loop around the golf course.

Up ahead, PJ saw a little pond, where a giant alligator was sunning himself. When the gator smelled the cat, and the blood from PJ's open head wound, he opened up his eyes. Golden eyes, lizard eyes, a black slit through the middle. He took a step toward PJ and the cat. PJ scooped up Pancakes. He would protect the cat at any cost. "Shoo," he told the gator. "Shoo!"

The alligator opened his mouth, as if about to laugh, but he did turn his giant lizard head away, and crawled off.

"That's right!" PJ called after him. "Go on! Eat someone else!"

41

Sophie, Ollie, and Luna had finally gotten to the front of the line, where Mark Stackpole was waiting in all his orange-spray-tanned glory, smiling with his perfect white porcelain veneers. Luna introduced herself while Ollie and Sophie hung back. "My name is Luna Meeklin," she said confidently, like she'd practiced with the statue of Abraham Lincoln. "Age ten and a half. We drove from Massachusetts. My mom was Elaine Meeklin."

"So, *to Elaine*?" Mark had asked, his Sharpie hovering over the glossy paper, ready to sign it. "Elaine with an *E*?"

"Sorry, her name was Elaine Duggins, not Elaine Meeklin, when you knew her. She changed her name when she married my dad. Do you remember Elaine Duggins?"

He put down the Sharpie and looked at Luna. He did not smile. "So, you're the girl," he said. Then he gestured for a man in a suit to come over. Maybe his security, or his agent, or his lawyer, or all three. "This is the girl who keeps writing to me about paternity. Go get Christine."

"Christine is here?" Luna asked. "Are the kids here too?" The only one whose name she knew was Sassafras, but she knew there were four others. Her half-siblings.

Mark Stackpole shook his head. "The kids are in LA with the nannies."

"Nannies," Luna whispered. Really rich people had multiple nannies. Her mom had always complained and said she wished she had a nanny and a maid too. Luna nudged Sophie. "Tell him," she said. "Tell him we're great kids."

Sophie blushed hard, but she did it. "They're great kids. Both Luna and her brother are great kids."

Mark Stackpole didn't look at Sophie but kept talking to Luna. "Listen, kid, we'll address your concerns. But I do need you to step aside now, so I can finish signing things for the fans of the show. After this, we'll talk it over." Mark Stackpole smiled again, but it looked forced. "I'm very glad you came. How is Pondville doing, anyway?"

"It's good," Luna said, beaming. The man who might be her father was so glad to meet her. He wasn't telling her to get lost, or to go drown herself in the nearest ocean, as she imagined he might. She'd imagined he would say all kinds of horrible things, and he hadn't. He had simply told his lawyer to go find his wife and had asked her to step out of line so he could talk to the rest of the fans. That hadn't been so bad. The next woman in line had a stack of bras for him to sign across the cups, and Luna watched with interest. He did it without complaint, despite what Jesus might say about touching another woman's underwear. Maybe Mark Stackpole could love Luna after all, despite her many sins.

As Sophie and the kids stood to the side, waiting for Mark Stackpole to finish with his fans, they watched what was happening in the other lines. Things were getting rowdy on the other side of the tent. This was why Elvira and Betsy and all the other women volunteered year after year. Because it was always a spectacle.

Taylor Selfridge from *Invitation to Love* had taken his shirt off, and everyone was screaming about that, egging him on, and ignoring the actor right next to him, Dallas Fieldstone, also an actor on *Invitation to Love*, in direct competition for screen time with Taylor. Taylor was younger and fresher, and Dallas was beginning to feel washed up. He could not let this younger guy ruin his career. If Taylor had a strong enough fan base, they might write Dallas off the show to give Taylor the limelight. Dallas wasn't safe, even though he was a main character. Even a main character could get killed off at any time.

Dallas decided to take his shirt off too, and although he was older than Taylor by nearly a decade, he was still an extremely fine specimen of a man, with so many muscles his abdominals had abdominals. And soon Dallas was performing a lap dance on one woman while other women whipped his abs and his butt—he'd taken off his pants, too, was wearing only his Calvin Klein boxer-briefs—and the women were whipping him with their I ♥ BEEFY HUNKS jerky sticks that had come in the welcome goody bag. It was getting awfully hot in the tent, and one woman fainted from heat stroke and would die by the time they got her to the hospital.

But for now, everyone was having a wonderful time, it was shaping up to be the best Meet the Hunks event ever, and then T. Boone Pickens entered the white tent. The alligator was looking for something to eat if he couldn't eat the cat, and he had smelled all the dried beef sticks. He crawled into the center of the white tent like a too-drunk wedding guest, opened his mouth, and let out a sigh, which sounded like a dragon's breath of fire.

For a second, everything was still. No one could run. There was one entrance to the tent, and the gator was standing right in the middle of it. The gator hissed again.

People started to crowd into the corner, screaming and panicking, and then a woman with a short red dress and Tina Turner legs stepped forward and everyone was quiet again. "Sex Bomb" by Tom Jones was playing over the loudspeaker.

"It's Christine," Luna whispered.

Christine Stackpole was wearing six-inch stilettos. "Hey, bucko,"

Christine said to the gator. "Over here." Christine Stackpole was a native Floridian, had been Miss Florida before she was Miss USA, and she wasn't afraid of any gator. They were lazy animals; they ate chicken giblets on gator farms. Christine had toured plenty of gator farms, back when she was Miss Florida. She saw what this gator wanted and unwrapped a few of the jerky sticks that the women had been whipping Dallas Fieldstone's abs and butt with and threw them one by one into T. Boone Pickens's open mouth. The gator swung his head back and forth in appreciation. He had not wanted to eat anybody. He was a golf-course alligator, practically domesticated. He wanted to be fed.

"She might be our stepmother," Luna said to Ollie, nudging him. "She's going to take such good care of us."

Sophie felt an unexpected pang of hurt to overhear that. But did *she* really want that job? Be their caretaker, worry about them all the time, tell them endless stories, drive them everywhere, give them constant snacks, deal with it when other kids were mean, talk to the principal when Luna punched someone again, make lunches every morning and help with their homework every night? Did Sophie even remember how to do basic math? No, she didn't. No, thank you. It would ruin her life.

"Christine Stackpole homeschools her children," Luna said as they watched her feed the gator.

Ollie nodded, in awe. Maybe living in a closet would be fine.

42

Back in the parking lot by the Volvo, the women and their floral dresses were getting in their cars and driving away. Pancakes watched the women go, straining at the leash in PJ's hand. Luna excitedly told PJ about Mark Stackpole, how he'd said he was glad she had come to see him.

"He said that, did he?" PJ asked. "He'll take the paternity test?" He looked at Sophie.

Sophie shrugged. "I think so. He said he'd find us afterward."

"This might be him!" Luna said, pointing to a black tour bus pulling across the parking lot.

The bus stopped near them with a big sigh, as if it were disappointed. The doors opened, and Christine and Mark Stackpole emerged down the bus stairs and began walking over. They were sauntering over, even. PJ imagined they were two rival cowboys, and it was time for a duel. PJ, of course, was without a gun. PJ hadn't owned a gun since Vietnam. But the Stackpoles didn't appear to have a gun either, or any kind of weapon. There was only a man in a suit walking a few paces behind them, holding a manila folder.

"You're really beautiful," Ollie said to Christine Stackpole, once she got close.

"Yes," Christine said.

"Thanks for saving us from the gator," he added.

At that, Christine smiled. "You're welcome. He was just hungry."

"So, these are the kids," Mark said to his wife and the lawyer, or perhaps he was a bodyguard. "But only the girl would be mine. The boy is a spitting image of Frank Meeklin."

"Hi," Luna said.

But Christine wasn't looking at Luna, instead she looked Sophie up and down, and wasn't smiling anymore. "And you're their mother."

"No, no," Sophie said. "Not me. I'm their babysitter."

"Oh," Christine said, looking a tiny bit friendlier.

"I'm their parental guardian," PJ explained. "I'm their great-uncle, and this is my daughter. And this is Pancakes, our cat."

"What happened to Elaine?" Mark asked.

"Tragic murder-suicide," PJ said.

Mark looked a little gray underneath the spray tan. "He killed her?"

"Vice-versa."

Mark put his hand to his mouth.

Sophie took the box out of her army bag, the one with a smiling dad snuggling a baby on the front of the box. "Are you willing—"

"Oh, sure, always glad to take a paternity test," Mark said.

"I told you he would!" Luna said.

"But I'll need you to sign this first."

The lawyer stepped forward with his manila folder, the papers inside. "If it comes back negative, we'll tear it up and forget this ever happened. But if the test comes back positive, it's a document that says my client, Mr. Stackpole, waives all parental rights. You will receive payments of five thousand dollars a month until the child is eighteen."

"It's more than fair," Christine said. "It's the arrangement we have with both other mothers of Mark's other children."

"Other children?" Sophie asked.

"Other children?" Luna asked.

"My husband is, unfortunately, extremely, extremely fertile," Christine said. "It's a problem." She gave Mark a dirty look.

"You can't be mad about this one," Mark said, throwing up his hands. "This was way back in high school. Before we met." Mark and Christine had met when they were twenty-one on the set of a movie, and that's when they started spitting out kids.

"Wait, you're really going to let me raise your kid?" PJ asked.

"That's what we are proposing, yes," Christine said. "You raise her, and we have no contact or obligations, other than financially."

"You're going to pay me child support? Even though I'm an old man? An alcoholic? This bandage on my head? I was hit by a car last night. You really think I can take good care of two kids?"

"I don't think that's our business," said Christine. "They'll be your kids."

PJ was doing the math. Five thousand dollars a month. They wouldn't be rich, but they could make it work. But maybe he could squeeze a little more out of them. "Seven thousand dollars a month," he said. "There's two of them."

"But the boy isn't Mark's."

"You pay me, and I'll take them," he said. "You pay me seven thousand a month and you'll never have to see them again."

"Fine," Christine said.

Luna's eyes watered. "You don't want me," she said. "Even if I'm your kid, you don't want me." Inside Luna, there was a hope and dream of a mansion, a mansion where she was wanted and loved by her real father and a kind and beautiful stepmother who could tame alligators, and now the mansion disintegrated. It disintegrated like the mansion was made of sand.

"Well, sweetie," Mark Stackpole said, bending down and getting close to Luna's face. "You see, I have my own family. I have my own kids. I love them and their mother very, very much, and they are made out of that love, marital love, and what happened between me and your mother was a long time ago, and it was a terrible mistake."

"Oh," Luna said, and then she looked up at him with fire in her eyes. Her hands clutched, and she was wearing both Sophie's leather bracelets because Ollie had given her his bracelet to borrow for the day for good luck, after he felt bad that the cat had jumped out the window. "You can have your DNA back," Luna said. "I don't want it." And with the help of the strength of two Wonder Woman bracelets, Luna Meeklin spat right in Mark Stackpole's face. Got him right in the eye.

Mark Stackpole went red, and a vein in his neck bulged, and Sophie worried he might hit the girl. She moved in between Mark and Luna as quick as she could.

"Hey now," PJ said.

"Oh my," Christine said. "That wouldn't fly in our house."

"Go wait in the car," Sophie told Ollie and Luna. "Let us deal with this. Get in the car now and stay there."

"Okay," Ollie said.

"I hope Sassafras dies," Luna said, and bent to pick up the cat. PJ dropped the leash so the cat could go with the kids. "I hope you all die," Luna added.

"Like I said," PJ said to Christine and Mark, "you pay me 7K a month, and you'll never hear from the girl again. Best money you ever spent."

Hearing that, Luna immediately broke into a sob and slammed the Volvo door.

"Dad!" Sophie scolded.

"I was joking! Hey, Luna, I was joking!"

Ollie opened the car door and followed his sister into the backseat, but PJ didn't go over to the car to do damage control right then, because the lawyer continued: "And also attached is a nondisclosure agreement, that you can't talk to the press about this."

"I don't think we will," PJ said. He took the papers and looked them over. "Can I use your back?" he asked the lawyer. The lawyer turned around and let himself be used as a clipboard. PJ signed at all the highlighted parts. It reminded him of when he'd won the lottery, all the paperwork he'd had to fill out. They weren't giving him a free sweatshirt, though.

"But wait, Dad," Sophie said. "What about the person the social workers have lined up in September? That person is supposed to take care of them, if Mark didn't want them."

PJ looked at his feet.

And as Sophie said it out loud—she understood. The person lined up to take care of them in September was Sophie's own mother. The bastard was going to pawn the kids off on his ex-wife, once she was back from her trip. "You're an asshole, Dad," she said, her laser eyes coming out, but Ollie wasn't there to see them. He was in the Volvo with his sister. "You're a real asshole." She hoped she said it loud enough so the kids could hear.

"I won't deny it," he said. "But I've been doing my best."

Sophie shook her head in disgust.

"Let's get this show on the road," Christine said, tapping her foot. "You people can argue later."

The lawyer looked everything over, and he gave Mark the go-ahead to take the paternity test. Mark removed the cotton swab from the box. He stuck it in his cheek and rubbed it around. He handed it to Sophie, who held out the sample-collection tube. She put the tube back in the box and sealed it. "It takes seven to ten days," she read.

"We'll need a copy of the test results," the lawyer said. "And don't try to pull a fast one and get fancy with Photoshop. I'll be confirming with the company."

"We wouldn't do that," PJ said. "I'm not very good with computers. But it's your loss, if she's your kid and you don't want to be part of her life. She's a special kid, and I hope you'll reconsider down the line. I'll keep the door open. A father should know his kid." *He's a jackass to not want to know his own kid,* PJ thought.

After that, Christine and Mark and their lawyer walked off back to the Hunks tour bus, kicking up more dust as they went. Mark Stackpole didn't even bother to knock on the window of the car to say goodbye to Luna, but maybe it was for the best. He didn't want her. He had paperwork that said he didn't want her, and PJ Halliday had signed it.

PJ was getting ready to talk to Luna, about how Mark Stackpole was a dipshit anyway, that men with teeth that white can't be trusted, but then he looked in the backseat, and where the children had been, only a minute ago, there was only an empty backseat and a piece of paper decorated with colorful cutout magazine letters. Luna had been using the scissors for the past few days in the backseat to make this project, in case she and Ollie needed to buy themselves some time while they ran away to Mexico, a country Luna had never been to, but she knew that's where everyone goes when they run.

WE WERE KIDNAPPED, DON'T BOTHER LOOKING, the note said. $1.5 MILLION RANSOM. And then at the bottom, in pencil, Luna had added: *You're an asshole Uncle PJ.* And then, on a second line, she wrote: *We took the cat.*

43

"We lost them!" PJ wailed. "We lost them! Sophie, how did we lose them? Do you think they left with one of the women from the event? Got in one of their cars?" PJ thought of those women, and all their floral outfits felt so menacing now. Maybe those women were Venus fly traps. They were the sort of animals that eat their young. The kind that stole children. They were all that was wrong with the natural world.

"No," Sophie said. "Dad, they didn't leave with one of the women. They didn't get in anyone's car, they just ran off somewhere. Stay calm, Dad, stay calm." Sophie was saying that to herself as much as she was saying it to him. She felt a desperate panic, but the kids had to be around here somewhere. They had to. And she had to find the kids and make her dad apologize to Luna for being an idiot. His fucking $7,000 negotiation. They couldn't have gone far. She should not panic, she could not panic, panicking wouldn't help. Sophie needed to think fast and find the kids. "You look around the golf course," Sophie commanded. "Ask the golfers. Go look in the clubhouse. Look in the bathrooms. Look in the restaurant. I'll look on the golf course and in the tent." *And in the gator pond,* Sophie thought but didn't say. She did not want her dad having a heart attack over the possibility of the children drowning in the gator pond.

"Okay," PJ said, trying to pull it together, and he hustled into the country club clubhouse, where men in pink polo shirts were having small sandwiches and beer in green bottles. There were women with some of the men, beautiful women, wearing white and pastel purple outfits, drinking Chardonnay. No one had seen two children, ages nine and ten, names Ollie and Luna. No one had seen an orange cat. They wanted to know if PJ's head was all right, and why it was bandaged like that, and then one of the employees asked him politely to leave, claimed he was disturbing the guests. PJ jogged back to the car, his white undershirt soaked through, and Sophie came back from the woods and the pond. No luck.

Sophie wanted to throw up. The golf course seemed to be spinning. Terror gripped her throat. *Where the fuck had they gone?* They were just here. They were really just here. "We'll go to the police station," Sophie said. "Let's go to the police station."

"We can't do that."

"Why not?"

"Because the social worker is already mad at me for not having them in school. I guess there was still a little school left before summer break, and if the social worker, this woman named Belinda Bell . . . if she found out I lost the kids and had to go to the police, I am very, very sure she would take the kids away from us forever."

"Dammit, Dad. You took the kids out of school for this?"

He shrugged. He thought this was important. He stood by his decision. And truthfully, he'd always known there was still three weeks of school left when he took the kids on the trip. Because he knew exactly when the last day of school was. It was two days after prom, which was always the third Tuesday in June. The day Kate had died. But PJ had chosen not to think about it. Sometimes he just didn't think about things.

Sophie raked her face with her hands in frustration. "Okay, okay, no police, not yet. We'll find them. We can find them on our own."

"It's my fault we lost them. I shouldn't have said—"

"Yes, Dad," Sophie interrupted. "It's your fault."

PJ felt stabbed in the chest. It was all his fault, it really was. He sat down on the curb and waited for a heart attack to kill him. He prayed for a heart attack, a brain aneurysm, a stroke, a bolt of lightning, a sinkhole to open up and take him into the earth. "I can't do this. I can't do this again." He was sucking in air. "Why would they run away?"

"Dad, you hurt Luna's feelings when you said you needed money to take her from Mark Stackpole. We need to find her and apologize. She'll forgive you if you apologize. Kids are good at forgiving. Now, stand up and get your ass in the car."

"Okay," PJ said, and he did. He hoisted himself up and he got into the Volvo. He was glad to listen to Sophie. It took the pressure off him.

"They can't have gone far," Sophie said. "They took their suitcases." Sophie wished she hadn't bought them suitcases with wheels. Heavy duffel bags would have slowed them down more, but both suitcases were rollers.

"And they have the cat," PJ pointed out. It wasn't easy to travel with a cat.

"And they don't have much money," Sophie said. "Just the hundred bucks each you gave them in the beginning of the trip, right? You didn't give them more?"

He shook his head. He didn't give them more. He would have if they asked, but they didn't ask. And they would need money for food for themselves and for the cat. And then he remembered something. *The Lost Cat poster*. The bus stop! "They probably got on the bus," he said. "They have enough money to get on the bus."

But that wasn't good news. It meant they hadn't gone on foot, and they could be anywhere in Sugar Land. Anywhere the city bus went.

"Shit," Sophie said. "Let's go." A frantic fear gripped her throat.

They had to find them. What if they couldn't find them? Where had they gone? Sophie and her father peeled out of the country club parking lot in the Bird Barn Volvo, out of the iron gates and onto the road. "Fuck that place," Sophie said under her breath.

Okay, PJ thought, trying to stay calm. No, they weren't in Pondville, but Sugar Land, Texas, wasn't the world's biggest city. It wasn't Times Square. They could find the kids. Sophie was right, he had to stay calm.

Sophie realized she was driving aimlessly, she didn't know where the bus had gone, so she pulled over to look up the bus route on her phone. As she did that, PJ looked out the window. On the corner, there was a group of kids clustered together, all of them holding skateboards. There was a boy wearing a red T-shirt in the middle, the color of Ollie's ketchup-bottle T-shirt—*had Ollie been wearing that?* The boy wore that T-shirt most days. Maybe it would be that easy, and the kids were standing right over there. Maybe they had run away and immediately found some friends. That's how kids survived in the world without adults, didn't they? They relied on one another. "Ollie!" PJ called out the window. "Ollie! Hey, you in the red T-shirt!"

The boy in red looked nothing like Ollie, but he approached the car anyway. "Did you lose your dog, sir?" the boy asked. He was holding a skateboard.

Kids in Texas were very polite, PJ thought. "No, Ollie is a boy," PJ explained. "Have you seen a boy and a girl about your age? Maybe a little younger? And a cat? An orange cat."

"Oh," the boy said. "I'm sorry, sir, I haven't."

"How old are you?"

"Fifteen, sir."

"Oh, so you're much older than they are. Well, that's why it's so important that we find them. They're too young to be wandering around alone. I'll give you two hundred dollars if you help us look."

"Dad!"

"What? Sophie, we need help here. We're strangers in a strange land. Do you know anyone else in Texas who can help us look?"

Sophie did not know anyone in Texas. She only knew people back in Massachusetts, because she almost never left Massachusetts. She wished she never had. She rested her forehead on the steering wheel.

"Sure, sir, I'd be glad to help," the boy said. "We lost my dog once, and I found him."

"That's the spirit." PJ took out his wallet, and he handed the boy two hundred dollars and Sophie's phone number on a piece of paper. "Call me if you see them," he told the boy. "What's your name, kid?"

"Alexander Laboso, sir, but my friends call me Zander."

"Zander, huh?" And right, the boy had friends. All those other kids over there, staring at them. All his friends could help too. "Tell your friends, whoever finds those kids, there's more money where that came from. Five-thousand-dollar reward."

The boy's eyes went wide. Then he saluted and returned to his friends. He showed them the money, told them what they needed to do, and then the boys and the two girls in the group all went skateboarding off in different directions. Each of them typing on a cell phone as they skateboarded. It was beautiful to see.

"Now we have a search party," PJ said proudly.

Sophie closed her eyes and shook her head. She could not believe any of this was happening. This extended nightmare.

But PJ was feeling hopeful. The teenagers would find the kids. He had a good feeling about that boy in the red shirt. Zander. He'd been so polite. He had saluted like a real soldier. They had an army on the streets of Sugar Land. This was a war, but it was a war they were going to win. Sophie had to keep driving now, and they would look for the kids, and wait for Zander and his army of friends to call. It would only cost him $5,000 to find the kids, which was probably about most of what he had left in his bank account at this point. But so what. All that mattered was that PJ got those kids home safe.

Sophie was driving down Beechnut Boulevard, following where she was pretty sure the bus had gone, and that's when she saw the red-and-blue lights flashing in her mirror. "Oh my God," Sophie said. "We're being pulled over."

"What did you do?" PJ asked, turning around.

"Nothing!"

"You must have done something," PJ said. "You're not drunk, are you? The cash bar at the meet-and-greet?"

"No, Dad. I'm not drunk."

Sophie pulled over. Maybe the Volvo's taillight was out. Maybe she had run a stop sign. Maybe the cop just wanted to say hello. Maybe she should tell this cop right now that they had lost two kids. But she agreed with her dad. If the social workers found out that they had lost the kids, they would put them back in foster care. And Ollie and Luna might not even go to the same home. She had heard about that, that sometimes siblings were split up. The worst thing she could imagine happening was if Ollie and Luna didn't have each other anymore.

God, she loved those kids. Even though they had cut her hair and driven her nuts in the car, she loved them. She wasn't just fond of them, like she'd always liked the kids she babysat, but she loved them. She loved how weird they were, and how funny, and how Ollie kind of smelled like cheese, and how Luna was a little mean, and she loved them. She needed to find them.

The cop was tapping on her window. Sophie took a deep breath and rolled it down. The cop was wearing aviator sunglasses like a cop from a movie, and he pulled them down to look in the car.

"What seems to be the problem, Officer?" PJ asked, leaning across Sophie, and Sophie was glad to let her dad talk. She was freezing up in this situation, like a deer in headlights, like she had when her boss lit himself on fire. She was able to reach into her wallet for her license, at least, and her dad took the registration out of the glove box and handed it to the officer. His gold name tag said Officer Curtin.

"I'm going to need to search your vehicle," Officer Curtin said.

"What for, Officer?" PJ asked.

"Drugs," the cop said, as if it were obvious.

"What makes you think we have drugs?" PJ asked.

"I saw you give that gang of teenagers back there a wad of cash."

"But we—" Sophie started, but she didn't know how else to explain why they had given the kids on the street the money. If they didn't want Ollie and Luna to be taken away by social services, they couldn't explain it.

"Oh no, sir, we're not drug users," PJ said. "I'm a million-dollar lottery winner, and I like to give money to kids in need."

"My ass, you are," Officer Curtin said. "Driving an old Volvo shitbox?"

"He is," Sophie said.

PJ rummaged in the backseat.

"Keep your hands where I can see them!" the cop said, putting his hand on his gun.

"Oh, I wanted to show you the sweatshirt they gave me. It's proof I'm a lottery winner. A million and a half bucks in the Massachusetts State Lottery."

"I'm definitely going to need to search the vehicle."

So, Sophie and PJ put their hands up and got out of the car. Officer Curtin put on latex gloves before he gave each of them a patdown. Officer Curtin was a germaphobe, and it was hard for him to touch other people and their belongings, so he had a box full of latex gloves in his cruiser. The other officers on the force always called him Condom-Hands Curtin, a nickname he didn't like.

As Officer Curtin started his search, Sophie remembered the weed gummies she had in her bag. He hadn't looked in her bag yet, but he would. She did not think marijuana was legal in Texas. They were going to jail, and the kids would never be found.

Officer Curtin picked up the ransom note in the backseat, and that was certainly a red flag. There were empty Happy Meal boxes everywhere. There was a litterbox underneath the passenger seat, which was a little strange, but lots of people traveled with their pets. Officer Curtin found the sweatshirt PJ had mentioned. MASSACHU-SETTS STATE LOTTERY WINNER, it said on the chest. "No shit, you weren't lying," Officer Curtin said, looking back at PJ.

"No, sir," PJ said, feeling like he'd learned something from Zander. How important it was to say *sir*.

Officer Curtin was about to let them go, because it checked out that this was a rich guy giving away some money to hungry kids, which wasn't a crime, it was nice, actually, and that was refreshing for Officer Curtin, but then, when he reached under the driver's-side seat for one last sweep, something grabbed him. "What the heck?" he asked, jumping back from the car. "Is there another person in the vehicle?"

Sophie wondered if the kids were hiding underneath the seats, but no, there was no way. The kids couldn't fit underneath there. "No," she said. "There's definitely no one else in the car."

"Well, someone grabbed me. A hand. I felt fingers. Someone's fingers grabbed me, I'm telling you."

"Huh," PJ said. "That's strange, sir."

"Can I look?" Sophie asked.

Officer Curtin nodded, his face pale. He was afraid. His mother had some paranormal experiences in her house recently, and Officer Curtin had been feeling jumpy about it.

Sophie reached underneath the seat and pulled out a hand, severed at the elbow.

Officer Curtin screamed.

"It's just a wax hand," Sophie said. "Don't worry." It was indeed a wax hand, missing its pinkie finger. Sophie knew immediately that Luna had stolen it from the wax museum. ABE LINCOLN RIGHT ARM was stamped in small black letters on the wrist.

"Can I see that?" PJ asked, and Sophie handed it to him.

"I promise there are no drugs in the car, Officer," Sophie said, feeling like she was in charge now, now that she had saved him from the wax hand that he had said had grabbed him. It was impossible for a wax hand to grab anyone. It wasn't even very lifelike.

Officer Curtin was embarrassed; Sophie could see that. "I'll be back," he said, taking the license and registration with him. He walked back to his cruiser and got in.

PJ and Sophie waited. Watched him. It was taking a long time. He was talking to someone on his radio. Then he was talking to someone on his cell phone. *His wife?* Sophie wondered. She peeked into her bag, and she didn't see her baggie of gummies. "Did you take—*anything*—out of my bag?" she whispered to her dad.

"No," he said, still holding the wax hand and pretending to give it a handshake. "Oh wait, yes. I ate some of your gummy bears."

"Jesus," Sophie said, but an ocean of relief washed over her.

"He's trying to make us sweat," PJ said, watching the cop talk on the phone in the car.

Finally, Officer Curtin got out of his cruiser and walked back to them. He handed Sophie back her license but held on to the registration. "Are you aware that this car is registered to someone named Mr. Fred Sharp?"

"Yes," PJ said. "I am aware."

"Did you steal it?"

"No, no, no," Sophie said. "Fred Sharp is my mom's boyfriend. Her fiancé. Practically my stepdad."

"It's my best friend's car," PJ said. "We're borrowing it. He's in Alaska."

"That's a little strange."

"How so?"

"He said he was in Minnesota when I just spoke to him on the phone. And he didn't know you were using the car. He said—pretty explicitly—that you did not have permission to take the car out of state."

"You're mistaken, Officer. Fred's in Alaska until the end of the summer. Did you have a bad connection on the phone? They don't have much service up there."

"I could hear him fine."

"Was he mad about the car?"

Officer Curtin pointed his finger in PJ's face. "So, you did steal it."

"No." PJ shook his head. "No, no, no. You can't steal something from a family member. I'm the best man in his wedding."

"You *sure can* steal from a family member. In my line of work, that's pretty much eighty percent of the theft cases I see."

PJ wondered if Minnesota was the name of a town in Alaska. That could be right. He knew there was a Boston in New York State, which must be awfully confusing for the residents there. They must rarely, if ever, get their mail.

"You can't borrow a car if the owner doesn't want you to take it," Officer Curtin said. "This is a stolen vehicle."

"All due respect, sir, but Fred Sharp is my best friend in the world, and if he knew the situation, he would want me to have the car."

"What's the situation?"

"We're borrowing the car," Sophie said to the officer, interrupting her dad. "I promise we're just borrowing it." She did not want to go to prison for taking Fred's Volvo. That would be so stupid. So fucking stupid, stupider than going to prison for weed gummies. Fred wasn't using it. He was their family. They were all a family. Sophie felt like she was about to cry, but she knew if she started crying, she could never stop. "Let me call him," Sophie said. "Let me call Fred now."

"Sure," Officer Curtin said. "Go for it."

Sophie took out her phone and dialed. Her dad and Officer Curtin watched her. Fred didn't pick up, but a second later, the phone dinged with a text:

We will talk about the car when your mother and I get home, Fred had written. *I do not want to deal with it right now. I do not know what you and your father are thinking, or why you're in Texas, but I do not want to deal with it right now.*

"Um, Fred's busy," Sophie said, feeling sheepish. "But we weren't able to tell him why we took the car because he doesn't know about the kids and—"

"What kids?" Officer Curtin asked.

"The kids we gave the money to," PJ said, thinking fast. "We've been traveling around the country, giving out money to kids in need."

"You know, that's really lovely," Officer Curtin said. Condom-Hands Curtin was a sensitive guy. "That's the loveliest thing I've heard in a long time. You really won a million and a half dollars? And you're giving it all away to children?"

"I did and I am," PJ said proudly. "My daughter here, she's never been impressed."

"It's very impressive," Officer Curtin said, nodding. He wanted to shake PJ's hand, but PJ was still holding that creepy fake hand, and Officer Curtin didn't want the hand to grab him again. He didn't know how it had grabbed him the first time, if it was wax, but he didn't want it to grab him again. Officer Curtin sighed. "Well, folks, I'm not going to arrest you, because Mr. Sharp said not to, and I really like that you've been giving money away to kids who need it, but I'm still going to need to impound the vehicle. That's the policy regarding stolen vehicles. There's really nothing I can do about it, after everything Mr. Sharp said to me on the phone. I hate getting involved in family matters, I really do."

"Okay," Sophie said, defeated, because she feared if she argued with him, Officer Curtin could change his mind about arresting them. She did not want to lose the car, but she really, really didn't want to go to jail.

"All right," PJ said, because there was nothing to be done. They were losing the Bird Barn.

A tow truck was along only two minutes later and loaded up the red Volvo.

"I don't know how Fred is ever going to get his car back if it's impounded in Texas," PJ said to Sophie after the tow truck and Officer Curtin were gone and PJ and Sophie were left standing together on the side of the road with their suitcases. At least Officer Curtin had let them take their suitcases.

"Fred will do anything to teach us a lesson," Sophie said. Fred was a judge and he believed in justice and punishments for bad behavior. And Sophie knew Fred was not to be messed with right now, not at that moment. Sophie knew how mad Fred must be. He had asked for quiet time alone with Ivy for a few months, and they hadn't been able to give him that. She felt horribly guilty for what she'd done.

But she was pissed at Fred, too, because now it would be so much harder to find the kids. Fred didn't know what she was going through. He had asked her to not bother him and her mother while they were on the trip, but you know what, what if she needed them? She was allowed to need people. *We're never going to find the kids,* Sophie thought. Everything is a lost cause. They would have to call the police, and the kids would be taken to foster care, and she and her dad would go to prison for child endangerment. And they would both deserve it.

The Sugar Land city bus arrived, and PJ and Sophie got on. They sat side by side on the orange plastic seats. The AC was a relief, but everything else felt miserable. This would be an impossible way to find the kids. Wherever they'd gone, they had a huge head start.

"If we don't find them by nightfall . . ." PJ decided, "we'll call the cops. We'll call Officer Curtin. We've got a friend on the police force now."

"He's not our friend, Dad." Her dad would never get it. "A friend doesn't impound your car. And you were right before, if we call the cops, they'll take the kids from us. They'll take the kids and they'll put them in foster care. Sometimes siblings go to different homes."

"Oh," PJ said. That was worse than bedbugs, thinking of Ollie and Luna in separate homes. "But they need each other."

"I know."

"It's all my fault—"

"Shut up, Dad. Just shut up for now."

Miraculously, he shut up. They sat there on the bus. They waited for the next stop. They hoped they would get lucky, somehow. PJ knew he'd gotten lucky a few times, winning the lottery, getting Ivy to marry him, surviving three heart attacks, but he'd also been unlucky many times. He looked out the bus windows at all the normal life going by on the streets of Sugar Land, Texas. People walking their dogs. A woman pushing a stroller. A man smoking a cigarette. How simple things are for other people, PJ thought. People who don't know what it's like to lose a child.

44

Sophie looked up at the map of stops along the bus route above her head. A list of street names on a line. *Freeman St., Pressier Garage, Beechnut SC, HWY 36, Hillside Road.* None of those names meant anything to her. How could she know which stop they'd gotten off at? There was no way to guess. There were twenty stops and none of them looked right.

As the bus drove on, hurtling through Sugar Land, Sophie closed her eyes. In therapy, Blanche had told her that if Sophie felt overwhelmed, she should close her eyes and pretend to be somewhere else. They had practiced it in Blanche's office, and Blanche had chimed a bell when it was done.

Sophie imagined she was at a picnic bench, on the beach at a lake. Sophie knew the lake. Ossipee Lake. It was a memory; they were on vacation in New Hampshire. Her sister was there, and their mother had brought submarine sandwiches for lunch from the pizza place. The sandwiches were wrapped in white butcher paper. It was the first time Sophie had an Italian sub, and she announced to the table that when she grew up, that was all she would be eating. Subs like that one. How salty and oily it was.

Someone's phone chimed, and Sophie opened her eyes to the bus around her. She wasn't much calmer, and it wasn't a useful memory. Everything was still terrible.

But wait, the kids hadn't had lunch that day. No sandwiches of any kind. There hadn't been time to stop for lunch, they were rushing to get to the meet-and-greet. By now, Ollie would be whining for food, and Luna would have to deal with it. Sophie looked out the window to see where they might have stopped to eat. She prayed to see the golden arches of McDonald's appear. If the bus passed by a McDonald's, that was where they would have gone. Ollie would have demanded it, and Luna would have given in to shut him up.

Outside the bus, it began to rain.

"Oh no," PJ said. "They'll be wet and miserable."

If they're wet and miserable, Sophie thought, *at least they're alive.*

No, stop thinking like that, Sophie argued with herself. *Of course they're alive.* This wasn't like it always was, looking for her father. They were healthy and young and they hadn't actually been kidnapped. They knew how to use a crosswalk to safely cross the street. Luna was right on that very first day of the road trip: They weren't babies. They could take care of themselves. For a short while at least, they could take care of themselves. Eventually something bad would happen to them, but Sophie was sure nothing bad had happened to them yet. She and her dad just had to find them before something did.

The bus stopped, but there was no McDonald's in sight. And there were no other restaurants around either; it was a residential neighborhood.

"Get off here?" her dad asked.

Sophie shook her head no, and she watched out the window. A grandmother and a small child were about to get on, but the child was holding an open umbrella, and she wouldn't let her grandma close it, even though her grandma tried to explain that one of the metal spokes could put out someone's eye. The girl was only about three years old and she didn't care about anyone's eyes. She cared about holding an open umbrella.

"IT'S FINE, MA'AM," the bus driver said with an extraordinarily loud voice. "JUST GET ON. WE'VE ALL BEEN THERE."

The bus had filled up with passengers, so PJ stood up and offered the woman and the child his seat.

"Such a gentleman," the woman said, smiling. "Say thank you to the gentleman, Abby."

Abby didn't say anything. But Abby was now sitting right next to Sophie, and Sophie had an open umbrella in her face. Sophie didn't want to stand up and give up her seat, because she needed to look out the window for a McDonald's, but now she was stuck with an open umbrella in her face. *As if this could get any fucking harder,* Sophie thought.

Maybe she should pray to someone that she could find these kids, could find them safe and sound, but she didn't have much of a relationship with God or Jesus or any of them. But maybe she could pray to Kate. She talked to Kate sometimes, when she was alone and had no one else to talk to. It would have been nice to have a sister. Someone who could have commiserated about their idiot father. *Please,* Sophie thought. *Please, Kate, help me now. Help me save these kids. They are scared and they're mad at Dad—you remember what it was like to be mad at Dad? How he never listens and always does whatever he wants? How he thinks he's so funny? How everyone loves him, but no one knows what it's like to have him as a father, the person you're supposed to count on but can't?*

"I remember," the little girl with the umbrella said, clear as day, Sophie swore she heard her say it, and a shiver went up her spine. *Remember* was a big word for a three-year-old, but Sophie was sure she'd said it.

"You do?" she asked the girl. "You remember?"

But the girl didn't answer. She was picking her nose instead.

"Abby, you remember riding the bus?" the girl's grandma asked.

"Shit," PJ said, patting the pockets of his cargo shorts. "Shit. Dammit. Shit."

Sophie looked away from the girl, uncomfortable that the grandma was involved, and looked up at her dad. "What now?"

"The ring. It's gone."

"What ring?"

"I had a ring in my pocket."

"What kind of ring?"

"I showed it to the kids one night. The night we watched the movie about the killer whales. They were excited about it. Excited that I'm going to ask Michelle to marry me."

"You bought Michelle Cobb a ring?"

"No, no, no. I didn't buy it. Or I did buy it, a long time ago. Luna's probably going to take it to a pawn shop and get cash for it."

Sophie understood exactly where he had gotten the ring from, and her eyes turned into her usual lasers. "You stole Mom's old engagement ring to give to another woman?"

"She wasn't using it."

"You are so fucking selfish, Dad. So unbelievably fucking selfish. You can't give Mom's engagement ring to another woman. It's hers. It's Mom's. Those memories are important to Mom. Important to *me*."

"Please watch your language," said the umbrella girl's grandmother.

"I'm sorry," PJ said. "I didn't think either of you would care. She doesn't wear it. She never wears it."

"Because you aren't married anymore. But it's hers, Dad. You can't take anything else from her. She has given you so much. She has given you everything she has, and sometimes I think . . . I think it's hurt her, to spend so much of her life looking after you. She's spent so much of her life stressed out."

"I doubt she's stressed out in Alaska."

"She probably is, Dad. She's probably really stressed out because she's probably worried you've gotten into some huge mess back home. Which you have! You have gotten us into a huge fucking mess!"

The umbrella girl's grandmother stood up and said something to the bus driver.

"YOU TWO!" the driver called to the back. She could have been an opera singer, with lungs that size. "YOU TWO ARE GETTING OFF AT THE NEXT STOP! NO CURSE WORDS ON MY BUS!"

"What's the next stop?" PJ asked.

"THE MALL!"

"The mall?" Sophie repeated. On the map, the stop was called Beechnut SC, which had meant nothing to Sophie, a stranger to Sugar Land, didn't know that *SC* stood for shopping center. But at the mall, there was fast food for Ollie. There usually weren't pawn shops in malls, but Luna probably thought she could sell the ring to any jewelry store. She had probably gone up to the counter at Zales and asked what the clerk would pay for it. And maybe Zales actually would buy it from her, maybe they had a program where they bought gold, many jewelry stores did. And then the kids would have more money, to keep running. Shit, what if they had enough money to keep running? If they left Sugar Land, it would be impossible to find them without the police. This was hopeless. It was probably fucking hopeless.

Then, Sophie's phone dinged. *Hi sir. Zander here!* the text read. *Possible sighting! My friend saw a boy in a ketchup bottle T-shirt throwing up outside a trampoline park.*

Sophie gasped. *Which trampoline park?* she texted back.

The bus pulled up to the next stop and screeched to a halt. "TIME TO GET OFF, BOZOS," the bus driver said.

Sophie paused, waiting for Zander to answer. If the trampoline park was somewhere else in Sugar Land, a stop farther down the line, perhaps she could beg the bus driver and the watermelon umbrella grandmother to let them stay on the bus. They couldn't lose any more time, if they knew where Ollie was, or where he had been recently. Standing hunched over outside a trampoline park, vomiting. He must have jumped on the trampolines right after eating. Luna must have promised him McDonald's and trampolines if he went with her. "Come on, Zander, answer me," Sophie said, looking at her phone while the bus driver waited for her to unload. Her dad had already gotten off the bus, was standing with his suitcase in the rain. "Come on, come on, come on," she begged as the three dots to show he was typing right then appeared.

The FunTime trampoline park, Zander wrote. *In the Beechnut Galleria Mall.*

Sophie grabbed her suitcase, but before she jumped off the bus, she took one last glance at the little girl with the watermelon umbrella, who had tried to take out her eye with the spokes. She'd heard little kids were like that sometimes, that they could see ghosts and read minds. But Sophie didn't have time to communicate with Kate right now through a child medium. She had living children to find.

45

The parking lot at the Beechnut Galleria Mall was an ocean of cars, so many people at the mall on a late Saturday afternoon.

"We should split up," Sophie said to her dad. It was a huge mall. A city itself, practically. "You start at this entrance; I'll start at the other one. I'll go talk to the mall security. They'll help us. They're not the real police." People lost their kids in the mall all the time, the mall cops understood that. They wouldn't call child services over something so routine.

PJ nodded. He appreciated Sophie taking charge. Sophie was right, he never should have taken Ivy's old ring to give to another woman. Their marriage was an important memory, and the ring was a trinket of their happiness. And they had been happy once. When he saw Ivy again, he would apologize for taking it out of her jewelry box, and for so many other things.

He walked into the mall alone. The inside of the building was all white, escalators connecting the two floors, and an open railing all around the top. Mostly stores he recognized, many of the same stores they had in the South Coast Mall back home, down in New Bedford. He went there once a year for Christmas shopping.

Up ahead in the mall, there were ladies in pink velour tracksuits sitting on a bench.

"Have you seen two small children?" he asked them. "And a cat?"

"A cat?" the first woman asked.

"No," the other woman said. "I don't think I've seen a cat today."

"Yes, a cat on a leash. An orange cat. And two children, ages nine and ten. Both fourth graders. Irish twins."

"Oh," the first woman said. "Their poor mother. So hard to have children close in age."

PJ knew he should keep walking. The women in pink velour had nothing to do with this, and they weren't helping, but he had to say something to these old bags: "You shouldn't assume it's their mother who takes care of them. It's *my* job. It's *my* job to take care of them." The women were startled. PJ moved on, kept walking through the mall.

He saw a jewelry store, where Luna had probably tried to sell the ring, but the Zales was empty, other than the glass cases and a bored-looking employee in a black polo shirt. PJ looked in the next window. And then another. No children in the Gap, or in the Apple Store. No children in Lucky Brand Jeans. It seemed like the mall was full of teenagers and middle-aged women and old people, no children. What happened to the children? Did no one take them out of the house to go shopping anymore?

PJ looked ahead, and at the far end of the mall, in front of the Macy's, right next to the escalator, there was a crowd around a small waterfall on the first floor. PJ wondered if they were throwing pennies into the waterfall, wishing for better luck. Hoping to win the lottery. To fall in love that year. Get pregnant. Get into college. For this to be the year they get out of this town and never, ever, ever come back.

But no, the crowd wasn't throwing money in the waterfall. Instead, they were all looking up, above, to the second floor of the mall. PJ looked up too. A little redheaded boy was standing against the railing and holding an orange cat over the edge, like the monkey holds Simba in *The Lion King*.

"LISTEN TO ME, LUNA!" Ollie was yelling. "LISTEN TO ME OR I WILL DROP THE CAT!"

"Don't drop the cat!" the people below yelled. "Listen to him, Luna!"

Up above, on the second floor, PJ could see Luna was standing near Ollie, about ten feet away from the boy.

"I'm listening," Luna said. "Please don't hurt the cat. The cat is a hero, remember? He saved our lives."

"I don't care! I am not going to Mexico. We had something good, and we ruined it. We had a family!"

"We weren't a family," Luna said, her arms crossed.

"What were we then?"

"We're just two kids. Just two kids no one wants!"

PJ's heart was in his throat. He had found the kids, but he would kill Ollie if that boy dropped the cat. But he didn't want the kids to think he was mad, or they'd run again, and PJ would never stand a chance, chasing them. He was old and they were young, he was slow and they were fast. He had to say the right thing. He could be jokey about it. "Hey, Annie Edson Taylor!" he yelled. "Do not throw that cat over the falls!"

"Uncle PJ!" Ollie said, but he was still holding the cat over the edge. "You found us! She made me go! I didn't want to go!"

Luna looked over the edge. "*How* did you find us?"

"I'll always find you!" PJ yelled up. "Now, please put the cat on the ground."

"What took you so long?" Ollie asked. "We've been here forever!"

PJ had thought it was remarkable how quickly he and Sophie had found the children. Against all odds, they'd found them. And that he was lucky he'd gotten here before they killed the cat. "Ollie, buddy, can you bring the cat over to safety? He must be scared. Cats don't like heights so much; it's not true that they land on their feet, not if dropped from so high."

But Ollie had watched enough movies to understand how a hostage situation worked. "NO!" he said. "I have demands!"

"Okay, bud, what are they?"

"I want to swim in a hotel pool."

"We'll talk about it. Put the cat down and we'll talk about it."

"And I want my sister to be happy! She's always sad or angry and I want her to be happy!"

"That's a tough one, buddy. People in your life aren't always going to be happy. Sometimes we're going to be heartbroken, or depressed. I think your sister is both those things."

"So why doesn't anyone put her on Prozac? Or get her a therapist? That's what they do on TV when somebody's depressed."

"We should get her a therapist, you're right. We should probably get you both a therapist. Heck, we all need help."

Ollie sniffed. He was starting to cry, and he couldn't wipe his eyes because he was holding the cat. "I wish it had never happened. I wish my parents never died."

"Me too," Luna said. She was inching closer to Ollie. Trying to figure out how to grab the cat. Trying to tell Ollie what he wanted to hear.

"But I'm also glad we don't live with them anymore."

Luna stopped inching. "Yes," she agreed. She was so glad she did not live in that house anymore. She did think that maybe some people are better off as worms. She had hated her dad after he broke Ollie's arm. There were a lot of things Luna could forgive that adults did, but she couldn't forgive that. She never would.

"And I want to live with Uncle PJ and Michelle Cobb in Arizona," Ollie said.

At that, Luna's face turned red. She was furious. Ollie had not listened to her. She had told him everything on the bus on the way to the mall, how he needed to think about things, how they were alone now, that they had each other but no one else, no one else in the entire world, and he hadn't listened. "Uncle PJ doesn't want us, Ollie! Face it! He tried to give us away to Mark Stackpole. He drove us all the way to Texas to get rid of us. He told Mark Stackpole he wanted money to take care of us! A lot of money! He wanted seven thousand dollars!"

"So?"

"That's not love! That's a job!"

"But you asked them to. They drove us all the way to Texas because you asked them to! You can't get mad at people for doing what you ask them to! You're not the boss of the universe!"

"I should be! Things would be a lot better if I was!"

"Hey, Luna, it *is* love," PJ said. "I want to take good care of you. And I need money to take good care of you. I'm an old man without a license. I'm unemployed. It's not easy for me to get a job. And also—I was scared. I wasn't sure I could do it. Parenting again. I messed it up so bad the first time. One of my daughters died and the other one—well, she hates me."

"Sophie doesn't hate you," Ollie said. "She's just mad that you can't stay in your bed all night."

"Appreciate that, Ollie. But I'm going to try to do better this time. I'm going to stop drinking, and I'm going to do a better job this time. Will you let me try to do a better job?"

"You've said that before!" Luna called. "You always say you're going to stop drinking!"

"I've been messed up for a long time. It's hard to change."

"I don't think you can ever change!"

PJ felt wounded to hear this from Luna, struck by how much she sounded like Sophie, but perhaps it was true. "I'm going to try," he said. "I'm going to really try. Is that okay?"

"No. It's not good enough. It's scary when we wake up and you're not there."

"He's going to try, Luna," Ollie said.

"And why do you need money from Mark Stackpole?" Luna asked. "You're a millionaire."

"I'm not. Not anymore. I have twenty thousand dollars in my bank account, last I checked, and we've been spending it since."

"You spent it all?" Ollie asked.

"Most of it."

The crowd stared at this man in Birkenstocks and cargo shorts, an undershirt. He did not look like a man who had spent a million dollars.

"So, you didn't want us because you can't afford to take care of us?" Luna asked. "That was the only reason?"

PJ rubbed his beard. The truth was, of course, that he hadn't wanted the kids at first. Not really. He had wanted to get to Arizona and spend the rest of his days playing shuffleboard and massaging Michelle Cobb's feet. He bet Michelle Cobb had great feet. That was the easy life, the one he could still imagine, still almost wish for, but now that the kids were part of his life—now that they were people, *real* people to him, with personalities, likes and dislikes, things he liked about them and things that annoyed him about them—he felt he couldn't live without them. He felt like he would be incomplete without them. Wherever they were, he wanted to be too.

"Yes," he said. "That's it. I mean, would you want to live with me if I don't have any money? If I can't buy any more trampolines or PlayStations or pineapple purses?"

"No," Ollie said. "I wouldn't like that."

An officer from mall security was walking up now, with Sophie beside him. "Oh my God," Sophie said. "Oh my God."

The mall cop's mouth fell open when he saw the child dangling the cat over the waterfall. He was going to get fired for this shit if he didn't put a stop to it soon. There had been a rash of shoplifting in the mall recently, and his boss had been really hard on him for that, but this was next-level. There was an animal in danger. Animals weren't even allowed in the mall, except service dogs, and that, up there, was not a service dog. That was a cat. An orange tabby. An orange tabby who was looking right at him.

"Shit," the mall cop said. "I'm fucked." He turned around right then, to go back to the security office and get the big fishing net. He hadn't known before why they kept a big fishing net in the office, but he understood now. It was for shit like this. In case you needed to catch a cat. He would get his taser, too, in case anyone resisted him confiscating the cat. But you can't bring a cat into a mall. Sprinting back to the security office, he ran past the entrance to the FunTime Trampoline Park. He ran right over the spot where Ollie had thrown up an entire vanilla milkshake. There was the usual plastic yellow Caution sign, but the mall cop still slipped on the freshly mopped floor and cracked his head open on the hard vinyl mall tile. He was dead a minute later.

"Will you love us, even if you can't buy us stuff?" Luna asked PJ.

"Of course I will."

"How will we know you love us if you can't buy us anything?" Ollie asked.

"You won't, I guess," PJ admitted. "But I'll tell you what loving kids is all about," he said. He was preparing a speech. His best-man speech. This was his moment. Everyone in the mall was looking at him. "Loving your kids is protecting them from stupid shit that they think they want to do, like run away to Mexico or jump off the top of the stairs or go on a boat without a lifejacket or when they're in high school and they want to drink hard liquor. Loving kids is teaching them new things, and being delighted when they learn it. Loving children is when they hold your hand with their little sweaty, meaty paw and you feel a direct wire to your heart. Loving children is even though they drive you up the wall, and life was so much easier before they were around, you hope they always, always come back home, and you miss them as soon as they're gone. You miss them as soon as the school bus takes them away in the morning, and you worry about them, you constantly worry about them, hoping and praying that, somehow, they will be one of the lucky ones. One of the lucky ones who is happy, and safe, and stays off drugs and lives to a hundred and two and never knows any heartbreak or pain."

"So, you do want us?" Ollie asked. "You want to love us like that? You want to miss us when we're at school?"

"Yes!" PJ said. And he found it was true, he really did. PJ had always loved children, all children, they were the jewels of the world, but now he loved these particular ones the most. He loved how strong-willed Luna was, and how sweet Ollie was, and how smart they were, how kids could pick up new words and new facts all the time. He loved that they did thoughtful things, like bring him beignets from the Cracker Barrel in Tennessee, even though he had hoped to try the French donuts somewhere a little classier, like a bakery in New Orleans. He loved their weird interests, although Luna would not be allowed to cut and paste any more ransom notes. They made his life harder; they made his life so much harder, and still he wanted them. "I want you. I need to figure out how I can afford to raise you, but I want you. I really do."

Sophie wasn't surprised her dad was out of money. She knew it was a matter of time. Maybe now he'd finally get it together. Maybe this was the rock bottom they'd been waiting for.

The crowd started cheering, because the boy had brought the cat back over the railing. Ollie was trying to hug the cat. "I'm sorry," he said. "I'm sorry, I'm sorry, I'm sorry. I'm so sorry." Pancakes squirmed, his claws out. *You ungrateful twit,* he thought. He jumped into Luna's arms.

Luna held the cat and started to cry. She cried and cried and squeezed the cat.

It's okay, little girl, the cat thought. *The kitty wasn't hurt. The good kitty wasn't hurt.*

The crowd kept applauding. They hadn't really understood the script, but it had been a while since there had been performance art in the mall. There had been a flash mob dance a few years back, but nothing like that ever since.

PJ was running up the escalator now, toward the kids. He was going to hug them, he was going to hug them and never let them go. He was going to make them know how precious they were, and he was never going to let them forget it. He would tell them every day.

Sophie started running up the escalator, too, right behind her dad. They had found the kids. Somehow, they had found them. PJ ran to Ollie, and Sophie ran to Luna. The cat jumped out of Luna's arms and went to rub against PJ's ankles, thankful for being saved.

Luna was still crying, and Sophie hugged her and felt the girl shaking. "You're all right," Sophie said. "Shh. You're all right now. You're safe. We found you."

Luna whimpered. "I want my mom," she said.

"I know. I know. It's terrible that she isn't here."

"I don't want *my* mom."

"Oh."

"I want *a* mom. I want the mom I see in movies. I want the mom other kids have."

"I get it," Sophie said, pulling back and looking at the girl. "You want someone who will make you feel safe and loved. You need someone you can count on."

"Yeah."

"You can count on me, you know."

"I can?" Luna sniffed.

"And you want someone who loves you even when you make big mistakes like stealing a two-thousand-dollar pineapple purse."

Luna met Sophie's eyes. "How do you know I stole it?"

"I don't think anyone would let a kid put two thousand dollars on a credit card. No one is that stupid. But, Luna, you have to stop stealing. You could get in real trouble. You know that. Your dad was a cop."

Luna nodded. She had been waiting to get in real trouble, but she hadn't so far. "I'm sorry," she said. "Are you mad?"

I am not your mother, Sophie half wanted to say, like she had said other times on this trip. *I am just the nanny. The babysitter.* She would never be their mother, no matter what. But she would like to try to keep Luna and her brother safe. She would like to do that. *Someone to love, something to do, something to look forward to.* The kids would give her all of those things in one package.

"It's fine," Sophie said. "No, I'm not mad. I'm just so glad you're safe. I don't know what I would do if something bad happened to you." And she hugged Luna again and squeezed her even harder this time. She still could not believe they had found the kids. It had been worse than any time she had to go looking for her father, because if her dad was found dead, choked on his own vomit, it would have been at least half his own fault. He had made the life choices that would have brought him to that end. But you can't blame kids for anything they do. They are just kids. It's their job to test limits, to shoplift and try drugs and drink jungle juice out of trash cans, and most of them still turn out okay in the end.

Part III

ONE DAY CLOSER TO THE END

46

In the mall parking lot, PJ wrote a check to the boy Zander for $5,000 and told him not to spend it all in one place. He said he wouldn't, and he had to split it with his friend who saw Ollie vomiting outside the trampoline park anyway. Meanwhile, Sophie called around to cab companies for someone to take them to a hotel with a pool, but none of the cab companies wanted to pick them up if they had a cat with them. She had called six cab companies already.

"My uncle will do it," Zander offered. Zander said his uncle Enzo wouldn't care about a cat. He owned a limousine service. If he didn't have a wedding, Zander's uncle Enzo would take them anywhere.

"Anywhere?" PJ asked. "All the way to Arizona?"

Zander shrugged. "Probably. He drives people to Vegas all the time and that's really far away."

"If we took a limousine, we could drive all night," PJ said. "We wouldn't need a hotel. We could sleep in the limo. We could be at Tender Hearts Retirement Community by morning. It would be so romantic to drive all night to see Michelle Cobb in the morning."

"Why can't you ever be normal?" Sophie asked.

"Because he's our Uncle PJ," Luna said. "He's a wacko. And he's loved Michelle Cobb for a million years. It's a beautiful love story. Better than a thousand greeting cards, no offense."

"None taken." Sophie never wanted to look at a greeting card ever again.

"Come on, Sophie, let's do it," Ollie said. "Wait, does Michelle Cobb have a pool?"

"I don't know what a retirement community would be without a pool," PJ said, smiling.

"Please?" Ollie and Luna both asked.

And it broke Sophie, the love these kids had for her father. They were fools for loving him, but they did anyway, and she didn't want to mess with it. "Fine," she said. "Let's finish the trip." She called Green Bean Limousine and Enzo picked up immediately. He said he was glad to drive them all night to Arizona, no problem.

"Limo or party bus?" he asked.

"Limo or party bus?" Sophie asked her dad.

PJ remembered, originally, he wanted to drive up to Tender Hearts Retirement Community in an antique Jaguar convertible, to show Michelle there was so much life they still had to live. If he couldn't show up in a Jag convertible, a black stretch limo was a pretty good second best. Yes, PJ Halliday would show up in a limousine to Michelle Cobb's front door, with grandkids in tow, the grandkids she'd probably always wanted. Michelle had never had kids of her own, PJ had used Sophie's phone to read the rest of Gene's obituary online, the last few lines he had missed. Gene Bartlett was survived by Michelle Cobb and his father-in-law, Ed Cobb, the man who had once owned the pie shop in Middleborough, just over the Pondville town line, and also some nieces and nephews, but no kids or grandkids. PJ was surprised Michelle's dad Ed was still alive, he must be over ninety now.

"Limo," he told Sophie. "Black if they have it."

* * *

Ten minutes later, the black stretch limo pulled up into the parking lot of the mall. "Your chariot is here," Enzo said. Enzo had crooked yellow teeth, tufts of gray hair, and he was wearing a suit. He held the door open for them like they were royalty. Sophie loved Enzo immediately. It would be so nice to have someone else drive. Someone who wasn't her father.

"There's so much room," Luna said, climbing in.

"We should have gone like this the whole way," Ollie said. "Why didn't we?"

The cat found a spot on one of the seats and curled up. As Zander had promised, Enzo didn't say shit about the cat. Running a limousine and a party-bus company as long as he had, a cat in the car was not a concern. People always wanted to do something a little out of line in the back of a limo, and it was Enzo's job to pretend he didn't see it. Enzo pretended not to see the cat.

They pulled away from the Beechnut Galleria Mall. The lights on the ceiling of the limo glowed and twinkled like stars. "Close your eyes," Sophie told the children. "Before you know it, we'll be in Arizona."

"What's Arizona like?" Ollie asked, already drowsy. It had been a long day.

Sophie had never been to Arizona, but she'd seen some photos. She said there were cactuses, and strange-looking trees straight from Dr. Seuss, and big red rocks, and endless sand, and desert animals, prickled lizards with forked tongues, jackrabbits with black-tipped ears. It was like another planet, and they would be there soon.

47

The children were asleep, the cat curled up like a donut, but PJ and Sophie were still awake in the limo. They had been sitting there in the quiet, recovering from the day. They were somewhere in the middle of Texas, a long way still to go to Arizona. Texas was its own country. PJ looked at his daughter, the outline of her beautiful face in the dark. The new haircut suited her, he thought. "That was amazing," he told her. "It was amazing how you found those kids. I'm very proud of you."

"We both did it, Dad. It was a good idea to pay Zander and his friends."

"Nice to work together," PJ agreed.

Sophie sighed. She was still mad at him, but she couldn't have done it without him. She would never have found the kids alone. *Your father is a good man,* her mother often said, *who sometimes wears the suit of a really shitty man.* Even though her dad never actually wore a suit, just cargo shorts and white T-shirts and his sweater with the polar bears on it. Her dad loved to tell people about the polar bears, and their plight of survival, and how much it hurt his own heart. Sophie knew her dad wasn't a bad person. She knew he loved her. She knew he wanted her to love him. But her dad had also hurt her, over and over again, with his drinking, his unreliability. How many times she'd had to walk into the house on Clear Pond Road expecting to find him dead. "Dad," she said. "I can't keep doing it."

"Can't keep doing what?"

"Driving around town trying to find you after you go drinking. Walking into the house and waiting to see if you're dead."

"Sophie, I never asked you to do that. I don't need you to take care of me anymore. It's not your job. It never was. If I'm half-dead on the side of the road, leave me there."

"I don't do it for you, Dad. I do it for Mom. I'm taking care of Mom, not you. So that she doesn't have to be the one to find you dead."

"Oh, Sophie—"

"If and when I find you dead, I've practiced what I'll do. I will open up your eyelids and look you right in the eyes and say I told you so. But Mom . . . if Mom saw you . . . it would kill her." Sophie barely got that last part out, because she was crying now. She was sobbing. Some dam inside her had cracked. She was sobbing and she didn't know if she would ever stop.

PJ slid across the seat and took Sophie in his arms. He held her as she cried. His poor daughter. His only living one. He let her cry for a while. "I'm sorry," he finally said. "I'm so sorry. I know I've been selfish. I know I've taken advantage of you and your mother and Fred."

"Yes," Sophie said. "You have." Her crying slowed. She was getting it back together. She wouldn't cry forever, it turned out. No one could. She pulled away from him, embarrassed she'd let him hold her.

"Sophie, I know you stayed near Pondville all this time to help out with me. I see that now. You weren't codependent on your mother. It was because your mother needed your help with me. Sophie, I owe you a lot."

Sophie considered this. It was good to hear her dad blame himself.

But Sophie had also been afraid to leave. She had felt she needed her mother, and that her mother needed her. At the time, it was hard to imagine how she could cope so far from home. Her dad wasn't the only one who was fucked-up; Sophie was fucked-up too. Her mom had never wanted Sophie to be defined as the girl with the dead sister, but of course she was.

"How will I ever make it up to you?" her father asked.

Sophie sighed. A month ago, she would have told him to stop drinking, and maybe they would talk. But he had been trying to do that; maybe that's why they were talking now. He hadn't been totally successful at not-drinking, but he was making an effort. For the first time since she could remember, he was making an effort. "You can make it up to me by taking care of the kids, Dad. If you can really love them and take care of them, I can forgive you. If you can do that, that will prove that all that grief wasn't for nothing. It's a choice, Dad; you can let Kate's death make you love people less, or it can teach you to love them more. Kate's death was not the end of things."

"It wasn't," he agreed. Somehow it hadn't been.

"I'll help you with the kids. I won't let you do it alone. They're mine now too."

"Okay. You'll help me. I can do it if you'll help me."

"Do you really think you can stay sober? You'll need to stay sober."

This was the problem. PJ didn't know if he could stay sober. He honestly didn't know. He had vowed to get sober other times and failed—why should this time be different? There was the old-dog-and-new-tricks problem. But staying sober wasn't a trick. It was just something you did. "I'll do it," he agreed. "I promise. This time I will."

"Okay," Sophie said, and she tried to believe him.

Sophie and PJ looked at the two children, lying on the long seats of the limousine, sleeping while not belted into seatbelts, as if a stretch limo would be different from any other kind of car in a crash. As if it were safe just because it was fancy.

"You think they'll be all right?" Sophie asked. "After everything that's happened to them?"

"I think they will. Kids are resilient."

"They're not, Dad. Kids *aren't* resilient. That's something adults like to say to make themselves feel better. To pretend that kids don't feel as deeply as adults do. But kids are everything that happens to them. They're sponges. Everything bad, everything good. Every hurtful thing you say. Every loving one."

PJ was ashamed he'd said the wrong thing again. "Kids aren't resilient," he repeated. "Why do people say they are?"

"Because people can *learn* resilience. They learn resilience by feeling safe, having time to bounce back and recover. So that's what we can do for the kids. We can give them safety. Like Mom did for me, although Mom made some mistakes, not letting us talk about Kate. Not letting us properly remember. But we'll give them consistency and a routine. We'll listen to them. We'll love them. We'll love them exactly as they are, even when they fuck up."

PJ put his arm around Sophie, and she let him. PJ would like to do all those things his daughter had described. He hoped he was capable of it. Because Sophie was right: Kate's death was not the end of things. There had been life afterward, and some of it was even good.

DAY SIX
SUNDAY

48

They crossed the border from New Mexico into Arizona, and PJ watched the desert as the sun rose. He looked out the window of the limo and imagined the men who had traveled out there in the desert on horse or donkey or mule, and how many of those men must have died of thirst. The limo was stocked with mini bottles of water, and PJ drank seven of them. He figured they were complimentary. He had not asked how much the limo ride would cost. He would figure the money situation out when he got to Arizona, he'd promised himself that. He would not worry about it now. Perhaps the child-support payments from Mark Stackpole would work out. They would have to find a post office to mail the paternity test to the lab address on the box.

When they finally arrived in Tucson, PJ hugged himself. He had done it. He had survived the journey. He had made it to Michelle Cobb's front door. "Thanks for coming with me, Sophie," he said, looking over at his daughter. "It's meant a lot."

"You're welcome, Dad," she said. "It's certainly been a journey."

"Once in a lifetime," he agreed.

The kids were still asleep, but here they were in the limo at the base of the hill, the entrance of the Tender Hearts Retirement Community. There was a little gray tower with a man inside, a white security gate across the road. Protecting Michelle Cobb. The princess in the castle.

PJ readied himself to tell the security guard the story, how he was here to win the heart of a girl he'd met at a high school dance. But what if he called up to Michelle Cobb and she turned him away? What if she was still grieving old Gene? It was possible. The lump in PJ's throat grew.

"Who are you here to see?" the man in the tower asked.

"John Smith, he's expecting us," Enzo said with confidence. The man in the tower raised the gate.

"We're in!" PJ said. Michelle Cobb still didn't know he was coming. She didn't have the chance to turn him away at the gate. He was within the castle! But he couldn't go into the castle looking like he did—a dirty, sweaty undershirt and a bandaged head. He rummaged through his bag. *There, there it was.* The perfect shirt. Fred's blue silk Hawaiian shirt with the pink flamingos on it. PJ had stolen it from Fred and Ivy's closet when he'd taken her engagement ring. Luna had given the ring back when they first got in the limo, but he wasn't going to give that ring to Michelle Cobb now. That ring was Ivy's. Inside the gold band, it was engraved with their old motto: *Don't Worry, We'll Figure It Out.* It was something Ivy and PJ used to say to each other, before real tragedy happened.

But PJ thought maybe it didn't matter that he didn't have a ring for Michelle Cobb, because in this blue silk shirt with flamingos on it, what woman could resist him? PJ only wished there was a place to shower. He took off the bandage on his head, and Sophie assured him the head wound didn't look so bad. He was no longer actively bleeding.

PJ shook the kids awake so they could see the retirement-community grounds, which were quite beautiful. A pond with a fountain, a little Japanese bridge that could be good for kissing on.

There was a shuffleboard court, and tennis courts, and yes, a pool. The cat looked out the window. He liked the look of this place.

Enzo took them to the main building, which had two tan pillars on either side. "Here we are," he said.

Before PJ got out of the limo, he put the cat in his carrier. He hoped Michelle was an animal lover. He gave Enzo his credit card for the fare and didn't ask how much it was. Enzo processed the card, and then he took out the suitcases from the trunk and handed them over, wished them all the best of luck. But then Enzo looked around. "If you don't mind," he said to PJ. "Just between us, I might stick around and try to meet a woman. I heard these retirement communities are . . ."

"Hotbeds of sexual activity," PJ finished. "I saw the same *60 Minutes*. And of course, no we don't mind. The more the merrier. But I've got dibs on Michelle Cobb. Anyone but Michelle. Michelle Cobb is off-limits."

"Gotcha."

Together, they all went inside.

"This place is like a really fancy hotel," Ollie said, looking around the lobby. "Wow." There was a crystal chandelier above their heads. There was a room off to the left with a pool table. There was a bulletin board advertising karaoke night coming up, and a sign-up sheet.

"Karaoke night? That sounds fun," PJ said.

"Oh yes, it is fun," the receptionist said from behind the front desk, a young woman in a crisp white shirt. "I see some new faces. Are you visitors of a resident here, or are you interested in Tender Hearts, sir? I would be glad to set you up on a tour with our recruitment officer."

"That's all right," PJ said. "Not right now. I'm an old friend of Michelle Cobb's. We're here to see her."

"Oh yes," the receptionist said, nodding. "Of course, of course. Go on in the chapel. It's right down the hall. They'll be starting in a minute."

"The chapel?"

"Yes, it's right down the hall. You'll see the stained-glass doors, looks like a real chapel, you can't miss it."

His heart pounding, PJ walked down the hall toward the doors, which did look like church doors. Brown wooden doors curved in an arch, with stained-glass windows inserted in the middle. There were white flowers on either side. Sophie and the kids followed behind PJ, each kid holding one of Sophie's hands. Enzo had gone off to get the lay of the land. He had spotted a group of women in the common area playing cards.

The chapel doors swung open; PJ walked through. People were already sitting in the pews, and a few people turned to look at them walking in, but then resumed talking when they saw it wasn't who they were waiting for. Organ music was playing.

Goddammit, said the baseball cap on his head. PJ took it off. That was another new word for the baseball cap, and PJ also knew you weren't supposed to wear baseball caps in a chapel or use the Lord's name in vain. "Oh no," PJ said, as the organ music played. It was Bach. "She's getting married again. We're too late."

"Maybe Michelle Cobb is just a guest at this wedding," Sophie said, trying to keep her father calm.

"I think it's definitely her wedding," Ollie said, and pointed to the front of the room where COBB was written in pink flowers.

"Oh no," PJ said. "We have to leave. I'm so embarrassed."

But the organ music changed, to Mendelssohn, so Sophie pushed everyone into a pew. "Sit here in the back and be quiet. We'll leave when it's over." Sophie didn't want to be rude. No one would notice them in the back, and maybe watching Michelle Cobb get married would give her father some closure on this delusional journey. They weren't leaving now.

PJ put the cat carrier on the floor, and then sat slumped in the pew, looked at the front of the chapel. A priest in a black robe was standing at the front next to a young man in a suit, the man much too young to be marrying Michelle. Much, much too young. Practically pedophilia. He looked to be around forty. He was crying. And then the chapel doors swung open again, and in came four men, carrying a mahogany coffin.

PJ gasped. "No," he said.

"She's dead," Luna said, hammering it home.

Goddammit, said the baseball cap in PJ's hands. PJ sat on it.

It comes for us all, said Pancakes in the carrier.

"Oh my God," Ollie said. "Uncle PJ, I'm so sorry." The boy started to sob. Sophie held him to her.

"Michelle!" PJ called out. "We came all this way to see you!"

"I'm sorry, can we have quiet in the back?" the priest said. "This is a funeral."

"We thought it was a wedding!" Luna told him.

"Who came all this way to see me?" a woman said, who had just walked in behind the coffin. "Who are you?"

"Michelle Cobb, as I live and breathe," PJ said, and he couldn't believe his eyes. There she was, her hair still red—although not a very natural shade—and her blue eyes still blue. He would have recognized those blue eyes anywhere, even now with all those wrinkles gathered underneath. She was sixty-three, and still alive. Wearing a nice black dress and pearls. She was a woman who wore pearls. She was not in that coffin, which was making its way down the aisle. Someone else was. "It's PJ Halliday," he said when she didn't recognize him.

"Pauly Halliday?" Michelle asked. "You're here. Oh my, you came to the funeral. How did you know he passed?"

"I read Gene's obituary in the paper," he said, forgetting that Michelle knew him as Pauly, but of course everyone back in high school had. PJ had only changed it when he went off to war and became a man. "I sent flowers when I read about poor Gene. You're just burying him now?"

"Oh, no. It's my father's funeral. He died a few days ago. Ninety-one years old."

"Mrs. Bartlett, let's get started," the priest said at the front.

Right, Michelle was Mrs. Bartlett now. Cobb was her maiden

name. Her father's name. The flowers in the front were for her father. PJ was getting his bearings. He remembered Ed Cobb fondly. But the man was over ninety. He'd had a good run. No one was even wearing black at this funeral, except for Michelle, and the men in suits. That's why it had looked more like a wedding. It was a celebration of life. PJ didn't even look that out of place in his blue silk shirt with pink flamingos on it.

"I'm so sorry for your loss," Sophie said to Michelle while still holding Ollie, who was still crying, even though he didn't really know why.

"We'd like to get started," the priest said again, and Michelle walked to the front and sat down in a pew. "We are gathered here today in remembrance of Edward . . ." the priest began.

"Can we leave now?" Luna whispered. She didn't want to sit through a funeral for a man she didn't know. Ollie was still crying.

A woman in front of them turned around; she was wearing a yellow silk scarf over her head like an old movie star. She had oval-shaped sunglasses. She looked on the younger side for the fifty-five-plus retirement community, could even pass for late forties. She held open her purple velvet purse. "Would you kids like a lollipop? Might help with the tears," she whispered.

Luna smiled and nodded. She stuck her hand in, and the lollipops went up to her elbow. It was a bottomless pit of lollipops. She pulled out a handful, and then Ollie took a turn. He put a red one in his mouth and the crying slowed, like a baby with a pacifier. The woman put the bag of lollipops back in her lap. Sophie wondered what this woman was doing with a purse full of lollipops. It gave her a Hansel and Gretel vibe. She hadn't seen anything else in the purse, except for lollipops.

"Wow," PJ said, straining to look at Michelle Cobb in the front. "Ed Cobb. Did you ever go to Cobb's Pie Shop?" he asked Sophie. "Was it still around when you were a kid?"

Sophie shushed her father. The priest was talking about Ed's life, how loved he was.

"He was a good pie maker," PJ said.

The woman with the velvet bag of lollipops turned around again, and looked over to PJ and held the bag open. "Would you like a lollipop too? It might help with the talking."

"Sure," PJ said, looking at the woman with the lollipops. And when her eyes met PJ's, even through her oval sunglasses, when PJ saw her face, PJ felt his soul leave his body. "Oh my," he said.

The woman put her gloved finger to her perfectly red-lipsticked lips, and then turned back to pay attention to the priest.

PJ waited a second to gather his breath, but then he tapped the woman on her shoulder again. She was wearing a polka-dotted dress, one PJ remembered from photographs. He recognized the purple velvet purse; the same one had been on display in the purse museum back in Little Rock. "I'm sorry," he whispered. "Are you—I know you couldn't be, but have you ever been to Pondville, Massachusetts?"

"Pauly," the woman said, sternly, using his childhood nickname, maybe because she'd heard Michelle Bartlett call him Pauly. "It's a funeral. We have to pay attention and give our respects."

"Yes, ma'am, of course. I just wondered—you look just like—"

The woman put her finger to her lips again to shush him.

"Please, for the love of all things holy, can you be silent in the back," the priest said. The grandson was about to read a passage from the Bible. The grandson, Michelle's nephew, was the forty-year-old man in the suit.

When it was Michelle's turn to give her remembrance, she said her father had been a good man, a noble man, who loved his wife and kids and had run a pie shop and then had come out west to help with Gene's shoe company once it took off. He had a knack for small business. "But my dad never forgot his community back in Pondville," she said. "He tried to go back every year, and it means a lot that one member of the community is here today. Pauly Halliday was very important to him, and his mother, Regina Halliday, too. Please, Pauly, stand up so everyone can see you. He's all the way in the back."

Everyone shifted in their seats. PJ stood up, blushing, but also glad for the attention. He was glad to hear his mother's name said out loud. He had to ask the woman in front of him if she was related to Regina Halliday somehow. Because the woman looked just like his mother, a spitting image, before she was badly scarred from the burns from the housefire her older son, Chip, had set. The woman looked beautiful, like his mother had when PJ was growing up. The way PJ liked to remember her.

But when PJ sat back down, the woman in the seat in front of him in the silk scarf and oval sunglasses and the polka-dotted dress was gone. He hadn't seen her walk out; *how had he not seen her walk out?* She had been sitting right in front of him and the kids. But she had disappeared. He must have imagined her. He must be going crazy again. He knew he heard things sometimes. The cat talking to him, the house, the baseball cap. Maybe now he was seeing things too. The ghost of his mother. It must be because he'd barely slept all night in the limousine. He hadn't had much sleep all week on the road trip either. It was only sleep deprivation, alcohol withdrawal, and his imagination running away with him.

But when PJ turned, Ollie and Luna still had their lollipops in their cheeks, given to them in order to keep them quiet at the funeral, which was just like something Regina Halliday would have done. She had been the first to build a lollipop tree. She used to make one every Easter morning, as part of the egg hunt, in the bush in their front yard. It was not as extreme as the lollipop trees all over Pondville that PJ would come up with later, but it was still astounding to PJ as a child, that an ordinary bush could sprout candy overnight.

49

After the funeral, there was a reception in the dining room of the Tender Hearts Retirement Community. Ed Cobb was to be cremated, the coffin was only a rental, so his interment would be the next day, and they could go straight to the party. It was held in a large, beautiful room, with a maroon carpet, and huge windows that looked out over the golf course. There were round tables dotted throughout the room, with pink tablecloths and fake flowers on every table.

PJ scanned the crowd for the woman in the yellow scarf, but he didn't find her. She was gone. If she'd ever been there at all, she was gone.

"What's going on with you?" Sophie asked, noticing her father looking around. "Don't you want to talk to Michelle?"

"I saw a woman. I need to find her—"

Sophie couldn't believe it; they had come all this way to win back Michelle Cobb, and her father was already on to another woman. "You dirtbag," she said. "You unbelievable fucking dirtbag."

"It's not what you think—" PJ said. "It was . . . I swear it, I swear, this woman was my mother. She looked just like your grandmother."

"Dad. Now is not the time to lose it, please. Let's keep it together. Grandma is dead and has been dead for a long time."

"I know," he said. "But—"

"But nothing. Don't make me put you in a home. It won't be nice like this one."

"This is a retirement community, Sophie. Not an old-folks' home."

"I said it won't be like this one."

PJ kept scanning the room, but with no luck. The kids brought over a big plate of pastries, and they all sat at a table. Enzo sat with them too. He hadn't connected with a woman yet.

Michelle had finished with all the cheek-kissing and condolences from her friends, so she came over to the table. Sophie introduced herself, and said she was sorry they had interrupted the service.

Michelle said it was fine, they saw the same service practically every week.

"Great funeral," Luna said. "Thanks for the lemon squares."

"You're very welcome, dear," Michelle said, and smiled. "You know, I've known your grandfather for a long time."

"Actually—" Ollie started, about to explain that PJ was just their uncle, and his real grandfather was dead and so were his parents, that they were all worms now, but Luna put her hand over her brother's mouth.

"Our grandpa told us all about you," she said.

"Good things, I hope!" Michelle said.

"Good things," Luna agreed.

PJ smiled. This was going exactly as he hoped it would, except for the part about the possible ghost of his mother wandering around the funeral reception. PJ hadn't planned for that.

"And who are you?" Michelle asked the other man at the table, who was deep into a tuna sub.

Enzo finished chewing the best he could. "Sorry, I'm the limousine driver. I'm used to being invisible. No one ever asks about the limo driver. I'm sorry about your father, ma'am. He sounds like he was a great man."

"He was. Kind and good. Not without his flaws, but kind and good. So, Pauly, you took a limo from the airport? Who were you trying to impress?" Her hands were on her hips.

"We took a limo all the way from Texas. Long story, but we drove to Texas to meet her biological father." He put his hand on Luna's head. "But he might not be her father; we'll know in a week. It doesn't matter either way, I'm keeping the kids. And then our car got impounded, and well, we needed a ride."

"For heaven's sake, why didn't you fly?"

"I don't do air travel. And I wanted to see some of the country."

"He's afraid of flying," Sophie said.

"Oh, it's not so bad," Michelle said. "It can be pretty relaxing, actually, if you fly first class."

"First class?" Luna asked. "You're rich?"

Michelle laughed. "My husband owned a successful shoe company. Bartlett Shoes. We sold it to one of the big shoe empires a few years ago, so, yes, I always fly first class. But, Pauly, why did you come, if you didn't know my father had died?"

"Michelle," PJ said, gearing up for it. "I sent you those flowers because you were always the one that got away. And you sent me those flowers too, when Kate died, but I was still married, and so were you."

Michelle shook her head. "Pauly, oh Pauly. We all felt so terrible when your daughter died. We kept getting *The South Coast Daily Sun* out here, because my dad would get so homesick for Pondville, and we saw the article. I had to hide the newspaper from my father so he wouldn't keep reading about it, it upset him so much, even though he'd never met the poor girl."

"Sounds like someone we know," Sophie said quietly.

"But, Pauly, dear, I wasn't the one who got away."

"No, you were, Michelle, you were. And we're still young, or young enough. I don't have a ring to give you, because the one I brought belongs to my ex-wife, but I intend to get another . . ."

Michelle laughed. "Oh, Pauly. No, no. This isn't happening."

"No?"

"No, Pauly."

"Why not?"

Michelle sighed. "My father was adamant that your mother didn't want you to know about this. He said he would take it to his grave. Well, I suppose he did."

"Didn't want me to know what?"

"There was a very simple reason I picked Gene. After we had such a good time at the dance, and Gene and I got you out of jail and took you to the hospital, and you both asked me out on a date, and I said I'd have to decide the next day."

"I remember," PJ said.

"Uncle PJ told us the story," Ollie said.

"It's true then?" Luna asked.

PJ shrugged. They could believe what they wanted to believe.

"After that night," Michelle said. "I went home and told my mother about these two boys I'd met at the mixer, and that things were over for me and Ricky, and how he was on life support at the hospital."

"Ricky's still in a coma," Ollie said. "Sometimes Uncle PJ goes in and combs his beard."

"Oh," Michelle said, and she looked confused.

PJ had changed just a few small details when he had told the kids the story. In fact, Ricky had only lived for three more days in a coma after his head hit the sink, before he was declared brain dead and they unplugged him. But PJ never liked to talk about that. He never liked to admit he had killed a man, so he changed the story when he told it to the kids.

"Well," Michelle continued, "I went back home after Gene dropped me off, and I went straight to bed, but when I woke up, I told my mother about the two boys I'd met from Pondville High School, and how they both wanted to go out on a second date, and how one was going to Vietnam and the other had gotten a medical deferment because he had bone spurs, but the one going to war was such a good dancer and we had such a connection—my mother was elated. She always wanted to see me in love. 'What are their names?' she asked.

"'Pauly Halliday and Gene Bartlett,' I told her.

"And my mother went stone-gray then. 'Michelle,' she told me. 'You are never to go out with that boy again.'

"'Which boy?' I asked.

"'The Halliday boy.' And she said she had a story about him, but I couldn't tell anyone, not as long as I lived. I crossed my heart and hoped to die and said she could trust me. But I think she'd agree, it's time you know."

"Okay."

"Many years ago, my mother had a friend named Regina Halliday," Michelle began. "They weren't best friends, but they were friends. Both members of the women's club."

Everyone in town liked Regina, but Regina Halliday had a nasty husband; his name was Roy Duggins.

Everyone in town knew Roy beat poor Regina, which everyone felt sorry about, but apparently, he had never laid a hand to their little boy, little Roy Jr., who they always called Chip—Chip off the ol' block. Roy said Regina could leave him if she wanted, she could leave the family anytime, but if she tried to take the boy, he'd kill them both. Regina believed him, so she left on her own. It must have killed her to leave that boy, but she did. She packed a leather suitcase and left Chip with his father. There were no shelters for battered women and children back then. It was 1950. The rumor was she'd taken the train out to California; that was the rumor she'd asked her friends to spread around town.

* * *

But really, Regina hadn't gone anywhere. She couldn't afford to go anywhere; she didn't have the money to travel. She had only rented a room above the barbershop in Middleborough, the very next town over from Pondville, and she got a job at the barbershop. She swept all the hair up after hours, would sweep after the customers were gone so no one would see her and tell her husband she wasn't very far from Pondville at all, and he could come after her anytime. Regina swept up so much hair that every night she would make a little sculpture of the hair, a little dog or sometimes a cat, and she was so lonesome that one day, the pile of hair turned into a real dog. She named it Arthur, and then she had a friend.

"Artie," PJ interrupted the story. "That was my childhood dog." He snorted. "He did look like a little pile of human hair."

And after Regina was done sweeping up hair, she and Arthur would walk over to Cobb's Pie Shop for the early morning baking shift, her second job. She and Ed Cobb would roll out the dough and make the filling and feed Arthur scraps of the crust. And then, twenty minutes before the shop opened—they served coffee and breakfast pastries as well as pie—just as the sun was rising, Regina would walk back to her apartment above the barbershop, and she and Arthur would sleep all day while the barber cut hair below.

Some days, Regina wouldn't sleep the entire day, and would put a scarf over her head and sunglasses so no one would recognize her, and she would walk Artie all the way down to the White Rock Elementary School in Pondville, a long six-mile walk from her apartment, so she could watch her little boy play on the swings, but she stopped going after she saw how cruel the boy Chip was to other children, how much he was learning from his father. She did hear her husband had remarried, and everyone said he didn't beat the new wife like he'd beat his last. Regina wondered if the problem had been her. It was too easy for women to blame themselves back then, they didn't have the resources for domestic-violence victims that they do now.

Still, Regina was happy to hear that Roy had moved on, and that

Chip had a mother-figure, and everything was all right for a while. Every day, Regina kept on sweeping hair, she kept on rolling out pie dough, taking Arthur on walks. Sometimes customers would complain about the hair they regularly found tucked in the pie dough, but Ed Cobb was too kind to fire Regina. He was sure eating a little human hair had never hurt anyone. And he had grown awfully fond of Regina Halliday. Perhaps too fond, for a married man.

Then, one night, Ed's wife, Nancy Cobb, couldn't sleep. She was very pregnant with her second baby, and she had an awful craving for cherry pie, and they had none in the house. Her husband was already at the bakery, and she knew she shouldn't leave her four-year-old daughter, Janey, sleeping alone at home, but she would only be gone for less than an hour, and little Janey always slept through the night. She was a good child, had been an easy baby. So, Mrs. Nancy Cobb walked down to the pie shop, and when she walked in, Regina Halliday and her husband were rolling dough out together, side-by-side, elbow to elbow. They were laughing. Nancy Cobb saw that Regina Halliday—her friend she hadn't seen in months—was quite pregnant, too, almost as pregnant as she was. In anger and disgust, the baby twisted inside Nancy Cobb's belly, and Nancy's water broke all over the floor of the pie shop. Regina would have to mop it up, as Ed rushed out with his wife.

"I was born three hours later, a month early, at the hospital in New Bedford," Michelle Cobb Bartlett said. "My mother always thought I'd recognized my kin, so she was surprised when I didn't recognize my kin eighteen years later when I met him again at the dance."

"Kin?" PJ said, gulping.

"You and Michelle are brother and sister?" Luna said. "Gross!"

"Ew," Ollie agreed.

Sophie grimaced.

"Half-siblings," Michelle said, holding up a finger.

"That's not any better," said Luna.

"Did you ever kiss?" Ollie asked.

"No," Michelle said. "We never did, thankfully. Just a dance."

"So that means we . . ." PJ said, trying to sink it all in. "That was my own father's funeral. That's why you had me stand up like a moron in front of everyone."

"Yes," Michelle said, blushing. "I didn't know what else to do. When you showed up, I thought maybe you already knew. But you didn't know. Maybe it was time for you to know."

PJ put his hand to his forehead. "I missed meeting my father by a few days."

"Oh, Pauly," Michelle said. "There wasn't a lot of him to meet at the end. His mind had been gone for years. Best you didn't see him that way. And you knew him, you'd been in the pie shop. You can remember him as he was. He was a good man. He gave your mother money as often as he could. And my parents worked it out. My mother forgave him. She wasn't vengeful. She helped my dad get your mother set up in a house in Pondville, so she could see her older boy, Chip, grow up too."

"I see," PJ said. "That's good." He didn't remember Michelle's mother. Perhaps he'd never met her.

Pancakes appeared from under one of the tablecloths and jumped in PJ's lap. PJ held the cat. The cat had freed himself from the carrier, made his escape, had been making his rounds around the dining room, rubbing against different people's legs, getting acquainted with the folks of Tender Hearts. It reminded him of the nursing home in Pondville, but everyone—mostly everyone—was a lot healthier here. Some of them could still play tennis. But after surveying the residents, the cat had come to find PJ and the rest of his family.

"That means," PJ said, realizing, "my mother never saw the country. All those stories about traveling by train and being in a movie and meeting Frank Sinatra. Those stories weren't true. She never pet every horse in America."

"No." Michelle shook her head. "She didn't go anywhere. My

mother said Regina Halliday never even left Massachusetts once in her life, but she would bite her tongue when she heard Regina tell the stories at the women's club. They still traveled in the same circles, even if they were never friends again. But my mother kept Regina's secret. She knew what Regina had been through."

PJ's heart broke for his mother, that all those stories she'd told him at bedtime hadn't been true. All those fabulous stories, all made up. Regina Halliday had only gone to Middleborough. She'd worked at a pie shop and a barbershop on the red-brick Center Street. She'd made herself a dog as a companion, out of nothing but a pile of hair clippings mixed with loneliness and the impossible grief of leaving her first son behind with his father. His abusive father. "I can't believe she lied to me," PJ said. "All those years, she never told me the truth."

"Your mom was trying to give you a better life than she had," Michelle said, putting her hand on PJ's shoulder. "Which meant you had to believe that a better world was possible."

"Are all your stories true, Dad?" Sophie asked, because she'd heard a few she wasn't sure about.

"Most of them," he said. "All of them have truth to them."

"You always said it doesn't matter if the stories are true. It matters if you believe them."

PJ considered it. Like the man at the Half-Moon Bar had said, about trotting out old World War II veterans to tell their stories: You need a story about your own life, or the bad stuff in your head writes the story for you. He got it. He did. Why his mother had told a different story from the one she'd been given. She had made her story better. PJ himself had put more lollipops in the trees, pretended the boy he'd fought with at a high school dance was still alive in a forty-five-year-long coma. He had changed some details, but it didn't make the stories untrue. The truth of the story was that Regina Halliday was a very brave woman. A survivor. That's what she wanted her son to know about her, and her granddaughters, too, later, so she told them in a way children could understand. PJ could see that now.

"I'm sorry I never told you, Pauly," Michelle said. "I'm sorry you never knew who your father was."

"Not too late to tell me now, I suppose."

"No," she said. "Not too late."

PJ started to cry, and Michelle went to hug him. "Hi, sis," he said.

"Hi, brother. Thanks for coming all this way."

THE NEXT TWO WEEKS

50

They were staying in Ed Cobb's empty condo for the time being; Michelle Cobb extended her father's lease. PJ and the kids and the cat could stay there forever, actually, if they wanted to. The community was fifty-five-plus, but exceptions were made for dependents of residents. But Sophie wasn't a dependent, so she could only stay in Ed's condo for two weeks. They had a strict two-week visitation policy at Tender Hearts.

Or, most of them were staying in Ed's condo; the cat was spending more time in Eugenia Daly's apartment, even though Eugenia Daly was loud and smelly and obnoxious, but Pancakes loved her. Eugenia and all the residents were thrilled by the friendly cat. Not as much as they loved the kids, though. The kids were the real stars. Everyone wanted to bake brownies with them. Teach them to knit. Watch their tricks in the pool. PJ had finally accepted that kids need swimming pools for their happiness. And Sophie was using the treadmills at the Tender Hearts fitness center, open twenty-four hours. This place had everything they needed. It was too bad Sophie couldn't stay.

PJ had called Belinda Bell back, and he explained that he had left town with the kids for a family funeral. Belinda was so glad to hear from him, so glad that the kids were safe and doing well. She agreed it wasn't a big deal to miss the last few weeks of school after what they'd been through, especially if it was for an important reason like a funeral.

"It was my father's funeral," PJ told her. "I really couldn't miss it." It felt good to PJ to say that phrase, *my father*, and know who the man was.

"Of course, of course. I'm so sorry for your loss," Belinda Bell said, before she hung up.

They interred Ed Cobb's ashes into the Tender Hearts mausoleum in the cemetery in the back, a plot of land that was watered every day so the grass was green even though that was unnatural in Arizona. PJ should have realized long ago his father was someone local. A postman should have known that white envelopes full of cash don't arrive to Massachusetts from any other state with no return address and unstamped, but sometimes it's too hard to see what's right in front of you. He'd had to go on this whole long journey in order to figure it out.

PJ started going out to the mausoleum wall every day, to talk to his father. "Ninety-one, huh?" he asked the copper plaque on the wall. "What's your secret?"

Lots of pie, the copper plaque joked.

PJ laughed. "Good one, Dad."

But that wasn't the whole truth. Ed Cobb had stopped drinking, in his sixties. Michelle had told PJ about her father and his struggle with alcohol. Maybe the apple hadn't fallen far. It was good to hear Michelle describe her father as a good and noble man, despite his mistakes. Perhaps Sophie could still remember *him* that way. There was still time. PJ was going to the AA meetings they had in the morning at Tender Hearts. All the members had been Ed Cobb's friends, and PJ wanted to hear stories about his father. And it was also good to talk to them about his drinking, and trying not to do it.

The Longhorn had been right about the stories PJ needed to tell and needed to hear.

With the help of his AA friends, PJ survived June 15, fifteen years without Kate. They even had a cake that night, which felt a little strange, celebrating the fifteenth anniversary of his daughter's death, but Tommy Knoll, one of the guys in the group, said it was a day worthy of celebration. It was the first June 15 in fifteen years that PJ had spent sober.

One afternoon, a week into their time at Tender Hearts, PJ and his sister sat in lounge chairs to watch the kids in the pool. Ollie and Luna were riding the back of a woman named Phyllis Mumford, who was wearing a pink floral swim cap and trying to stay afloat. The kids were pretending Phyllis was one of the killer whales in SeaWorld they'd watched the documentary about.

"They're strong swimmers," PJ said. "I would worry more if they weren't such strong swimmers."

"Pauly, you'll always worry about them," Michelle said. "You'll always worry because part of loving children is worrying about them. Worrying about them and hoping for them. I feel that way about my niece and nephew. I worry about them still, even though they're grown adults."

"I'll always worry," PJ said, repeating it. Maybe if he accepted that he was supposed to worry about them, that it was part of loving them, it wouldn't be so painful.

"But, Pauly," Michelle said, reaching out and grabbing his hand. "I hope you're not worried about money. I've got plenty of money."

PJ laughed and squeezed his sister's hand. The paternity-test results hadn't come back yet, but who needed Mark Stackpole and his dirty soap opera money when they had Michelle Cobb and the Bartlett family fortune.

It was two days later that Sophie got the email. She had to read it again, especially because it was worded in such a confusing way. *The alleged father is not excluded as the biological father of the tested child. The probability of paternity is 99.9%.*

Sophie ran to find Luna.

"Oh my God," Luna said. "I was right. No one ever listens to me, and I was right."

"You were," Sophie said. "And we did listen to you."

"I guess you did," Luna agreed.

Luna took it well, for the most part, everyone thought, that Mark Stackpole was her real father, and still didn't want her. Luna didn't need him, or his terrible wife and stupid kids, not when she had Sophie, whom she could really count on, and Ollie, who was still her brother and her best friend, even if they were only half-related. And she had Uncle PJ and Aunt Michelle and Pancakes and all these people at Tender Hearts who said she was smart and delightful and a really good singer.

"Are we still Irish twins?" Ollie asked.

"Yes," Luna said. "All that matters is that the mother has two babies a year apart. No one cares who the father is."

Sophie wasn't sure that was true, but the kids wanted to keep their cosmic connection, and who could blame them? They had lost so much.

Luna did go a little crazy one afternoon when Eugenia Daly was watching *The Tears of the Rich* in the common room, and Luna almost put a golf club right through the TV, but Ollie reminded her of the money they would be getting from that soap opera, and it would probably be enough to pay for college, or whatever else Luna wanted. That was enough reason to make Luna put the golf club down, leaving the TV unharmed and Eugenia Daly only shaken. But when Eugenia passed away later that day, some people said it was from the fright.

51

Sophie was in the Tender Hearts dining hall having a sandwich when her phone rang. "Hi, Fred," she said, picking up as quick as she could. "Everything okay?"

"Is your father there?" Fred asked.

"He's sorry about the Volvo—"

"Put your dad on."

"He's not with me." Her dad was upstairs with Natasha Eskolsky, his fling from his first week at Tender Hearts.

"Well, go find him," Fred said. "I need to talk to him."

Upstairs, Natasha Eskolsky greeted Sophie warmly. "Oh, dear Sophia, so glad you could join us! Can I make you a cup of tea?"

Sophie did not want any tea. She handed her father the phone. "It's Fred."

"Freddy? Did you tell him I'm sorry about the car?"

"Yeah, Dad, he knows."

"Freddy's my best friend," he told Natasha. "He's marrying my ex-wife in the fall. I'll need a date. Do you have a dress?"

"Sure, I have a dress," Natasha said.

"Fred, Freddy, Fred," PJ said, into the phone. "I'm so sorry about the car, I really am, and I hope Alaska is wonderful, but someone better be dead, because you're interrupting something special with a woman friend—What? You didn't . . . why?" He looked at Sophie. She looked away. "Ivy," he said. "Not my Ivy." He put the phone down and laid himself flat on the thick beige carpet of the condo. "Not my Ivy," he was saying, over and over again.

"Is he all right?" Natasha Eskolsky asked, in the doorway. She had come out of her bedroom with three dresses in her arms to show him the options. "Ivy is his ex-wife?"

"He'll be fine," Sophie said. "He just needs a minute to make it all about him."

Sophie's mother wasn't dead, not yet.

Everyone else had been hiding it from PJ for months. PJ hadn't been told, because Ivy didn't think PJ could handle the news, and she couldn't handle him not handling it.

Ivy had brain cancer. Inoperable. Twenty years after she'd beaten it, cancer had come back for her, in a new form.

Ivy and Fred had gone to Alaska for only ten days. It was their big vacation, a big last hurrah if there were going to be no more hurrahs, and after that, ever since then, they'd been in Rochester, Minnesota, at the Mayo Clinic for an experimental study. They had pretended to be unreachable, because, well, Ivy needed to focus on herself. Not on answering PJ's phone calls about every little thing. Her odds weren't good, but she needed to give it a shot. Fred had begged Ivy to build a wall around herself. He had begged her to let him guard her from the rest of the world, even from Sophie, who had her own issues, and definitely from PJ. Sophie was told not to call them, to pretend they were in Alaska, and PJ wasn't told the truth about the circumstances at all. They nicknamed the brain tumor Alaska, and they told all their friends and neighbors they would be in Alaska for several months. They weren't going to be reachable, because they were in Alaska, so don't bother to call.

But they were back in Pondville long before the trip was supposed to be over. It was clear after only a few weeks of the experimental treatment, it wasn't working for Ivy. The tumor was twice its size. "We really should have named it after a smaller state," Ivy had said at the news as Fred had held her and cried. "We should have called it Rhode Island." PJ and Sophie would hear her make this same joke later.

Sophie realized as her dad was on the phone, that if Fred was calling, it meant the treatment hadn't worked. He wasn't calling only to tell PJ; he was calling to tell them both that Alaska hadn't worked. She knew the odds hadn't been good, but she'd still had hope. She thought someone should get a miracle, and if anyone deserved one, it was her mother. Sophie needed to go outside and get some air. Or maybe she needed to go downstairs and dunk her head in the pool and scream. Her mother was dying. It hadn't worked. The worst was happening. She left her dad with her phone and Natasha Eskolsky and went downstairs alone. She would find one of the residents who liked to get high for medicinal reasons and bum some weed from them.

"When were you going to tell me?" PJ asked Fred, still lying on the ground but having picked up the phone off the carpet. Fred had waited on the other end of the line until PJ was ready to talk. Fred knew he had to be patient with PJ.

"I'm telling you now," Fred said. "Ivy is ready to tell you now. She wants you to come home."

"What for?" PJ said, angry he'd been left out. "Because you need the car? Well, Fred, I don't have the car."

"It would be nice to have a car. But we need you home because we need you for the wedding. We want to do it while she's still feeling good. You should fly home. Fly home tomorrow and help us get ready for the wedding."

"I prefer not to fly—"

"Fly home. I'm not asking. I'm telling you."

"Okay. Okay." And then PJ took a deep breath and told Fred

about the two dates he would be bringing to the wedding. Ages nine and ten, Ollie and Luna Meeklin, his new grandkids.

"Where did you buy grandkids?" Fred asked, but he was only joking. Fred and Ivy had gotten home to Pondville a few days earlier and found the bunk beds in Fred's office. And the trampoline in the backyard. Then they found the whole town was talking about how PJ Halliday had adopted the poor Meeklin children, and how PJ had such a good heart. Practically a saint.

"That's me," PJ agreed, wiping his eyes. "I'm a giver."

52

After PJ hung up, he went to find Sophie. The woman at the front desk pointed him outside, and he found her sitting on a stone bench by Ed Cobb's copper plaque. It was a lot like the stone bench for Kate back home. PJ could see Sophie had been crying, her eyes red. "Can I sit?" he asked.

"I won't stop you."

"Well, Sophie."

"Yup."

"I can't believe you didn't tell me."

Sophie knew what was coming, and she waited for his annoying rant about how he really should have been the first to know any health news about his ex-wife. Waited for him to say he couldn't believe he had been left out, that he had been her husband first, and had everyone really forgotten all about him? Sophie couldn't stand it. Even though her dad was still healing from being run over by a car, she might still punch him right in the head.

"I can't believe you've been dealing with this all on your own. Sophie, that must have been so hard," he said, instead of everything she thought he was going to say. "You've been very brave dealing with Ollie and Luna and with me while you were also dealing with this. You are an extraordinarily strong person. Brave. You've been very brave."

Sophie unclenched her fist, relaxed her jaw. She was surprised to hear what she needed from her father. To hear that she shouldn't have been expected to deal with this all alone. She had been left behind while Fred and Ivy had each other, and she had been alone. She had been tough, and alone, and she should feel proud of herself. Sophie sniffed. "I wanted to tell you," she said, because she *had* wanted to. It would have been nice to have someone to talk about it with.

"I understand why you didn't."

"Thanks, Dad."

"We're going home tomorrow. Your mother will need you."

"She needs you, too, Dad. That's why she asked Fred to tell you."

"I'm not so sure about that. I can't imagine what your mother would need me for, after everything I've put her through."

Sophie didn't answer that. She didn't want to hurt him more than he was hurting. She knew her dad loved her mother, that he always had. There were a lot of things Sophie hadn't been sure about, but she had always known that.

So instead of talking they just sat there, listening to the birds. Even in Tucson, the dry desert, there were birds. Birds were proof of life. PJ could understand why Fred loved birds so much. Sophie leaned her head on her father's shoulder.

"You think it's our fault?" she finally asked him. "That Mom got brain cancer? From stress?" Sophie had googled this many times, and the answer was always the same: *While stress can cause many health problems, including high blood pressure, heart disease, and depression, there is no conclusive evidence to support the claim that stress causes brain cancer.*

"Well, there's an exceptionally dark thought," her dad said, considering. "But no, Sophie. I don't think your mother got brain cancer because of you. For the amount of stress you've put her under, you've brought her just as much love and joy. Much more love and much more joy."

"That's nice, Dad," Sophie said, and she hoped it was true.

They were quiet again for a minute.

"I bet she's going to be so proud of me for getting off the booze," PJ said. For the twelve days they'd been at Tender Hearts, PJ had been going to AA every day.

"Of course she is. Everyone's proud of you for that."

"Thanks, Sophie. I couldn't have done it without you." And PJ finally believed that he could stay sober. He'd been going to AA, and he had a story about getting sober, one he loved to tell. It involved two orphaned kids, an alligator, a gas leak, and driving cross-country thinking he was in love with his sister. It was a long one, but in the end, PJ realized he had to stay sober for the kids, and that there was no other woman in the world for him except his ex-wife. He would never move on from Ivy, not really. She'd been the love of his life, and always would be.

"I can't believe your mother is dying before me," PJ said. "It's terribly unfair."

"Yeah," Sophie agreed. "It is."

The cat watched PJ and Sophie from above. He was sitting on top of the mausoleum, was perched up there so he could hunt the cactus wrens who were singing nearby. The cat was amused at these two idiot humans, talking about how unfair death is, when it's one of the few things everyone gets. Death is a magnificent invention, the cat knew, because it's the impermanence of life that makes it beautiful.

53

The plane had landed in Boston and PJ was amazed how easy that was, flying across the country. "I think I'll fly everywhere from now on," he said, and Sophie rolled her eyes.

They found Fred waiting at baggage claim. He'd gotten a minivan. "It's just a lease," he said. "But I figured we need a minivan if there are kids in the family."

"That's nice, Fred," PJ said, grabbing his friend and kissing him on the forehead. "I missed you, buddy."

"I missed you too," Fred said, tearing up. "It's been a rough couple of months."

"I understand," PJ said, and then he surprised himself by saying: "I can't imagine." It didn't mean that PJ wasn't capable of imagining it — it really meant *I recognize that you have had an incredibly difficult time. I recognize that you had to dredge up more strength than you knew you had, and I am impressed that you are still standing. I don't think I would be if that happened to me, but look at you, standing! On two feet!*

On the way home in the van, the hour from Boston to Pondville, the kids talked most of the way. They told Fred about everything they'd seen when they drove across the country. The humming alpacas, the best pie in Kentucky, the funniest bulletin boards, the wax museum, the swimming pool at Tender Hearts. Fred was surprised by how buoyed he felt by the kids and their talking, after these weeks of quiet and intense sadness.

When they came into Pondville, they drove past the bogs at the edge of town. PJ looked out the front window. *Hi, Pauly,* the cranberry shrubs said. At this point in the early summer, the cranberry fields were blanketed with pink flowers, before the white pinhead berries would come in, and those would turn red in the fall, and then the farmers would flood the bogs and people would drive down from Boston to see how beautiful the berries looked, floating up to the top.

I wish—said the cap on PJ's head. It was hard to listen to the hat jabber all the time. PJ would hang it back on its doorknob when he got home. Back in its rightful place, where Kate had left it.

PJ looked for a silver flick of tail in the bog trenches, but the water was still. PJ couldn't wait to tell Ivy he'd seen the mermaid. The mermaid he'd looked for all his life, he'd finally seen her in the bogs where she didn't belong. The mermaid his mother had told him about. Regina Halliday had swum with the mermaid once, skinny-dipping after dark. She told PJ she had touched the mermaid's hair, said it was slimy like seaweed. PJ still believed that story.

At the bogs, the kids stopped talking to Fred, and they looked out the window too. *Home,* Ollie thought, nervous, not at all soothed by the thought, and then Luna took his hand.

"It won't be like it was," she whispered.

"It won't?"

"Not at all," she promised. "Not even close."

"Okay," he said, and he trusted his sister. Everything was different now. Almost everything was different, even if Pondville looked pretty much the same.

They drove past Old Man Charlie Rust's house, on the right, and Fred slowed down there when he saw the outline of the cop car. Years ago, Charlie had made a life-sized wooden cutout of a Crown

Victoria and had painted it like a police car. Everyone slowed down in front of Old Charlie's house, even though almost everyone who drove by knew the car wasn't real. On the side of the cruiser, where it should say PONDVILLE POLICE, it said: SLOW DOWN, DICKHEADS!!! instead. Charlie's young son had been hit by a car thirty-five years ago when his basketball rolled out into the street. Charlie had not forgotten. He had tried not to let the town forget.

Bad things had always happened in Pondville.

Farther down the road, a bouquet of balloons was tied to a mailbox. IT'S A BOY! read one balloon. IT'S A GIRL! said another. "The Nielson family just had twins," Fred said, pointing.

PJ knew those balloons would likely end up in the belly of a sea turtle, the string wrapped around the neck of a dolphin. But there was good news in Pondville. New babies were good news. A hopeful thing, to add a baby to the world. Especially hopeful to add two.

In PJ's lap, in the cat carrier, Pancakes began to wake up from his drug-induced slumber. The vet in Tucson had recommended drugging him for the plane ride. *Where in the devil am I,* Pancakes thought, but as he got his bearings, he could smell it, because the windows in the van were open a crack: He was back in Pondville. He was home. He looked out through the mesh of the cat carrier and out the car window at the group of three buzzards circling the van overhead. *Alive! Alive! Alive!* the birds chanted, in celebration at the Meeklin children's return. Pancakes thought about what it would be like to kill a bird that size.

When Fred turned left onto Clear Pond Road, he drove past PJ's house first, the little blue house with the white porch on the corner, but he didn't stop there. Someone had mowed his yard, PJ noticed; it looked neat and suburban. PJ's old drinking buddy, Hank, had done it, but PJ wouldn't find out about that until later, how his friends Hank and Moose had been cleaning up the house after they found out about the Meeklin children left in PJ's care. Moose had a key.

"Hello, house," PJ said, but the house didn't have time to respond, since Fred kept on driving by.

Fred pulled the car into the driveway of his own house on Clear

Pond Road, the brown house with green shutters. Ollie was out of the car first and he ran around the side of the house straight to the backyard to the trampoline.

Luna didn't run after her brother; instead she bent and unzipped the cat carrier so she could check on Pancakes after the sedative drugs, and she tried to pick him up and hold him, but the cat was fully awake, alert, and jumped down from her arms and weaved through everyone's legs, pushed his way past Fred, who was opening the front door of the house. The cat was the first one inside.

"Since the day I met that cat," PJ said, "he's been trying to sneak into your house. He knows where the good food is, I guess."

Fred smiled, although their cupboards were currently bare. Someone would have to go shopping. Maybe PJ could do it.

Pancakes skittered right upstairs, to the master bedroom, where Ivy was resting.

"Oh my, hello, kitty," Ivy said, opening her eyes when something landed on her covers. Of course her ex-husband had brought her a cat as a gift. A cat was certainly not what she needed right now, but what could you do with PJ? She did appreciate that he'd flown home when he had always been so afraid of flying. She wanted him there for the wedding. She needed him there, even if she didn't need the cat he'd brought home with him, not to mention these two kids. She could hear the children outside in the backyard, yelling at each other on the trampoline. Ivy didn't have to take care of the kids, she reminded herself. She could just enjoy them; it wasn't her job to take care of them. That was PJ's job, and she had faith that he would rise to the challenge. She had seen him be a good father once, a wonderful husband at one point, and she was sure, in this situation, he would manage to pull it together. There were people around who would help him, even if she couldn't. He would figure it out.

And then, strangely, when the cat curled up against Ivy's frail body, Ivy found she did feel a little bit better. Comforted. Warm. She stroked the cat, and he purred.

Here you are, Pancakes thought. *I've been looking everywhere for you.*

ACKNOWLEDGMENTS

First, I want to thank a house I used to live in. Not thank you as in "Thanks for giving us a roof over our heads, a place to sleep, and a cozy place for me to write," but thank you as in "Thanks for not killing us despite your many attempts."

In the fourteen months we lived there, from 2020 to mid-2021, that rental house gave us two gas leaks, two basement floods, a gang of rats who nested in our car and caused $1,400 in damage (not covered by insurance because the car "didn't explode," *F U, GEICO*), black mold on the walls, lead in the water, three trees that the arborist said were going to fall on the house after he came to cut down one, poison ivy that blanketed the yard, a neighbor who stabbed her sister on the day we moved in, and a teenager who crashed his car driving too fast and died at the base of our driveway. When we moved out, I sent the new tenant a message to make sure she filtered her water, and she wrote back: "Did you ever have any paranormal experiences in this house?"

"No," I wrote back. "But that could explain some things."

My daughter turned one and two in that house, and as a new mother during those events, it felt like death was hunting us down. And it felt like I had to get between death and my child so it could take me first.

When we broke our lease and arrived in our new rental house in Lakeville (yes, the real-life Pondville! A random town I found on Zillow, close enough to Providence but with cheaper houses), I felt safe for a minute—I didn't see a swarm of rats in our driveway, plotting to eat my child—but then, I would read the news and think . . . well, no. We're not safe. No one is safe anywhere. It is foolish to let your guard down.

So I decided I would take all those fears and anxieties and put them into a novel. I decided to take all my worries about not being a good enough parent or a generally capable enough person and put those worries in a book. And I decided I would make that novel as funny as I possibly could. That was my challenge to myself: to put everything bad I could think of in there and make it my funniest book yet. Humor is how I have always coped with anxiety and fear and terror and discomfort, so I wanted to make it all terrible but also very funny. *Things are so horrendously bad, let's laugh about it!*

So if you laughed at this book . . . I want to thank YOU for reading and laughing with me. It feels good when we can laugh together about hard things.

And now, thank you to everyone who helped make this book—first, to my supremely wonderful editor, Sara Weiss, who showed me where to dig deeper and had the faith that I'd get there. You are such a wise editor and an extraordinarily kind person. And a special big shout-out and welcome to your babies, who arrived just after we finished the edits. It is a hopeful thing to add a child to the world. It is especially hopeful to add two.

And an enormous thanks to everyone on my team at Ballantine. Thank you to Jesse Shuman for writing me that beautiful letter and picking up the end of the editing journey and giving me a pep talk when I really needed one. Thank you to my core crew: Taylor Noel, Melissa Folds, Emma Thomasch, and Sydney Collins, thank you for working so hard for me and my characters. And many thanks to Kara Cesare, Kara Welsh, Kim Hovey, Michael Harney, Elena Giavaldi, Rachelle Mandik, Cindy Berman, and Elizabeth A.D. Eno. Thank you to Nada Hayek for the cover art, which I am completely obsessed with. Thank you also to everyone else at PRH . . . Thank you all for the work you've done for this book. Shout out to the amazing sales reps . . . I see you hustlin'. And thanks to all the bookstores and booksellers who have helped get my work into readers' hands and brains.

Thanks to Katie Grimm, my beloved agent, and my treasured friend and confidante. I cannot imagine writing a book without you. I love how tough you are *and* what a sweetie you are inside. I am so glad we found each other so many Decembers ago. I can't wait to be old ladies on a porch together while you tell me to make the book funnier or make it sadder or put the scene back in where the girl kills all the chickens.

Thank you to Tessa Fontaine, my accountability partner and co-business owner, and my sacred friend. You are The Redwood and The Cannibal, more powerful than you realize, and I just want to keep you in my attic and take care of you forever. To Clare Beams, the friendly, sage, wisest friend. I will be asking you for advice for the rest of my days. To Rufi Thorpe, thank you for your wild stories and your bravery and general badassery. I can hear your laughter in my ear right now.

Tasha Graff, the best person I know, and there are a lot of other good ones. Two types forever. Natasha Sokol—thanks for always listening, for always texting back, and for being an emotional mastermind. Ellen O'Connell Whittet. Man, do I love you. Thank you for being a longtime constant. Jordan Wade, Lauren Fletcher, Susan Pienta: Our text chain sustains me. Thanks for putting up with my hijinks all these years. I can't make any decision without you three. Thank you to Kristen Hartt and Jessica Manly, my beauties, for speech pathology tips, talks about the book, being there always. To the PVD crew: James, Taylor, Lucas, Otti, Jade, and Nick, the smartest club I've ever been part of. I'm so grateful for you all. To Rebecca and Brian, your friendship is better than a unicorn or a rainbow. Chris and Courtney Crowell (& Co . . . and also Bryan), for always being enthusiastic and supportive and generous. Aimee and Conor, for being wonderful neighbors. And to the FA Community—thanks for making this corner of Massachusetts feel like we found ourselves a real home.

Thank you to my Accountability Workshop family. You are all so special to me. The co-workers of my dreams. I can't wait to show up in *your* acknowledgments.

I am so grateful to MacDowell, who gave me an emergency stay when I really needed one. MacDowell is a gem on this planet, and I'm so grateful to the place and the people.

Thank you to these babysitters (who have become dear friends!) who gave me extra time to work and who love my kid so well: Jill Fury, Maddy Owens, and Abby Lawrence.

Thank you to the kind folks at the Lakeville library who figured out a way to print my mammoth manuscript. And to the people of Lakeville, I hope you don't mind the ways I've fictionalized our town. Please don't take any of it too seriously. Do go look for the mermaid.

Thanks to every friend I ever made at summer camp, middle school, a random college party, a friend I made on the internet, my dad's old roommate, my mom's co-workers, my uncle's friend from work... anyone I know tangentially who reads my book. Every time someone sends me a message about my books, I want to write back that we should be best friends—*hey, are you free for Thanksgiving?*—but that always seems like overstepping. Just please know how much you reading these books means to me. My heart is tied to yours by a string.

Thank you to my grandparents: Paul John Hartnett Sr. (the first PJ), and Regina Hartnett, John Callahan, and Eleanor Callahan, plus my great-aunt Claire Hartnett. They are all gone to wherever we go next, but they left behind their many stories and the tradition of lollipop trees. Thank you to my parents, Liane and Paul J. Hartnett Jr. (the second PJ), for their love and support and shared sense of humor. I appreciate you both more than you know. Thanks for always telling us how loved we are. Thank you to my brothers, Jake and Michael, and to Nomin and Sway. Thank you to the extended Hartnett, Callahan, and Linsley families. Special shout-out to all the sweet kiddos we have in the family: Rowan, Desi, Tengis, Alessandra, and Viviana.

ACKNOWLEDGMENTS

Thanks to Mrs. Nancy Criscitiello (Mrs. Cris), my next-door neighbor growing up who is like family to me, who read aloud to me and two other girls every Wednesday after school and who started my first writing club. You and Dr. Cris are models of how to live a great and meaningful life. It was Dr. Cris's advice that everyone needs "something to do, someone to love, something to look forward to," which will always guide me. How fortunate I am that I got to grow up across from the red house with piano music coming through the open window.

To my husband, Drew, man, I sure did get lucky with you. Thanks for telling me never to stop writing, to not get off the train while it's still going. Thank you for putting Leora to bed, for cooking dinner and cleaning up so I can write, thank you for being an equal partner, and for highlighting all the lines in the book you think are funny because you know it jolts my heart to make you laugh. Thank you for being brainy, funny, sensitive, and a total hunk. You are the complete package. They should consider a cloning program. I would give them as gifts.

Thank you to Willie, our beloved dog. You are a very good boy and the perfect writing companion. Also, I am sorry to the readers of this book for not having a cat. My dad is allergic.

This book is dedicated to Leora, who is five years old as I write this. I love you more than I ever thought possible, and I was already a person who loved with great zeal. The very best thing about having an only child is there is only one person I love the most, the single person I love more than anyone else on the planet, much more than all those other jokers I listed above. You are the most joyful corner of my heart, the part of my body where all the sweetness lives.

INTERIOR IMAGE CREDITS

https://stock.adobe.com/images/cat-crosses-the-road-sketch-png-illustration-with-transparent-background/583573184?prev_url=detail&asset_id=583573184

https://stock.adobe.com/images/vector-illustration-of-a-healthy-human-arm-with-elbow-and-its-bones-medial-view-for-advertising-medical-publications/239962082?prev_url=detail

https://stock.adobe.com/images/vintage-open-scissors-isolated-hair-cutting-tool/525098697?prev_url=detail&asset_id=525098697

https://stock.adobe.com/images/curled-worms-set-pink-wiggling-earthworms-isolated-on-white-background-flat-vector-illustration-for-soil-nature-wildlife-fishing-concept/380860450?prev_url=detail

https://stock.adobe.com/images/handcuffs-silhouette-vector-illustration/923727989?prev_url=detail

https://stock.adobe.com/images/bus-coloring-page-city-bus-side-view/447822355?prev_url=detail

https://stock.adobe.com/images/image-of-pineapple-fruit-vector-black-and-white-illustration/116000975?prev_url=detail

https://stock.adobe.com/images/realistic-lollipop-candy-on-the-stick-with-packaging-in-black-isolated-on-white-background-hand-drawn-vector-sketch-illustration-in-doodle-engraved-vintage-outline-style-children-yummy/558657775?prev_url=detail

https://stock.adobe.com/images/solid-black-outline-cactus-wren-ancow-animal-silhouette/860179914?prev_url=detail

https://stock.adobe.com/images/icon-of-a-carrier-for-cats-dogs-in-doodle-style-soft-bag-with-mesh-and-handles-for-carrying-animals/937617694?prev_url=detail

https://stock.adobe.com/images/set-of-hand-drawn-sketches-of-travel-luggage-handbags-suitcases-travel-bags-vector-ink-isolated-illustration/243951459?prev_url=detail

ABOUT THE AUTHOR

ANNIE HARTNETT is the author of *Unlikely Animals,* which won the Julia Ward Howe prize for fiction and was longlisted for the Joyce Carol Oates Prize, and *Rabbit Cake,* a finalist for the New England Book Award and a *Kirkus Reviews* best book of the year. Hartnett has been awarded fellowships and residencies from the MacDowell Colony, Sewanee Writers' Conference, and the Associates of the Boston Public Library. Along with the writer Tessa Fontaine, she co-runs the Accountability Workshops for writers, helping writers commit to routines and embrace the long, slow, joyful, terrible process of doing the work. She lives in Massachusetts with her husband, daughter, and dog.